Praise for JOHN BURDETT

"John Burdett's crime novels . . . are lovely and complex. . . . The reader is transported to a foreign world made familiar through the voice of his guide."   —*The Denver Post*

"Nothing is simple in Burdett's bawdy, wild fiction."
                                    —*Pittsburgh Post-Gazette*

"You might find yourself addicted to Burdett's sizzling prose."
                                    —*San Antonio Express News*

"John Burdett is writing the most exciting set of crime novels in the world."   —*The Oregonian*

"Time and again, John Burdett breaks the crime-thriller mold. And then reassembles it, piece by piece. His narrative becomes more than the sum of its parts. . . . Thoroughly enjoyable."
                                    —*New York Journal of Books*

Books by John Burdett

The Royal Thai Detective series
Bangkok 8
Bangkok Tattoo
Bangkok Haunts
The Godfather of Kathmandu
Vulture Peak

A Personal History of Thirst
The Last Six Million Seconds

JOHN BURDETT

THE LAST
SIX MILLION SECONDS

John Burdett was brought up in North London and worked as a lawyer in Hong Kong. To date he has published seven novels, including the Bangkok series: *Bangkok 8*, *Bangkok Tattoo*, *Bangkok Haunts*, *The Godfather of Kathmandu*, and *Vulture Peak*.

www.john-burdett.com

JOHN BURDETT

•

THE LAST
SIX MILLION
SECONDS

•

VINTAGE CRIME/BLACK LIZARD
Vintage Books
A Division of Random House, Inc.
New York

DISCARD
CARLSBAD CITY LIBRARY
CARLSBAD CA 92011

M
BURDETT, J.

For Laura

FIRST VINTAGE CRIME/BLACK LIZARD EDITION, MAY 2012

Copyright © 1997 by John Burdett

All rights reserved. Published in the United States by Vintage Books, a division of Random House, Inc., New York, and in Canada by Random House of Canada Limited, Toronto. Originally published in hardcover in the United States by William Morrow and Company, Inc., New York, in 1997.

Vintage is a registered trademark and Vintage Crime/Black Lizard and colophon are trademarks of Random House, Inc.

This is a work of fiction. Names, characters, places, and incidents either are the product of the author's imagination or are used fictitiously. Any resemblance to actual persons, living or dead, events, or locales is entirely coincidental.

Library of Congress Cataloging-in-Publication Data
Burdett, John.
The last six million seconds / by John Burdett —
1st Vintage Crime/Black Lizard ed.
p. cm.
1. Hong Kong (China)—Fiction. I. Title.
PR6052.U617L37 2012
823'.914—dc23
2012001207

Vintage ISBN: 978-0-307-74529-3

www.weeklylizard.com

Printed in the United States of America
10 9 8 7 6 5 4 3 2 1

NOV - 2 2016

PREFACE

THE SECOND TREATY of Peking of 1898 was one of the more bizarre treaties of the British colonial era. The British had already occupied Hong Kong, a small island off the south coast of Canton in southern China, by 1841, and extended their occupation to a small part of mainland Canton, known as Kowloon, by 1860. The purpose of the occupations, which were carried out by force of arms, was to establish a base from which to continue the sale of opium to the Chinese mainland, in the teeth of opposition from the emperor of China. The trade had grown so successful by the 1890s (twenty million Chinese were addicted to opium) that the British required more land, principally to ensure that Hong Kong and Kowloon could be defended in case of attack. What they extracted, more or less at gunpoint, in the Second Treaty of Peking was a lease of a larger area of land contiguous with Kowloon and stretching thirty miles north into mainland China. Although the newly acquired territory included some of the more ancient cultivated lands in the world, the British named them the New Territories. The lease of the New Territories was dated July 1, 1898, with an expiration date ninety-nine years hence: June 30, 1997.

By 1982 Hong Kong, as the entire territory was known, had become a financial miracle. The infrastructure had developed in such a way that Hong Kong Island and Kowloon could not survive without the New Territories. The prime minister of Great Britain at the time, Mrs. Margaret Thatcher, was therefore forced to negotiate the return of the entire territory of Hong Kong at midnight on June 30, 1997, by means of a document known as the Joint Declaration of 1984.

ACKNOWLEDGMENTS

ANY DISCUSSION OF *Laogai* probably begins with Hongda Harry Wu's fine and courageous book of the same name (Westview Press). My own certainly did. In addition, I thank John Carroll for telling me more about the RHKPF and Mongkok Police Station than I had found out in twelve years in Hong Kong; H. K. Law was a mine of information on all aspects of Cantonese culture; and Kay Mitchell told me how laser fingerprinting works in practice. If any of the help I received is not accurately represented in the text, it is my fault.

Special thanks too to Jane Gelfman for selling the book and to Ron Bernstein for selling the film rights almost as soon as there was a book.

AUTHOR'S NOTES

HONG KONG IS A SMALL PLACE. There is but one governor, one political adviser, one chief secretary, only a handful of international law firms of any size and, I daresay, not very many Eurasian chief inspectors of police. To make matters worse for a writer earnestly trying to avoid defaming anyone, the manner in which Cantonese surnames are translated into English results in a narrow selection of single syllables: Wong, Chan, Lau, Kan, etc. In such circumstances one is left with no resource other than to state with even more emphasis than usual that this is a work of fiction and that no character depicted herein bears any relation to a living person.

It is not possible to write about Hong Kong without using the word *gweilo*. Literally translated from the Cantonese, it means "foreign devil" or "foreign ghost." These days it is used in a nonpejorative sense to describe all Westerners.

It is frequently used by expatriates living in Hong Kong to refer to themselves.

An' the dawn comes up like thunder outer
China 'crost the Bay!

—RUDYARD KIPLING, "MANDALAY"

THE LAST
SIX MILLION SECONDS

I

Typhoons—"big winds" in Cantonese—start to gouge holes in the South China Sea in early April and are well into their stride by the end of the month, when the sea is already the temperature of bathwater and humidity runs at between 90 and 100 percent. Everyone avoids the water during typhoon warnings. Except fools, Chan thought.

He looked at his watch, a fake gold Rolex flaking at the edges: 3:30 P.M. *Ayya!* What had started as a search and recovery operation expected to last no more than a couple of hours had turned into a dangerous drift toward Chinese waters that was taking all afternoon.

Standing at the bows of *Police 66*, a fast motor launch belonging to the Royal Hong Kong Police Force, he moved his eyes in an arc from the sea to the sky. Darkness piling upon darkness. Sometimes the turbulence could be five hundred miles away yet drag down local clouds so dark that visibility disappeared in the middle of the day. Clouds like solar eclipses, except they lasted longer and fascinated no one.

By his side Inspector Richard Aston, twenty-four years of age, blond, imitated his movements.

"Not looking good, Chief."

"Not good," Chan agreed.

Ignoring the best principles of leadership, Chan failed to disguise from the young recruit that he was nervous and unsure what to do next. Alan, a tightening whorl of trapped wind spinning around a dead eye, had been more than four hundred nautical miles to the southeast when they had started out and tottering toward Taiwan.

If it kept its present course, it would miss Hong Kong by a safe margin, but name a typhoon that was predictable. Name too a typhoon that did not kill at least a few people, especially at sea.

The wind was freshening. The first whitecaps were dancing on top of stubby waves. Small whitecaps for the moment, but that could change. Chan yelled in Cantonese to the captain up in the wheelhouse. Aston smirked.

Chan glanced at him. "You understand that?"

"You said, 'Slow the fucking boat down. Can't you see it's as black as a Chinese vagina?' "

Chan nodded. It was typical of a young English cop that he would know the word for the female part; it was what they learned after "please" and "thank you." But Cantonese was rich in double meanings and the captain had understood a slightly different message: *Don't get us trapped in the crotch of China.* Chan knew six million people who would say amen to that.

"Better go back," he said without conviction.

"Yes, we better. Could get blown halfway up the Pearl River if we hang around here."

"Don't say that." Chan's hand shook as he lit another cigarette. "You see it anywhere?" Smoke and words tumbled from his mouth in a rush.

Aston gazed into the gloom. "To be honest, Chief, I can't see a bloody thing."

Chan grimaced. "It's there, though." He turned to the bridge, shouted in Cantonese: "Where are we now?"

"Due north of the Soko Islands, heading west at three knots."

All aboard understood the tension in the captain's voice. Every map of Hong Kong shows that the territorial waters belonging to the People's Republic of China begin very close to the western end of the Soko Islands. Private and commercial craft from Hong Kong passed regularly across the invisible line in the sea, usually on their way to Macao, but it was forbidden for officials in uniform to do so, especially aboard craft bearing the queen's arms. The Chinese Navy, always sensitive to foreign incursions, had never forgiven the theft of Hong Kong by bullies in British uniforms more than a hundred years before.

"A clear plastic bag, very large and of industrial quality, with apparently gruesome content," the tourist had said. American tourists gave the most precise reports to police. They had more practice.

"Gruesome"? Neither Chan nor Aston had taken the report. The message had been redirected by the local Lantau police station to the RHKPF's headquarters in Arsenal Street on Hong Kong Island and then on to Chan's desk at Mongkok. It had been his first break in a triple murder inquiry with which Chan had conspicuously made no progress for over a week. With a disposition like Chan's frustration was hard to disguise, and the nature of the crimes did not help his state of mind. "Atrocities" was the word English journalists were using.

From the boat they had seen the bag four or five times off in the distance drifting toward the west, but it had eluded them, and then the cloud had come down like a curtain.

Aston gave him another five minutes. "Well, Chief? Do we go back?"

Chan flicked his cigarette into the South China Sea. "I guess." There was nothing to be achieved in a state of blindness; only gravity provided a guide to the difference between up and down. But the cloud did seem to be slowly dissolving and growing lighter, from black to slate gray. "Five more minutes, okay? Want tea?"

They stood together at the bows, drinking green Chinese tea from two tall glasses the boat boy brought. As they drank, the cloud in front of them dispersed, leaving a heavy cloud bank to stern, not necessarily a good omen. The freshening wind was cutting the mist into scarves that floated around the boat and tore against the radio mast to reveal a corpse-gray sky. The only unchanging element was the heat. In a short-sleeved white shirt with epaulets, shorts, long socks, Aston leaned gratefully into the spray that had started to rinse him every time the bows bashed against the burgeoning waves. Chan was in plain clothes: a pair of shorts and a money belt where he kept his wallet and police identity card. His naked torso was olive. A small blue butterfly hovered on top of one bicep and covered most of the faded Chinese characters of an earlier tattoo, now illegible. His feet were bare, the better to grip the wooden deck.

A shout went up from the crew. Aston had seen it too at the same time as everyone else, gray and almost entirely submerged about two hundred yards to the west. It appeared and disappeared with the rhythm of the waves: the top of a bag with a dab of green from the ropes that tied it.

On the bridge bank notes changed hands, those who had bet against finding the bag again paying out to those who had gambled that it would be found.

From the bows Chan called over his shoulder: "Slowly ahead. Get the nets. No hooks. Don't damage the evidence. No more gambling."

About ten minutes later in a world without coordinates it seemed to Aston that it was the floating bag that drifted alongside the boat, rather than the other way around. He watched as three Chinese constables leaned over and with little trouble captured it in a large green nylon net attached to a long bamboo pole. Cantonese expletives exploded in the muggy air when those closest saw what was in the bag. Then, as they drew it up, Aston saw too and retched loudly over the side.

When Aston had choked up the last of his stomach's contents, he turned again, half disbelieving, to look at the bag, now sitting on the center of the foredeck not two yards away from him. Three waterlogged and decapitated heads with drooping mouths and wide-open eyes stared out through the transparent plastic like the distorted faces of children pressed against glass. Revulsion, and the curiosity it inspired, took him two steps closer. To judge by the shapes, two pairs of eyes were Chinese, one pair Caucasian. But the mouths were not drooping; he'd been misled by seawater trapped between gray folds of plastic. The faces had no lips at all. Or noses. The eyes were staring because the eyelids had been cut off. So had the ears.

The Chinese constables who had recovered the bag from the sea retreated to the other end of the deck. They stood in navy blue shorts smoking and swearing copiously, making jokes Aston could not follow, although he understood enough to guess at their obscenity. Behind the obscenity, fear. Behind the fear, awe. Extreme cruelty was a manifestation of power, after all.

"Help me," Chan said. "Bloody Chinese won't touch it. Bad luck."

Aston swallowed hard and grunted. With Chan holding one side of the bag, which was tied at the top with thick polyester rope, and Aston the other, they picked it up. The change in pressure forced gases out through the closed mouth of the bag. Both dropped it at the same time, gagging. A cloud of nauseating sweetness hung in the air for a moment before the wind blew it away. Holding his breath, Chan bent the opening of the bag over on itself, used the ends of the nylon rope to retie it. They started again and were carrying it slowly toward the cabin, lurching to accommodate the rolling of the boat, when the staccato rattle of a submachine gun rang out across the water.

Half cocooned in mist, its motor still inaudible over the threshing sea, another launch, similar in size but older and less well kept, rolled with the waves not more than fifty yards to stern. Three Chinese men in shabby green uniforms, one of them with a cigarette hanging from his mouth and an AK-47 cradled in his arms, stood staring at them across the water. Aston made out a red star painted on the bows of the boat. Chan signaled to Aston to put the bag down. The heads made a squelching sound as they hit the deck. Aston put out a foot to stop the bag from rolling and trapped dark blond human hair between the plastic.

Chan staggered to the rail, held on while he shouted to the other boat in Cantonese. "What's the problem?"

"Problem, Firstborn, is you're lost. This sea belongs to the People's Republic of China. What did you just pick up from it?"

"*Lap sap* [rubbish]. And we're not lost."

"I don't think it was *lap sap*, Firstborn. And you're in China. How about you just give us that bag and we'll let you run back home instead of arresting you like we should?"

"Okay." Chan made no effort to move.

"Okay what?"

Chan pushed his hair back. "Okay, arrest us. Arrest us and eat shit for the rest of your life. Because we're in Hong Kong waters."

"Frog shit, Firstborn. Ask your crew for a compass reading."

Chan summoned an expression of profound disdain. "We have satellite positioning, good to the half inch. Hey, Captain, tell the man in green where he is."

From the bridge the captain yelled a set of numbers in Cantonese.

The three coastguards on the other boat conferred, shook their heads. Chan's captain was no fool. To a man the crew of the police boat maintained implacable stares focused just above the Communist launch.

"That's not our reading."

"So where was your compass made?"

"China."

"Exactly."

The three coastguards conferred again.

"Just give us that bag, Firstborn, and stop insulting the Revolution. Ten years ago we would have killed you."

"Why do you want it?"

The coastguard shrugged. "Orders."

"Did your orders tell you to cross into Hong Kong waters?"

The coastguard took a long drag on his cigarette, threw the remains into the sea.

"What's your name, Firstborn?"

"Charlie."

"What?" The coastguard tried to repeat Chan's rendering of his nickname. "Gar-ha-lee?"

"Don't they teach you anything over there?"

"I told you, don't insult the Revolution."

The coastguard pulled the trigger of the AK-47. Chan and Aston hit the deck. Chan heard guffaws from across the water.

"Power comes out of the barrel of a gun," the coastguard said.

Chan used the rail to pull himself to his feet. "I bet you made that up yourself."

The coastguard stiffened. "No, Chairman Mao."

"Who's he?"

"I'm warning you, Firstborn."

Chan held up a hand. "Don't shoot, I have bad nerves. Look, it's teatime in Hong Kong. Let's all go home."

"Give us the bag, Firstborn."

"We could discuss it over a beer."

"Nothing to discuss. You picked up something from Chinese waters. It belongs to us."

"A thousand dollars," Chan said.

"No."

"And two cases of Carlsberg."

"What's in the bag?"

"Nothing you want."

"We have orders."

"Don't tell them you saw us. Look, there's a typhoon. We have to get back. So do you."

The coastguard rubbed his hand on the stock of the gun, then looked at the sky.

"What's in that other bag, the one protecting your crotch?"

"Money."

"How much?"

"A thousand dollars."

"I think there's at least two thousand dollars in there keeping your balls warm."

The crew on the Communist boat chuckled.

Chan's twitch subsided somewhat. "Okay."

"And all your beer."

"Okay."

"Now tell us what's in the bag."

"Three human heads."

The coastguards guffawed again.

"You're a real comedian, Firstborn. How're you going to bring the money and beer over here?"

Chan gestured toward the stern. "I'll send the tender."

He ordered the inflatable lowered from its davits. The crew

didn't need to be told to hurry; they had the outboard roaring within a second of its entering the sea. Two constables handed some twelve-packs of Carlsberg to the crew in the tender. Chan extracted all the notes from his money belt and borrowed some more from Aston. The wind had started to moan.

"Did he say, 'Ten years ago we would have killed you'?" Aston spoke in a half whisper.

"He was being macho. It's not true."

"Right." Aston waited while Chan watched the tender reach the Communist boat, his black eyes fixed like stones. He relaxed as soon as he saw the beer unloaded and the tender put off again from the other boat.

"Twenty-five years ago they would have killed us, though." Chan caught Aston's gaze. "During the Cultural Revolution it wasn't a good idea for Hong Kong police to stray over the border."

2

Chan and Aston carried the bag to the box situated under the fixed awning amidships, dumped it inside and packed it around with dry ice. White smoke rose up around the three heads that formed a triangle back to back, as if guarding a mystery.

"Should take the pictures really." Chan rubbed his hands, cold from the ice. "Even chilled, the evidence is decomposing. I guess it can wait."

"I'll do it," Aston said.

"You really want to? It's a shitty job."

"I know. It was a shitty job to stand up to those coastguards too, but you did it." Aston swallowed. "Me, I never would have had the guts. There's no point risking the evidence after all that. It could be a while before we get them back to Mongkok. In this heat . . ."

Chan nodded.

"Just answer one question. It wasn't a coincidence, was it, those guys showing up today?"

"No." Chan seemed on the point of saying more, then turned instead to leave Aston with the heads.

The trick, Aston told himself, was to regard them as objects. Not to hear their pain, above all not to identify with the misery of those grinning lipless mouths. He opened the bag standing as far away from it as he could, took out the first by the hair. It swayed in his hand to the motion of the boat.

It was bloated from its voyage in the warm sea and had developed marine hues: purple, mauve, green-gray, the colors of sea slugs. Aston set the Caucasian on a table, attempted to align it along the Frankfurt plane as the handbook required. To keep it from rolling, he borrowed a life belt from the side of the boat and adorned the head with a Day-Glo orange ruff. He followed the protocol as best he could, taking shots in profile and face-on close-ups of the gashes where the nose, ears and mouth were supposed to be. He gagged on the stench. The Caucasian's blond hair was longer than the others'. Did hair continue to grow after decapitation? Probably. Aston didn't want to think about that.

Within minutes they started to arrive: small, black and zooming straight to the eyes. Even at sea the flies came from nowhere, in ones and twos at first and then in winged armies. They loved the heads of mammals. From his forensic science course Aston knew that with perfectly designed needles they injected instar larvae into the eyes, mouth and nose. Aston was particularly angry that they should violate the blond-haired head, but not for reasons of race. The more he photographed it, the more he suspected it of having belonged to a woman. He hit out at the swarm that divided around his hand and continued to grow. Then, giving up the fight, he worked more quickly, trying to complete the job while the ice was still smoking. By the time he had finished with the last head he was working inside a black, buzzing cloud.

Aston went below to change. He rejoined Chan on the bridge, where he was smoking and talking to the captain. He stood apart from them and tried to follow. He had spent his regulation six months learning the local dialect and was able to say, "What is your honorable name? I am now going to arrest you," and many other useful phrases, but Chan cursed a lot and indulged in word-play. Chan threw him a glance from time to time yet made no effort to slow his speech or include him in the conversation.

Behind them Chinese constables kept their distance from Aston, the man who handled the dead. He heard a word repeated over and over that sounded like the number "four," pronounced *say*. It was almost identical in sound to the word for death, which was why four was an unlucky number. Aston's apartment block was the forty-fourth building in his street, but the postal address was forty-six; few Chinese were prepared to live in a building twice named death.

Aston kept his eyes on the chief inspector. One thing about Chan Siu-kai, nicknamed Charlie by his British colleagues: He was not inscrutable. Under pressure a slight twitch appeared under his left eye, and his lean face expressed every mood. He was the product of an affair, they said, between a wandering Irishman and a Cantonese girl and had benefited from the conjunction of opposing genes, although he would never have put it that way himself. In the mess they whispered that he often cut himself shaving because he hated to look in a mirror at a mostly Western face, albeit a handsome one. Aston could testify that Chan frequently bore signs of such mishaps.

For all his good looks, Aston guessed that the chief inspector did not much like himself. But then Aston, who had been a policeman now for nearly three years, had begun to wonder who on earth over the age of thirty did. Still more intriguing to the young Englishman, who had no problem with mirrors, was the way the Eurasian's rugged self-disdain sometimes attracted the fiercest and most desirable women; Chan, divorced, never paid them any mind.

Finally Chan left off talking to the captain. Aston shouted in English over the noise of the engines. "I guess those heads fit the other remains."

"Either that or we have six homicides instead of three."

"Well, the DNA will tell us. There's plenty to do now, even if we still don't have any fingers to print. I'll get to forensic first thing tomorrow for the odontological profiles. Some of the missing persons lists actually include dental records."

"Okay." Chan twitched but showed no enthusiasm.

"At least we've got a good chance of finding out who those poor bastards really were."

Chan exchanged glances with the captain. "Sure."

"And when the forensic artist's produced some drawings, we'll have something to fax to the foreign consulates. The Caucasian was probably from overseas." Aston finally detected embarrassment in Chan's mobile features. "Hey, is there something I'm missing?"

Chan shrugged. "Just that the investigation may be over."

Aston froze. *"Over?"*

"You heard what the coastguards said. They had orders to intercept that bag."

"So what?" Aston's voice had risen an octave. "You bribed them. We have the bag."

Chan pushed the hair back from his forehead. "Yeah, I bribed them." He looked out to sea, hesitated, spoke into the distance. "But the people who gave them orders to intercept the bag, they're the ones who'll be running Hong Kong in two months' time. See?" He looked at the young Englishman, so typical of the raw recruits who had been coming out of England for as long as he could remember. "Everything has already changed. The rules are different now; they just haven't got around to telling us yet."

Chan waved a hand in the direction of Hong Kong Island, which had begun to appear full ahead. "Enjoy the view, why not? You don't have to live here after June. This is a vacation for you."

Aston gulped at the implications of what Chan was saying, then obediently stared out through the bridge window. For the moment the wind had died again, a calm before the storm. In the twilight of an early tropical evening lights were being switched on from Aberdeen to North Point, burning electricity and money with an exuberance like nowhere else in the world.

It was an awesome skyline, not dissimilar to Manhattan's except that it was surmounted by a mountain and the scores of office towers presided over a huge harbor where some of the largest ships in the world lay at anchor. Neither the city nor the harbor ever slept. And it all happened on a rock not ten miles long that hung west to east off the south coast of the largest remaining Communist country in the world. Thirty miles north there lived 1.4 billion people whose collective attention was focused on Hong Kong just two months before its reversion to rule by the People's Republic of China. It was like living in a spiritual wind tunnel: You could feel the pressure of uncontainable envy, loathing and longing pressing in from over the border. Somebody said Hong Kong was a borrowed place living on borrowed time. That time was now being measured in hours: about fifteen hundred at the moment, but reducing quickly. The Communists were coming; they were almost here.

He left Chan to his private chat with the captain, stood at the bows again, where he had spent most of that afternoon. Hong Kong was the first hot country he'd visited. Standing in the warm, damp breeze created by the boat and gazing at the constellation of lights on the island were like a dream he'd never dared to believe could come true. He didn't care that he'd be made redundant in June. He would have had almost three years. Three years! He couldn't believe his luck.

Swinging around into the harbor itself, they slowed to the regulation four knots. Aston watched a tiny woman in a wide-brim straw hat fishing from a sampan, her silhouette balancing against the bucking of the tiny boat. The Star Ferries, lit up from stern to bow, were crossing from Hong Kong to Kowloon and back every fifteen minutes. A jetfoil bound for Macao rose up on its skis like a praying mantis. There, crawling up the mountain toward a saddle near the top, were the lights of the Peak Tram, a funicular railway that had put the coolies with their sedan chairs out of business nearly a hundred years ago. To the far west a fleet of green fishing trawlers, just visible in the dusk, was making for the typhoon shelter at Aberdeen where they'd raft up until Alan was spent.

As the launch drew closer to Central, comparisons with Manhattan no longer held. There was no grid system; the jam-packed futuristic city had sprung up without any planning at all. It was as if a giant spaceship had stopped by one day and hurriedly unloaded ten thousand assorted buildings for storage; from the sea it was hard to understand how traffic, or even people, managed to squeeze between them.

It was this intensity, physical and mental, Aston knew, that gave the place its fascination. There was no time to stand still and no

space to stand still in. Weeks, then months, then years had flashed
by at ten times the speed to which he was accustomed. He had
been drunk with excitement since arrival; he liked the sensation of
never quite catching up with himself. But it was true what they
told you when you first came out: The longer you remained in the
Far East, the less you understood. Take today. A detective he had
never thought of as brave had stubbornly, cleverly held on to evidence in an inquiry that the same detective expected to be aborted
for political reasons. Perhaps he'd risked his life and Aston's too.
It didn't make sense.

During the transit of the harbor the rain returned, a sticky, wet
blackness that swallowed huge tankers and cut the launch off again
from land. He'd told his mother she wouldn't believe what fell
from the skies out here. And it was warm. What in the world could
be more exotic, more wonderful, more mysterious than the warm,
stench-enriched rain of this tropical city?

It was weird how the East changed you. There was more life and
more death, and you felt twice as real for it. Soaked to the skin in
a second and clutching the safety rope as he made his way back
over the flooding deck to the wheelhouse, he caught Chan's eyes
and grinned. *God forgive me for loving these Hong Kong storms full of
money, sex and corpses*. If there was a way to stay after June, he
would find it.

3

At Queen's Pier Chan showered and dressed in the cabin, then told Aston to stay with the heads on the boat while he found a car to collect them. The captain dropped him off at the concrete steps, then backed out into the harbor to escape the crowd of small craft using the public pier. It was rush hour in the rain; all streets and pavements were flooded with people who seemed to be fleeing some disaster over their shoulders. Above high-rise office buildings the remains of a savage light glared between charcoal clouds. In half an hour it would be night.

At the Star Ferry Terminal, next to Queen's Pier, the sergeant at a small police incident cabin let Chan telephone for a car to meet Aston at the pier to collect the heads and take them to the morgue.

"Heads?" The sergeant was accustomed to writing out reports of pickpocketing and loss of credit cards. He stared at Chan, silently begging for details. Replacing the telephone, Chan mimed decapitation.

"Then they cut off the lips, ears, nose, eyelids."

The sergeant let his mouth fall open. "Fuck your mother."

Chan nodded. He had made one man happy this day.

He knew there was no point trying to find a taxi, still less to hope for a car to collect him within the next forty minutes. Aston would be on the boat with the heads until the rush hour was over. On the other hand, he wanted to discuss those Chinese coastguards with Chief Superintendent John Riley at Arsenal Street Police Headquarters without delay.

Ordinarily Chan would have reported to his immediate superior at Mongkok Division, the assistant district commander/crime. Recently, though, headquarters had required officers in charge of sensitive cases to report important developments to a designated officer at Arsenal Street. After the media interest arising from the extreme cruelty of the murders he was investigating (CNN and the BBC both had carried clips of Chan saying, "I have no comment to make at this time"), and following his discovery that his telephone had been tapped and case files tampered with, he had been ordered to bypass the command line at Mongkok and report directly to Riley. He decided to walk to the complex of buildings that constituted headquarters for the Royal Hong Kong Police.

Edinburgh Place, City Hall, Murray Road, Queensway: British names whose sell-by date was fast approaching. Queensway Plaza was an air-conditioned Oriental shopping mall crammed with Chinese tailors, Chinese takeouts, Chinese computer stores, Chinese jewelry shops and Chinese pedestrians. People moved in tidal waves in both directions. As Chan allowed himself to be carried forward into the mall, the cool from the air conditioning froze the rain and sweat on his body. He could smell on himself and everyone near him the musty odor of tropical damp as it cooled.

In their rush to escape the wet and hurry home, people pressed against him and closed off all movement to the left or right. If he had wished to enter one of the shops, it would have required an extreme and antisocial effort of will. There was a hard knot of people who weren't moving, though, immediately in front of Wong's Watches. Chan allowed himself to be deposited on the outside of this crowd, where he paused for a moment. The fashion for countdowns had started in Beijing some years before; now almost every street in the territory had at least one large digital clock recording how many days, hours, seconds until midnight June 30, 1997. Wong's was extralarge, filling half his shopwindow. Chan realized why everyone had stopped when he saw the "seconds" panel: six million and twenty seconds. The woman next to Chan started counting down in Cantonese: nineteen, eighteen, seventeen. When the panel registered a clear six million, a small cheer went up, and the woman turned to Chan: "One second for each of us—and disappearing." Chan broke away as the crowd dispersed.

On the other side of the twin office towers called United Center the walkway toward Arsenal Street lost a little of its human density. Chan thought about how to handle the chief superintendent, who would surely be alarmed by the problem with the coastguards. Riley? Chan had known him on and off for ten years, had watched him grow and change in the manner of *gweilos* since he first stepped off the plane at Kai Tak. His nickname in Cantonese could be translated as "rubber spine." A permanent condition of self-doubt made him especially sensitive to political sea changes, which was why he was appointed to supervise delicate investigations. Not so much a willow bending in the breeze, this Riley, as an artifact of empire broken by the storms of change. Chan didn't hold it against him; there was a disease that went with expatriation and grew worse as the years passed: schizophrenia.

"You went into Chinese waters?" Riley said when Chan had finished.

"It was a mistake."

Chan watched the Englishman try out various responses: a blink; a frown; a sedate placing of the hands together in prayer; a muted thump on the table.

Finally Riley bit his lower lip. "But they were expecting you, you're sure?"

"Someone must have been listening in to our ship-to-shore and given orders to those coastguards to take the bag from us. I told you, this isn't an ordinary investigation. Last week someone bugged my phone, and they've been in my files; today they listened to the ship-to-shore. As it happened, the coastguards were just dumb thugs."

"But they didn't seem to know what was in the bag?"

Chan shook his head. "They asked me several times. When I told them, they laughed as if I was joking."

Riley stared at the wall, then back to Chan, then back to the wall. Chan watched Riley. Taoism posited a center of energy in the human body called chi. Riley's chi was like a Ping-Pong ball bouncing between two identities: master race/indentured servant.

"You were incredibly brave. Or incredibly stupid. Time will tell." He drummed on his desk. "I have to say it does make my blood boil, though. What business do those Communist bastards have interfering in my investigation? Excuse me, *our* investigation—well, yours really. Five years ago I would have been behind you all the way. Even twelve months ago I would have supported you." Riley's eyes were more pleading than annoyed. "But we've only got two months left, Charlie. *The Commies practically run the place already!* Now they could have my arse for this—well, yours really. I'll have to see the commissioner. Please stay home tonight, in case someone wants to see you."

When Chan had gone, Riley sought and obtained an immediate interview with Ronald Tsui, Hong Kong's first Chinese commissioner of police.

Half an hour later Riley was sitting at a huge desk in the largest office on the fifth floor of Caine House, the most prestigious building in the Arsenal Street complex. On the other side Commissioner Tsui sat in a leather chair under an oil painting of the queen of England in full ceremonial dress. Tsui, who had been educated in England, spoke in that language to Riley.

"And you say that these coastguards had orders to intercept this bag with its incriminating contents?"

"Yes, sir."

"A bit of a coincidence, isn't it? I mean, Chief Inspector Chan just happens to follow a lead that just happens to take him toward the Sokos at the same time that these chaps just happen to be in the area?"

Riley looked at the desk, then up at the commissioner. The game they were playing was a kind of double bluff that penetrated every aspect of life in government. Tsui knew that the coastguards had deliberately intercepted Chan's search, but he wanted to report the allegation as Riley's, not his own. Riley wanted to report it as Chan's, not his.

"I believe I told you, Commissioner, according to Chan, there have been a number of other attempts by an outside agency to monitor the investigation into these murders."

Tsui nodded. "Yes, you did. At least you convinced me that he convinced you that someone had tapped his office telephone and copied some of the confidential files related to the case."

"Well, if this other agency went so far as to tap one of our phones as he alleges, which presents some logistical problems for them, it's not farfetched to imagine they were intercepting ship-to-shore radio reports that Chan was issuing every half hour from the time he left Queen's Pier. After all, ship-to-shore can be monitored by just about anyone with the right frequency on their radio."

Tsui nodded. "So?"

"I think you see the point, sir. If his radio reports were being intercepted, it would be a simple matter for them to issue instructions to the nearest Communist coastguards to keep an eye out and to be especially interested in anything he salvaged from the sea."

"That's how you see it?"

"That's how Chan sees it."

Tsui looked as if he were considering the possibility for the first time. "I think I follow you so far, Chief Superintendent. But one thing still puzzles me. If the coastguards had been given such instructions, why did they let him go?"

"Firstly, they weren't sure whose waters they were in, ours or theirs. He managed to bluff them. Secondly, and most important, these were not high-flying cadres with a passionate concern with national security. Chan describes them as the usual bunch of yobs in uniform who could be persuaded to betray just about anything for the right price."

The commissioner sighed. "This will have to go higher. The political adviser will have to be informed."

Riley saw that the interview was over. He stood up. "Yes, sir," he said in English, repeated the same words in Cantonese, turned smartly and left.

After he had gone, the commissioner sat for a moment. He tapped the government-issue blotting pad with his forefinger, then lifted the telephone.

"Get me the commissioner for security. When I've done with him, I'll need to speak to the political adviser. And I'll need a summary of Chief Inspector S. K. Chan's personal file, please."

4

Arsenal Street Police Headquarters was only a short walk from Wanchai, where Chan had trained as a cadet. On the surface the area was a red-light district of international renown, but Chan was intimate with its other features. He liked the old-style low-rise apartment blocks in the narrow back streets with their external chaos of air-conditioning units, hanging gardens, illegal balconies, chicken-wire aviaries and satellite dishes. In a side alley he opened his lungs to Chinese odors. Every neighborhood had its essence; Mongkok, where he lived and worked, was a full-bodied diesel with nuances of glutamate. Wanchai's was a lighter palette: fried cabbage, stale beer and hundred-year-old sex.

Despite his Caucasian features, he merged effortlessly with the pavement beggars and bag people, the street vendors and the small shop owners who rarely closed their narrow roll-down shutters before ten o'clock at night. Culture was a matter of personal history expressed through subliminal gestures; within seconds people who had never met him before accepted him as Chinese. His mastery of the street slang helped. He sank gratefully into a feeling of ethnic belonging. Speaking the language his mother had spoken to the kind of people she had spent her life with, he became almost loquacious. In the vegetable market that meandered for a quarter mile the length of Wanchai Road he bargained for pleasure at stalls selling half-black eggs that had been buried in the ground, jackfruit, garlic, ginseng, live frogs and chicks. He watched three women pick at bean sprouts; he discussed next Wednesday's racing at Happy Valley with men he knew to be triad members and matched them expletive for expletive. Chan would have turned down the governorship of Hong Kong so long as he could always be Chinese in an Asian street market.

He basked in anonymity for forty minutes before he admitted to himself that he had come to see the old man. He turned down a side street in which five men strolled toward him in single file, each carrying a bamboo bird cage containing a tiny yellow bird. A few yards down the narrow street he stopped at the Kwong Hing Book Store Ltd. The name of the company was the only Roman lettering in the store. Every book was printed on a Chinese press in Chinese characters. Chan liked the smell of Chinese books, subtly different from Western books. There were no pictures on the heavy paper covers, no commercialism at all; the print was everything. It was the way books should always smell: paper, binding and words, no frills.

There was no counter and no register at which to take money, only a cheap wooden desk in one corner and behind it an old Chinese man with a gray beard constructed of sparse hairs, some of which reached as far as his T-shirt, which was black and bore a portrait of John Lennon. He looked up.

Under the beard the skin was stretched over unfleshed bones. The eyes glinted like water at the bottom of a well. It was a face that shocked; it bore no sign of physical abuse, yet Chan could not look at it without seeing suffering beyond that which humans were designed to endure. The old man nodded.

"Well, well." He spoke English with an American accent.

"I was just passing."

"Bullshit."

"Aren't you pleased to see me?"

"The man who saved me from exile? Sure. I thought you'd dropped me. It's been a long time."

"Only six months."

"Too long." The deep eyes flashed at Chan. "I scared you last time, huh?"

"You scare everybody."

The old man sighed. "Not me. Truth. That's what scares every-body." Chan nodded. "But you came back. I knew you would."

"Did you?"

The old man chuckled. "Actually, no. But I hoped you would. You're not an ordinary Chinese. You're half Irish. Sometimes the Irish are attracted to truth. It's a kind of minority reaction against the main bias of their culture." He smiled. The American English was perfect and somehow dated. Chan thought of American films set in small towns in the fifties. "And then there was my little problem last year. You showed character. You're different, for sure."

"They were abusing the law. You were right."

" 'They' being the government of Hong Kong. Your employers, as a matter of fact. They were looking for a pretext for deporting me, and you spoke up for me. It could have damaged your career. That showed guts."

Chan shrugged. "They didn't hold it against me. The British aren't vindictive."

The old man turned his head thoughtfully as if considering the point. "True. They're hard to like, but they have definite qualities. If the Third World had remained at the emotional age of thirteen the British Empire could have lasted a thousand years."

"You've been writing?"

He nodded emphatically. "I've found a new publisher in San Francisco. Outrage doesn't sell the way it did in the sixties, but he thinks the whole China thing is more marketable than it was." He held up his hands. "I do what I can."

Chan smiled, despite a sense of doom. "If they try to deport you again, they won't listen to a cop like me telling them you're an honest citizen and you loved your mother. They'll find a way. The British only take so much democracy; then things happen be-hind closed doors. They're like that."

The old man harrumphed. "I would like them to deport me for publishing a book. Think of the publicity. Someone might actually buy it."

Chan nodded. "Well, no one can say you're a quitter."

The old man frowned. "I told you why. You steal a man's soul only once. Second time he fights to the death. I told you that."

"Yes. I remember."

"That's what scared you?"

"No."

"So what scared you? I like to know these things; it helps refine my marketing."

"The photographs, of course. Photographs scare more than words."

The old man looked at Chan. "I don't really believe I scared you. I know every shade of fear, every nuance. I'm a world authority on fear, and you weren't afraid. You were upset but not afraid."

Chan shrugged. "Perhaps. Perhaps I need to see them again. You still have them?"

"Even more. I get photos like that almost every month now." Chan remembered the old man's curious way of sliding his eyes over him. It was like a radar scan that was over in less than a second. Chan knew it as a survival skill developed by long-term prisoners. "Something happen to you today?" The old man looked away as he said it.

Chan shrugged. "Just a case I'm working on."

"So?"

"There's a China dimension; at least there might be."

"Ah! The dragon blew on you. Now you want to know more about the dragon?"

"Maybe those pictures will focus what I'm feeling. I don't know."

With difficulty the old man stood up. "You're a good boy. A little slow but good. I'll show you those pictures, and some new ones, on one condition. I have a potential recruit coming next week with his wife. I would like you to be here."

"Why?"

"Don't pretend to be dumb. On my own I'm an eccentric old

fart with poor Cantonese and an American accent. I'm also a world-class loser, according to the value structures of this city. With a chief inspector of police in the room, though, I could look almost respectable.''

Chan looked the old man in the eye. "You're ruthless."

"You mean I'm using you? Of course. Not for any hope of personal gain, though. You'll come?''

Chan remained silent.

The old man smiled again. "You're a real old-style Chinaman, even if you do have Irish genes. You bury gold under old rags. I bet I'm the only one in this whole town who knows you have the heart of a saint."

"You're right, you need to refine your marketing. Me as saint isn't even vaguely credible."

He followed the old man into a tiny bedroom adjacent to the bookshop. The old man pointed at black-and-white photographs strung on lines across the bed. Chan gave the old man a sharp glance.

"You took them out of the box?"

"I sleep with them," the old man said gruffly. "Weird, huh?"

Chan did not answer. In the picture in front of his nose he recognized the fallen features of someone condemned to death. A printed caption at the bottom of the photograph read: "Female prisoner being escorted by military policemen in an execution parade held in Baise Municipality of Guangxi Autonomous Region on August 29, 1990." As his eye took in the other photographs on the string, he saw that each one recorded an execution. Some of the captions recorded executions that had taken place as recently as a month ago.

The old man's hand was gripping his arm because Chan had started to shake. Blinking down tears, Chan pulled himself free. "I better go."

The old man followed him back into the bookshop. He looked into the black tunnel eyes. The old man made his features plead. "Try to make Thursday."

At the door Chan left without saying good-bye. Out in the street he lit a cigarette and inhaled deeply. China: The Hong Kong experience was like camping in the mouth of a cyclops's lair. Survival required meticulous study of the creature's habits, but everyone came sooner or later to the same conclusion: The cyclops was insane.

5

Although it was fairly late in the evening before a slot could be found when all three men would be free, the commissioner for security, the commissioner of police and the political adviser all considered the matter sufficiently urgent to meet that night. Tsui picked up Caxton Smith, the commissioner for security, in his chauffeur-driven white Toyota. Together they entered the lift lobby of the government buildings in Queensway, which, at 10:00 P.M., were almost deserted. On the twenty-first floor they walked down the corridor to the office of the political adviser.

Of all the many hundreds of English men and women working for the Hong Kong government, only the political adviser was appointed directly by the Foreign Office in London out of its diplomatic service. He answered not to the governor but to the colonial masters in London and was intended to be the mother country's eyes and ears. He oversaw every action by the colonial administration that could conceivably have an effect on the precarious relationship between London and Beijing.

Like the political adviser, the commissioner for security also spent 90 percent of his time preoccupied with Chinese matters, but for opposite reasons. Almost all of Hong Kong's frontier, land and sea, was shared with the PRC and it was the C for S's job to deal with the many border incidents that arose, from smuggling to illegal immigration to calculated border intimidation by Beijing.

Tsui, who had come from home, wore an open-neck shirt and casual trousers. The two Englishmen were still in their business suits. They sat at a long table in an anteroom to the PA's main office.

Milton Cuthbert looked up from the short briefing Tsui had been able to send over before the meeting.

"Tell me, Ronny, about the murders first. That seems to be where it all begins."

Tsui cleared his throat and hesitated a moment before speaking. "Apart from the sensational aspect, not that remarkable. You read about them in the papers. The so-called Mincer Murders. A vat of human flesh, which forensic analysis showed to be the product of three different bodies, was found decaying in a warehouse in Mong-kok. The bodies had been put through an industrial mincer and were therefore totally unrecognizable. Further examination showed that all three had been minced while still alive."

Cuthbert jerked his head up and raised his eyebrows. "You can tell that?"

"It's all a question of the condition of the nerve endings and blood composition. When the body is in extreme pain, the nerves literally shrink in terror, just like the owner himself, and some sort of chemical is secreted into the blood. The mincer left fairly large chunks, permitting a minimal forensic examination. The mincemeat in the vat showed consistently clenched, terror-stricken nerves, and blood analysis supported the view that the victims were alive when minced."

"Dear God," Cuthbert said.

Caxton Smith rubbed his knees nervously. "Dreadful business."

"Go on, Ronny."

"There was one other startling revelation by forensic. The bodies had been decapitated during or after the mincing. That is to say that the heads were not minced. No cerebral matter at all was found in the vat."

"Just a minute," Caxton Smith said. "These victims were still alive whilst being minced, but decapitated?"

Tsui shot Smith a sharp glance. "Hardly. The only explanation is that at a certain point in the mincing—probably when the victims had already bled to death—the heads were removed."

"And not found by the investigating team until today?"

"Evidently not," Cuthbert said, "but let's not jump the gun. Historical sequence, if you don't mind, Ronny."

Tsui paused to take a cough sweet out of a small box before proceeding. He sucked it as he spoke. "Preliminary investigations suggested that the murders were drug-related. At first we assumed the triads—who else? The district commander at Mongkok appointed Chief Inspector Chan to lead the inquiry. However, with the intense media interest and the discovery by Chan that his telephone was tapped and that someone had been copying the case files without his consent, I gave instructions that Chan should report directly to headquarters, a precaution I habitually take with high-profile cases. I appointed Chief Superintendent Riley to supervise the investigation."

"How did he discover the illegal copying?" Cuthbert asked.

Tsui smiled. "Chan's basically a streetfighting man. He came up through the ranks and has a hundred tricks up his sleeve. I seem to remember he pasted a hair over the file—something like that. I forget exactly what, but it was sufficient to convince him that there had been some copying done."

"What was done about it?"

"The tap was removed, and the files were kept in a safe from then on. As far as we know, there's been no further interference— at least until today."

"The coastguards and all that?"

"Yes—it's all in the briefing paper I sent you."

The three men sat silently for several minutes. Caxton Smith was the first to break the silence. "Just to set my mind at rest, Ronny, why did you think it was a drug-related case?"

"It's not a question of what I think. You simply have to start with a reasonable hypothesis to give your investigation direction, and drugs were the only one. First, Mongkok is a notorious triad center. Second, with the premeditated torture of three people it just doesn't look like a crime of passion. Third, the perpetrators would have had to buy or borrow a large industrial meat mincer— an indication that money was no object. There are plenty of cheaper

ways to intimidate and murder. Fourth, there had to be a degree
of organization. Organized crime is financed in large part by drug
dealing.''

"But it could have been a gangland vendetta?''

Tsui sucked loudly on his sweet. "Which brings me to my fifth
and probably best reason. There have been no gangland reprisals as
far as we know, and our intelligence is pretty good. Which suggests
that the victims were murdered by their own organization.''

"Why?''

Tsui shrugged. "Who knows? Betrayal? Hands in the till? Knew
too much? Tried to usurp someone higher up the triad pyramid?''

Cuthbert tapped the table. "Very well, three drug-related murders seem an eminently reasonable hypothesis. That doesn't encroach on my patch at all.''

Tsui looked at him with something approaching amusement. Caxton Smith also smiled. Cuthbert looked from one to the other.

"Well?''

Caxton Smith spoke. "You know very well it doesn't encroach
on your patch, Milton, until you include in your list of suspects the
world's largest criminal organization specializing in the transporta-
tion and sale of heroin in Southeast Asia. Some call it the biggest
triad of all.''

Tsui swallowed the last of his cough drop. "I believe he's talking
about the People's Liberation Army, Milton.''

Cuthbert sat back in his seat, looked from one of his colleagues
to the other, then fell into thought. One of the advantages of working for a benevolent dictatorship, which was what the colonial system amounted to, was that there was not a great turnover of
personnel at the top. One saw the same faces at meetings year after
year until what was left unsaid became more significant than anything in the minutes. There were also disadvantages. It was really
not possible, for example, for him to maintain that the rumors of
the extensive criminal interests of the People's Liberation Army
were untrue. All three men knew perfectly well that PLA generals
these days sold sophisticated weaponry to the highest bidder by

taking the Middle Eastern potentate, terrorist, whomever on a tour of his army and having him pick out the rocket, bomb, grenade, tank, whatever of his choice. *And all this without the consent of anyone in Beijing.* And then there were drugs.

The fact was that ever since Deng Xiaoping had seen what Mikhail Gorbachev had seen in the USSR—namely, that a conventional socialist economy sooner or later ends in bankruptcy— the natural genius of the Chinese people for every aspect of capitalism had been unleashed. And one of the commodities of the bad old times introduced by the British themselves—namely, opium, these days in the form of heroin—was suddenly doing a roaring trade all along the old route from northern Burma through Yunnan and overland to Hong Kong and Shanghai, hence by ship to just about anywhere west. In Yunnan the army was openly involved, but in Hong Kong the generals had to make use of the triads.

The problem, if you were political adviser to the governor of Hong Kong, was how to play down the delinquency of the three-million-man Communist army in order to avoid confrontation between the forces of law within the colony and the crooks in green over the border. This was the meaning of the silence around the table: The commissioner of police had brought with him the nightmare Cuthbert had been carefully sidestepping for the past ten years.

Caxton Smith broke the silence. "Let's face it, it was bound to happen, sooner or later."

Cuthbert grunted then stared at Tsui for a moment. "I think we need to know more about Chief Inspector Chan."

Tsui nodded. From a slim plastic folder he drew a single sheet of paper.

"Chan Siu-kai, nicknamed Charlie by just about everyone after the ridiculous fictional character, is thirty-six years old. Divorced— from an Englishwoman. No children. He's half Chinese, half of Irish extraction, but his loyalties and identity are entirely Chinese. His father disappeared without marrying his mother although he stayed long enough to provide Chan with a younger sister, Jenny Chan Wong. She's a celebrated beauty and an ex-Miss Hong Kong, by the way, married to a wealthy Chinese lawyer.

"Most of Chan's early life was spent in a squatter hut in the New Territories, not far from Sai Kung on the east coast. There's a tragedy, I'm afraid. After the Irishman left her, Chan's mother was killed by Red Guards during an ill-advised return to her native village in Guangdong. Charlie was fifteen years old at the time. Charlie and Jenny were left to be brought up by an aunt, who also lived in a nearby squatter hut. Chan joined the police as a constable when he was seventeen and rose steadily to his present rank of detective chief inspector. He's not thought to be especially ambitious. His relatively rapid promotion has been due to a natural intelligence, tenacity in solving crimes and willingness to work long hours. Not especially social. Only hobby as far as we know is scuba diving, although in his twenties he won the police karate championship. Spends even more time at work now that his marriage has failed."

Tsui put the paper down, waited.

"I see." Cuthbert pressed his lips tight until the corners of his mouth turned down. "I did rather wonder why a perfectly ordinary chief inspector had bothered to stand up to some Communist thugs in their own waters. He hates them, I suppose?"

"I've never asked him. But how would you feel about the organization that directly or indirectly murdered your mother?"

Cuthbert glanced sharply at the commissioner. "Quite. But that does rather make him unsuitable for the present case, doesn't it?"

Tsui's features went flat. "You could say that. Although an administration with a little backbone might take the opposite view."

Cuthbert stared at Tsui. Tsui stared back. Caxton Smith stared at the floor. There was a long silence.

"I think I understand Ronny's point, Milton. And I agree with him," Caxton Smith said eventually.

"Oh, really! What point is that?"

"That when it comes down to it, we British can be the world's most nauseating cowards."

Cuthbert looked from one to the other, tapped his pad, muttered unintelligibly, stood up, went to a window, stared out. The large ships in the harbor were lit up from stern to bow in garlands of light, like Christmas trees. Beyond them lay Kowloon, the other part of the colony of Hong Kong. And thirty miles to the north lay the People's Republic of China where lived one quarter of the world's population with an army of over three million and an enduring resentment against Great Britain dating back to the Opium Wars. Unlike the other two men, he regarded the land over the border as part of the constituency with which he worked. He understood Tsui's point of view, but as a senior diplomat one had . . . other considerations.

He turned back to the table, drew his chair near to Tsui, who was sitting stiffly. When Cuthbert spoke, it was in a soft, almost consoling voice.

"Think about it, Ronny. If he finds out who was behind the killings, and he probably will, and if it's who we think it might be, he'll find a way to tell the world. I really can't have a chief inspector with a twenty-odd-year-old grudge against the Communists upsetting the relationship between Great Britain and China. Not now, not barely two months away from the handover of power. Anyway, suppose the cat is let out of the bag. What is Britain supposed to do? Arrest the Red Army?"

It was Tsui's turn to stand up. "Maybe letting the cat out of the bag is what matters. I'm Chinese; you're not. On fourth June 1989 those old men in Beijing ordered the massacre of thousands of peaceful young demonstrators. They ran over them with tanks— minced them up, you might say. In eight weeks' time those same old men will be running this place, where six million of my people have sought refuge. Every one of us sitting here will be gone. I'll be retired, and you'll be following your careers elsewhere. We can afford to make a fuss now, when there's a chance of focusing world opinion on the problem. I would consider it a betrayal of my people to miss an opportunity to expose the nefarious activities of those thugs over the border. However, I've taken my oath to the queen and all that, and I'll obey orders. But if you want me to take Chan off the case, I want it in writing, signed by the governor."

Cuthbert's face hardened. "Very well, Ronny. You'll have your orders. Signed by the governor. But I'll have to fax London first. Just hold Chan off for twenty-four hours, would you? And in the meantime I suggest you appoint this Chief Superintendent Riley to work closely with him. Just in case he gets a little too creative even for your taste."

In the glacial silence that followed, it was Caxton Smith once more who intervened.

"What's he like, this Chief Superintendent Riley?"

Tsui coughed. "Reliable, hardworking, sensitive to political nuances."

"That sounds like an official line, Ronny," Cuthbert interrupted. "Off the record, what sort of man is Riley?"

Although bilingual, Tsui thought first of a Cantonese word that he took a couple of seconds to translate into the English vernacular.

"He's a jerk." He looked from one to the other. "If that's all, perhaps you'll excuse me, gentlemen? Caxton, d'you mind finding your own way home?"

"Not at all, Ronny," Smith said. He smiled.

"Good night, Ronny." Cuthbert was able to sound cheerful, as if there had been no disagreement at all.

Tsui paused at the door. He seemed about to say something, then thought better of it and left. Cuthbert and Smith exchanged glances, like two men who after a long wait could finally get down to business.

6

"He's a terrific chap, Ronny. I'm really very fond of him, you know," Cuthbert said.

"And so am I, Milton. I'm afraid your ruse didn't work. It was you alerted the Commie coastguards, I take it?"

"My people were listening to Chan's radio. It seemed like a chance worth taking. Without those heads the investigation would have ground to a halt. Now . . ." He raised his arms, let them drop, shook his head. "Damn and blast!"

"Those Red coastguards have always been the lowest of the low. They're all as bent as a two-bob watch. Look, I hope you didn't think I went too far tonight, playing devil's advocate?"

"Certainly not. You summoned exactly the right amount of verisimilitude. We can't have them thinking we're ganging up on them at this stage."

"Quite."

"This Charlie Chan—a problem?"

Cuthbert shrugged. "I really don't know. He sounds too good for what we want. And then there was a little thing Ronny conveniently left out. You remember that old chap who's trying to raise awareness about *laogai*? The one we were thinking of deporting last year, until the press got hold of the story and some damned busybody MP threatened to ask a question in Parliament?"

"Matter of fact I do."

"Chan vouched for him. The old man instructed lawyers, and the lawyers obtained an affidavit from Chan, who swore he'd known the old man for years and could vouch for his character. My chaps were furious, but Ronny protected his man. Chan hates the Reds all right. Very telling for Ronny to leave it out of Chan's curriculum vitae."

"So you do know all about Chan?"

Cuthbert's eyes darted. "Yes, I do. I didn't want Ronny to know how closely I've been watching him. It seemed important to act ignorant."

They sat in silence for a minute.

Smith tapped the table. "Just out of curiosity, Milton, how did you swing it with those coastguards?"

"I rang their headquarters, told them to watch out for a Hong Kong police launch chasing a plastic bag." He smiled. "Piece of cake."

"Impersonating?"

Cuthbert took out an old silver cigarette case, selected a Turkish cigarette, lit it with a silver butane lighter. In doing so, he illuminated his long face, aquiline nose, case-hardened eyes: the disdainful features of an eagle.

"General Xian. I was phoning from Hong Kong after all. It had to be someone very senior who was based here."

He produced a long phrase in Mandarin that Caxton Smith didn't understand. The rough accent of an aging Chinese peasant general was instantly recognizable, however.

Smith shook his head. Ever since the beginning of the nineteenth century when the Great Game of intelligence and counterintelligence operations on the borders between the British Empire and Russia and China had begun, the Oriental Department of the Foreign Office had attracted the brightest and the best—and the most eccentric, men with double firsts from Oxford or Cambridge who behaved as if it were still 1897.

"You're a damned clever chap, Milton. Damned clever. Of course it was you tapped Chan's telephone and copied his files?"

Cuthbert inhaled on the fine Turkish tobacco, looked away. "Not clever enough, it seems." Caxton Smith raised his eyebrows.

With his free hand Cuthbert pinched the narrow bridge of his nose. "I've been stalking or shadowing Xian, whichever way you want to put it, for more than half my career. I've got taps on his telephones and electronic surveillance to cover him twenty-four hours a day. I was convinced that the general couldn't eat a spring roll without my knowing about it. But I'm damned if I understand what he's up to this time."

"You're totally convinced he ordered these murders?"

Cuthbert dropped his hand. "No, I'm not. At first I thought that must be the reason he's so obsessed with Chan's investigation. Then I began to wonder. What does he care if he gets found out? Nobody's going to prosecute *him*. So why the interest in the case? The old boy's in a frenzy about it. Acting purely on instinct, I'm trying to block the investigation because after thirty years in diplomacy I can smell a scandal when it's creeping down the Yangtze, and this one is big, whatever it is. In diplomacy, Caxton, a scandal is worse than a holocaust. One hint in the press of what Xian is really doing in Hong Kong, and there'll be the biggest imaginable row. Can you imagine, *eight weeks before handover?*"

"Ah! Yes, that would land us in a bit of a pickle. And might one ask, strictly off the record, what exactly Xian *is* doing in Hong Kong? I think I've been wanting to ask you that question for as long as I can remember."

Cuthbert studied the end of his cigarette. "Off the record, Caxton, he's taking over whether anyone approves or not, and the West can shove its democracy up its arse. That's a very rough translation from the Mandarin." He put the cigarette to his lips and inhaled reflectively. "I couldn't tell you the precise moment when my career became devoted to the study of General Xian. China was my business, with particular reference to Hong Kong. At first all one did was watch Beijing and read all the diplomatic dispatches. Then things began to fall apart, Chinese style. That is to say, you wouldn't have known they were falling apart except for the subtlest signals that China watchers look for. Little by little Beijing was less powerful; there were centers of power elsewhere in the country; people began to talk about a return to the old warlord system. Xian is an extremely secretive man. By the time it became clear that he was a major player, he was already in control of most of southern China. Not officially in control, of course, but he more or less runs the place. All the senior cadres answer to him, and in a fight his troops would side with him against Beijing—which is why Beijing leaves him alone. China wasn't my business anymore, he was."

7

When Chan emerged from Central underground station that same evening in response to Tsui's summons, Typhoon Alan had meandered a hundred miles closer. The wind had freshened, and the meteorological office had issued a Typhoon Signal Number Three. Although it was now past eleven o'clock in the evening, workmen were fitting vertical wooden slats to protect the plate glass windows of the shops all along Queen's Road. Planters, portable advertising signs, anything unable to resist hundred-mile-an-hour gusts had already disappeared from the streets.

Chan walked up the slope under the Hong Kong Bank, crossed the street, took the stairs by the side of the branch post office to the officers' mess, where Tsui liked to hold informal meetings. The commissioner was standing at the bar talking to the Chinese barman when Chan entered. After ordering a pint of lager for Chan, Tsui led the way to a small table far from the bar. He carried his own glass to which a cardboard beer mat had attached itself.

"Quite an adventure you had today," Tsui said.

Chan twitched. "Mind if I smoke?" He lit a Benson & Hedges. "Scared me."

Tsui watched Chan closely. "You know, you have quite a reputation."

"Me? What for?"

"Fanaticism. Is that what possessed you to go into Chinese waters today?"

"I wasn't checking our position. It could only have been a few yards. We needed that bag for the investigation."

Tsui's frown conflicted with the pride in his eyes. "But you could have got yourself killed. You know what they're like."

Chan swallowed the first inch of the lager, was about to put it back on the table, then gulped another inch. "Look, you tell me to stop the investigation, I'll stop. Until then—I mean, I'm not going to be the one to give in to them. The British can, you can, but I won't." Under the commissioner's gaze he added reluctantly, "Unless ordered, of course."

Of course obedience was a Confucian virtue. During the siege of Nanking, Chan had read, Japanese machine gunners had fired down narrow streets into charging Chinese soldiers until the roads were blocked with mountains of bodies like sandbags and some of the guns had melted. Any other race would have taken cover after the first casualties, but the Chinese kept coming. Why? Because they had been ordered to. It was this self-obliterating obedience the British would rely on when they turned six million free people over to the criminal regime in Beijing. Anywhere else the riots would have started long ago.

Tsui dropped the frown. He smiled. Chan wondered if the tiny diamonds in his eyes were the beginning of tears. "You have my support—and my blessing. But please remember, we are a small tribe."

"Chinese?"

"No—free Chinese. And I'm afraid there's a compromise that has to be made." Chan swallowed more beer. "If the case is allowed to go ahead, you'll have to work more closely with Riley."

Chan used a Cantonese word. It was identical to the one Tsui had recently translated in his head. Tsui laughed.

When they left each other on Queen's Road, Central was deserted. Chan walked aimlessly down the main street in a western direction. It was fear, not the time of night, that had cleared the city of people: The tropical storm had intensified, and there was a rumor that it would go up to eight during the night. Even though the wind was not yet at typhoon level, it pulled at Chan's hair, and he leaned into it as he pressed on all alone with his thoughts. Arabs feared the sun, Russians the cold, Californians earthquakes; in

Southeast Asia wind could become a ferocious beast stronger than buildings. He had read a contemporary Chinese poem in which wind was a billion invisible people in a stampede, smashing everything in their path. The poet had not needed to stress the point: In ancient mythology wind was a manifestation of the Dragon; the Dragon Throne had belonged to the emperor of China.

Tonight, though, Chan had a feeling that Alan had changed course, as typhoons often did, leaving him the freedom of the streets. He could not remember the last time he had experienced space to spare. It was an eerie sensation, as if the lights of the city had been left on exclusively for him. A chrome-plated pillar on Connaught Road curved the light streaming from an empty Pekinese restaurant; in the bright pillar five hundred fragmented and wind-blown Chans populated a town full of lurid lights, small restaurant tables and the illuminated Chinese character for Beijing, repeated to infinity.

8

Two hours later Milton Cuthbert had composed and sent a fax to the Foreign Office in London over a secure telephone line. The fax recommended that the FO take the unusual step of ordering the governor to order the commissioner of police to take Chan off the case. Without an explanation the FO, Cuthbert knew, would have trouble believing that a Hong Kong policeman of any race could pose a threat to international relations.

Cuthbert admired the chief inspector's tenacity. Indeed the commissioner of police had not done the Eurasian detective full justice in his short résumé. Cuthbert had discovered that Chan achieved a 90 percent success rate in the detection of serious crime. It was said that in regard to the remaining 10 percent Chan usually identified the culprits but lacked sufficient evidence to prosecute. Chan was a brilliant policeman or a dangerous fanatic, depending on what desk you sat at.

The diplomat was renowned for his ability to express on a half sheet of paper the essence of any problem no matter how subtle and complex, and it was the exercise of this gift that had taken up the bulk of his concentration since the meeting with Tsui and Caxton Smith. It was only after he had sent the fax and was relaxing in his apartment with a glass of cognac that he began to question his fundamental assumption during the meeting. There was absolutely no way that London wanted to risk public exposure of what was well known in all diplomatic circles where the Far East was discussed: The army of the People's Republic of China, the PLA, was the largest criminal organization in the history of the world.

If that news emerged from an official source—a medium-ranking Hong Kong policeman would do—even at this eleventh hour Britain might be expected to do something to protect the six million people who lived in Hong Kong from the predators over the border. But London wanted most not to have to do anything at all until the colony had been safely handed over to Beijing at midnight on June 30. After that the UK could deplore the growth of corruption and the likely loss of human rights in its ex-colony from a position of zero responsibility. At present any crime in which General Xian was interested was, by definition, a source of concern because detection would likely lead to revelations about his extensive criminal connections both in and beyond Hong Kong. With Cuthbert's guidance that was the line London would take.

Or would it? Over the past year the influence of General Xian had increased to extraordinary levels. A hundred subtle clues had forced Cuthbert to entertain an almost unthinkable possibility: Xian possessed the means to go over his head to his masters in Whitehall, and Xian, more than anyone, wanted Chan to complete his investigation for reasons Cuthbert could only guess at.

The answer came sooner than expected. When he returned to his office at eight-thirty the next morning, a top secret fax was waiting to be signed for. It read: "In the view of the Service, Chief Inspector Chan is eminently qualified for the investigation in question. We see no reason to alter our policy of noninterference in internal policing matters. Your recommendation is rejected."

Cuthbert pondered the fax for a long moment. He had been too long in the Foreign Office to regard such an instruction as final. The hierarchical structure of the FO was Hindu in its gradations of seniority, its shades of status, its jealous retention of caste distinctions. The writer of the message, he noted, was of exactly the same rank as himself. As an experienced paper warrior Cuthbert quietly decided to take the matter higher with arguments that would appeal to the Brahmins at the top of the tree. He had not intended that the removal of Chief Inspector Chan, for whom he had the highest regard, should become a mission, but in diplomacy as in life it was not always possible to choose one's enemies. In any event, it could only be for the chief inspector's own good. After June, Hong Kong would not be an ideal refuge for a man who knew too much.

From a drawer under his desk he took out a single sheet of paper that consisted of a blurred photocopy of a note written in inelegant Chinese characters. The copy had been stamped "Top Secret" by MI6, which had obtained it and passed it on to Cuthbert as part of a routine intelligence-gathering exercise over the border. In truth the document was not especially secret since its contents was probably a matter of common knowledge throughout the Communist administration in South China. Cuthbert had kept it without being entirely convinced of its relevance to Chan's investigation.

The note, written by an officer of the Communist Ministry of Public Security, recorded, in language bordering on outrage, that two senior Communist cadres based in Guangdong had suddenly gone missing and—here was the rub—their disappearance did not seem to have been precipitated by any investigation into their activities by the MPS; on the contrary, there was strong evidence to suggest that they had been kidnapped by counterrevolutionary or criminal elements. The kidnapping had taken place at about the time that the victims in Chan's inquiry had met their ends. Cuthbert had no evidence to indicate that the disappearance of the two cadres was connected to the Mincer Murders, but he could not think of a better reason why General Xian should take such an interest in Chan's investigation.

As with most successful careers, Cuthbert's had been much assisted by the patronage of someone of power and influence who liked him. With a fountain pen he wrote a note on a blank sheet of paper and instructed his secretary to post it to a private address in London. The note read: "Michael, we'll have to talk. If you can possibly get away for a few days I'd be eternally grateful. Milton."

9

They called her Polly because they had found her in a polythene bag. Her two Chinese companions Aston named Jekyll and Hyde: English humor.

The forensic artist, Angie, healed all wounds. With an airbrush she blew new life into Polly and restored her youth. Twenty-eight, twenty-nine, not much over thirty anyway. Green eyes with generous lids smiled above high cheekbones, bouncing hair parted in the middle over a noble brow. Her new nose was fine and Anglo-American; it pointed to the sky. From her cheeks Angie released postmortem swelling; with a pencil she cured the bruises over her temples. She placed small pearls in holes in her brand-new ears. She took special care over Polly's new lips: thin with a knowing curve.

Aston fell in love with her. Chan stared at her in preference to Jekyll and Hyde. Who was she? He propped up the posthumous portrait with those of her two companions on the left side of his desk, in front of the photograph of a very young Eurasian constable receiving an award for bravery from the then Governor Sir Murray Maclehose.

A black industrial-quality government telephone dominated the other side of the desk. Nothing had changed in police offices during the past twenty years. There were the same metal shelves, gray filing cabinets, buff-colored cardboard files, crumpled law manuals, a small metal wardrobe where Chan had kept the same white shirt and tie for ten years. Forensic science had made giant strides, but the only effect technology had had on Chan's personal environment

was the typewriter; it had disappeared. Nobody trusted cops with
word processors, which were jealously guarded by the typing pool.
The old black Smith Coronas that had faithfully recorded the worst
of human nature for seventy years had been thrown on the scrap
heap, and with them had disappeared the lightning two-finger stab
that police officers had shared with newspaper reporters. Another
hard-won skill superannuated in this breathless century, Chan
thought, like Himalayan trance jogging and platonic love.

The typewriter had been replaced by a Sony Dictaphone. One
look at the tiny plastic grille froze his thoughts like stage fright.
Sometimes Chan couldn't believe how Chinese he was. When the
wheel was invented, the guy who said it wouldn't catch on was
surely named Wong, Kan—or Chan.

The artist's impressions of the three victims had arrived that
morning. Every twenty minutes or so Aston found an excuse to
walk around behind Chan's desk and stare at Polly. The exercise
was accompanied by a pursing of the lips and an inward hiss at a
frequency where anguish and lechery meet.

"What a waste!" Aston said on his fourth visit.

Chan sighed and looked up from the file. "In old China to fall
in love with the dead was considered one of the worst fates. Ghosts
can sap your strength, Dick. Be careful."

Aston grunted mournfully. "No safe sex even with the dead."

Chan leaned back in his chair. "Didn't you get laid last night?
I've noticed that stressful cases seem to activate your gigantic allocation of hormones."

"D'you blame me? On a case like this you need all the R and R
you can get."

"As long as the lay was not procured by waving around your
police identity card?"

Aston's features flattened. "Course not, Chief. I know how you
feel about that sort of thing."

"Me and the commissioner of police. Just a sniff, the slightest
suspicion, and you're on the plane back to Romford, Essex. I'm
not getting heavy, just advising; it's part of my supervisory duty."

"*Back to Romford?*" Aston feigned unendurable distress. "I'd rather cut it off."

Chan nodded gravely. "Your preference for castration rather than repatriation is noted. By the way, what's so terrible about Romford, Essex?"

"Nothing . . . until you've been somewhere else. Even Luton. When you've been here . . . I tell you, honest, I'd give ten years of my life to stay on here."

"On this filthy, polluted, Chink-infested, superficial, crass, materialistic, overheated rock?"

"You know why? Life! The place is buzzing with it, night and day. It's crawling with it, bursting. People flying all over the place earning a crust, nobody has time to sit around moaning. England's on Valium, America's on Prozac, here people still act human. There's youth, ambition, drive. Eighty percent of the population is under thirty."

"So it has nothing to do with the women?"

Aston passed a hand through his hair. "Now I didn't say that, did I? I explicitly didn't say, 'Nothing to do with the women.' "

Chan watched the young man's eyes stray once more to the sketch of Polly.

"I think I understand. Would you mind taking your erection back to your own desk now, before you have an accident?"

At his desk opposite Chan's Aston checked through *The Murder Investigator's Bible*, an American publication that Chan refused to touch. He had Aston refer to it on his behalf.

"DNA stands for deoxyribonucleic acid," Aston explained.

Chan didn't ask what RFLP stood for, or even PCR. It was enough to know that PCR was the short DNA test; you got the results in a day. RFLP took much longer but was more reliable. A detective was put to an election between the two only when he had a shortage of specimens. Chan had a whole vat full, a vat and three heads. Already he had the PCR results and doubted that the RFLP would produce any surprises.

The PCR test had been positive for all three. That is to say, the unique double helix that God stamped like an engine number on the nucleus of every human cell matched. Matched what? Three different double helixes had been identified in the mess in the vat, and each of these was replicated by DNA found in the hair follicles of one or other of the heads. Polly, Jekyll and Hyde were the mess in the vat.

Aston faxed all the foreign consulates in Hong Kong with all three faces, emphasizing Polly because she was probably from overseas. For the American and West European consulates he added a special request to check for missing persons thought to have disappeared on vacation in the Far East. He checked available missing persons lists for Hong Kong, Manila, Singapore, Taipei and Bangkok, the four closest cities most popular with foreigners.

Chan read the odontological report and understood little. He lit a cigarette and dumped the paper on Aston's desk. "You did the course recently; what does he mean, 'Her upper sixteen has amalgam missing'? Which is the upper sixteen?"

Aston read aloud. " 'First bicuspid lower 28, crown missing. Central incisors 9, 24, 25, 8, all broken. Also lateral incisors 10, 23, 26 and 7.' Also what? Broken? Those bastards punched her in the mouth?" Alert now, Aston stared at Chan.

Chan held out his hands, caught the report, turned the pages. "Same for the others. Look. They all got punched in the mouth?"

With Aston standing by his shoulder he flicked through the report, studied the front and back pages. He looked up at Aston.

"No idiot's summary." He sighed. "It'll mean going over to Arsenal Street."

Aston grunted and with the capriciousness of youth lost interest. From Chan's desk his attention was drawn to the large diagram on the wall between the desks.

Chan followed Aston's gaze. The title of the diagram read "Hierarchical Organization of a Typical Triad Society." Underneath someone had scrawled, "What do fireworks, foot-binding, noodles and organized crime have in common? Answer: They were all invented in China."

Chan had no idea where the diagram had come from. It had

appeared one day years ago, and he'd never bothered to take it down. It was the shape of an emperor in a traditional gown. The emperor's toes were the foot soldiers, or *sze kau*, who were referred to as 49's. The value of the numbers rose with status so that a general, known as a red pole, was a 426. Still-higher status attracted higher numbers until the emperor's head was reached.

Aston asked: "Is it true that organized crime started in China?"

"Don't you know?"

Usually English recruits came equipped with detailed knowledge of triads: the rebellion of the black monks of the Shao Lin Monastery, the ancient triad city of Muk Yeung Shing and all the medieval paraphernalia of bloodstained white robes and the initiation ceremony that went on for days. Half the *gweilo* detectives who had passed through his hands planned to write novels featuring the triads and the drug trade.

"Well, I know about the rebellion of the monks at the Shao Lin Monastery, the Five Tiger Generals—all that."

"Of course you do. Have you started your novel yet?"

Aston blushed.

Chan leaned back in his chair, looked up at Aston. "China didn't need to start organized crime; people did it all over the world all by themselves. Our triads authenticate themselves through history because they're Chinese. But it's easy, you just find someone who knows the story and appoint him the incense master. If it wasn't easy, there wouldn't be so many of them."

Next to the diagram was a list of most of the known triad societies operating in Hong Kong: Sun Yee On; United Bamboo; 14K; Fei Lung . . .

"But they do go back a long way, the triads. They were political, right?"

"So they say. Certainly they supported the Kuomintang during the Civil War. But then organized crime and Communists usually hate each other."

"Is that still true? The Commies hate the 14K and all that?"

"They've always loathed each other. The 14K is huge; worldwide it's as big as the People's Liberation Army. Maybe bigger. And they're sophisticated capitalists these days. Sure, they despise the Communists, and the Communists hate them.''

Chan was aware of Aston's continued gaze. Fascination was so stubborn in the young. No use explaining that the exotic was a function of ignorance and distance; sooner or later the Chinese screen would rip, and that gleam in Aston's eye would fade.

"So there'll be some fireworks in a couple of months if the 14K are still here?''

"I wouldn't bet on it.'' Aston raised his eyebrows. "I'm not an expert, but the rumor is that they've found some kind of uneasy accommodation. After all, now that the Communists are not really Communists and the 14K are sophisticated businessmen, maybe they've seen the wisdom of working together.''

"Really?''

"It's just a rumor. In Hong Kong rumors are usually true.''

Aston stood when he saw Chan do so and inwardly girded himself for the coming struggle. It had taken him a while to accept that certain acts that were simple enough in less crowded places in Hong Kong required mental preparation; leaving the police station was an example. Even the compound was crowded day and night with police in and out of uniform: antitriad squads; regional traffic teams; community relations and staff relations officers; police tactical unit; narcotics bureau members; and of course civilians who were allowed to join the mess and who would come and go in various states of inebriation at any time of the day or night.

10

Mongkok is the most populated part of the earth; Chan supposed it offered humans what the caves of North Borneo offered bats: low rent, zero unemployment, refuge from predators. Ninety percent of those who lived there had either fled the PRC or were the children of parents who had fled. With numbers of refugees during the Cultural Revolution reaching tens of thousands per week there had been no time for town planning. The residents were thankful that the sewage system was still functioning.

Every Chinese clan or tribe was represented, from the Muslims of Kashgar in the west to the Chiu Chow from Shantou in the south, from Mongols of the far north to Shanghainese from the coast. Then there were Sikhs from the North-West Frontier, Gurkhas from Nepal, Filipinos, English, American, French. Japanese was the only nationality Chan never came across in Mongkok. There was no golf course.

Many buildings were illegal structures, and those that were not housed illegal businesses. Restaurants flourished over pet shops; car repair workshops ventilated dry cleaners with exhaust fumes; clothing factories the size of living rooms produced copies of designer brands as good as the original; garages housed watchmakers who would produce a thousand copies of any timepiece you liked within forty-eight hours. Pharmacies sold prescription drugs whether or not you had a prescription, and there wasn't a narcotic in existence that you couldn't buy if you knew where to go. Chan and the other homicide detectives agreed in private that theirs was the easier job on the force. Suppose you were trying to stop drugs, smuggling or forgery when your suspect list included every inhabitant?

Mongkok Police Station dominated the corner of Prince Edward and Nathan roads. As far as Chan knew, Edward was the English queen's youngest son, who had yet to turn his private life into an international soap opera; he had no idea who Nathan was: someone grand, white and elsewhere, no doubt. The white man's genius for misnaming the lands he stole was well documented: New York for the Algonquians' country; George Town for everything that was not called Victoria or Albert; America for an Italian who thought he was in India. Did Edward and Nathan know they were trampled day and night by a million larcenous Asians? Or care? He and Aston emerged from the station gate into the crowds and were instantly separated. Like the corpses in the vat, they found it hard to maintain the frontier of self; the river of bodies took you, a corpuscle in a hemorrhage of humans gushing through streets, sidewalks, alleys, basements, shops, buses, cars, taxis. Lunchtime was a locust storm of people choking every orifice of the city, and Chan was suddenly part of it, indistinguishable. Thank god for DNA, the inner proof of personal existence, though rats had it too. He bought his cigarettes from his usual street corner vendor, waited for Aston at the underground.

Aston was searching for him, trying to see over the crowds. They descended the escalator together, slipped through the queues. The underground railway was the only form of transport not gridlocked at this time of day.

On the train the benches were stainless steel. Without other passengers a person would slide from one end to the other, but that circumstance seldom occurred. Chan and Aston were locked in standing position, every motor option paralyzed by the pressure of other bodies. Only eye muscles could move without restraint. Chan found his face twisted slightly upward, condemned to read the underground map over and over. English colonial names competed with Chinese names and lost: Lai Chi Kok, Waterloo, Diamond Hill, Mongkok, Tsim Sha Tsui, Tsuen Wan, Choi Hung.

From Admiralty they walked. The crowds over on Hong Kong

Island were less ferocious, but not much. The four-building complex of Arsenal Street Police Station with its conical gun towers grafted onto the perimeter walls of the compound was a magic castle where a policeman could find refuge from the surging masses. It had air conditioning too.

Chan paused for a moment in the reception area in Arsenal House. He had asked for three-dimensional impressions of Polly, Jekyll and Hyde, in the form of plaster busts. This was expensive, and he'd expected to be refused. But the request form had returned the same day with an endorsement by the commissioner himself.

He telephoned Angie, the forensic artist, whose studio formed part of the corridor occupied by the identification bureau, then asked a female constable at reception to ring down to forensic. The dentist, a part-timer who ran his own private practice two blocks away, was waiting for them. They took a lift, emerged into a government issue corridor: linoleum the color of lead, cream paint that had oozed down the walls like lava and dried in waves. At the end was a door marked "Government Laboratory."

The lab had its own reception. The options were odontology, toxicology, forensic anthropology, serology. The ballistics and firearms identification bureau was in another building. For disciplines not in frequent demand it was still possible for experts to be brought in on retainer from outside government service, which was the case with odontology, although over the years the government laboratory had built up an autonomous expertise in most branches of forensic science.

Dr. Lam was in the small laboratory off the reception area. Chan noticed the white coat, thick lenses, hard features of an old pro indifferent to pain. Other people's anyway. Three plastic jaws were laid out on a Formica bench top. Each jaw carried a neat red tag with a number printed in black. A copy of his report was open next to them.

"How can I help?"

Chan lit a cigarette, saw a no smoking sign, put it out, twitched instead. "Great report, really good. It helps us a lot. Just a couple of questions. I mean, we need to know the state of the teeth—

what d'you call it? the dental profile?—before they were tortured and killed. We also need to know about any damage to the teeth and jaws that happened during the murder." Never at ease with strangers, he looked at Aston. "Right?"

Aston nodded. "And the numbers. We're not too clear about them."

"Numbers?" Dr. Lam frowned. He flicked through his report. "What numbers?"

Aston took out his copy, read: " '31, 32, 16, 17 all have amalgam missing.' "

Lam looked from Aston to Chan. "You never had to deal with forensic odontology before?"

Chan cleared his throat and stopped himself on the point of reaching for a cigarette again. "Not really. Not in Mongkok. People bite each other only rarely. For identification, victims usually have identity cards, fingerprints. Now, ask me about fingerprints. Loops, deltas, ridge counts, bifurcations, islands, tented arches, ulnar loops. See, usually we know who the victim is, we just don't always know who did it."

Lam pushed his spectacles up to the bridge of his nose. They were so thick both eyes were magnified and distorted. It was like looking at two oval fish in a tank.

"I see. Look."

From a briefcase he took out a laminated diagram of a human mouth. "It's easy. Easier than fingerprints. The human mouth has thirty-two teeth. Half of them grow from the top part of the jaw, called the maxilla; the other half from the mandible. Half of them are on the right, the other half on the left. Clear so far? So, the convention is to count from upper right to upper left, then from lower left to lower right. That way the upper third molar number one crunches against the lower third molar number thirty-two. The Caucasian female had fillings missing or seriously eroded from most of her molars."

"Does that indicate violence?"

"Not at all. It indicates neglect. In her youth she had some first-class dental work performed on her mouth. Later she stopped going to a dentist. You have to look elsewhere for signs of violence." He picked up the larger of the three jaws. "Here."

He fitted the jaw around his left hand, opened it, pointed at the upper and lower front teeth with an index finger. "I had these plastic replicas made up of the deceaseds' jaws. See, all four central incisors broken." He scraped the teeth with his finger. The plastic bones vibrated like a cracked tuning fork. "In the actual mouths the remains of all four incisors are still sharp. Not yet worn smooth by use. The breakages are therefore recent. Now, look again."

He replaced the jaw on the table with a rattle. The two parts fell open in a grin. He picked up another set, showed the same damage. There was similar damage to the third. All three victims had suffered breakages to all four front teeth.

Chan scratched his head. "Mind if I smoke? There's no one else here."

Lam shrugged. "Go ahead. But it's bad for your teeth. Leaves a heavy deposit that fosters decay."

Chan lit up, inhaled gratefully. Of all the drugs, nicotine hit the brain quickest. He'd read that somewhere.

"Doesn't make a lot of sense, does it? I mean, if you want to beat someone up, fine. A woman is especially sensitive to damage to her mouth, any part of her face. But if your intention is to murder three people by grinding them up in a mincer, why begin by breaking their front teeth?"

Lam sat back and placed his small hands over his stomach. Behind the spectacles Chan deduced self-love fed by professional snobbery.

"I don't think anyone broke their teeth."

"How's that?" Chan drew again on the cigarette, hoping it would help him to keep up.

"Look."

Lam took up the larger of the three jaws in his left hand as before. He opened it wide. Holding it in that position, he walked across the lab to a small bookshelf with glass doors. He slid open one of the doors, returned with a book. He placed the book in Polly's mouth. He made her chomp down on the book.

"You see, broken, the teeth make a relatively level bite. The incisors don't protrude beyond the other teeth."

"So? You're saying all three victims bit on the same piece of stone hidden in their noodles?"

Calmly Lam sat down, still holding the book and jaw. "Think about it. As we know, they were minced up. Alive." He closed the jaw down again on the book. "Minced up alive." The dentist looked from one to the other to see if either had caught his meaning.

Chan caught Aston's shudder. He could see understanding dawn in the young man who loved women; and after understanding, rage and revulsion. Chan too could hear her screams, those piercing screams they tried to suppress by placing something hard—wood, metal or plastic—between her jaws. When the pain reached an extreme pitch, she didn't notice that she was biting so hard she had broken her beautiful white teeth.

It was cold in the lab with the air conditioning. Cold and damp. Aston, who had turned white, looked as if the walls were closing in on him. Chan gripped his arm.

"Go upstairs. Get some air. I'll see you in a minute."

When he had gone Chan picked up another jaw, fitted it over his thumb and forefinger, closed it down on the wedge of his other hand.

"All three?"

Lam nodded.

It happened every time they gave Chan a recruit. Young Englishmen came to the East looking for adventure. What they lost was their virginity, that strawberries-and-cream innocence that had no counterpart anywhere in Asia. East of Athens even college kids knew that life was made of nuts and bolts, pain and suffering, hunger and rage. At least Aston was the last. They'd stopped recruiting overseas in preparation for 1997.

He found him in the courtyard, but it wasn't the same boy. He seemed to have grown thinner in five minutes. And about ten years older. That youthful bounce that everyone found so charming had finally hit Asian steel and burst. The blue eyes were unfocused; the mouth was pinched, the skin an ugly puce. Everyone snagged on his own special detail.

"You okay?"

"A bit shaken, that's all."

Chan took out two cigarettes, lit them and gave one to Aston. "Smoke, it's good for you." Aston nodded doubtfully and took the cigarette. "Really, it can settle your nerves."

He watched while the Englishman inhaled. A mild nicotine rush brought life back into the eyes. "That dentist's a cunt. He didn't need to do that."

Aston looked at Chan, wiped water from his eyes with his sleeve. "Thanks, Chief."

Chan touched his arm. "Why don't you wait here? I want to collect those busts if they're ready."

Aston nodded. Chan hoped he wasn't going to be sick in the courtyard. He didn't mind, but there were other Chinese cops who would never let the Englishman forget it.

On the third floor, next to the identification bureau, the forensic artist, the Australian named Angie, kept a studio. Policemen liked to visit her. You wouldn't have described her as beautiful, but she glowed with a womanly softness that was beaten out of the female cadets in the first six months.

Instead of a desk, telephone and files, the FA had an easel, chalk, airbrush, charcoal, acetate paints and a lot of natural light. She worked as close to the window as she could. Under her hand the dead came to life, the unknown fugitive acquired features that could be shown to eyewitnesses. A sideline was cartoons that the men liked to show wives and girlfriends, proof that cops were human too.

Chan had persuaded her to draw Sandra in the early days of their marriage. He still had the sketch. Somehow it was more alive than all the photographs. Angie had caught her eyes: large, Caucasian, sly, hungry.

"Ah," Angie said when she saw Chan. "The man who thinks in three dimensions."

Chan smiled. Everybody liked Angie. "Are they ready?"

"As it happens, yes. It'll cost you a beer, though. Haven't done plaster busts for ages. Quite a challenge. Three dimensions just isn't the same as two, as Michelangelo pointed out. I was here at the break of dawn finishing them. Want to see?"

Angie crossed the room to a heavy varnished cupboard. She took out three identical cardboard boxes, each apparently a perfect cube.

"Turn your back."

Chan turned to face the window. He glanced at the sketch on the easel. A Chinese in his early forties with a low brow frowned out. There had been a number of rapes on a housing estate in Junk Bay; eyewitness accounts all mentioned the low brow and the frown.

"Okay, you can look."

It was true, three dimensions were not like two. There was Polly on a table between her two Chinese companions, smiling, without a care in the world. Jekyll and Hyde were more serious but happy to be by her side. Somewhere in ancient Taoism it was said that all man's problems came from having a body. Well, these three didn't anymore.

"Very good."

Angie smiled. She removed the wigs, put the busts back in their boxes, laid the wigs on top. "Charlie, look, I know it's been a while, but I was really sorry to hear about you and Sandra. I know how much she . . . well, I'm just sorry."

Chan shrugged. "It's not easy being married to a cop. Not in Hong Kong."

"Oh, don't blame yourself or the police. Look, it's none of my business, but she was a wanderer. Nice, good-hearted, but a wanderer. Believe me, I'm Australian. We don't know much, but we do know wanderers."

Chan took his eyes off the boxes to hold Angie's smile. Men talked about her, adored her, even fantasized about her, but not in the usual way. Policemen thought they could be sane and happy with a woman like her: soft, big-hearted, overweight, unambitious, Australian. In Hong Kong underachievers were like gold.

Angie laid the boxes one on top of the other. He could carry them like that until he found help. "Don't forget, you owe me a beer." She smiled.

Chan picked up the boxes, nodded. He hesitated. There was that housewarming party his sister insisted he go to. Her husband and his rich lawyer friends would be there. It would surprise them if he turned up with a woman. She would be someone to talk to at least. He put the boxes back on the table, pushed his hair back. He hadn't done this since Sandra left. He couldn't believe how hard it had become.

"If you're free tonight, I have to go to a party. It's my sister; they've bought a new apartment. We wouldn't have to stay. I'd like it. I mean, I'd appreciate it. It would be great if you would. We could slip away early and have a beer somewhere."

Angie smiled. "That would be real nice, Charlie. Great. Look forward to it."

In the courtyard Chan gave two of the boxes to Aston to carry. The dignified thing would have been to find a police car to take them back over to the Kowloon side of the harbor, but even with the siren blaring it would take over an hour. From Angie's studio he had seen how slowly the traffic was moving toward the tunnel. A siren couldn't move that kind of jam; there was nowhere for it to go. As they were walking along Lockhart Road, Chan caught sight of Riley in the back of a police car stuck in traffic. Chan pretended not to see his gesticulations.

Walking toward the underground, Aston almost dropped Jekyll and Hyde. Chan held Polly close in the press of people on the train.

II

The party was worse than he'd expected. Male lawyers and businessmen, Chinese and British, talking about money and vintage wine stood in small groups with their women hanging on their arms in pearls and low-cut dresses. The women lawyers wore somber-colored business suits, shared negative judgments about their male colleagues and waited to see who would come to seduce them. About one half of the room was filled with Chinese people who Chan could tell were even richer than the lawyers; they wore the same kind of clothes and jewelry, but their eyes never bothered to check if they were impressing clients or colleagues. They were safe in their castles of cash, and it was the world's job to impress them.

Chan knew that he was being measured, in the second it took to blink at him, against a scale of money—and instantly discarded, with a sardonic turn of the head. Dress had a lot to do with it. The men wore suits with labels like Kent and Curwen, Ermenegildo Zegna, Yves Saint-Laurent; Chan's white and blue butcher's stripe had been hip when he'd bought it for Jenny's wedding, but sweat darkened it in patches under the arms, and there was a small stain on the left lapel. He could have carried it off, though, if like these people, he'd lived with money long enough for it to slow his movements, mellow his nerves, condition all his reactions as if life consisted of swimming through liquid gold.

Instead he endured the sort of rudeness that justified homicide. While Angie visited the bathroom, he leaned against a wall with a glass of beer in his hand and conjured from memory gratifying cameos of murderers he had known: gunmen, knifemen, stranglers, bludgeoners, kickers, artists of the four-inch meat cleaver. Such expertise wasted on domestic disputes and gangland vendettas when it could have been put to good use at a party like this.

The Chinese waiters in white jackets, hired for the evening, disconcerted him. With the alertness of fighter pilots they could spot an empty glass from the other side of the room and close in from behind with a fresh shot. Their courtesy and dedication were impregnable and, to Chan, profoundly depressing. When he was seventeen, his aunt had given him a choice between two careers: police constable or waiter. It could have been he in the white jacket with the obsequious smile masking malice aforethought.

When Angie returned, he showed her around the apartment, dwelling longer in the emptier rooms. The new flat was too big for just one couple and servants, but that was the point. No amount of expensive Italian furniture, which his sister and her husband already owned anyway, could make the statement as well as a four-thousand-square-foot flat. Most families lived in spaces one tenth of that size. In Hong Kong real wealth expressed itself through space.

Pushing open a door to a fourth spare bedroom, Chan heard a murmur, an intake of breath. Angie held back, but Chan entered the room just long enough to glimpse a couple, a Western man with a Chinese woman, in an airtight embrace. It was the man, apparently young and blond, who was showing the most flesh with his shirt nearly off, backed up against a window while the woman pushed against him. The woman turned at the disturbance, raised her eyes at Chan, then turned back to the man. Chan had glimpsed a long jaw on a Chinese face; from the back she was mostly black hair, strong shoulders and a silver dress that shimmered like water and revealed 80 percent of her vertebrae. He closed the door with care until the last inch, which he completed with a malevolent bang. Angie grinned.

They returned to the party, but after forty minutes Angie admitted she was hating it too. The women sneered at her cheap cotton dress, and the British men cringed at her accent. The Chinese noticed only that she didn't have money and ignored her.

Chan used his chin to point to the door. "Let's go."

Angie gave him a grateful smile. "It's all right, I can stand it for another twenty minutes. Hadn't you better talk to your sister and your brother-in-law?"

"I guess."

"That's why we're here, isn't it?"

Chan shrugged. "You know . . . parties. I don't know why she invited me."

Angie looked baffled. "But she's your sister, Charlie. She loves you, mate."

Chan nodded. "Sure, you're right."

He found a criminal defense lawyer he knew for her to talk to while he went to the kitchen to hunt for Jenny. She was there supervising the Filipino maid. Her husband, Jonathan Wong, was talking to a famous Chinese woman whom Chan now recognized from newspaper stories about the glitterati. He recognized her from her dress too. It was silver and shimmered like water.

"This is my notorious detective brother-in-law," Wong said when he saw him. "Charlie Chan, meet Emily Ping." Chan summoned a smile for the famous Chinese woman, who looked into his eyes, winked once and held out her hand. "Pleased to meet you."

Chan glanced around the kitchen for her blond friend. Apart from the Filipino maid there were only Chinese in the room. "Hi. Look—"

"It must be fascinating to have a lawyer and a detective in the same family," Emily Ping said. "What do you talk about?"

She was tall for a Chinese woman, over five feet seven, but she would have been striking at any height. Her black hair was swept back from a high forehead, the silver dress dipped almost as deeply in front as at the back, revealing most of two ivory globes that Chan found difficult to ignore; she stood straight as a post with a jaw you could hang a Chinese lantern from. More Rambo than bimbo, Chan decided. She was older than he would have guessed from that first glimpse. Mid- to late thirties with an unbroken history of money and power; only the very rich were quite so shameless. She gazed at him for a moment with a kind of nonspecific lust, then smiled. The blond boy? Eaten and forgotten already?

"Oh, he has all the interesting cases. We only talk about *his* work; mine's too boring for words." Wong spoke in English with an impeccable Oxford accent. He pretended not to see the brazen gaze in Emily's eyes.

"What are you working on right now, for instance?" Emily asked Chan.

"The Mincer Murders. Maybe you read about them. Three people fed live into an industrial mincer."

She was tough. She blinked, smiled again. "How interesting. Yes, I remember. In Mongkok, wasn't it?"

"Where else?"

"And have you solved the mystery yet?"

Despite himself, he was held by the authority in her manner. In an unbroken motion he drew a packet of Benson & Hedges from his pocket, flipped open the top, knocked it against the palm of his left hand, withdrew the cigarette with his lips, lit it with the lighter he'd lodged in the other hand in preparation: the expertise of an addict. Then he looked into those fearless Chinese eyes. To his surprise they seemed genuinely interested.

"No. We don't even know who the victims were. No fingerprints, no ID tags—nothing to go on. They were shredded. All we have is a vat full of human hamburger." He didn't mention the heads. He was keeping them out of the public domain for the moment.

The other people in the kitchen had stopped to listen. There were muted squeals and winces all around, except from Emily Ping. She was amused by his provocation. Or perhaps she enjoyed gore. The rich could have strange tastes.

Chan turned to Jenny, drew her into a corner. "I'm sorry, I've got to go." He spoke in Cantonese, exaggerating tones to carry his point.

She made a face. "Is it really that bad? Jonathan had to invite all these people; it's business. You're my only real guest."

"I don't believe you. They all love you, and you're a perfect hostess. Look, it's just me, isn't it? I'm sure they're all great, wonderful, warmhearted, humble—like most billionaires.''

Jenny's eyes pleaded. "Don't go yet. Let's go somewhere private for a moment. I need a real person to talk to, and I have news.''

Her eyes searching his face expressed something close to adoration. He noticed Wong looking at her, a husband's complaint in his expression: *You never look at me like that.*

"Okay.''

Chan followed her to the same corridor and eventually the same room as that where the seduction of the blond young man had so recently taken place. Chan sniffed at a fading odor of sex and perfume and told her about it as they entered the bedroom together. Jenny winced as she closed the door.

"She has a hell of an appetite. I think I'll lock the door. God knows what people would accuse us of if they came barging in.''
She looked up at him and cocked an eyebrow.

She turned a bolt, then held his hand to lead him to a small window with a view over a mountain at the back of the apartments. The room was unlit except for safety lights from the grounds of the apartment building and from lamps that lined a mountain road. About every thirty seconds a car rounded a certain point in a bend and illuminated the room. He stood still while she kneaded his hand. Her dress was a deep crimson that contrasted with her black hair. It was as expensive as any other woman's, but, on her, twice as beautiful. Standing so close to her, he could smell her perfume and underneath it a faint musk that he remembered from childhood. Odors could be like fingerprints.

Her voice was full, rounded, confident; she was a natural princess who found it easy to charm these people. When she was in the mood, anyway. Tonight there was a glint in her eye.

"We're going through a bad patch, Jonathan and I. I'm not sure how much of all this socializing I can take. He lost his rag with me when I refused to wear a triple string of pearls that he bought me last week.''

"How selfish of him.''

"I refuse to be got up like a pet poodle. I don't mind the odd

party, but it's every night, sometimes cocktails at one place followed by dinner at someone else's—it's so artificial. What are you
grinning at?"

"The problems of the rich—how can you stand it?"

"I'm serious. We'll have to reach a compromise."

"Two strings of pearls?"

"Smart-ass. You know, sometimes I feel, living this life, that I'm
being disloyal to Mum."

He lit a cigarette without offering her one. "That is a little
farfetched."

"Is it? Okay, you being so street-wise, tell me what you noticed
about all those people out there tonight, especially the Chinese."

"Apart from wealth, arrogance and a serious lack of depth, nothing. They all looked disgustingly happy to me."

She lowered her voice. "Exactly. They're mostly Emily's people.
Jonathan invited them because of her. Her main business is with
the PRC; she's well in with some big shot general called Xian. Only
two months to go till the Communists march in, and these people
alone are happy, not a care in the world. Why no June neurosis?
Because they've made their connections, their *guanxi*, as everyone's
calling it now, with the killers over the border. Their positions are
secure after June. That's why they're so happy."

Chan shrugged. "There's no money in heroic resistance. They're
smart; to survive an invasion, you have to befriend the invader."

Jenny scowled. "You don't really think that; you're just saying
it because you know I'm stuck with these people, for better or
worse. To me, it's like collaborating." She looked him in the eye.
"You loathe them as much as I do. More, probably. You don't
really approve of Jonathan. Why did you encourage me to marry
him?"

Smiling, Chan looked her in the eye; she knew the Chinese answer to that question. Since her early twenties her looks had raised
her above her class. She was a natural member of the aristocracy
of beauty. Not only her looks; her grace, elegance, a kind of poise
that cut through social strata. It would have been stupid not to
capitalize while she could. How many attractive women from their

background ended by working in bars and nightclubs? That would have broken his heart. It wasn't the job of older brother to be romantic on younger sister's behalf; his duty was to save her from poverty and shame, a duty he'd discharged in a rare act of social shrewdness by persuading her to enter a beauty competition. Quite amazing, the respectability that a title could bestow: Miss Hong Kong. The wealthy suitors alone would have filled a house. Not all eligible from Jenny's point of view, though; Wong had been among the prettiest.

She was safe now; even if the marriage didn't work, she'd be protected by a share of Wong's money. Chan was still proud of himself. Would marriage to a pauper have been less stormy?

"Okay, he was a good catch, and you were being the Chinese patriarch. Well, I have real news. I'm probably pregnant."

"Whoopee."

"Right word but not much feeling. Are you pleased or not?"

"Of course I'm pleased."

"You're going to be the godfather."

"Honored."

"And in addition to your usual duties, you will make sure that he or she grows into a real person. If I catch them prancing around like those creeps out there, you'll be in trouble."

"Agreed. I'll be a blue-collar street-cop uncle. Weekends we'll spend at the morgue."

She smiled and kissed him, held his arms while she gazed into his face. He made to move away, but she held him still. She wore no pearls, no jewelry at all. A neckline like that could not be improved.

"No one compares to you." She said it in a hurried whisper, before he could stop her.

He admonished her with a finger, tutted, returned to the door to release the bolt, let Jenny out first. She led him back down the hall to the huge reception room, which had filled since he'd left it. "You didn't even introduce your new girlfriend," Jenny said.

Chan looked for Angie over the heads of the other guests. Finally he saw her talking to the young blond man, who was now fully dressed. "She's not. This is the first night—I mean, she's a colleague."

Jenny smiled. "I'm so glad. I hope she stops you smoking."

Chan pushed his hair back. "It's not that serious."

He saw Angie say something to the young man while keeping her eyes on Chan. The blond boy—he was hardly more than that—took his leave of her before Chan arrived. A pity, Chan thought, they seemed to go well together. The boy looked Australian too.

"We can go," Chan told Angie, feeling suddenly nervous; it was so long since he'd had to entertain a Western woman on his own.

12

Three hours later outside the Bull and Bear Chan stood with Angie in the taxi queue. Nearly midnight and still as hot as a sauna. In the pub she'd felt instantly at home and talked for hours. He'd forgotten almost everything she'd said. Something about family and Australia, with an unlimited collection of sports anecdotes that had grown cruder as the alcohol took effect. Apparently she was homesick.

He'd never seen a woman drink so much beer. There was something almost professional about the way she poured it down; she held it well too, except for a moment on the steps of the pub when she'd swayed and almost fallen. Now she stood very close, a hint having condensed to an assumption without any help from him. He didn't want to offend her. How did you explain that you were just too Chinese to take a woman to bed on the first night? Or that your complicated sensitivity found drunkenness a turnoff even in the last years of the twentieth century? Or that your flat was designed for Chinese-size lovers?

The hand that had been stroking his arm suddenly gave up.

"You're not going to take me home, are you?" Chan appreciated the effort she was making to keep the slur out of her speech.

"No."

She turned, put her arms around his neck. "Why not?" He felt the weight of her heavy breasts on his chest, as if she'd decided to make them his problem.

"I can't."

"Why? Still destroyed about Sandra?"

"Maybe."

She dropped her arms. "You don't like me."

"I do. A lot. Can we talk about this another night?"

She overlaid a pout with a smile. "Sure."

"I thought, I mean, you're very popular with the men. Surely there's someone?"

She shook her head. "Ain't that easy, mate. The white men chase Asian women like there's no tomorrow, and the best Chinese stick to their own."

"Leaving me?"

She squeezed his arm, buried her lips in his neck. "You're so intense, Charlie. It turns me on."

A small hand slipped between his thighs to find the outline of his penis expertly. He caught the hand, wrapped it, for want of a better place, around his waist. "Didn't that blond guy get your phone number?"

She sighed deeply with undertones of irritation, looked up at the black sky. "You never go off duty, do you?"

In his mind's eye he saw them, two Australians far from home comforting each other with rugby jokes and drunken sex. The fact was that Hong Kong only pretended to be superficial, crass and transient. Underneath there was a depth of cynicism that began to frighten after a while. And then to appall. When the beautiful blond boy and Angie swapped stories about the predatory Emily Ping and the intense Chief Inspector Chan, it would be with an Anglo-Saxon relief at having escaped from some complex Oriental trap. They would look into each other's blue, round eyes and see—well, to the bottom anyway. It would have been better if she had been rude enough to go off with him directly from the party.

"He'll ring you tomorrow," he said with a smile as he put her in a taxi. He was about to take the next one when he decided to walk to the underground instead. Free from the pressure of seduction, his mind leaped back to the case. There was an adage by Confucius—or was it Raymond Chandler?—Never dwell on a mystery that has been solved.

In other words, forget the front teeth. Forget the muffled screams of agony. Why had Polly, an attractive Westerner, allowed her fillings to fall out? Self-neglect placed her in a specific category in her culture. Like where? What caused a young woman to fall into the drifting class, to become indifferent to her own well-being? Not thwarted love—not these days. Self-indulgence, an aversion to work, an adolescent need for adventure untamed even in adulthood?

It all came back to drugs in the end. Drugs sold provided the funds; drugs abused provided the adventure; drugs shared provided the company; drugs prescribed provided the cure. The First World was a drug addict. Illegal drugs were only the tip of the iceberg. Take into account the barbiturates and the amphetamines, then add in the spectrum of antidepressants; in other words, make a list of all the popular tranquilizers and stimulants of prescription, and you had not so much an epidemic, not even a pandemic, as a colonization of the human species by traders in chemicals, from the multinational pharmaceutical companies at the top to the street corner dealers at the bottom. And it had all happened in the last years of the twentieth century.

It was a five-cigarette meditation that took up most of the ride home. Emerging at Mongkok station, Chan realized he was short of cigarettes. Only one pack left and only two left in that pack. He'd forgotten to add the tobacco companies to the list. And the brewers and distillers too. Was there a single person left on earth who took reality straight? Some thoughts led to mountains too high to climb. Especially without a nicotine stash.

In the small hours of the morning the streets of Mongkok were less crowded. It was possible to distinguish individuals as opposed to clumps of humans, although it was not in the nature of Asians to be solitary. The heat upset everyone's sleep rhythms. Lovers walked hand in hand as if on an early-evening tryst; children played; an old woman in rags begged. A swarm of starlings chattered around a streetlight while small bats swooped. Only Chan was entirely alone, walking quickly toward a small supermarket near his block that sold English cigarettes. Only Chan and a Western woman, in her late forties or early fifties as far as he could tell, who emerged from the shadows as he passed.

A habit from his patrolling days produced an automatic description: about five eight, dirty blond, baggy black shorts and red T-shirt, no bra, an extralarge money belt slung around her waist, slight stoop, slim with heavy breasts. Sensual. She wore sneakers and socks and was therefore American. In this heat every other nationality wore plastic thongs, but Americans feared foreign soil. Morose but healthy. Not lost, for she was not examining street signs; purposeless. She didn't fit. Tourists stayed on Hong Kong Island or in Tsim Sha Tsui, not Mongkok. He turned once to catch her face in the glare of a streetlight. Possible drink problem.

She followed him into the supermarket. He walked to the end of an aisle to pick up some Rickshaw tea bags. The cigarettes were behind glass at the cash desk at the other end of the aisle. Looking up into a convex security mirror, he saw her pocket a quarter bottle of whiskey. By holding her arm against the large pocket in her shorts, she disguised the heavy weight of the bottle. Chan paused over the tea bags. A civic duty was being invoked, but on the other hand, the owner of the store was a wealthy Chiu Chow named Fung who could look after himself. Also, it was late, and he could do without filling in reports for the rest of the night. He looked up again into the mirror. This time it was a toothbrush and toothpaste. Such huge pockets on those shorts.

Chan shrugged. Fung was rich enough to be able to afford electronic security. Chan had told him so more than once. He strolled to the cash desk, pausing as he passed her. They exchanged glances. Tired eyes. Very, very tired eyes. No sign of fear. It was a mystery too many for one night. He bought five packets of Benson & Hedges, carried them in a plastic bag back to his apartment block in a side street off Nathan Road.

In the ground-floor hall he paused to open his thin steel letter box: an electricity bill and a postcard from Sandra. In his Chinese way he had assumed that divorce meant finality, but the English tended to cling to their failures as proof that all effort was futile. The cards arrived at about three-month intervals from exotic beaches where drifters gathered. They could be wistful ("last night I dreamed of you riding on a Chinese carpet") or slashing ("so glad you're not here to frustrate me"). This one was from Ko Phangan in the Gulf of Thailand: "Not missing you at all." He categorized it as one of the slashers, put it in the bag with the cigarettes.

Running his hand around inside the box, he crumpled a single sheet that was almost stuck to the back. He saw it was the cheapest paper imported from the PRC. In the center of the page in Chinese script there burned the single word *Laogai*. Underneath in English handwriting: "Please don't forget Thursday." Chan stared at it for a moment, then threw it into a waste bin that was bolted to the floor between lifts.

All his life Hong Kong had been a magnet for different political movements. The British commitment to freedom of speech meant that just about any fanatic could buy a printing press and develop a cause, although the big struggles for hearts and minds were inevitably between the local Communists and the Kuomintang, those losers of the Civil War who now ran Taiwan. He had received pamphlets, though, on paper of similar quality, from Seventh-Day Adventists, Buddhists, an animal action group trying to wean aging Chinese men off powdered rhinoceros horn, Muslims from the extreme south of the Philippines, Moonies, someone selling fresh monkey brain—another illegal, and probably ineffective, cure for impotence. He took the lift to the tenth floor.

Three keys tumbling three dead bolts let him into the 450-square-foot cubicle. The kitchen barely accommodated a fridge and a double-ring gas burner. The living room was filled by the television set and one couch. In the bedroom he had to climb over the bed to reach the other side. He was glad he hadn't invited Angie back. Where would he have put her? In Hong Kong only the rich had space for plump lovers.

His jacket was soaked through. He threw it over the sofa, peeled off the Saran Wrap shirt, trousers that stuck to his thighs. Naked he faced the Mongkok dilemma: stew or freeze? On all but the hottest nights he managed without the window-mounted air conditioner with its chamber music like a canning factory.

As always his exhaustion on the street failed to conjugate smoothly into sleep. As he lay on the bed, naked except for a cigarette, his mind accelerated in tightening circles. He was in a museum full of white busts of Western women, Sandra, Polly and Angie in particular. They spun in front of him demanding a decision, but his only response was dizziness. Then the door buzzer rang. He jumped; a facial muscle twitched.

He pulled on a pair of shorts, padded barefoot to the front door, looked through the dirty spy hole. Distorted by the fish-eye lens, the American woman was a demon from Chinese opera. A huge face leaned forward hungrily, orangutang lips curled under a squashed nose, hands like claws folded over the money belt. He opened the door to the limit of the security chain.

"Chief Inspector Chan?"

Chan nodded.

"Maybe you could let me in. I have some information for you."

Now that she had spoken a full sentence he could identify the kind of accent American actors assumed when they made a film about the Bronx, a curious drawl that threatened to make a syllable last for minutes.

"Information? At this time?"

"It's important."

Chan stared.

"I'm Clare's mother."

"Clare?"

She opened the zip on her money belt, took out a crumpled sheet of paper. It was a fax with the Royal Hong Kong Police letterhead on the top. She held it up. On the top right-hand corner the words "All enquiries to Insp. Aston, Mongkok CID," and in the center a blurred picture of Polly. Chan felt a blip of the hunter's excitement at the first faint scent of quarry; he repressed it, though. Patience was the only virtue worth cultivating; he was with the ancients on that. He closed the door, released the chain, let her in.

She held out her hand. "Moira Coletti. Pleased to meet you. I apologize for being here so late, but the plane didn't get in till this afternoon, and when I tried the station, they said you were out for the night. I'm afraid I spun them a yarn to get your private address. I even got to see your desk and that big photograph of you receiving an award for bravery from the governor. Easy to recognize you from that. Didn't figure on you being so late, though.''

Chan gestured to the sofa, sat down on the coffee table.

She looked at the floor. ''You saw me in the supermarket, right?''

''Quarter bottle of scotch, toothbrush, toothpaste. I should have reported you.''

''That was the downside risk.'' She took the items out of her pocket as she spoke, placed them on the floor. ''I paid for them, of course, right after you left. See, I know cops. I don't know Chinese, but I know cops, and there aren't many homicide detectives going to start filling in arrest statements for a minor larceny after two in the morning.'' She paused, looked him full in the face. ''Sorry about that. I just wanted to know how good you were. American arrogance, I guess. We just don't want to believe that any nation is anywhere near as good as the old U.S. of A. at anything. Damn near ruined Detroit till they had the sense to admit the Japanese could make better cars than them. Now you get Japanese quality control even at GM.'' She paused, sighed. ''I'm rambling. That's always been my problem. Reason I never made it higher than sergeant. You're good, though, really good. Even got the toothbrush. I was especially careful with that.''

Chan, twitching, lit a cigarette.

''Well, since neither of us is on duty—you mind?'' She held up the scotch. ''It's been a long day—and night. Hate to think what time it is in New York.''

''About twelve hours earlier than now. Two, three in the afternoon. Yesterday afternoon. You better open the scotch.''

''Right.'' She undid the screw cap. ''Wow, yesterday afternoon. That's how it works? I must seem awfully ignorant to you. Never traveled out of the United States before except once to Acapulco to divorce Clare's father. But you don't need to hear about that. Want some scotch?''

Chan declined, went to the fridge to fetch some beer. ''You better have this with it. Neat it won't last.''

''Thanks. What you want is fingerprints, right? Clare's dead, I guess, or you wouldn't be going to all this trouble? Didn't say so on the fax, at least not on the sheet I got out of them on the sixth floor. I bought this book Clare read all the time when she was staying with me—*The Travels of Marco Polo*. I guess she and I are the only ones who have ever touched it, other than the bookseller. If you take my prints, you'll be able to work out which ones are hers. I brought dental records too.''

''You did?'' Immediately he regretted his enthusiasm.

Moira's face fell. ''That bad, huh? Man, it sure hurts even to contemplate what might have happened. Don't tell me yet, though. I need to be real drunk.''

Tears streamed as she poured the whiskey down her throat. Somehow she managed to keep the emotion out of her voice. ''Don't mind me, please. It's just a reaction. Americans are encouraged to let it all out. All means all too. Over here you do it different if those kung fu movies are to be believed. Never show weakness, huh? Might be right. Never saw tears get anyone anywhere, and I've seen a few. Manhattan these days is a jungle, a jungle. Say, what do I call you? Chief? Chief Inspector?''

''Charlie. Everyone else does.''

''Charlie? Like Charlie Chan?''

''British humor. I'm a detective, they couldn't resist. Look, Mrs. Coletti, we don't know if we're talking about the same person at all. You just saw an artists' impression.''

''Call me Moira. That's what I've been telling myself. But you tell me, what would you think if you saw a fax like that? Ever since Clare disappeared, I've been making them give me every Identi-Kit from Asia that comes in. I bet I can check out artists' impressions as good as anyone.''

Out of her money belt she took an envelope with photographs.

''This is her at sixteen. I brought it for me really.''

Chan saw a thin-faced girl in a purple and green tracksuit, dark blond hair falling over one eye, large trees in the background, trees of a kind he'd never seen except in pictures. He paused over the smile. Perfect American dentistry.

Moira took back the picture, stared at it. ''Central Park, 1986.''

''A jogger?''

"Skateboard. Now, here she's twenty-one. Graduation. NYU. That stands for New York University. B.A. in sociology."

Chan glanced quickly at the scotch bottle. He didn't need another drunken woman on his hands; she took the scotch well, though, apart from a single burp half suppressed. Her eyes and hands were steady. He picked up the photograph. The child had turned into a young woman in cap and gown. She was gazing not into the camera but into a future full of promise. Only Americans smiled like that. Only Americans had that kind of future.

"Now here's the most recent. Two years ago, when I went to see her in San Francisco."

Something had gone wrong. Only a few years down that sunny road life had failed. She was still smiling, but it was wan, uncertain. Her hair was brutally short; two dabs of silver shone in each ear. This time she was looking straight into the camera, trying to say something to whoever was going to see the picture. Help me?

"I know what you're probably thinking, Charlie. Any cop would. But it wasn't drugs. It was just the tail end of an affair with a married man that was chewing her guts out. She snapped out of it pretty soon afterward. It's just that I haven't got any pictures more recent than that."

Chan nodded. No point in asking questions until after positive identification. He placed the most recent photograph next to the fax that Moira laid out on the floor. Photographs could be as deceptive as eyewitnesses. The human eye saw what the mind told it to see. Urban Man spent his life trapped in an internal dialogue from which he emerged only for the purposes of survival. On the fax sheet he covered over the hair that Angie had given her: a possible identification. If anything the young woman in the photograph was better-looking with a finer chin, chiseled nose, large eyes. A beauty.

"How long has your daughter been missing, Mrs. Coletti?"

"Please call me Moira, Charlie." She touched his hand. "It feels funny not using first names in this tiny apartment. The British really did a job on you people with the formality, didn't they? About two years." She swallowed. "No, I'm kidding myself. Must be two years six months since I saw my Clare."

"But you spoke to her on the telephone, received letters?"

"Oh, sure. Sure. All the time. Look, we both know you're going to see your forensic department tomorrow with whatever I'm able to give you—"

"Everything can wait till after that. Sure. I'm sorry."

She waved a hand at the same time as blowing her nose on a man-size handkerchief. "No, no. I shouldn't have rushed it, but what else could I do? Haven't thought about anything else since I saw that fax."

Chan saw that the whiskey bottle was empty. In an ashtray he saw a nest of butts that had collected since her arrival. With a hand she covered a yawn. He felt tired himself; perhaps even tired enough to sleep. "You want another beer before you go?"

She nodded. "That would help."

"Where's your hotel?"

She coughed. "Haven't had time to get hold of one. Haven't even thought of it."

She waited. Chan looked at his fake Rolex, which he'd left on the coffee table: 3:20 A.M. In Hong Kong it wouldn't be difficult finding a hotel, even at that time, but what would be the point? It would be 4:30 before she could lie down, and she'd want to be in his office by 9:00.

"That couch doesn't open up into a bed. You'll have to put the cushions on the floor. If you want to stay."

"Oh, that's real kind of you, Charlie. Real kind. I won't make a sound once I'm settled."

"There's a bottle of vodka in the fridge, if you need it. It's the only spirits I keep."

She looked away with a grunt. "In the morning I'll go straight to the identification bureau with your fingerprint samples. And the dental records. May as well take them just in case the prints are smudged."

She was already making up her bed on the floor, kneeling and

JOHN BURDETT

80

placing cushions from the couch end to end. She lay down with a
sigh. "You're a kind man, Charlie. You don't look kind, but you
are. As one damaged person to another, let me give you one word
of advice: You smoke too much. Good night."

He lay on his bed, smoking. He could hear her snoring on the floor
while he lay wide-awake. It was possible to envy her. His mind
flicked from the case to other things. Angie, Sandra. What had the
postcard said? "Not missing you at all." That was because like all
Chinese, he was emotionally stunted. She had been careful to explain that to him before she left. She would be surprised that a total
stranger had called him kind.

13

At his desk at Mongkok Police Station, Chan played with a black government ballpoint. As yet he had told no one about the American woman and her dental records except Lam, the odontologist. Ninety percent of detection was waiting. At his flat Moira Coletti was waiting too. On the other side of the office Aston sat at his desk, also waiting.

There was a knock on the door. Chan looked at Aston. In Mongkok nobody knocked.

"May I come in?"

Riley's face was almost featureless, like a description by a myopic witness. On it he inscribed the mood of the moment. He was tall, slim, stooped with hands that flapped at the wrists.

"Good morning, sir," Aston said.

"Morning, Dick." Riley rubbed his hands together. "Morning, Charlie. *Nei ho ma?*"

"Fine, how are you?" Chan did what he could to discourage the chief superintendent's Cantonese.

"*Ho ho.*"

"What?"

"*Ho ho.*"

Chan looked at Aston.

"It's Cantonese," Aston explained, "for 'good.' "

"Oh—*ho ho.* I'm *ho ho* too. Dick—*ho ho?*"

Aston busied himself with *The Murder Investigator's Bible.*

"I was just passing," Riley said. "I thought I'd pop in."

Chan waited. It was important to know which Riley one was dealing with.

"Heard you're having a little trouble with the investigation. Perhaps a little brainstorming would help?"

Chan lowered his head in a controlled nod. "Sure."

Riley stood in the middle of the room. Chan stared at him. He was not sadistic by nature; it was rather that self-doubt was the only part of Riley he could relate to. The temptation to draw it out was usually irresistible.

"D'you know what DNA stands for?" Chan asked with a smile.

"Deoxyribonucleic acid." Riley smiled back.

Chan bit his lip: Never underestimate an Englishman in a quiz. "We already have the results of the PCR."

"Good."

"The heads fit the bodies in the vat."

Riley's face lit up. "That's what the PCR says? Excellent! Bob's your uncle! The crime's as good as solved."

"Not quite. All we've done is restore three heads to three bodies. Their ghosts can rest in peace. On the other hand, both the minced and the unminced share the same anonymity. Faceless, you might say." Chan let a beat pass in case Riley wanted to change personalities. "The DNA doesn't tell us their names, you see."

Riley blinked. "Sure, sure." He wrung his hands. "What about fingerprints?"

Chan scanned the room for a moment, saw that Aston was suffused with a sympathetic blush, then returned his attention to Riley. He held up both hands. "No fingers, no prints."

Riley's beam leaked like a punctured tire. "Quite." He wrung his hands again. Sweat exploded in small pods over his forehead. "Anyway, you're making progress. That's what counts." He twisted in his seat, searched the wall for relief from Chan's gaze. "Triads."

Aston lowered his book.

Chan watched the two *gweilos* exchange a common gleam. He remembered the adage: Put three Chinese together and you have two conspiracies; two Anglo-Saxons and you have a secret club.

"Did you know that Sun Yat-sen was a Four-eight-nine?" Aston asked. Chan noticed how anxious he was to relieve the chief superintendent's discomfort. There was a social worker in most Englishmen.

"I'm going to buy some cigarettes," Chan said. "Then I'm going to the scene of crime." He turned to Riley. "Why don't you join me there?"

Chan was prepared to bet that the "scene of crime" was the only empty space in Mongkok. The building was about eight years old, ten reinforced concrete floors suspended from a reinforced-concrete structure 130 feet high. For the owners it was a 96,000-square-foot money box. At the lift area on the eighth floor police No Entry signs painted on barricades that rested on trestles still guarded all four gates. Chan had calculated that the owners must be losing ten thousand Hong Kong dollars a day in rental income.

Moving the barricade to one side, he pushed open one of the large steel doors.

"Hello? Hello?"

He called out just in case Riley and Aston had already arrived. There were no windows; his greeting fell into a black void. He remembered a heavy-duty switch at shoulder height on the wall near the entrance. All over the floor fluorescent tubes flickered into life. Over the area where the vat had stood the strip light flashed on and off and made a sound like hornets buzzing. At the far corner Chan found a stepladder with the letters RHKPF engraved on every step. He carried it to the chalk square that marked the position of the vat at the time of first discovery, climbed up to extract the fluorescent cylinder. It was held by two plastic clips containing the electrical outlets. He pulled out a long plastic plate to reveal the starter and electric cord above it. Next to the starter someone had taped a small plastic bag. He used a handkerchief to remove the bag. There was a movement on the far side of the warehouse near the door.

"*Wai? Wai?*"

Riley's Cantonese reminded Chan of a cat fight.

"Over here."

Aston followed Riley to the center of the empty floor. They stood under Chan's stepladder. A patina of sweat covered Aston's face. Lakes stained the chief superintendent's shirt under the arms and contributed to the inland sea on his back. Chan replaced the plastic strip and the light. He held the handkerchief with the plastic bag in one open palm while he descended. He showed them the bag, then snatched it away from Riley when he tried to touch it.

"Prints," Chan said.

Cradled in his handkerchief, he held the bag up to the light. A white powder too fine for sugar or salt, too coarse to be flour. If Riley was the next person to speak, it was number four heroin.

"What is it?" Riley said.

"My guess is number four heroin. Pure. Finest quality. But we'll have to check with forensic."

"Funny it wasn't found before."

"The tube wasn't flickering before." Chan disguised his professional shame with an aggressive tone.

He picked up the ladder. As he did so, he noticed the blue-black corpses of beetles scattered around the perimeter of the white rectangle. The light caught them and transformed them into tiny iridescent carapaces, like beads from a broken necklace. He saw Riley staring at them too. He put down the steps, picked one up, beckoned to Riley.

"Clue," Chan said. Riley blinked. "The beetles told us the remains had been here for about seven days. Day one, flies arrive to deposit larvae. Word passes to the ants, who eat the larvae. The ants attract the wasps. By day five or six the feast's in full swing. People who never gave dinner parties in death feed millions. Beetles are slow, though; it takes them about seven days to get here." Chan held the beetle like a toy car. "Here they come now, trundling over rough terrain. The best has already been eaten, but they don't mind. They prefer dry skin. When we took the vat away, they died of starvation."

Riley swallowed.

"We've been over the place with a fine-tooth comb," Chan continued, tossing the beetle carcass back onto the floor. "We didn't check light fixtures because we weren't looking for drugs. We were looking for signs of struggle, ropes, gags, scuff marks, shreds of clothing, claw marks from fingernails, torn fingernails, blood traces. Not the sort of things you find in light fixtures. We found nothing. The place is as clean as a whistle."

"Who owns it?"

"A small company owned by a family who run a Chinese restaurant in Albuquerque, New Mexico. They've all been in New Mexico for over a year waiting for citizenship."

"Tenants?"

"They're between tenants."

"Other floors?"

"We checked them all."

Chan took the stepladder back to the far wall, returned to where Riley and Aston were standing looking at the floor. He gripped Riley's arm.

"See, this is how it works. We rope off the warehouse. We establish only one route to use to and from the scene of the crime. We assign an officer to guard the scene and record all persons coming and going. We photograph and videotape the whole scene. We divide the area into zones; we search each zone. We check doors and windows. Before leaving the area, we make a list of all license plates of vehicles in the area; we obtain the names of all businesses and persons working around here; we interview everyone in the vicinity."

"You've been very thorough."

"Routine."

"And what have you come up with so far?"

"Nothing. Except the heads that were spotted at sea—by a tourist."

"Any theories?"

"The murders took place somewhere else. In Hong Kong or over the border—who knows? With lifting gear and a refrigerated lorry the vat could have come from a thousand miles away."

Chan and Aston watched Riley walk to one of the far walls, his footfall echoing off the raw concrete. It was like watching someone walk to nowhere from nowhere. When he reached the wall, there was nothing to do but come back again.

"I see," Riley said.

On the way out Chan looked again at the flickering light and shook his head. Normally he would have checked light fixtures. The stench from the vat had driven everyone to take shortcuts.

After agonizing, Chan slipped home midmorning with the case file. He was glad Moira had gone out. He'd said that she could stay another night—why not? He was hardly ever home. He'd given her a spare set of keys. She'd cleaned the flat during the morning, left a note to say she'd gone for a long walk.

After leaving Riley, he had been to see Dr. Lam. There was no doubt about it: Clare was Polly; Polly was Clare. Chan knew that a brave man would sit down with Moira, put his arm around her, tell her everything, absorb some of her pain.

He placed the file and a large bottle of scotch on the coffee table, left right away.

14

At the identification bureau at Arsenal Street, Chan had no trouble persuading one of the technicians, Raymond Tsim, to give up his lunch break. It was a Chinese deal: Chan would buy and deliver the takeaway noodles and pay two to one on Tsim's bet that the plastic bag would carry no prints in common with *The Travels of Marco Polo.*

In the lunchtime crowds Chan knew where he could have Tsim's noodles in their Styrofoam box under his arm in less than five minutes. But Tsim was particular about his noodles. It was Mimi's or the deal was off.

Chan didn't blame him. Mimi's had all the characteristics of a restaurant the Cantonese respected. The waiters wrote nothing down but remembered the orders with precision. There was a deafening noise of chopsticks on plates, plates being stacked, customers sucking loudly on fish heads and egg yolks. Spittoons on the floor awaited the products of the incessant hoicking that provides background birdsong throughout Asia. The noodles were, quite simply, the best in the world. For every seated customer there was at least one other standing behind him, breathing down his neck and exerting whatever psychological pressure he could devise to make the seated one finish quickly. All over the restaurant taste buds were mercilessly excited by steaming dim sum baskets wheeled around on trolleys by scowling old ladies, who used the spittoons from time to time.

Chan joined the takeaway line and tried to resist the temptation to jump the queue. After five minutes he took advantage of a distraction caused by the collapse of a construction of plates on a trolley near the kitchen. While everyone stared and laughed, he slipped in behind a woman who was about thirty places closer to the front. Even so it was twenty minutes before he returned to the identification bureau with the noodles.

He was disappointed that Tsim had not yet begun the tests. The technician was absorbed in a glossy magazine with airbrushed centerfold. Chan crept silently up to where Tsim sat on a stool at his bench and admired the sensuous lines of the new IBM Thinkpad with Pentium chip, active matrix screen and sixteen megabytes of RAM with a 1.2 gigabyte hard disk.

"Noodles," Chan shouted in his ear.

In a process that had more in common with inhalation than digestion Tsim finished the noodles in less than eight minutes, burped five times, put away the computer magazine, switched on the terminal by his right hand.

Even a technological Neanderthal like Chan had come to pronounce one acronym with awe: CAFIS. With imported software Chan could use the computer assisted fingerprint indexing system to cross-check in seconds with every print known to central records, a task that in his early years with the RHKPF had taken days with a high risk of error. All you needed was the print from which to start the inquiry.

Here there had been advances too. Dusting powder was still extensively used, but many of its limitations had been overcome through the use of other techniques: the marvelous Magna Brush, the astonishing argon-ion laser, iodide fuming, silver nitrate, ninhydrin and superglue. With each new invention the rate of detection spiked for a while, until the crooks caught up.

With tweezers Tsim lifted the plastic bag (emptied of its contents, which had been sent to the chemists at Arsenal Street) out of the cardboard box that carried the case reference number and Chan's name. With Chan watching intently by his side, Tsim jammed the top of the bag in a clamp on a small tripod. He lifted the tripod into a glass box the size of a small wardrobe and closed the box door. From outside the box Tsim was able to adjust the focus of the barrel of the laser that was inside. Also inside were a camera that automatically focused with the laser and a metal dish of superglue. With the laser focused Tsim pressed a switch that heated a hot plate under the superglue. Fumes rose and clung to tiny impressions on the plastic bag, which impressions were enhanced by the laser. Tsim pressed another switch, and the camera flashed several times.

The technician peeled a pair of plastic gloves onto his hands, took a small retractable cutter from a drawer and sliced off the cover of *The Travels of Marco Polo*. Flicking arbitrarily through the thirteenth-century masterpiece, he cut out thumbed pages from the "Prologue," "The Middle East, Kublai Khan" and "From Peking to Bengal."

At a chair further along the bench he used Chan's cigarette lighter to light a small spirit lamp under a glass box. At the bottom of the box was a grill under which iodine crystals had been placed. He opened the lid on the box, inserted the front cover of the book. When violet fumes rose from the grill, Tsim blew out the spirit lamp. Chan watched while fatty matter absorbed some of the fumes. In a minute the secret record of the book's handlers appeared: a mass of prints one on top of another as if a word-hungry army had fought over it. It was unlikely that Tsim would be able to retrieve ten clear points of identification from the chaos, but he took a photograph anyway. He removed the cardboard cover and replaced it with the first page that he had cut out.

As Tsim worked, Chan saw that at its heart the book, handled by many, had known only one lover. The same fine finger- and thumbprints appeared at the top or bottom of each page. In the bottom corner a slim thumb had spread the spine. Chan held his breath. Here she was at last, that troubled young woman with the short hair. Still calling for help? Chan continued to look even after Tsim had taken all the pictures he needed. The violet whorls were like ridge lines on an ordnance survey map; each print was a tiny mountain of identity.

Back in his office in Mongkok, Chan remembered to ask Aston to find the telephone numbers of the New York Police Department and New York University.

By midafternoon Chan was restless. Moira hadn't telephoned. That was understandable; what was there for her to say to him? But still he worried. How to explain the suicide of a victim's mother in the apartment of the investigating detective? His twitch was at maximum mobility by the time he reached his apartment, sweating from the effort.

She was sitting on the couch poring over the file and only grunted when he entered. He stood behind her, tried to see how far she'd read.

"It's all right. I already read it twice. I appreciate you doing it this way—much better than to have to break down in front of you. I already did that too—break down, I mean." She looked up. "But you do good work over here. File's in better shape than I've seen in a long while. Real quality control."

He glanced at the floor. The bottle of scotch was half empty.

"I'm sorry." His English was perfect but, on occasion, stale. There must be some other phrase *gweilos* used at moments like this? He said it again: "I'm sorry."

She grunted, stood up. Her legs were not as steady as her voice. She staggered a little on the way to the window.

"No." He started forward, but it was too late. She swung the window open until it crashed against the frame.

Essence of Mongkok flooded the flat: diesel, burned monosodium glutamate, fried rice, fried noodles, dry cleaning fluid, burning rubber, burning petrol, fumes from the underground railway ventilator, hamburger, cooking oil, every human odor. In Mongkok nobody opened windows.

Moira leaned out, screamed at the world once at the top of her lungs, coughed violently, closed the window.

"That's what I was waiting for you for. Didn't trust myself to do it alone."

She walked back across the room toward him, steadier now. Her arms embraced him, clutched him tight. Her tears flooded down his neck. She made hardly any noise apart from the soft sucking sound of the sobs. It was minutes before he heard her voice, her face in his ear so close he could feel the fine hairs around her mouth. The voice was soft, caressing, comforting, as if the pain was his.

"I'm going to ask you to do a terrible thing, Charlie. You can say no. But when you come home tonight, will you make love to me? I think if I don't do one life-affirming thing today, I'll just dry up forever."

15

Although by no means the largest law firm in Hong Kong, Jonathan Wong's catered exclusively to CIPs. As a litigation partner Chan's brother-in-law divided the commercially important people who sought his advice into three groups. There were the rich, the very rich and the fabulously wealthy.

Only the rich paid for their own lunches; the higher categories expected to be wined and dined, Emily Ping in particular. She was fabulously wealthy on a number of counts, but most recently her friends in Beijing had appointed her managing director of a PRC-owned development company registered in Hong Kong. The new company would raise funds in Hong Kong to develop large tracts of land along the Pearl River. As proof of her faith in the project she had put a huge slice of her own money into it.

The Wong-Ping relationship was of a kind better understood in Asia than the West. Their families were distantly related, and they were lifetime friends. They had sat together in primary school, they had been close at grammar school, they had taken exams together and they had studied in England together, although at different universities (Emily at Cambridge, Wong at Oxford). They had never been lovers. Emily had acted as "best man" at Wong's wedding to Charlie Chan's sister, Jenny. In Asia some aspects of human life could still be innocent, if innocent meant uncontaminated by sexual innuendo.

Money was different. Although Wong was from a wealthy family and would one day inherit more than a million U.S. dollars, she was infinitely richer. He owed his partnership in his firm to Emily, who insisted on channeling all her commercial work through him. In the circumstances Wong didn't mind buying her lunch, which was on the firm in any case.

Wong waited for her in the China Club, which occupied a complete floor in the old Bank of China building. The waiters dressed in Red Army uniforms; a huge portrait of Chairman Mao stared down on the diners; Democracy Wall posters competed with more abstract paintings from Beijing. Wong was fond of Chen Guanzhong and other PRC artists who painted with Chinese sensitivity in a Western style. The furniture was blackwood with marble. Everyone said it was a clever idea, to invoke nostalgia for Chinese communism before it was officially dead.

Wong ordered a Bloody Mary. At a table nearby he recognized the English wife of one of his partners, to the other side of him a table for six included two lawyers and three businessmen all well known to him and in the far corner he saw his intellectual property partner, a slim Englishman with the embarrassing habit of wearing a monocle. Hong Kong was a small town where the superrich occupied a social archipelago in which they bumped into one another all the time. As Wong sipped his drink, he saw an Englishman whom he knew to be the political adviser to the governor walk in with the mayor of Shanghai. Behind them was Emily.

Her black Chanel suit with wide gold belt matched black stockings and black and white high heels, her substantial bust filled out a white blouse with gold buttons, she walked as straight as a ramrod and what one noticed most of all was what some claimed was her greatest business asset, her jaw. Sunbathing on the deck of a yacht, she still looked ready to climb a mountain.

Wong heard her call out in Mandarin to the mayor of Shanghai. He turned, beaming. Cuthbert, the political adviser, stepped aside while the two old friends greeted each other. She knew Cuthbert too; the three stood exchanging pleasantries for a few moments until Emily pointed to the table where Wong sat and made her excuses.

"Mayor of Shanghai," Emily said, offering each cheek for Wong to kiss.

"And Cuthbert, the political adviser." Wong held his hands palms up. "You always know more important people than I do."

"I have a magic secret. It's called working your buns off. If you'd eaten your *fahn* like your mummy told you and hadn't watched all those movies, you might have got to know the mayor of Shanghai too."

"Boring. Anyway, how're the tits?"

Emily put a finger over her lips. "Shh! Not so loud!" She grimaced. "Not that good. It's humiliating. God knows what persuaded me to have those implants; I wasn't exactly flat-chested before. It's not like me at all."

"I told you not to." Wong pointed an accusing finger. "The feminists would shoot you."

"Feminists? What do I care about feminists? To be a feminist, you have to believe that men have all the power. My problem is I'm too formidable. I can kill an erection on an Italian in two seconds flat. Eighteen months ago I persuaded myself that it wasn't my chain saw personality that ruined my sex life but the size of my bust. So I had implants and discovered that it was my chain saw personality after all. And to make matters worse, they're giving me trouble, and I'm thinking of joining a class action against that surgeon in Los Angeles who performed the operation. There are about sixty women like me all with pains in their chests and feeling nervous."

"No one in your life at the moment?"

She raised her shoulders, lifted her hands. "Are you kidding? I'm too busy."

"What about that blond?"

"A mere Kleenex, darling." When Jonathan winced, she added, "He's a new recruit to the government's prosecutions department. Hardly my style."

"Ah! Really no one else?"

She smiled. "You know why I love having lunch with you, Johnny? You're the only man in this town under fifty who isn't scared of me. All right, there was a guy last week in Shanghai, very sensitive, artistic—reminded me of you. I had to drop him, though. Clinging. Gave him some money to get lost. How's your partner- ship going? I might have some work for you—something big. Even bigger than last time."

Wong put down his drink, used his chopsticks to pick up a tiny piece of pickled ginger. He looked around the room. In total the men and women gathered at the club represented a wealth equal to the gross national products of some European countries. To- gether they could have bought Manhattan, if they had not done so already. But with all the frantic energy that Hong Kong created it had never made a single significant contribution to any form of science, art or literature, with the doubtful exception of Bruce Lee movies. Each of the hundred or so conversations taking place in English, Cantonese, Mandarin, Fukienese, Shanghainese, German, French and Italian was centered one way or another on the same thing, and it wasn't love or the improvement of mankind. He often wondered if he would have been happier if he'd been less lucky. Perhaps struggling to make art films somewhere in Europe; a tor- tured affair with a woman who talked about her feelings; friends who worried about the state of the world.

He looked at his friend, smiled. "I can never thank you enough, you know that."

She beamed. "Now, more important, how's Jenny?"

Wong beamed too, leaned forward. In matters of intimacy he and Emily spoke in Cantonese. "We're pregnant. It's official."

Emily let out a cry, stretched both arms over her head. "Bravo."

Everyone turned, looked at Emily and turned back to their food. She grinned. With a hand half cupped she beckoned a waiter and ordered champagne. He returned immediately with a silver ice bucket on a blackwood pedestal. People turned again when the cork popped.

They clinked glasses.

"And what are you going to call the bambino? Are you going for the traditional Hong Kong hybrid of English stroke Cantonese?"

"Probably. For the sake of the family we'll have one of the usual

Chinese ones." He reeled off a list of traditional Cantonese names. The girls' names always included the name of a flower; the boys' invoked wisdom.

Emily nodded approval. "By the way, thanks for the party the other night. You know that was the first time I met your brother-in-law. I must have missed him at the wedding."

"It's easy to miss him. He never stays long at social events."

Emily swallowed some more champagne. "An intense-looking type. Does he talk to you much about his work?"

"Only if I let him."

"Interesting?"

Wong grimaced. "Don't tell me you fancied him?"

"He told me he was investigating those Mincer Murders. *Gorree!*"

"You want me to introduce you properly? He loves to dole out reality sandwiches to the pampered classes."

"Oh, I'm not that interested. Weird, though, mincing up three people like that."

"Triads."

"I guess." She picked up a piece of pickled ginger with her chopsticks, glanced around the room. She leaned forward, whispered: "So, you haven't had a chance to find out what's behind the Mincer Murders from your manic brother-in-law?"

Wong stopped eating. "Emily, what is this? Are you going through some kind of change? Since when did you care about what the criminal classes got up to?"

She sighed. "Oh, you know, as I get older, I wonder about how the other half lives. Don't you? We're pretty cushioned, people like you and me, aren't we?"

Wong shrugged. "From wayward meat mincers? I hope so. Can we change the subject now? I'm looking forward to my braised abalone."

Emily laughed. Toward the end of the meal she revealed that on this occasion she was paying. She insisted that they end with Wong's favorite brandy, Armagnac.

16

Emily left Wong in the lobby of the China Club to refresh herself in the ladies' room. She checked her Longines gold watch: 2:45. She had five minutes to reach the new Bank of China, which was ten minutes away walking slowly in the heat. It didn't matter that she would be a little late; punctuality was something Communists rarely worried about.

She checked her face in the mirror, smoothed her blouse over her sore breasts, took the lift down to the ground floor. At the new Bank of China building she showed her ID card to the old man at reception, who telephoned up to the top floor. She was shown to a private lift at the back of the building. Unlike the lifts in the public lift bank, it stopped on only one floor: the top.

Fear made her stomach flutter. The meeting with Wong had not gone as well as she had hoped. His news about the pregnancy of his wife had taken her by surprise and made it difficult to talk about money and murder. The fact was, she had little to report, except that in the end Jonathan Wong would do whatever she told him to do.

She stepped out at the top floor. As a state-owned bank the Bank of China was more than a commercial branch of the PRC; it was a center of intelligence gathering and surveillance as important in its own way as the New China News Agency, which functioned as the PRC's consulate in Hong Kong. The new bank building had been designed to accommodate visiting cadres. There was a sauna room, Jacuzzis, large bedrooms with videos and televisions, a huge kitchen that was manned twenty-four hours a day and a cocktail area with the best views of Hong Kong that money could buy. Better, the new Bank of China was the tallest building in Central. From the start it was envisaged that the People's representatives would not suffer during their frequent visits to the despised British colony.

She was shown upstairs to the glass-enclosed cocktail area on the roof of the building, where the old man was waiting. Seventy stories below, toy cars sped along Connaught Road; tiny ships lay at anchor in the harbor; the richest city on earth lay at the feet of the seventy-year-old man lounging in an Italian leather-and-chrome armchair. The owner of possibly the largest personal fortune in the world after the sultan of Brunei's, he wore an open-neck shirt of the kind that could be bought in Stanley Market, khaki slacks. His worn sneakers rested on a suede footstool hand-stitched out of brown and beige triangles.

He did not rise to greet her. Nor did he offer her one of the cigarettes that he shook out of a flimsy pack: Imperial Palace, unavailable outside the PRC.

"So?"

She took a seat opposite him, sat straight, tried to attract his attention. Some kind of sexual chemistry might have been useful in these interviews, but he had never shown the slightest interest. His age didn't help either. Mass murderers do not necessarily mellow with the passage of time. His wiry form reminded her of a ginseng root. She recognized in it the will of her people at its crudest. Her striking looks, enlarged breasts, billions in assets, the respect she was able to command throughout Hong Kong and anywhere else in the world where money was revered had no effect at all on this ugly old man. Still without looking at her, he started to pick his nose.

"You had lunch with your little friend the lawyer?"

"Yes."

"And?"

"I told you, he'll do whatever we want."

"Yes, that I already know. How did you develop the matter today? That's what interests me."

"I'll phone him in a day or two; he'll come to see me at my house. If you're really serious about this."

The old man grinned. "What could be more serious than five hundred million American dollars?"

"In cash? It's pure provocation."

He laughed with a whinny like a horse. "Not provocation. Convenience. I'm tired of these *gweilo* games. Why should we hide anymore? With only two months to go, we've won already. Now we can start enjoying the victory."

"I know. I guess I don't understand why you need to move five hundred million again so soon. Less than a month ago you also moved half a billion dollars."

An expression of intense fury passed over the old man's face. He caught himself. "I'd forgotten I'd told you. There was no laundering involved on that occasion. We were paying for something. In cash. This next consignment I want to be clean and official. There are still parts of Hong Kong we haven't yet bought."

Emily breathed in deeply. "I can't think what."

The old man twisted his features into a smirk. "Now, tell me, this interesting piece of luck with that detective—did you explore it at all?"

"The only lucky part is that Chief Inspector Chan is Jonathan Wong's brother-in-law. The rumor is that Chan himself is a dedicated fanatic, who hates Communists. I don't know what you expect Jonathan to do."

"Do? They're in the same family, aren't they? Your friend is rich; the detective is poor. How much does he want?"

She watched while he took a long draw on his cigarette.

"I told you, he's dedicated. I don't think he takes money."

The old man kicked the footstool away, turned to look at her for the first time. "Everyone takes money. Anyway, he's half Chinese, isn't he?" He laughed again, then made a long retching noise in his throat. About to spit, he remembered that there was no spittoon. He swallowed instead. "Cuthbert will have to deal with it."

"He won't. Aiding and abetting isn't part of the deal; you know that. He'll turn a blind eye, but that's all he'll do."

The old man had a way of looking with one eye closed, immobile as a lizard on a rock.

"Are you telling me we may be driven to something more decisive?"

Emily felt her cheeks burning. She rose, stood directly in front of the old man, who blinked.

"Can't you people get it through your skulls that you can't just kill everyone who gives you trouble? Yes, I'm daring to yell at you; are you going to kill me too?"

He laughed then. "Who said anything about killing? I want the little detective to carry out his investigation. I want to know who died in that mincer. I want him to tell me first—perhaps exclusively."

He stared at her. She felt the fear again, a sense of doom in the pit of her stomach. Never raise your voice to a psychopath. She sat on the footstool, kept her eyes below his.

"I'm sorry. Everyone thinks *you* had them killed. Give me another few weeks. I'll see what I can do. I have a few ideas."

The old man sneered at her. "What ideas?"

"Wong needs to get to know his brother-in-law better first. They're not great friends. I'll try to set it up."

The old man grunted. "It's not urgent until the little detective gets close. I want to know what happened to those three before Cuthbert is told." He stared at her. "D'you still fuck him?" He smirked at her discomfort. "Pity. You could have kept me informed about how much he knows, our little English diplomat. They're going to make him *Sir* Milton Cuthbert when he goes back in July. If you'd managed to marry him, you would have been Lady Cuthbert." He sniggered.

"I don't understand. Why are you so interested in those killings if you didn't do it? It was probably just triads; people like that get snuffed out."

The old man turned his face away from her. "Maybe. See what you can do about the detective anyway—make friends with him, find out what stage he's at. Fuck him if you have to. And as far as the five hundred million is concerned, I expect results. It's been hanging around for too long. You don't want to lose those development rights along the Pearl River, do you? You have a lot of money riding on that. All your money, taking the personal guarantees into account. I don't think you want to be poor.''

Seeing the expression on her face, he laughed again.

When she had gone, the old man picked up a telephone on a coffee table near his left hand, told his secretary whom he wished to speak to. When the telephone rang, he began speaking immediately in Mandarin, his voice heavy with condescension. At the end of the conversation he said: ''By the way, don't impersonate me again. I want this investigation to continue. I want to know who died and who did the killing.'' His reply to the question that followed was to hang up. After a moment's thought he pressed the intercom button again. ''Get me the other Englishman, the one in London. And stay on the line; I'll need you to translate.''

17

Moira was a generous lover. Generous and adventurous, the beneficiary of a culture that ordained that the over forties must have fun. Chan was surprised she'd had the delicacy to sober up before his return from work and more surprised that she'd been able to arouse him when Angie hadn't. She was unexpectedly sensitive, and then there was a self-sufficiency to her suffering that attracted him. Half dreaming beside her, he found it possible to believe he lay with a woman whose soul was as big as the world. He liked her breasts. They were large, pendulous, friendly. He formed a spoon around her body to hold them while she slept. She woke up once to say thank you, turned over, fell into a deep sleep.

As usual he remained awake. After a while he slid out of bed, closed the door, sat naked on the couch to smoke. He turned on the television with the sound off. Monks who had perfected the art of kung fu in the Shao Lin Monastery flew through the air, slaughtering their opponents against the usual impossible odds. On another channel an aging landowner in mandarin dress was taking his daughter to market when they were ambushed by a gang of robbers. Fear of rape, pillage and murder was amplified by the makeup. China dramas usually dug into the distant violent past. The recent violent past was too much for most stomachs.

He turned back to the monks of Shao Lin. He'd gone through his karate stage. To perfect the body to the point where you could defy gravity was a legend engraved in the imagination of every Asian boy. He lit another cigarette, coughed, wondered what to do about Moira.

The truth was, she was only the second Western woman with whom he'd been involved. Comparisons were inevitable. He wondered if the learning curve he'd been through with Sandra was applicable to an American. What he remembered most about his English wife was her complaining. She was very different from a Chinese wife; the problem did not seem to lie in lack of material possessions or social status. Sandra's moans emanated from high moral ground. Hong Kong was shallow and materialistic, greedy, inhuman. Chan deduced that the British Isles were a fortress of psychological depth, moral courage, human kindness. He set himself to understand more, to take advantage of his wife's wisdom and background. He found that she had an agile wit that ranged over English and American cultures with apparent ease. She used different voices, different accents to accord with certain moods. One funny little voice was used when she wished to convey affection. Chan wondered why she could not express love in her own voice, but he learned to live with it. A phony New York accent was used when she would have liked to be forceful; an upper-class British accent appeared when she thought he was being uncouth.

It was the videos that precipitated the end, though he could never have predicted it. He'd subscribed to a rental shop largely to try to alleviate the homesickness she complained of from time to time. She'd reacted with enthusiasm, renting mostly old videos of English comedy shows with a strong satirical, self-mocking bite. As he'd sat with her night after night, he'd begun to realize where her voices came from. Not only her voices. Her opinions, her moral postures—even her disdain for Hong Kong was a rerun of a BBC documentary. The English, it seemed, in their cold, wet climate spent hours in front of televisions being told what to think and who to be. He was married to a collage of *Monty Python, Spitting Image, Black Adder, Not the Nine o'Clock News* and a range of similar shows.

At the start she had been vehemently antiracist. Indeed Chan had worried that she had married him out of an excess of political correctness. Little by little, though, odd epithets had poked through the facade, like barbed wire through snow. English mockery was highly developed and embraced the world. French were Frogs, Germans were Krauts, Scandinavians were Hurdy-Gurdies, Italians and Greeks were Dagos, Chinese were Chinks or Chokies, Japanese were Nips. Was it possible that behind the television programs there cowered a mean-spirited people smaller than life?

Chan had probed further (he was looking for the woman he had married). Political opinions were reproduced verbatim from the *Guardian*; feminism was lifted direct from *Cosmopolitan*. Even her vegetarianism was tainted. She ate tiny dishes of vegetables to keep her figure, but when she discovered how well the Cantonese roasted duck, she stole morsels from Chan's plate with a self-forgiving smirk. Under questioning (she called it interrogation) she seemed to consist most of an appetite for sex, marijuana and Greek sheep's yogurt, with a nonspecific resentment that could fixate without warning on anything but most frequently targeted men and capitalism. Sobbing, she accused him of misogyny and chauvinism, two words that peppered her speech. He shook his head; it was worse than that. He'd married a piece of the West, and intimacy had bred contempt.

Although he'd remained a model husband, he knew that she'd fled from the profound disillusionment she saw in his face when he looked at her. If only she'd been able to let it go, all that absurd European pretension, but without those borrowed opinions and the energy of resentment, what would she amount to? The thought of being no different from any struggling Chinese housewife in the streets of Mongkok was unendurable to her. It was implicit in the way she talked and in the letters she wrote afterward: The last thing she'd expected from marriage to a Chinaman was that he would not be able to respect her, as if when all was said and done, disdain were a prerogative of the Raj. Moira, it was true, seemed very different, but there were reasons for caution.

Perhaps he had fallen into a doze or was merely thinking too hard. He didn't hear her enter. Her hands over his eyes made him jump.

"You're jumpy."

There was no light in the room except for the flickering images of the television and the eternal glare of Mongkok leaking through the curtains; she was no more than a voice and a subtle caress. Reaching behind him, he felt his raw silk dressing gown. Under it, those breasts that almost brought him sleep.

"My Irish genes."

"Irish people aren't especially nervous. Half the NYPD is Irish, including me. My maiden name was Kelly. They're no more sensitive than a sack of potatoes."

"I bet the murder squad is jumpy."

She sat down beside him. "Ever thought of changing professions?"

"Sure. I have great options. Security for a bank, adviser to the triads. I'd make a great hit man except for my stomach trouble."

"You have stomach trouble?"

"No guts."

She snuggled up to him. "I don't believe that. I saw that photograph of you receiving an award for bravery."

"I was very young. I just reacted. Probably caught between two fears. Fear of being called a coward was the stronger."

"But you saved a life."

"Maybe."

She caressed his thigh, moved on up until she reached his neck. Her fingers probed his facial muscles, pausing at the ones that twitched.

"You know, in the West, where I come from, we think it helps to talk about it."

He leaned forward, lit a cigarette. "Maybe because in the West you have 'its' to talk about. You think of problems like thorns. Just find it, pull it out and live happily ever after."

"And in the East?"

"Chinese call it 'being alive in the bitter sea.' It's not a thorn that hurts; it's the whole environment."

"In Hong Kong, the richest city in the world?"

"In China. Hong Kong is a Christmas decoration. Christmas will soon be over."

Moira grunted. "Nobody loses sleep over politics. That's what we pay politicians for. Was it a woman?"

He rested his head on the back of the couch. "Yes, a woman."

"Look, I'll be gone by tomorrow. We don't even need to meet again. I can be just a voice in the night. You've helped me, more than you know. Why not let me help you?"

He smiled into the darkness. "She was Chinese, through and through—not inscrutable, though. She had a big moon face, eyes that took you straight to the purest soul you could ever meet. Eyes that couldn't help believe everything you said because she didn't know how to lie.

"She was short and dumpy, about five foot two, and no matter how hard things got she always made sure there was steamed rice and pork or duck for her kids to eat. The only adventurous thing she ever did was to come to Hong Kong but that was because her big sister was here. She walked. Lots of them did in those days. They camped by the frontier, tried to keep out of sight of the soldiers; then, when night came, they'd make a break for the border fence. They knew that some of them would be killed. A bullet in the back from the People's Army, but most got through. The British weren't too gentle either. They sent them back if they caught them near the border, but they had a rule, one of those funny British rules like a school game. If they made it as far as Hong Kong Island and the Immigration Department, they could stay. And she did. The little dumpy Chinese girl with the moon face made it when tougher ones failed."

Chan stopped, moved from the sofa to find his Bensons. When he returned to the sofa, he smoothed the robe over Moira's breasts. She held his hand. "Go on."

He exhaled into the night. "No, it's not interesting to you. You wanted another story full of sex and torment."

She dropped his hand, let her own rest on his thigh. "That's not true. You're talking about your mom, right? You're forgetting, I'm a mother. Was. Mothers don't get such good press these days. It's encouraging to know that some men have a passion for the woman who gave them life."

Chan heard the catch in her voice. He squeezed her hand. "I'm sorry, I'm being selfish. You're the one with the grief."

"It's soothing to hear you talk. And it's not a story I've ever heard before."

He took a long draw, found the ashtray. "Mai-mai lived with her sister in a squatter hut for a while, until she met Paddy. Actually his name's not Paddy; I just think of him as a Paddy. I think he did love her, like a bastard can love his opposite. She really believed him when he told her he had to work nights during the week and could only be with her at weekends. It was believable to her because that's what Chinese men did. Of course, he was out whoring in Wanchai, but he liked the emotional security of the little girl with the moon face who adored him. I was born first, Jenny three years later.

"Thirteen years later Paddy just disappeared one day as Paddys do. Mai-mai went into depression. No one had ever seen her like that. She even forgot to feed us, and her sister had to do it. Eventually she decided that these big red-faced people with the round eyes really were devils, just like everyone said. She'd left her home village to wander into the land of the devils. So she went back. On foot again. Somehow she managed to avoid the guards at the border. I guess they weren't keeping an eye out for anyone who actually wanted to return to the PRC.

"When she reached her home village, it was infested with Red Guards. China's second civil war this century, called the Cultural Revolution, was in its closing stages. As a ruse to keep power Mao Zedong set his people against each other, the young against the old, brother against brother, pupil against teacher, wife against husband. It was an orgy of hate, Chinese style. But to some of the outside world it was a courageous socialist experiment. Wise men and women from Europe and America were taken to a kind of Walt Disney China where everything was wonderful, the people full of smiles.

"The real China was villages like Mai-mai's, where they arrested her for being a capitalist running dog. They put her in a dunce's cap and paraded her through the streets. Red Guards about her age, or younger. They made her confess, something she was glad to do since she believed everything they told her and supposed she must have been deluded by the wicked West.

"Ordinarily they would have let her go, but she made a mistake only the very innocent make. She told them she would have to return to Hong Kong to bring her children back. So they decided she hadn't really reformed at all and threw her from a fourth-floor room in a government building. The fall broke both her legs and her pelvis and made a hole in her skull, but she remained conscious. I have eyewitness accounts of her lying there, deciding to die because all over the earth from west to east there was no place for her. A pure soul with a big moon face who believed what people told her."

Chan went to the fridge, found a beer, came back. They sat in silence.

Moira coughed. "That's a lot of hate to carry around. Hate is a problem, like a thorn, at least to my Western eyes."

Chan shook his head, opened the can, swallowed. "No, hate's not a problem. If you're bad and you hate, you kill someone; if you're good, you forgive; if you're in between, you hesitate—but it's not the real problem."

"What is?"

"The way they've turned the world upside down. That's what drives you crazy."

"Upside down?"

"Sure. During the Cultural Revolution important people like film stars, famous BBC commentators with film crews, French left-wing journalists went to China and were deceived. We said, 'Okay, that's because the West is naive; they want to believe in the socialist experiment, and those cunning old men in Beijing, they're so good at the art of deception.'

"But even when the truth came out, nothing much happened; you didn't even hear any of those famous people apologize for being so stupid. We said, 'Well, what can you expect? They're embarrassed, and anyway what could they do about it? But next time those old men start murdering people, then surely the West will expose them to the world.' Which is exactly what happened when they killed all those students in Tiananmen Square in June 1989.

"The West was mad as hell. People went on television denouncing the violence; politicians talked about trade sanctions; nobody believed those murderous old geriatrics anymore. But in America and Japan and Europe there were people who said, 'Hold on, there are one point four billion people over there, the biggest single market in the world, and if you impose trade sanctions, some other bastard is going to be selling them the T-shirts and the sneakers and the pocket calculators and the mopeds instead of us.'

"So the trade sanctions didn't last long, and the murdering old men in Beijing laughed so hard you could hear them in Hong Kong. And in two months' time they'll be here with their tanks and their cynical sneers and their contempt for human life, and the Chinese screens will go up, and no one over there in your country will want to know what's really going on here. They'll be happy with the shadow play on the screens, glad not to have reasons for refusing to sell the T-shirts. That's the problem: how to live a life when you always have to pretend that the world is upside down and has always been that way."

Moira had stopped stroking him. He let the television lights flicker over his face. Her voice when she spoke was a Bronx rumble. "Kinda tough, that one, Charlie. Not sure there's anything I can do to help."

"Well, there's one thing that might help in a tiny way."

"Name it."

"You could stop lying."

A pause.

"Did you say stop lying?"

"Yes, that's what I said. You were a sergeant in the NYPD, but you took early retirement over two years ago. Your daughter, Clare, did go to NYU, but she didn't graduate in sociology; she graduated in business studies. Strange mistake for a mother to make."

The silence lasted so long Chan assumed Moira wasn't going to answer. It didn't much matter. He became absorbed in the images from the kung fu show again. Evil wasn't vanquished as easily as all that. There had been a counterattack by the bad monks from the black monastery over the hill. It was no problem telling them apart from the good monks because they always snarled when they spoke whereas the good monks oozed serenity. If he went into movies, he'd have to be one of the bad guys. Finally Moira made rumbling sounds preparatory to saying something.

"You checked the same day? With the university as well? Would have taken NYPD a month, minimum. If they'd bothered at all. Guess what made you suspicious was the stuff I pocketed in the shop downstairs, huh? You didn't believe I did it to test you, did you?"

Chan tried to look at her. "You mean I was supposed to?"

Moira grunted. "Guess not."

18

A million U.S. dollars does not buy a house on Hong Kong Island, not even a small one; almost everyone lives in apartment blocks. The few remaining houses, old colonial constructions (built by the taipans of yesteryear high up on the Peak and away from the cholera and malaria that made nineteenth-century Asia a threat to expatriate health), tended to be owned by international corporations and used by their top executives to entertain and impress. To own privately one of the three- or four-story mansions that clung to the side of the mountain was proof of membership in the local aristocracy, a demonstration of wealth staggering even by Hong Kong standards.

Jonathan Wong had organized the conveyancing when Emily first bought hers six years before. She had been excited, full of plans for improvements and visions of the many parties she was going to give. Since then she had hardly stopped adding wings, demolishing walls, changing decor. Her swimming pool was the largest private one in the territory, almost Olympic size, shaped in an oblong with Roman columns and terra-cotta tiles on the perimeter. The house faced southwest so that the view was not of the harbor but of the dense green drop to the Lamma Channel and the wide-open sea beyond.

A large awning close to the swimming pool gave some shade. She was sitting in a fawn bathrobe and Gucci sunglasses when her maid showed him in.

He pecked her on the cheek, sat down opposite her at the marble table.

"I've got the cook to give us Italian for once. Antipasto misto, spaghetti al funghi followed by fruit. I found some reasonable strawberries in Oliver's that you can have with cream à l'anglais if you like. Or have you given up cream along with every other middle-class male approaching forty?"

Wong took off his jacket, undid his tie. "I still eat cream. I hold the view that it's stress, not cholesterol, that kills. Anyway, I don't have the strength of character to give up cream."

She wasn't smiling today at his jokes. She even seemed irritated that he'd removed his tie. The stock market hadn't crashed; it must be a particularly heavy period.

He waited until the maid had brought an ice bucket with a bottle of Perrier. "So, you have more work to burden me with?"

"If it's not too much to ask." She studied him for a moment. "I'm afraid it's just a tad controversial, but I want you to do it anyway. Let's be frank: You owe me, and I need you to do this thing."

Under his smile Wong quaked. He couldn't tell how closely she was looking at him through the black lenses. "Shoot, this poor slave is only too eager to be of assistance." He was surprised at how little sarcasm he was able to invest in the words.

"You remember the Zedfell purchase of Chancery Towers?"

Wong shot her a sharp glance. "How could I forget?"

It had been about three years ago. Emily had introduced an important piece of conveyancing into his firm. As usual, she had channeled it through Wong, although he was not a conveyancer himself. He had assumed that the transaction was proceeding normally when his conveyancing partner had demanded a meeting with Wong and Rathbone, the senior partner. The conveyancing partner had been nervous.

"*Cash!* They want to buy a whole office tower *in cash!* It's bent, and I'm not prepared to carry on unless I get the full support of all the partners."

Wong had had to admit the conveyancing partner had a point. Zedfell Incorporated, the would-be purchaser of a substantial apartment building, was, on examination, owned entirely by an offshore company, which in turn was owned by sixteen Chinese men, all domiciled in the PRC. The problem arose from some recent legislation intended to crack down on money laundering. Nobody doubted that the sixteen gentlemen who owned Zedfell were corrupt Communist cadres who had accumulated a great deal of spare cash and needed to hide it. Nobody doubted either that Emily was helping them because she owed them favors.

Rathbone had found a way of describing the transaction that seemed to take it outside the antilaundering legislation. But the firm had looked on Emily in a different light from then on. In banking parlance she was no longer Triple A, and by extension neither was Wong.

Emily took off her sunglasses, looked him in the eye. "Well, Zedfell want to buy another three apartment blocks, two on Kowloon, near Castle Peak, one at North Point. They've also successfully negotiated for an office block in Kennedy Town."

"I see."

"Total price for all four transactions is in the region of five hundred million U.S. Payment will be in cash. Your firm will receive the money itself and bank it."

Wong took a sip of Perrier. Even under the awning it was hot. He was sweating and wished he'd brought his sunglasses.

He swallowed hard. "No, Emily. I'm sorry."

She replaced her sunglasses, stared out over the Lamma Channel. For a full two minutes he had her in profile, the jutting chin, the black glasses, the bathrobe.

"Emily?"

She turned back to him, pushed the sunglasses up onto the top of her head. He thought she was smiling until he saw it was a grimace. In all the years she had never shown him this side of herself, the side other people talked about, the killer instinct finely honed.

"We all have to grow up sometime, Johnny. I've helped you put it off for long enough. You were my innocence, but I can't afford you anymore. And anyway, I've made you lazy and dumb. So listen. You're going to do this thing. Understand? Of course you'll be paid your usual exorbitant fees, whatever they are."

Wong opened some more buttons on his shirt, wiped his palms on the Kent and Curwen jacket that he'd slung across a chair. In one of the pockets he found a cigarette, lit it. She had turned away from him again, presented him with her stubborn profile. He let the silence continue. Open defiance would only make her more determined. If he soothed her somehow, she would see how ridiculous she was being.

He lit a second cigarette from the first, stood up, walked around the table, knelt by her chair. To his surprise she put a hand down without looking at him, stroked his face.

"I've always loved you, Johnny, like the brother I never had."

"I love you too, like a sister."

"You'll do it?"

"Emily, listen, it's out of the question. Five hundred million U.S.? We only just got away with the Zedfell thing last time. And that was only about thirty million. I'm not going to ask questions about where this money is coming from, but you know and I know that it's hot. A sum like that gets onto the front pages of *Time* and *Asiaweek*. My firm would be blown away in the scandal. Remember what happened to Freeman's in the Nabian debacle?"

Wong remembered. So did every other lawyer of his generation. A senior partner who committed suicide after fleeing to London, two other partners arrested and unable to work for two years until the trial, when they'd got off by the skin of their teeth, the loss of major banking and other Triple A clients. All because of an illegal conveyance considerably less sinister than the one Emily was proposing. It had taken Freeman's ten years to return to genuine profitability, and even now it was doomed to remain in the second league.

She sighed, withdrew her hand. "I see."

He forced a smile, stood behind her chair, started to massage her neck. She liked that.

"Oh, I know you're the empress of Hong Kong and not in the

habit of being defied, but frankly, you don't own our firm. You give us a lot of work, you're one of our most valued clients, but if the partners were forced to choose between ruining our reputation by taking on these conveyances and losing your business, they'd choose to let you go, I'm afraid. You see, if we took it on, we'd be in danger of losing all our other clients. No one would understand, no one. It's as if Morgan Grenfell were to open a pawnshop; it just doesn't happen."

Emily let her head fall back until she was looking directly into his eyes. She pulled the sunglasses down to the tip of her nose. "It's only your partners you're worried about—nothing else?"

"I swear, nothing else." He half smirked. "Except that the whole thing scares me shitless."

She smiled. "Tell me about it, Johnny. You think just because I'm a filthy rich bitch I don't wake up in a cold sweat most nights?"

"You? You're pure Teflon."

She let her head drop further backward so that she was looking at the awning. "But the terror, my friend, is the cloud that always comes when there's a silver lining. Those deals where the green balls slide down your back every time you think about what you're about to do—those deals are the ones that really pay off. Because those are the ones nobody else will have the guts for. See?"

"If you say so. I don't have your nerve, Emily, we both know that. I don't even know why you carry on. God knows you have enough."

"Oh, but you do know why. You once said it better than I ever could. Don't you remember?"

"No."

"During your first year at Oxford, my dear. I remember getting a very distressed telephone call—"

"Don't, Emily—"

"A very distressed telephone call. A bunch of brutal English thugs after a night in a pub to which you should never have gone, wasn't that it? It was not so much the physical damage, though God knows they really beat you up. It was the psychological scars that remained with you—to this day, I would guess."

"All right, you've made your point."

"The point is that it was not your daddy or me who persuaded you to give up your dreams. It was racist England. Or simple human reality, whatever. I've never forgotten your words: 'If one must be Chinese, it is important to be a rich Chinese.' That's when you changed to law. The terror of big money is nothing compared to the terror of no money—especially for someone like you. Am I right?"

"Probably. You've said enough." He allowed himself to look annoyed. He didn't want to be reminded of the humiliation or of the deeper lesson that he'd been too ashamed to tell Emily about. After his wounds had healed, he had paid some thugs from a local Chinese restaurant who claimed to be part-time triads to avenge him. He remembered a garage late at night, four big beef-faced young Englishmen squeaking like pigs, actually shitting themselves in terror of the eight yellow men with steel pipes, bicycle chains, knives and, of course, meat cleavers, while he stood shaking with something truly awful: the realization that survival requires power and if you have no natural authority of your own, why, then, you must buy it.

It was after the night of his revenge that he'd told Emily of his vow to be a rich Chinese, leaving out the squalid details that lurked behind it. The whole chain of events lay so far outside his normal, mild-mannered approach to life that he preferred to look on it most of the time as an aberration. But the fact was, he was no different from her. With his back against the wall or his ego threatened he would cut, maim, murder; artistic aspirations were no help at all. He turned back to her and forced a smile. Her eyebrows were raised.

"So, if your partners can be persuaded, you'll accept?"

"Reluctantly, and with green balls already running down my back, yes."

"Then here's why they'll let you take the case."

• • •

When Emily finished, she handed Wong a cordless telephone with which to call Rathbone. True to his work ethic, Rathbone was in his office eating a sandwich. Wong set up the meeting for two-thirty with Rathbone, Savile and Watson, the Australian commercial partner, and Ng, the Chinese litigation partner. Then he had Emily's maid bring him a Bloody Mary. He took a pad and pen out of his briefcase.

"I'd better write down the names of the companies you mentioned. And those people you talked about—I'd had no idea."

Without referring to any documents Emily recited the names of more than one hundred companies and personnel without a pause.

"And they're all owned by or work for these sixteen men who own Zedfell?"

"All of them. I think you'll find that something in the region of sixty percent of your turnover last year was generated one way or another in the PRC and came through one or more of these companies. You're right to say that I don't own your firm. They do."

As Wong rose to leave, Emily put the tip of her sunglasses in her mouth and said, "By the way, I have a confession. I think I really do fancy the pants off your brother-in-law."

Wong forced a smile. "I'll see what I can do."

19

Lunchtime: Chan sat in his office alone with a laboratory report and two sets of photographs developed by the identification bureau at Arsenal Street. The lab report confirmed that the white contents of the plastic bag had been heroin. He turned his attention to the photographs. On the back of one set he wrote in ballpoint: "Taken after laser enhancement from small plastic bag found hidden in light fitting at scene of crime." On the back of the other set he wrote: "Taken from *The Travels of Marco Polo*, paperback book provided by mother of the victim, Clare Coletti."

Each photograph had been enlarged to three times actual size. Taking what looked like a thumbprint from one set, he set it against a thumbprint from the other. There was no point of identity between the two. Taking an apparently different print from the set originating with the plastic bag, he found again no points of similarity. There was a third thumbprint, quite different from the other two, that had been lifted from the bag by the laser beam. There were similarities even at a first glance; in both cases he noted a convergence of lines in a single delta. At the center of the print was a tight loop, the core. Working on one print, he counted the lines from the delta to the core, wrote: "Ridge count 18." Other idiosyncrasies of the print included three fragments next to the core, an island, an ending in the middle of the fifth ridge line, two bifurcations, two more islands near the eleventh ridge line, some more ridge endings. Chan put the photograph to one side, worked on the thumbprint from the book. When he finished, he compared the lists. He had found eleven major points of similarity, enough to satisfy even a purist like himself. Clare Coletti had clutched the bag of heroin, perhaps had even hidden it, before she was murdered elsewhere. Then her remains, together with those of the other victims, had been returned in a vat and placed under the fluorescent light where she had hidden her dope. Chan had never come across a case that made less sense. When Aston returned from lunch, he asked him to send another fax to New York with all the prints that had been lifted from the plastic bag.

At least the exercise might have helped identify the other two victims. And Tsim, the technician, owed him fifty dollars.

The four lawyers sat in silence at one end of the huge boardroom table. Jonathan Wong looked from one to the other, waited. For the chief eunuch to the empress it was a pleasure to watch a ritual castration.

When he had joined the firm as an articled clerk, these men—Rathbone, Savile, Ng and Watson—had already been senior and highly respected. As he had grown older and wiser, he had come to despise them. As lawyers the Englishmen hid behind the pompous postures that had served the British so well. But they had been in the East a long time. Something happened to Englishmen who stayed too long. The country they came from, that little island off the cold northwest coast of Europe, had proceeded without them with its own peculiar modern history, full of football hooligans and royal scandals, as far as Wong could tell, until the mannerisms they had retained and developed had no reference outside their own narcissism.

There was Rathbone, almost fifty with an adolescent fascination with his own musculature, who liked to boast about how many hours he spent in the office. There was Savile, the music hall Englishman with the three-piece suit and the monocle, an intellectual property lawyer. And there was Watson, the prima donna in the bow tie who thought of himself as an international commercial lawyer. His Chinese assistants joked that he was incompetent in nine separate jurisdictions.

Ng was different only insofar as he was Chinese. He was a few years older than Wong, but in terms of postcolonial evolution a chasm separated them. Although Wong spoke English with an upper-class accent, any English person foolish enough to assume that he wanted to be one of them was quickly put in his place. Ng, though, had invested his life energy into growing a British carapace at the center of which, Wong was fairly sure, lay nothing at all.

Each man in his own way defied a basic law of physics, possessing height and width but no depth. But people who wondered how they'd survived so long and grown so rich underestimated the inexhaustible appetite of the very wealthy for sustained groveling. The vulgar said that the four men who gathered around the boardroom table with Wong had the brownest noses in Hong Kong. Little by little, Wong knew, he was becoming one of them.

Watson rudely gestured to Wong to pass over the sheet of paper with the names of the companies Emily had given him. He took it to a computer terminal in the corner of the room, began punching in the names with heavy stabs. The others watched him, glad to have something to wait for.

"Amazing," Watson murmured.

"What is?"

He continued to punch in more names.

"Quite incredible." He punched in some more, then hit the top of the screen with his open hand as he stood up.

"Would you believe it? Taken in isolation, none of these companies is remarkable. Taken together, these hundred-odd firms represent stupendous wealth. In terms of assets they could compete with some of our biggest banks. If they really are all owned by the same people."

"I think you can assume that they are," Wong said.

"It's like a cancer."

"Not a cancer," Wong said, "an Oriental strategy. Like the game of Go, one surrounds by stealth and strangles. Clever, these Chinks."

Ng nodded slowly, as if the epithet could not apply to him.

"Why would anyone want to strangle us?" Rathone said, ignoring the irony.

Wong lit a cigarette, his tenth in the past two hours. "Not us, Hong Kong. Or, more likely, Southeast Asia. Whoever they are, they're taking over."

Savile glanced at Wong. Wong knew that behind the absurd monocle and the affected manners he possessed the cleverest brain of the three, which was perhaps not saying much.

"I think we'd better admit she's got us. If this lot took their business elsewhere, we'd be bankrupt. Literally, we couldn't pay the rent."

"Absolutely," Ng muttered.

Rathbone groaned, stood up, flexed his pectorals facing first left, then right, squatted with arms folded, stood, sat down again.

"We'd better move fast," Savile continued. "This must go no further than these four walls. What we do is agree to take the work but, when it comes in, act surprised that payment will be in cash. Let them bring the money at the last minute. Naturally we couldn't hold up the transaction, but we say we were assuming payment by check or banker's draft. We'll take our fees up front. And then . . . we'll see."

Savile didn't need to spell out the precautions that he and the others would be making that very afternoon: new numbered bank accounts in the Caymans or British Virgin Islands; vacations moved forward; personal effects, especially houses, put into the names of trust companies based in the Channel Islands. The storm, when it came, would take some weathering.

Rathbone looked around the table. "We're agreed then?"

"I think we are," Savile said.

Immediately after the meeting Wong called Emily with the news.

"I thought they might see it our way, Johnny. You did well."

On putting the phone down on Jonathan, Emily pressed an autodial button. A rough old man's voice answered in Mandarin.

"He'll do it."

"Of course he will."

"But they want the money exactly one hour before each contract is signed. Not sooner or later."

The old man answered with a grunt. "And the little detective?"

"Jonathan will set up a social meeting somehow. I might even find a way of bringing you since you're so interested in Charlie Chan."

20

F eeling mild excitement, Chan ordered a car to take him out to the fishing village of Sai Kung on the east coast of the New Territories; an English senior inspector had called with news of a possible sighting of a meat mincer on the seabed.

Once he was out of the vast conurbation that stretched from the tip of Kowloon in the south to Choi Hung, the land was green and relatively free of development. The road expanded into a turnpike that lifted up to the hills on the east coast.

At nine-thirty in the morning sunlight hurt. Behind them Kowloon radiated its usual glaucous haze, but up ahead the sky was the deep blue of glazed Ming. Under the solar onslaught the world wobbled. Silver pools shimmered in hollows in the road. Green tiled roofs undulated. Chan and the driver put on sunglasses, turned up the air conditioning.

Chan flicked the radio on to a Cantopop station and winced. "Please release me, let me go" lost everything in translation. He turned to an English-language information program. "Visibility good, fire risk extreme," a voice said in a London accent. Chan switched off.

The driver pointed to two large military helicopters racing from a funnel of smoke twisting up behind a hill to the left. Huge buckets hung from chains attached to their underbellies and swayed against the direction of the choppers dashing for the sea.

"Bad one. Started yesterday."

"By campers?"

"Probably. It's in the bush, not near any villages. No one's been evacuated yet, but the bush is very dry."

At the top of the hill the sea came into view: the Pacific coast of China. There was not much between here and Japan, Chan remembered, and if you missed Japan, America was probably the next stop. Not that the ancient Chinese had seen any reason to go even a fraction of that distance. The Middle Kingdom had been the center of the earth, where everyone wanted to be. Only Europe could have produced a Columbus, a man so dissatisfied his own continent wasn't big enough. Or a Marco Polo.

They turned right along a coast road called Hiram's Highway by the British, "the road to Pak Sha Wan" by the Chinese. Nobody knew who Hiram had been, not even the British, but Pak Sha Wan was a tiny fishing village with a large boat club. Each year the boats and the club grew larger and more expensive. Million-dollar sailing yachts hung in the heat next to cigar-shaped speed machines that the Cantonese called snakeheads. As a general rule Europeans owned the sailing yachts and Chinese owned the snakeheads. On a windless day like this the boats faced in all directions, their mooring ropes drooping. Sampans chugged between the floating parking lots, taking swimmers to beaches across the bay.

"You know this area?" Chan said.

"No, you?"

"Yeah. I was brought up near here. In a squatter hut overlooking the sea."

"That so? You were lucky. You got fresh fish and fresh air. I was brought up in Hak Nam, the Walled City. Nothing fresh there. Especially not the whores."

Chan laughed. Five years ago the government had knocked down the Walled City, a square mile of unplanned triad-built apartments with open sewers, fat rats, prostitution and drug addicts. But some people had loved it, as he had loved his wooden hut.

"You're right. I was lucky. I lived there with my kid sister. I told her stories about sea-monsters and taught her to swim. We never wanted to go to school. Didn't seem any reason to."

The driver nodded.

• • •

Chan was on his second Benson when they reached Sai Kung. It had expanded from a village into a town since he had lived nearby, but the covered market and the fishing fleet still flourished. The driver swerved to a halt at the end of the car park near the main pier. Chan got out. Chinese kids in black full-face helmets lying over the fuel tanks of Kawasakis and Yamahas practiced side skids in the center of the new concrete square. To one side skateboarders in silken black leggings with Day-Glo knee pads had set up a ramp from which they launched themselves into space. Opposite, the Watson's supermarket had risen from the ashes of a wooden Chinese village house where the headman had lived. On either side tinted glass and chrome video and music shops offered relief from the heat and a direct line to the twentieth century. For twenty years he had never been more than ten miles away, but he felt like a man who'd returned after spending a lifetime overseas. He remembered paddy fields that came up to the village square, a banyan tree under which the elders spent their days talking and playing Chinese chess, children so shy that even in early teens they were afraid to leave the house. The West had wrought a cultural revolution more drastic than Mao's. It took only a couple of decades, apparently, to replace a five-thousand-year-old civilization with the shocking new.

He searched down the length of the dockside where the past waited. Most of the fishing fleet was out; only a half dozen of the trawlers were anchored near to the market; the old ladies in the sampans who brought vegetables, duck and pork to the boat wives were plying between the high green walls of the trawlers that had remained behind, each twisting a long single paddle at the back of the curved sterns, where they stood bow-legged and imperturbable. From the distance he saw they still had permanent hairdos and smiles full of gold.

He walked the length of the pier to where a small police launch was waiting.

He nodded to the captain, stepped on board, immediately fell into discussion with the English senior inspector, who was stationed at an outpost in Mirs Bay. They had always made a point of putting an Englishman into this post, the closest to the Chinese coast.

Higgins showed Chan a marine department map.

"Just here." He stabbed the map at a point near the line that divided the PRC from Hong Kong. "Pure coincidence, a couple of police diving enthusiasts were near there over the weekend, trying out their ultrabig underwater spearguns, not to mention their Gucci colored wetsuits and their accurate-to-a-thousand-feet underwater Seikos. Youngsters, not long out of training. Sharp, though. They saw extra marine life a little further to the north, and although they weren't supposed to go so close to the border, they did, hoping to find something bigger to shoot than prawns. The fish were feeding out of what looked like a large industrial mincer. Got a bit closer; and Bob's your uncle; it *was* a large industrial mincer. One of them remembered that you were looking for one such, so they contacted me as the officer on the spot. I sent a couple of chaps down to take a look, and the sighting was confirmed. I thought you might like a day on the water to supervise the salvage operation."

"How big? How old? The mincer, I mean."

Higgins shrugged. "Not clear. But if fish were finding food in it, I would say it hadn't been down that long."

Chan lit another Benson, ignored Higgins's frown.

"Thought you might be interested in the positioning," Higgins said.

"I am."

"Bit of an odd coincidence, seems to me."

"What is?"

"Well, you find a bagful of heads in the sea at the extreme west of the territory; now you find the mincer at the extreme northeast. Both right next to the PRC border."

Chan didn't want to talk about that to an Englishman. "Just a coincidence, I expect."

Higgins shook his head. "Well, if I were investigating, I would consider it a lead worth following."

On an inhalation Chan took in Higgins. After four hundred years of empire the British bred Englishmen who would not feel at home unless in a colony organizing the natives. Where would they all go in two months' time?

"Thanks for the tip. How are you organizing the salvage? Divers to hook it up, gantry, all that?"

Chan counted five emphatic nods from Higgins. "Exactly that. Small floating gantry towed out of Tolo Harbor by a tug we borrowed from the marine department. Couple of police divers on board. We estimate it at about a hundred and twenty feet, so it's not a problem for the divers. Don't even need to worry about decompression apparently."

"That's right. You ascend slowly after the dive and wait at certain depths. Probably it's enough to spend twenty minutes waiting at about fifteen feet. Look, I'd like to go down with them; they're bound to have a spare kit, it's standard procedure."

"Go down? You?" Higgins surveyed Chan, the twitch, the cigarette. "I'm not sure—"

"I have a certificate. It's my hobby. Look."

Chan took his Advanced Open Water certificate out of his wallet. Higgins inspected it.

"I see. Any particular reason for you to go down? I mean, these men are perfectly competent, you know."

It's my case, Chan almost said. Then he remembered the English Way. "Just thought I'd use the opportunity to get in a free dive, I've missed it every weekend this month cooped up in Mongkok. And it's so fucking hot."

"Ah!" Higgins smiled for the first time. "What a wonderful idea! You know, I'd go down myself, I think, if I wasn't scared to death." He laughed. Chan laughed back. You had to if you were following the English Way.

The launch had already backed away from the pier as they were talking and was now clearing the harbor. Chan walked to the rail at the bows, gazed through sunglasses at the green archipelago that surrounded them. Fishing villages older than Britain huddled against the sun, a blinding white hole in an azure sky.

They had chosen the launch because it was the fastest available. The captain eased it up to about twenty knots.

Higgins came to stand by him. "That's improved the air conditioning."

The breeze raised the Englishman's thin straw hair, revealed the bald pink patch at the top. He had plastered his nose and hairline with white zinc.

Chan undid most of the buttons on his shirt, let the wind blow between his skin and the cotton. He never admitted how guilty he felt about his smoking. Fresh air around the chest gave the illusion of cleansing the lungs. He breathed in as far as his abdomen, let the air out slowly, held back a cough under Higgins's gaze.

There was a laugh from the crew on the bridge. Chan looked up and shared a smile with a square-set Cantonese constable in long blue shorts, bare feet.

He was excited about the dive; it was going to be a long day. He wondered what Moira was doing. He would be lucky to be back for dinner, although he'd promised to try. What did she look like in daylight? Was the Bronx near the sea? Did men his age love women her age? If they were liars, crooks, alcoholics? Who cared? She would be gone in two days. They had discussed that at least.

The wind blew her away.

Chan turned his attention back to Higgins. "Good launch—we must be doing about twenty knots?"

The Englishman gave his brisk, short nods. "Maybe a little more. About twenty-eight is tops, but fuel efficiency goes right down. We've a fair way to go. The snakeheads do it in about two hours, of course—all the way to China, I mean."

"Still a lot of smuggling?"

"Are you kidding? After nightfall it's like the Santa Monica Freeway here. The latest wheeze is to build hulls that are molded around the car of your choice—or rather your customer's choice. Literally, the fiberglass is built up around a specific model car so it fits perfectly and doesn't move around when the boat hits the high speeds. No extra packing required, saves crucial minutes."

"No chance of catching them at sea?"

"With boats like this? Compared to them, this is a barge, a joke. Their boats can be seventy feet long with four three-hundred-horsepower outboards on the back giving twelve hundred horsepower total. Those babies can reach ninety miles an hour. We have nothing like that. Of course, if they'd let us use force, that would be different. At ninety just forcing them to swerve would sink them. But then you kill the smugglers, write off the car and risk the lives of the cops involved, just to save a rich man's car. It's politically unacceptable.''

Chan had heard the complaint before. In the old days the British would have stopped the traffic no matter how many Chinamen they killed. All of a sudden everyone had become so delicate—apart from the crooks and the party cadres who employed them.

''You can see the attraction, though, to a young desperado. Flying across the water at night to China at ninety miles an hour with a stolen BMW in the back, cradling an AK-forty-seven. I bet they queue up to join the gangs.''

Higgins grinned. ''You know, if I wasn't a cop . . .''

Chan smiled. Despite his bald patch, Higgins was young, maybe under thirty. He was a cop now, but in two months he'd be another expatriate bum with nowhere to go. Nobody was rushing to employ ex–Hong Kong policemen. And it was funny how they never wanted to go home, to the Land of the Setting Sun.

Higgins left him as they were passing Big Wave Bay on the left. Chan turned to rest his backside against the rail and watch the rhythm of the water. *I dreamed I was a butterfly. Or am I a butterfly dreaming that I am a man?* He'd read that somewhere. He could see the vertical characters floating on a slow wave toward China. He'd hardly slept the night before.

He made his way to the lower deck and lay down on some cushions in the back cabin. *I am a butterfly dreaming I am a man.* In seconds he was asleep. He awoke to Higgins shaking him.

''We're coming up to the site now.''

21

Chan shook himself, walked to the foredeck holding on to railings, stood next to Higgins at the bows.

The floating gantry was in place; the tug was letting go of the ropes as they approached. The Hong Kong coast was perhaps a mile to the west; the coast of China about the same distance to the north. The political frontier was closer, though, just a few hundred yards. Apart from the gantry, the tug and the launch there was no sign of man at all.

As the launch slowed only the diminished chug of its diesel interrupted the primeval silence. They were just thirty miles from Hong Kong Island, but there was no real estate here that anyone wanted to develop, no mineral wealth, no highway to somewhere important. Except at night.

The launch slowed to a bare half knot, gliding through clear blue liquid that lapped the sides. The temptation to dive in, naked, was almost irresistible. He remembered a skinny Eurasian boy and his sister, not a stitch on, diving for clams every morning and evening throughout one long hot summer, their mother's cries echoing in his ears all the way from China, all the way underwater.

"So, here we are." Higgins beamed.

This was what *gweilos* joined the force for, an adventure on some foreign shore under a tropical sun. No doubt that's why Paddy had come east thirty-six years ago. Thirty-six? He must be the same age now that his father had been when he deserted Mai-mai and them, a careless Irishman running from responsibility. Dirty Paddy.

On the gantry platform police divers were assembling air tanks.

Chan was glad to see they had brought plenty. At 120 feet one tank didn't last long.

He jumped from the launch onto the platform, introduced himself to the two Chinese divers. They nodded respectfully to the chief inspector.

"How many regulators did you bring?" Chan asked.

"Four, one each, one for the kit we leave under the gantry, one spare."

That was correct procedure, Chan remembered. If you dived more than thirty feet down, it was always a good idea to pause at fifteen feet to allow the nitrogen to evaporate from the blood before proceeding to the surface. But waiting for ten or more minutes at fifteen feet could be a problem after a deep dive when you wanted to use up every last ounce of air on the bottom. So good divers always left a tank rigged up with a regulator and a weight hanging from the bottom of the dive boat at about sixteen feet. That way two or more divers could hang there, sharing the air from the safety tank, for as long as the computer on your wrist required you to wait.

"I do a little diving myself." Chan took out the laminated certificate. The two divers, professionals, exchanged glances.

"You coming down?"

"It's up to you. Underwater you're the bosses—that's the rule. But if you don't mind."

They exchanged glances again. "It's deep—about hundred and twenty. You been down that far before?"

"Sure." Once, when he was training for the certificate. You had to do one deep dive. He hadn't enjoyed it. Nor had his body.

The two divers were unsure. How to say no to a chief inspector?

"See, I'm looking at it as if it were scene of crime. I'd like to look around."

"Oh. Okay."

The Chinese Way was opposite to the English Way. Work justified everything.

●   ●   ●

Higgins watched from the deck of the launch and listened. After five years his Cantonese was good even if his accent was imperfect. It was what he would take away with him when he left, fluency in a Pacific tongue. Someone would hire him for something. But not yet. He wasn't leaving until June 30, until he'd sucked every last glorious moment out of the place. With eight weeks to go he didn't need a chief inspector drowning on his watch.

He'd heard of Charlie Chan; everyone had: a Eurasian, said to be a fanatic. If it hadn't been for an antisocial tendency and a slight problem with authority, he'd be a superintendent by now. Even so, it was odd for a detective to assist in the retrieval of evidence under the sea. Men were trained for exactly that purpose.

Chan looked up at him, caught his stare. "A straight line, you said, due north?"

"What's that?"

"The smugglers' route. I guess this would be in their normal lane on the way to the PRC?"

Higgins was impressed. "Yes, that's right. They generally fly past about a mile from the coast. I hadn't thought of that."

Chan raised an arm, held it out straight at eye level, pointed at China.

"They wouldn't have been doing ninety, of course. Nothing like it. To raise something that heavy and chuck it overboard, they would have had to slow to five or less. That's assuming they were using a snakehead in the first place. Obviously they wanted to be as near to the PRC as possible, but not actually in the PRC. Probably they would throw the most important items last—to be nearer China and less liable to detection."

"Other items?"

"The scene of the crime in Mongkok was strangely bare. They tortured to death three adults, but there were no ropes, no handcuffs, no signs of struggle at all. Just a vat full of minced remains in the middle of an empty warehouse. No prints on the vat, of course. As a matter of fact, if someone hadn't bungled by putting those heads in a polythene bag to float in the sea, it would have been pretty much a perfect crime. Impossible to identify the bodies without those heads. Forensic took a while to be sure there were three victims rather than two or four.''

''I see.''

Higgins raised his face to the sun. How could anyone worry about a few little murders on a day like this?

The divers lent Chan a wet suit and a full scuba kit, including buoyancy jacket, mask and fins. There was no spare diving computer; Chan would have to stay close to the others.

While they were attaching the regulators to the tanks, Chan strapped the compass to his left arm, held it out in front of him, grasping his left wrist firmly in his right hand. A direct line to the PRC beaches at the other end of Mirs Bay would be north six degrees east. He put on the wet suit, sat on a bench at the side of the gantry raft while one of the crew from the launch helped him on with the tank. He watched while the other two placed hands over mask and mouthpiece, leaned backward on the bench and splashed into the sea. Chan put the mouthpiece in his mouth, commenced breathing the pressurized air from the tank at the same time as he leaned back.

He tore through cooling strands of translucent silk. Free-falling was a pleasure in slow motion. Below him the other divers were already near the bottom. Their shapes were vague in the distance, but the dual sets of air bubbles racing to the surface provided an easy trail. Every third breath he pinched his nostrils, used his lungs to push air through the ganglia of nasal and sinal tubes that connected his nose to his ears and throat. Pressure increased by the equivalent of one atmosphere every thirty-three feet. If a diver did not perpetually equalize, his lungs would crumple like a paper bag. Chan forced a path through the tar from a thousand cigarettes. In truth it had been more than a year since his last dive.

At fifty feet the sea was cooler, the pressure of the column of water overhead more tangible. Slightly more effort was required to suck air from the mouthpiece; limbs felt heavier.

At eighty it was colder. Joints compressed under ten thousand tons of water; nitrogen was squeezed from his blood into muscles, joints, bones. There was no pain; you just knew that the body was never designed to spend time down here.

At 120 he needed the flashlight. Sunlight still penetrated, but it was attenuated, dim, alien in this other world of the deep. Checking his pressure gauge, he saw he was using up air ten times faster than in shallower water because the air compressed too. The volume that would fill your lungs at the surface was crushed to the size of a golf ball at this depth.

Using the light to illuminate the air bubbles that rose like crystal branches from their mouths, he swam toward the other divers. Drawing closer, he saw the silhouette of something unnaturally regular near where they hung in the water. From it rose a single orange line from the marker buoy that the young police divers had rigged up after they had stumbled across it.

Refraction made everything look bigger than it was, but it would be big anyway, even on the surface. He'd checked with brochures; a four-horsepower electric motor was needed to crush bones the size of the human pelvis, and the funnel that fed them to the grinding wheels had to be over twelve inches in diameter at the narrowest point. With a heavy motor and a large funnel, a cast-iron base to tolerate the vibration and a wide aperture near the bottom out of which the mince poured, the machine stood over four feet off the ground and weighed more than four hundred pounds. Lying diagonally in the gravel, it loomed out of the seabed with the two divers hanging near it. The funnel doubled the height of the machine.

The divers held index fingers against thumbs, questioning. Chan made the same sign back: I'm okay. He swam to the funnel, looked in. All the fish were gone, having feasted on whatever had remained in the machine. He tapped the funnel. The steel gave off a watery echo. Something moved. An eel shot out of the funnel, flashed toward Chan's face; a miniature monster with silent screaming jaws, it diverted at the last instant. Chan's heart raced, using precious air. He caught the concerned look behind the masks of his two colleagues. He showed an index finger against a thumb again. They nodded slowly.

The divers turned their attention to the mincer. They had brought down with them two heavy-duty nylon ropes with stainless steel hooks that were capable of being snapped closed at the ends. The ropes were fixed at the surface to the gantry raft. Chan watched them for a moment while they looked for somewhere to attach the hooks. Then he held out his left arm at eye level, grasped his left wrist with his right hand, started to swim north six degrees east.

It was a technique taught at advanced level: In still water every swimmer proceeded almost exactly the same distance for each flip of his fins. Chan knew that for thirty-three complete flips he covered a distance of twenty-one feet. After three complete fin strokes he was out of sight of the two divers. He remained at the bottom, following the direction that the boat must have taken. He gave himself ten minutes, too long for the amount of air he had left but sufficient if he used the spare tank dangling from the bottom of the gantry. Returning to the boat would be simple; he would ascend using the ropes they were attaching to the mincer or the two anchor lines that moored the gantry raft, whichever he saw first. He kept his eye on the compass, continued to swim north six degrees east, following a Chinese hunch.

He didn't know why every time he dived he had the same thought as though it lurked like a shark waiting to ambush him: *Charlie Chan, this is your mind.* Just like the mind, the ocean bed fell away under him all of a sudden, leaving a void.

He hung at 120 feet about a yard beyond the submarine cliff edge, looking down into a fertile valley. With his torch he illuminated a steep slope on which purple coral grew. Rainbow fish darted among the coral. Farther down, in the gloom, large shapes moved. Sharks were common in these waters, but their dangers were much exaggerated. More pressing was the diminishing air supply. The needle was creeping into the red zone. He was moving his light in one last farewell arc when he saw it jammed half way down the cliff against a gray coral growth: a large steel traveling chest of the kind sold in the China Products shops in Hong Kong. A corner was badly crumpled, and much of the paint had been scraped off by the slide down the cliff. He calculated. It would take only minutes to get to the fifteen-feet level where the spare air tank hung. True, it was bad practice to leave his companions to sound the alarm for him, but evidence was evidence. He exhaled, dived downward and accelerated with a couple of fin thrusts. As he reached the trunk, the needle on his air gauge moved into the danger zone.

The trunk was not locked but tied with nylon rope. Bright green nylon rope, he noted. Then, when he checked his depth gauge, his heartbeat doubled. Without noticing he had descended to 150 feet, 10 more feet than was permitted for recreational divers. To avoid the bends, he must ascend slowly and wait at specific depths, although he could not remember which. The problem was that he did not have enough air. The needle on the air gauge was in the middle of the red zone. At this depth he had no more than a minute. Panic worked his lungs, using up more air. *Charlie Chan, fool, trapped in his own mind.* So what was new?

A hundred feet seemed like a good number to pause at. He waited at this depth until the needle struck the black pin at the end of the danger zone, at which point there was nothing left in the tank to suck at. With the last of the air in his lungs he swam upward, exhaling as gently as he could.

Turning, he saw two ropes suspended in the sea about ten yards to his right. He swam toward them. Remembering the golden rule, Never hold your breath, he tore open the buckle on his weight belt, let it drop. Exhaling freely now, he ascended the ropes like a cork. The ropes converged near the spare tank hanging from the boat. By the time he arrived his lungs were screaming; he was at the fatal point of sucking in water. For the split second it took for the mind to process the thought he paused on the brink of dissolving this misfit Charlie Chan in the vast and bitter sea, to have done with his irritating company once and for all. Then he grabbed the mouthpiece to the spare tank and gorged on air, the primal food.

He hung there fifteen feet below the friendly hull basking in sea-filtered sunlight, flooding his starved blood with air. Shock trembled his hands. Oxygen narcosis lightened his head. Underwater he could not stop laughing. Terror had cracked a carapace of anger he'd been carrying for twenty-three years. Whom did he think he was kidding? He loved air, light, life.

He was thinking of Moira when the others joined him. They saw the trembling in his limbs. Systematically they checked him: air tank empty; weight belt missing; heart still racing. The fixed needle on his depth gauge showed that he'd descended to 151 feet. Behavior consistent with hysteria.

They brought down a full tank of air, made him stay an extra forty minutes to burn off nitrogen. When they finally hauled him to the surface, all Chan could do was cough. He lay on the deck spluttering in frustration. He was lucky not to choke to death on old tobacco. He tried to stand up, but they kept him down, allowing him to sit only. When he finally managed to explain about the trunk, Higgins was unimpressed.

"You shouldn't smoke," he said.

Higgins called for help on the radio. He insisted Chan go back to Sai Kung on the second launch that was sent out from Tolo Harbor. If he developed signs of the bends, he would need to be airlifted to Hong Kong Island, where the Royal Navy had a decompression chamber.

Higgins promised that as soon as they had hauled up the mincer, they would use the launch to move the gantry exactly sixty-three feet, or ninety-six fin strokes, north six degrees east. Less than fifty yards from the PRC border. The divers would go down again to retrieve the trunk.

"Have you ever seen anyone with the bends?" Higgins said. "It's distilled agony. One twinge in any joint, even your little finger, and you go into the decompression chamber. You'll thank me." He nodded to the two medics who helped Chan onto the other launch. "No point killing yourself over a few murders," he called out as Chan went below.

Could the bends be worse than English humor? Chan reached for a cigarette. At least he'd be able to make the date with Moira. He had to admit he was looking forward to seeing her.

22

That night Chan wore a white linen suit, an Italian silk tie, brown Italian leather shoes, a silk shirt he'd had made in Hong Kong. Moira wore clothes she'd bought that day: long silk dress, beige with faint mauve stripes; high heels; a new bra. She wore exactly the right amount of lipstick and mascara, but what Chan liked most was the perfume. It was faint, sophisticated, mature. Maturity was a curious thing. Sandra, his ex-wife, had had few vices, worn no makeup, committed no crimes, never drunk alcohol. And he had never fully trusted her. Moira was a thief and a liar, and he would not have been afraid to share his blackest secret with her.

In the womb of trust libido thrived. Sitting next to her in the back of the taxi, he slid his hand between the folds of her dress, tried to reach her nipples but was thwarted by the firm new bra.

Moira took his hand out, held it.

"What happened to you today?"

"Nothing."

"Just a scratch?"

"What's that?"

"Something we say in the States, you know, like when a movie hero gets shot to pieces by the baddies and wanders into the saloon with blood pouring from twenty different holes in his body and the sheriff says, 'What happened to you?' and the hero says, 'Oh, it's just a scratch.' I mean, why does the blood drain periodically from your face when you remember whatever it is you remember and why is your usual nervous twitch magnified by a factor of twenty and why are you suddenly as horny as a pubescent kid?''

Chan thought it over. Personal directness was not part of Chinese culture. He had to work at it to do better. ''Because I nearly killed myself today and I'm so damned glad to be alive if I hadn't promised to take you out for dinner, I'd be at home fucking you to death.''

Moira looked at the driver's reflection in the mirror. He didn't look as if he spoke English.

''We could always turn around and go back. I mean, I've got only one more day here, and I would hate to waste even a couple of hours—''

Chan squeezed her hand. ''I'm also hungry, need a drink and want to look at you across a plate of noodles.''

''That's erotic for you?''

''No, just familiar. Every really good date I ever had started off with noodles.''

''Sorry if we've been putting the cart before the horse.''

The taxi climbed from Central up Garden Road to Magazine Gap. Apart from Government House, a white colonial mansion crouching under apartment blocks at every corner, there was nothing left of the Hong Kong Chan had known as a kid. No traditional two-story flat-fronted Chinese houses with yellow walls and green shutters; no British barracks with pillared terraces, mosquito netting and red-faced chaps reading *The Times* with their feet up and sipping a gin and tonic; no Chinese girls in cheongsams, the long silk dress with splits up to the thigh; no compradors; no taipans; no rickshaws. Sometimes he wondered if he really did remember that old world from his youth or had merely read about it. But it had all happened there on the very slopes where five hundred apartment blocks now soared, each one reaching over the other for a view of the harbor. Harbor views could add a premium of 50 percent to the retail value of a flat; it was a cityscape sprung from a pocket calculator. Yet at night it was beautiful.

At the junction with Magazine Gap Road they turned and climbed more steeply. The driver switched off the air conditioning in favor of more power, Chan opened the window. They were just above the pollution level. Moira breathed deeply, moaned.

"It's so balmy. In exactly thirty hours I'm not gonna believe this ever happened."

On the flat saddle under Victoria Peak the driver switched the air conditioning back on. At the Peak Café they were shown to the outdoor table Chan had booked; it was small, round and made of marble from the Philippines. Chan ordered champagne. It wasn't a real Chinese restaurant at all, although in an earlier incarnation it had been a teahouse for coolies who had dragged Englishmen and women up the ancient paths in sedan chairs. An American entrepreneur had renovated it into a chic international café with international prices and one of the best views in the world.

Moira took it in with a long, slow sweep. "Wow! Is this how Hong Kong detectives spend their spare time?"

Chan screwed his eyes to slits: "Velly old Chinese proverb: Too much workee make Wong dull boy."

Moira's eyes sparkled through the meal while Chan ate noodles with dumplings and she ate smoked salmon with warm nan and pesto, washed down with a bottle of Australian white wine between them. Chan wanted to ask if she needed more alcohol but didn't. He knew she knew he was waiting.

He paid the bill and led her to the footpath that circles the Peak and is walked at least once by everyone who visits the territory. They began at the harbor side. Two thousand feet below a man-made constellation sent light skyward in a million different clusters, a macrofax for extraterrestrials: *This is wealth*. The show lasted for about a mile, then began diminishing as the path bent around to the less developed side of the island. He found a bench with a view over Pok Fu Lam, held her hand while they sat down.

Moira gripped his palm. "So, is this my moment?"

"I guess."

She cleared her throat. "I brought some pictures. Telling stories is easier for me with visual backup. Here's the first."

She took some photographs out of her handbag, gave him one. It showed a young blond female cadet in the blue uniform of the New York Police Department. He noted the chiseled Irish jaw, the determined posture, the womanly shape despite the ugly uniform.

"And this is me at about the same time out of uniform."

She was in an evening dress that reached halfway down her thigh and plunged between her full and youthful breasts.

"Great tits," Chan said, practicing directness.

"Dad spoiled me. He said I could have any man I wanted. Well, girls who can have any man they want generally pick the wrong one. Of all the guys chasing me in the department I picked Mario. He was a captain, the only one who hadn't been married before, or wasn't still, but that's not why I chose him. I fell for him like— oh, like all serious girls fall sooner or later. Can I have one of your cigarettes?"

Chan offered her the open box, took one for himself, lit both.

"Well, I have to backtrack to tell you why I joined the NYPD. I joined because it was the religion I was brought up with. My father was a captain, three of my brothers were already on the force, one of them a sergeant, and we were that other kind of Irish family you don't hear too much about. I mean honest like an iron girder. So when a year into my marriage I found that Mario was taking money from the mob, I broke with him even though we already had Clare by then. I flipped from violent love to violent contempt in about twenty-four hours. After all, I'd heard my dad preach against corrupt cops every mealtime for as long as I could remember. And I was very young. The young think in black and white; Americans think in black and white; cops definitely think in black and white. Mario was wrong; I was right.

"Italians don't think in black and white, though. To them it's all negotiable. I think that was our real point of disagreement, looking back. He was shocked, pleaded with me, told me how much he loved me. But I turned myself to stone."

She smiled up at Chan, paused to inhale from the cigarette.

"There's nothing wrong with criminals," Chan said, "except that they break the law."

"Looking back, I think I could have saved him. I'm old-fashioned enough to think that a woman can do that for a man. Now let's fast forward a bit. Clare stays with me, sees her father weekends; I throw myself into my work. Sure, I go through a man-hating period, but it didn't last that long. I'm one of those women who actually like men. My feminism was the political, economic kind. Still is, for that matter. Equal rights, equal pay. A lot has to do with being a single-parent family and with some frustration I'm getting with my promotion prospects. This is still early days for women in corporate slash institutional America. I honestly don't believe I was especially strident. It just happens that Clare absorbed the message that men are rotten through and through and just there to be used."

Moira paused, musing. "The other stuff I tried to instill in her, like respect for others, respect for the law, be a good citizen, work ethic—the more challenging part of my message, you might say— that washed right over. And we were living in the Bronx. In the back of my mind I know she's doing bad things, but I have a life of my own. Men come and go; I'm losing a lot of my hard edges; I even dream of hooking up with Mario from time to time, although he's turned into a womanizer pure and simple. Clare still sees him once a week. He gives her money, more money than anyone on the NYPD payroll could afford to give a teenage girl. What does she spend it on? I don't even dare to ask. All I can do is check her body, her eyes, the color in her cheeks. As far as I can tell, she's not doing anything real bad. She even goes skateboarding in Central Park. Her coordination is excellent. I take some comfort from that."

Moira threw the remains of her cigarette on the ground, rubbed it out with her shoe. "Sure is beautiful here, Charlie. Kinda mind-blowing, considering that this trip, this moment, wasn't even in my thoughts five days ago. Where was I?"

"Clare."

"Right. So, the first time I find her making love with another girl I'm shocked, I mean shaken to the bones."

"Another girl?" Chan frowned. There were plenty of Chinese

who looked on male homosexuality as a recent Western import. Lesbianism was a vice so exotic it was hardly more than a myth. What did lesbians do?

"Correct. This is not something my Catholic upbringing prepared me for despite sixteen years on the force. I restrain myself, though, tell myself it's just a phase. But frankly I'm disappointed. I don't have a problem with gays anymore, it's not a moral issue for me, strictly speaking, but in Clare's case it just strikes me as so damn— well, selfish."

"Ah, yes."

"Still, what's done is done. Fast forward to her eighteenth year, high school graduation. She's a beautiful young woman. A beautiful young lesbian actually. But cunning. She's gotten herself a lot of street wisdom growing up where she did, and she sure as hell ain't going to join the NYPD. She can see the world is more or less still run by men, and being a lesbian isn't going to get her a whole lot of mileage in most conventional jobs. She goes to her father, who by now is deeply in with the mob.

"I mean deeply. He's a millionaire captain of the NYPD. It's only a matter of time before they catch him, but he doesn't care anymore. He'll do some time, not too much, and retire. What help can he give a girl just about to enter the real world? He assumes she wants money, but it isn't that. She wants entry. To the mob."

Moira paused again. Chan was aware of a diminishing of the intimacy between them as she retreated more deeply into her memories, and his cop's instinct made him wonder what was coming next. He didn't want to lose her, though. He wanted that touch of love for one more night, that mature caress. God knew there had not been many in his life. He drew her closer, and she smiled gratefully.

"Of course a lot of this stuff I didn't know at the time. I'm giving you the benefit of some years of research and a whole decade of soul-searching. Mario explains that the mob doesn't employ women, at least not on the executive level. It's a very old-fashioned organization. Now, I don't know how she got from there to being the mistress of one of the senior members in the Corleone branch, but Mario must have introduced her. For that I'm unable to forgive him. Nor do I know how she managed to fake it in bed all those years because this daughter of mine is very, very gay. I guess it was one of those dirty weekend affairs and she was only too glad when he went home to his wife.''

Moira sighed. ''I guess she gets plenty of money to live on and time to decide what to do with her life. One thing about her, she likes to learn. She's good at it. She reads a lot, and the mob is always on her reading list. She finds out that the way the American Mafia makes most of its dollars these days is by laundering money for less sophisticated operations, especially the Colombians. The Colombians have so much cash from the cocaine boom in the States and in Europe, they actually contract out the laundering to the Mafia, which charges twenty cents on the dollar. So Clare comes up with a proposition: Send me to college; let me learn about high finance; give me something to do, I'm bored. The consigliere shrugs, why not? The mob hires Harvard M.B.A.'s to count their cash; maybe she could be useful.

''So, she spends three years at the university and actually enjoys it. Her thesis was money laundering and the effect it had on the national economy. I think the mob really fascinated her.

''So she goes back to the consigliere, massages his ego, pours his favorite whiskey down his throat and talks about her future. We're in late 1989, early 1990 now, when the Berlin Wall came down and the USSR ceased to exist. There's a new boy on the block; he's called the Russian Mafia. In the NYPD we expected war between the mobs when the Russians started coming in with a whole new spectrum of drugs, scams, weapons of all kinds, multimillion-dollar frauds, swindles like Al Capone only dreamed of. But the streets are strangely quiet. There's no war. Why? Because even the Russian mob needs to launder money, and the local Mafia actually likes staying away from the heat. They've taken a few hits from FBI investigations, and anyway, they've got all the money they need. They've sent their own kids to college and told them crime doesn't pay. Why not sit back and rake in twenty or more percent on the narco dollar while the other guy takes the risk?

"This news excited Clare no end. After a hell of a lot of cajoling she persuades the don to take her to East Berlin in the summer of 1990, which is a high-level meeting between Russian gangsters and the heads of the five New York families and a few others as well. You don't have to take my word for it; this meeting was monitored by the FBI. Journalists have written articles, books about it. It sounds like a bad novel, but what happened at that meeting was organized crime from different countries carved up the Western world. The main play was between the Russians on the one hand and the Americans and Sicilians on the other. The Americans had the expertise in laundering, the Sicilians had access to every member state of the European Community and the Russians—well, they had everything that was left in Russia. There was no government there anymore. You could buy tanks by the dozen, rocket launchers, AK-forty-sevens by the truckload, gold, oil, silver, aluminum, copper— just about everything people want and need. Of course I didn't know at the time that Clare had gone to that meeting. I just re-member how proud of herself she was around that time. She looked like she'd conquered the world. Can I have another cigarette?"

Chan took the box out of the pocket of his white jacket. While Moira had been talking, the night had thickened. Lovers strolled past arm in arm, Japanese photographers screwed thousand-dollar cameras into tripods, trying to find an original perspective on one of the most photographed night scenes in the world. Sitting on the bench, he had heard about twenty different languages spoken by the people passing behind their backs. If Moira was telling him that there was a truly international dimension to the murders he was investigating, where would he start? People moved around these days almost as easily as money. Dual, triple nationality was com-mon, and most successful gangsters had upwards of fifty bank ac-counts.

He lit their cigarettes. Moira took a long pull. "Then the world came to an end for her. It happened all at once. The consigliere finally found her in bed with another woman. There's a fight, Clare threatens to inform on him—something you just don't do, right? A few days later she's busted for marijuana. Ironic, considering what she had been doing for most of her life. She maintained it was the mob planted it on her as a warning. Anyway, she was cut off, out in the cold. Not total excommunication but a punishment. They knew she couldn't survive without them; they wanted to make sure she knew it too. The message was pretty clear: Shape up, dahlin', or next time the frame-up will send you to jail for the rest of your life. I don't think Clare had ever shot up on reality before; she'd assumed she'd survive on street cunning and teenage luck forever. She wasn't free at all. They owned her, all of her.''

Chan grunted. Enslavement by organized crime was as old as China.

''Worst of all, the smack she'd been using for over ten years was pure, the stuff that arrives in bulk before it's cut with all kinds of junk. She'd been getting it through her mob connections and was able to pay for it with mob money. When she couldn't get it anymore, she got real sick. That's when she came back to live with me. She would lie on her bed most of the day shivering, groaning. Sometimes she would double up with cramps that lasted hours. Sometimes she would lash out at me with her fists. Elegance was only ever skin-deep with her. The best I could do was get her small hits off the street and some methadone to ease the sickness. I took time off work to sit with her. It went on for over a month, and during that month I think I aged inside about a hundred years because it was then that she talked, mostly in a semicoma.

''Little by little I pieced together everything I've just told you— and suffered my first clinical depression. I had to accept that even in the depths of her sickness all she could think of was getting back into the mob, shooting up on the best-quality smack, setting up a money-laundering operation bigger than anyone else's, finding some homeless young girl to seduce.

''Flesh, drugs, power—they were what she lived for. Well, for her the clouds dispersed one day. She'd been right about one thing: The mob wanted to use her services. They figured she'd been punished enough and knew a little more about the lines of power. If she belonged to a made member, she belonged to a made member, no more girls. She got hold of her favorite drugs, started to smile again, forgot about me. She moved out as soon as she could. Last I heard from her was about two and a half years ago. She came around, tried to give me a bunch of money, which I refused. I remember she was talking about China a lot, had been to a bookstore and bought a whole load of books. It seemed to spin off from the book I gave you, *The Travels of Marco Polo*, that she'd read over and over while she was sick.

"So, Clare was back on her feet, but I wasn't. I started drinking heavy. And stealing. The first time I did it I was so drunk I couldn't believe it the next day. On the third occasion I took early retirement from the NYPD so as not to embarrass the force. Crazy the way some of us cling to morality, isn't it? Why did I start stealing? My probation officer says it's common, a psychological reflex he calls flip-flop. People who've followed one rigid path all their lives when hit by a serious trauma do a one-hundred-and-eighty-degree flip. They act out the very behavior they've always deplored. Being a Catholic, I can't help seeing it as a kind of punishment for pride. I sure don't despise anyone anymore the way I used to despise Mario. I started lying a lot too, to cover up. I always wanted her to study sociology, to be interested in people. So often as a cop you get to thinking there must be a better way of helping pathetic people than locking them up—you ever think that?"

Chan inhaled. "And you haven't heard from her at all since she stopped by with the money?"

Moira shook her head. "No. Not a word. I can't give you any more help, Chief Inspector, because I don't know nothin'. I guess you're glad now I'll be out of your hair tomorrow, huh?"

Chan took her hand, gazed into her eyes. He reminded himself: Directness was a virtue with Westerners. "I've got a hard-on," he said.

23

Chan wanted badly to know if the divers had discovered anything at the second dive site where he had seen the trunk, but he resisted calling Higgins. It was Sunday. Moira's plane would be leaving early the next morning. He took her to breakfast in a large hotel in Central, then proposed that they check into the Grand Hyatt for a day and a night. Chan's flat wasn't designed for full-time habitation by adult humans. Moira agreed on condition she pay half the bill.

The Grand Hyatt was a Chinese impression of Renaissance Rome. Marble pillars soared past two mezzanines to a cupola also of marble. There was a marble font, a marble floor leading to a marble check-in desk. Small and large bronze cupids held up silk lampshades, Cantocamp statuettes slouched on every shelf. Only God was missing. Chan and Moira checked into a room on the executive floor. They spent the day like good lovers, took a swim early evening in the Olympic-size swimming pool with a view over the harbor. Chan said it was like being in an advert for cognac. They had dinner in the Italian restaurant on the second floor but raced back to the bedroom without bothering with dessert.

"It's fun being sixteen again," Chan said.

"Especially for me. I think I missed it the first time around."

She didn't disguise her obsession with his lean body. For him she offered the endlessly voluptuous experience of total acceptance. Nothing kept an erection better than unremitting appreciation by one's lover. They hardly slept, but the night was over in a flash. Moira took the wake-up call. Chan steeled himself to say good-bye.

At the airport only his twitch gave him away. They were careful not to promise to see each other again soon. Or at all. Nevertheless, in the taxi back to Mongkok Chan carried her with him: those generous breasts, long legs that gripped him close. Most of all, though, he retained a subtle memory of something entirely new: uncritical affection. And by a Westerner at that. To sleep with a woman who somehow knows all about you and forgives everything was—well, a lot better than being called a misogynist by a vegetarian grouch. He could still feel her strong American hands gripping his buttocks just before she slipped away to the security area.

At Mongkok he checked his watch: 10:00 A.M. on a Monday. He was due into work after lunch, but he would phone Higgins as soon as he reached his flat.

His detective's instinct told him something was wrong as he walked along the corridor to his flat on the tenth floor. Silence. It was as if the corridor had been evacuated.

There was no damage to any of the three bolts on his door. He tried to recall the best karate maneuvers to disarm an assailant; in Hong Kong the favored burglar's aid is the small meat cleaver. Then he pushed open the door. He had long enough to take in two people in white spacesuits with matching soft helmets and visors passing black instruments with luminous dials slowly around the kitchen before something hit him on the back of the neck and he slammed into the floor.

They were still checking him with the black boxes when he came to. The two spacemen took off their headgear, revealing the blotchy complexions, round eyes, receding hair of Englishmen in their early forties.

"He's clean. So is the flat."

"Clean? Well, well, well, isn't that a coincidence," a voice behind him said. He twisted to look.

"We thought you'd done a runner, old chap," the same voice said. "Mind telling us where the hell you've been?"

Chan twisted further, ignoring the pain. He had assumed that it was the owner of the voice who had hit him, but he saw that that was a false assumption. The owner of the voice was surely the slim, impeccably dressed Englishman with black polished shoes and sober tie whom he dimly recognized. The owner of the rabbit punch would be the tall and very muscular South African standing next to him whom Chan knew to be a senior officer in the Independent Commission Against Corruption.

24

The ICAC was created in the early seventies, when the Royal Hong Kong Police Force was known to be the most corrupt in the world. Desk sergeants were millionaires with Swiss and Taiwanese bank accounts; senior officers absconded at Kai Tak Airport with suitcases full of cash; outlying islands suitable for importing morphine were nicknamed Treasure Island by the wealthy constables who patrolled them. Questions were asked in Parliament; the governor, Sir Murray Maclehose, responded by creating an organization with powers of arrest without charge, with authority to obtain confidential documents from banks and to interrogate potential witnesses whether they agreed to it or not. It was an organization answerable to no one except the governor. It investigated allegations of corruption in the police force in particular and was loathed by most policemen for its aggressive tactics and envied for its successes. Hardened criminals who never gave statements to police had a way of talking after seven days in ICAC custody at its offices on Queensway Plaza.

It was said that policemen made pathetic defendants, being subject to a form of guilt to which hardened criminals were immune.

"Scum." The big South African spat a fleck of his contempt into the wastepaper bin. His name was Jack Forte. The other, the slim Englishman, was Milton Cuthbert, the political adviser. Chan had recognized him from numerous appearances on news flashes about the progress of talks in Beijing concerning the future of the colony. Such an honor, to be intimidated by a celebrity.

Forte stood up, walked around his desk, stood very close to Chan, who was sitting in a chair in the middle of the room. Languidly Cuthbert looked at his watch.

It was always instructive to watch a fellow professional at work. Chan had no idea what he was supposed to have done, but fear of Forte induced an ardent wish to confide in Cuthbert, who was always on the point of leaving him alone with the South African. Forte's nationality helped. In small bare rooms such as this blacks and coloreds had been beaten to a slow death in Forte's hometown only a few years ago, a fact it was not easy to erase from one's mind. In Forte's system Chan was colored. Ironic considering the rainbow of shades that, close up, could be found in the white man's face. As the South African bent down to breathe over Chan, the chief inspector discerned purple veins and russet blood vessels bursting in a spray of pink and blue under an alabaster membrane, a blue eye set in porcelain flared with orange and mauve; red, gray, white and black whiskers close enough to be counted twitched around the near-lipless rim of a small mouth with a prodigious capacity for loathing.

"I hate you as I hate all bent coppers."

The big fist slammed into the big open hand two millimeters from Chan's left eye. Chan knew fists from his karate days. There were fists that no matter how big never succeeded in inflicting more than superficial bruising, others that were weapons of assault capable of smashing rib cages, splintering sinuses, crushing skulls. Forte was proud of his fists.

Cuthbert stood up, stepped across the floor, bent down so that both men were staring into his face.

"Who's paying you?"

"Paying me?"

"Why?"

"Which agent are they using here?"

"Agent?"

"Where's the rest of the guns?"

"Guns?"

"What are the weapons for?"

"Is it heroin?"

"Heroin?"

"What do they want?"

"Who?"

"What does it all have to do with the bodies in the vat?"

"Ah!"

"Why did they kill the girl and the two Chinese?"

"What did they know?"

"Where did the other stuff come from?"

"Yes, Chan, the other stuff?"

"The poison, Chan, that kills everything, who owns it?"

"Who owns it?"

"Who told you where to find it?"

"It?"

"Who owns it?"

"I'm lost."

"Were they delivering or receiving?"

"Were you delivering or receiving?"

"Which one, Chan?"

"Which is it, Chan?"

"Who is Chan?"

"I'm going to leave now, Chan."

"He's leaving, Chan."

"I'm leaving, Chan."

Cuthbert stepped toward the door. Chan heard it open, then close. He made the mistake of looking behind him with pleading eyes. Cuthbert was gone.

"Oh, yes, Chan, he's gone all right," Forte said. He was leaning over him, leering.

Chan felt the twitch opening and closing his left eye. He was glad Moira could not see it. Where was she now? Somewhere over the international date line. Safe from Forte anyway. He drew in both feet under his chair, made sure both heels were firmly planted on the ground, bent his head slightly forward, sprang up, using the power of his thigh muscles to drive the top of his forehead into Forte's face. The South African stepped back with a squeal, blood spurting from half a dozen broken bones in his small nose. Chan skipped to one side, grabbed the chair, held it by the back with legs horizontal as he retreated into a corner. Forte stared at the blood on his hands. The door sprang open. One by one five large men entered the small room. Cuthbert was the last. Chan waited like a cornered cat.

"Get the chair off him. We'll take him to the hospital." The political adviser's voice wasn't languid anymore.

Handcuffed in the back of a tall van, Chan could feel a bruise developing at the top of his forehead. Inexplicably he worried that Forte's blood was matting his hair. He hoped Forte used condoms. The South African was in the front of the van with a white folded towel over his nose. Three other ICAC officers were in the back of the van with Cuthbert. Everyone glared at Chan. It occurred to him that he was surrounded by Englishmen and that smashing Forte's nose had been a faux pas, like farting at a dinner party. The English never forgave faux pas. Even Cuthbert had grown a layer of sweat across his forehead that seemed to signal a countdown.

He guessed with impeccable hindsight that Forte had never intended to hit him. Now he'd ruined Cuthbert's choreography, and they were chasing Plan B. Something had happened to threaten the security of the territory and disrupt the relationship between England and China, and it was all Chan's fault. That much was clear. Only details were missing. Like: What? Where? When? And why the hospital? As far as he could tell, only Forte needed medical attention. Not an observation it was advisable to make, though.

They removed his handcuffs before leading him out of the van, an ambiguous gesture since he was surrounded by big men who pressed so close around him he hardly needed to walk at all. The lift, not the public variety but the kind used by teams of medics attending a body on a stretcher, was particularly claustrophobic since everyone wanted to be near Chan. The doors opened to two more Englishmen in army uniforms holding small black automatic guns. They glanced at Cuthbert, then at Chan. Someone had definitely been spreading rumors about him.

There were two more armed guards at the entrance to the small ward. An English doctor in white coat walked toward them down a narrow corridor formed by light green screens on either side. Cuthbert left the group to speak to him for a few moments. Chan heard him call the doctor Major. A military hospital then.

"Bring him over here," Cuthbert said.

They took Chan behind the first set of screens. His eye traveled from bandaged legs hanging from wires suspended from a frame above the bed, to hands also bandaged and hanging off the edge of the bed, to the distorted face of one of the divers. He gurgled when he saw Chan.

The diver's face was a mass of lesions with yellow crusts. His mouth was permanently open, showing large ulcers that had eaten away part of his lips. The man was shivering.

Cuthbert did not take his eyes off Chan as the doctor spoke.

"Agranulocytosis-infective lesions, severe ulcerations indicating radiation dermatitis, taking into account the other symptoms."

"Tell him about the other symptoms," Cuthbert said.

"Acute anemia, swelling in the lymphatic system, severe pains in the gastrointestinal tract, low white and red blood cell counts, beginnings of exfoliation—shedding of the skin."

Cuthbert nodded, led the group back to the corridor.

"The others, please, Major."

They followed the doctor behind another set of screens. The other diver lay in similar condition. His eyes burned at Chan.

The last victim: Higgins. Skin had already shed from his face, hands and forearms, his hair was gone, his skull was bloated more on one side than the other, pink-blind eyes stared at nothing; he looked like a giant fetus. Chan would never have recognized him. On a square plastic board hanging on the end of the bed someone had written in black felt tip: "Higgins, James Malcolm, Senior Inspector, RHKPF."

Blood, uncontained by skin, was seeping from the remaining flesh of his face.

Chan gulped. "Why don't—"

"Because he's dying," Cuthbert snapped. He looked at the doctor.

"That's right. If we hadn't shot him full of morphine, he'd be screaming the place down. After a certain amount of exfoliation has taken place there's nothing we can do. Unpleasant way to go, frankly."

They marched Chan to a small room off the ward. A set of shelves at the back held dusty box files; there was a large white box with a red cross on the lid lying on the floor, what looked like some ancient sterilizing apparatus in a corner. No table, no chairs.

Chan's teeth were chattering. His eyes pleaded with Cuthbert. The political adviser handed him the packet of cigarettes he had taken away when they had arrested him.

The cigarette waved up and down in Chan's mouth. "What happened?"

Cuthbert stared at him. "You tell us."

Chan fumbled in a pocket. They had left him his lighter, a sure sign that they didn't mind if he committed suicide. He moved his eyes from man to man in the group. They all gazed steadily back.

As a skilled interrogator Chan kept an intuitive checklist of body language indicating dishonesty: flushing with anger, looking away in an evasive manner, overanxiety, confusion, the defeated shoulder slump, wringing of hands, tightly folded arms, displacement activities like heavy smoking. In the course of a couple of minutes Chan expressed the whole repertoire. He wondered how he would behave if he ever committed an offense.

"You're making a mistake." His voice cracked, and his tongue slurred the words at the same time. He could not recall ever sounding so dishonest. "I know nothing."

Cuthbert exchanged glances with one of the officers. "Possibly. But how do you explain your miraculous escape? You led the divers to the new dive site where you said you had seen a trunk. They found it, hauled it to the surface and, not unnaturally, opened it. They found some guns and other weapons—and a long lead case. Inside was what appeared to be a piece of pipe. They all handled it, but Higgins handled it the most. He wanted to help with your investigation, Charlie. He liked to play the fool—he's young—but he was keen, a good policeman. Everyone on the boat that day has some degree of radiation sickness; these three are the worst. Except you. You don't even have a rash.''

Chan gulped. ''I was taken off. Higgins insisted. I nearly drowned by diving too deep. He thought I might get the bends.''

''But you found the trunk. You. All alone at a hundred and fifty feet. After abandoning your two companions, against all the rules of scuba diving.''

Chan's eyes watered. His right hand juddered. ''A hunch. Why assume that only one object had been thrown overboard? They would never have let me dive if they'd known I was going to search around, but someone had to. It was an obvious thing to do. It's in all the manuals: 'Check the scene of the crime or the scene of evidence collection in an expanding radius.' '' He looked into Cuthbert's eyes. ''I'm a detective. And why would I have told them about it if I was bent? It doesn't make sense.''

''You could have been double-crossed, framed. The point is you knew where to look. Impossible that anyone would have found that trunk by accident; it was in a fault line half hidden by coral.''

''I followed the smuggler's route, for God's sake. I was looking for evidence thrown overboard along the line the boat must have taken when they dumped the mincer.''

''And then you disappeared.'' Cuthbert made a cathedral out of two hands, put the tips to his lips, discarded the gesture in favor of a wagging finger. ''That's what swung us against you. Charlie Chan's not the type to find a key piece of evidence and then just disappear. Everyone said so. Even the commissioner. Not even a phone call to check on progress? You haven't taken more than two days' leave in two years.''

''Since I divorced.''

"We had a full radio alert out for you, a stop at immigration at Kai Tak Airport; we even checked the fishing fleets."

"You should have checked the Grand Hyatt."

Detection was a tedious business, Chan thought, there was no doubt about it. Checking, double-checking, cross-checking. There was no art. Ninety percent of it could be done by a clerk or junior librarian. A detective's experience culminated in the knowledge that 100 percent of human adults were liars when it came to issues of personal comfort and survival. But each urban tribe habitually lied in a different way. As a general example, the blue collars lied about stolen goods, the white collars about tax. There lay the difference between a professional and an amateur; the pro always knew what kind of person he had before him and wherein lay the preferred lines of dishonesty. Would a chief inspector, for example, lie about checkable details?

Back at ICAC headquarters Chan sat in silence, politely unimpressed. In a room more inviting than the first only inasmuch as it possessed a window and no Forte, he sat in a chair identical to the one he'd raised in defense against the now-hospitalized South African. On the other side of the desk another officer made telephone calls, sent for Chan's working files, made more telephone calls. It was extraordinary how reticent people became when told it was the ICAC on the other end of the telephone. And Chan had thought the police had it tough.

Eventually the tiny pieces of evidence began to form a pattern. The life and times of Chief Inspector S. K. Chan took shape on the brown government desk. A dry life for the most part, full of work and little play, distorted by early trauma, slashed by divorce, with a red flash of romance toward the end. On the plus side, an unusual success rate in the detection of serious crime, black belt in karate, medal for bravery when young. On the negative, a self-destruct streak manifested in heavy smoking, occasional surliness toward superiors, failure to attend social gatherings that might have aided his career. Borderline antisocial.

"You're piecing it together?" Chan asked. The officer glared. "Want any help?"

Cuthbert had disappeared. Chan suspected him of lurking somewhere to avoid embarrassment. There was a motto his kind of Englishman followed, handed down from imperial times: Never apologize, never explain.

It was another half hour before the officer picked up the telephone and asked to speak to Mr. Cuthbert. Chan found it heartening when the English used reverential tones to communicate with mandarins. Give them another thousand years, and they'd be starting dynasties.

"It seems he spent the day and night with his lady friend at the Grand Hyatt, sir. His story holds together on the circumstantial evidence, sir. I don't think I have anything to hold him with, sir. Shall I let him go?"

He put down the receiver and looked at Chan. "You're taking a week's leave, home leave. Sleep every night at your own flat, and phone in twice a day. Don't go scuba diving."

25

The considerable bulk of Sir Michael Henderson emerged from the first-class compartment of Cathay Pacific flight CX250 from London and was immediately greeted by a senior immigration official who called the six-foot-three, 250-pound Englishman "sir" and asked if he'd had a good flight, to which the undersecretary nodded and replied in a booming voice: "Excellent."

The official quickly led the senior British civil servant to a door marked "No Admittance" and down a corridor that bypassed the interminable row of passport booths and led directly to the other side of the Kai Tak Airport buildings, where Milton Cuthbert waited. The two men shook hands warmly before Cuthbert showed his patron and boss to the waiting air-conditioned white government Toyota driven by Cuthbert's chauffeur. The two diplomats settled into the backseat as the driver made for Central.

"Just in time for lunch," Cuthbert said.

"It's mostly lunch that I've come for. You've no idea how unbelievably awful London's become; there's been a measurable decline in civilized values. Nobody dares be seen enjoying a good business lunch these days for fear of incurring some bloodcurdling epithet from the limited vocabulary of the politically correct: 'decadent,' 'wasteful,' 'conspicuous consumer,' would you believe? I've even heard a minister described as sleazy because he finished lunch with a cognac. There's a new fascism about, Milton, and it gives me the creeps. You don't know how lucky you have been, this past decade, stationed in this bastion of flamboyant laissez-faire.''

Cuthbert smiled. ''Will the club do, or would you prefer haute cuisine at Pierrot's?''

''My dear, to this long-suffering proletarian the club *is* haute cuisine. I snatched forty winks on the plane, and do you know, I experienced the most vivid dream of my entire life, the salient feature of which was that silver trolley at your club bearing a huge slightly underdone slab of roast Angus with bone marrow topping, light gravy and Yorkshire pudding crisp on the outside with a wickedly seductive softness at the center. The other memorable feature was a Bordeaux. I couldn't quite make out the label, but it looked very much like a St. Julien, or possibly a St.-Estèphe.''

''Perhaps a St.-Estèphe 1984, Cos d'Estournel?''

Henderson allowed his large hand to drop onto Cuthbert's forearm and grip it. ''My word, Milton, I do believe you're developing an Oriental clairvoyance.''

Cuthbert acknowledged Henderson's humor with a prolonged chuckle. Rank aside, Cuthbert admired the only man he knew who could solve the *Times* crossword more quickly than he could himself. And of course the fat man's mental agility manifested in other equally telling ways. Inside the pampered gourmet there lurked a paper warrior of extraordinary subtlety and cunning. Even if Cuthbert hadn't liked him, he would have been a fool not to cultivate him. The less influential desks of Whitehall were frequently manned by those who had neglected to pay homage to Sir Michael Henerson.

The driver stopped outside the revolving doors of the Hong Kong Club in Jackson Road and got out to open the rear door for Henderson. Cuthbert gestured him through the doors into the lobby of the club. To the right was a full-length portrait of the queen and the Duke of Edinburgh, on the left two bored Chinese cloakroom attendants. Four eminent Englishmen whom he recognized were waiting for guests. In the lift the chief secretary of Hong Kong was waiting to ascend.

"Come along, Michael, if you dare test Japanese technology with your bulk," the chief secretary said.

Henderson grinned broadly. "Peter, what on earth are you doing here?"

"I work in Hong Kong, Michael. Surely you knew that?"

"I did hear a rumor—some sort of secretary, aren't you?"

"Something like that," the chief secretary admitted. "What brings you to this quiet backwater?"

"He dropped in for lunch," Cuthbert said as the lift doors closed.

"In that case I'm going to order on the double, before he eats the whole of the daily roast."

The three men laughed on their way to the Jackson Room, where a Chinese maître d' greeted them with slick charm and showed Henderson and Cuthbert to the diplomat's usual table in a corner facing the room. Every diner they passed on their way to the table was male; women were not allowed in the Jackson Room at lunchtime.

They sat simultaneously, pulled napkins from rings, glanced up at the maître d'.

"Bloody Mary," Henderson said.

"Same," Cuthbert said. He smiled at a Chinese queen's counsel who was lunching with the attorney general at a nearby table.

"Your chief secretary is looking haggard these days," Henderson said, "I do hope he's not gone on a politically correct diet."

"I think rather it's the future of Hong Kong that's causing him concern."

"Oh, that! Yes, he always was a worrier, even at Eton. That's why I advised him to come out here, you know. Jolly glad I did; he's never looked back. He didn't have quite the sangfroid or the gravitas for the home team. Don't tell him I said so, though."

"Is that why you sent me out here, Michael?"

Henderson placed his large hands together on the table as if he were about to say a prayer. "My dear, you're out here because you are the only one who *does* have the nerve to preside over the last hours of the Holy British Empire—the runt of it anyway.''

"Really? You said at the time it was because I spoke Cantonese and Mandarin. 'Like a coolie' was the phrase you used, as I recall.''

Henderson tutted. "You never believed that was a reason. You know how I am about languages, especially Asian ones. How on earth you can have a decent crossword with ten thousand characters or whatever it is, I just don't know. Chinese cuisine, though, that does command one's deepest respect. Anyway, as I remember, you were keen as mustard. I assumed, to your credit, it was the food you were after, the Paris desk having been bagged by old Moffat.''

"The food—and China.''

Henderson allowed his eyes to rest on Cuthbert for a moment. "Yes, China. Well, shall we postpone business until after the main course? You know how strict I am about priorities.''

Discreetly Cuthbert checked his watch. Just after one. From the way Henderson watched the sommelier open the St.-Estèphe, Cuthbert guessed it would be late afternoon before the undersecretary was ready to talk shop.

Jonathan Wong also checked his watch for the fifth time in as many minutes. The trucks were due at one o'clock but had probably been snarled in the traffic on Queen's Road. He saw that Sowcross, the director whom the bank had appointed to oversee the operation, was also anxious. Twenty of the bank's usual security guards with pump-action shotguns stood in half attention around the underground entrance to the vaults, but Wong was most curious about five white men whom the bank had hired from a different kind of security company. They had taken up their own strategic positions in and around the vault and were waiting after their own manner. They slouched against walls and pillars, but Wong saw alert eyes constantly moving in lean faces. Black machine pistols with wire stocks hung around their necks. The white men had been flown in especially, according to Sowcross.

He heard a shout at the same time as he heard the security truck approaching the gate. Sowcross pressed a button on the wall behind the entrance to the vault; the steel gate rolled up; the small armored truck trundled up a ramp to the area next to the vault. Sowcross pressed another button; the steel gate rolled down. They were alone with the first consignment. Wong watched while some of the security guards unloaded crude cardboard boxes with Chinese characters on the side. Wong exchanged glances with Sowcross and followed him into the vault, where a team of clerks was waiting. Each clerk sat at a bench set against the wall; next to his or her right hand an automatic bill-counting machine also waited. Wong knew that the aperture of the machine could be adjusted for different-sized notes and the dial was adjusted to the currency.

Although it had underpinned and structured every aspect of his life for the whole of his life, having usurped the role that some cultures still reserved for God, Wong had never seen money in this quantity before. All around the room the machines whizzed through stack after stack of banknotes, many of them the dull green, black and white of the American currency, others the lurid colors of the Australian dollar, some French francs with the head of Delacroix, plenty of British pounds expressing the national obsession with their queen, small German marks, Dutch guilders, Italian lire, Spanish pesetas, Singaporean dollars—it seemed that all over the world crime paid. Wong realized that he was surrounded by money in all its mind-numbing banality. People died, slaved, prostituted themselves for this monotony. He saw that Sowcross was not of the same mind. The Englishman stared at the mountains of cash, impaled by fascination. When the last machine stopped whizzing, he roused himself to check the dials and enter the numbers on his pocket calculator. Having traveled in a circle, he returned to Wong.

"We'll do double and treble checks, of course, but on the first count I have two hundred million American dollars in various currencies."

Wong nodded. "Two more trucks."

"You'll have to sign—unless of course you want to check it yourself?"

He held out a form on a clipboard. Wong signed, on behalf of his firm, for the receipt and onward delivery to the bank of two hundred million dollars, broken down into various currencies. In his turn Sowcross gave Wong a receipt. With nothing further to say to each other, they went outside to wait for the next truck. On Queen's Road Central Wong finally recognized the sound that had been accumulating under the ground all his life. Too low to be detectable by the human ear, it nevertheless worked subliminally, exerting a remorseless power. The thunder of money.

By two forty-five Henderson had finished the last of his Stilton and was sipping his second glass of Dow's. It was usually over the cigar, Cuthbert remembered, that the fat man's booming voice turned quiet, discreet and serious. Sure enough, as soon as the waiter had clipped the Romeo y Julieta and lit it, Henderson leaned back slightly, looked around him in an unexpectedly quick movement and said: "So?"

"It's Xian."

"It usually is, Milton. Almost for as long as I can remember."

"This time it may be difficult to contain him. In the past he was merely teasing us with his infantile need to test our patience. Now I really do think he's angry about something."

"Something we've done?"

"Strangely enough, I don't think so."

"You'd better begin at the beginning, Milton. I have the greatest respect for your economy of speech. In any event we have all afternoon."

The diners at other tables in the Jackson Room had dwindled to a hard core of five or six. With the discretion of Edwardian butlers the Chinese waiters avoided Cuthbert's table; they would be left alone until six if necessary.

"Very well. I shall go right back to the beginning, if you don't mind. Point one, Xian and his sixteen cronies run southern China. Two, the major blunder of the Foreign Office when negotiating the return of Hong Kong to China was in failing to include Xian in the discussions. Three, as soon as the Joint Declaration between London and Beijing was made public, Xian threatened to open the borders and allow Hong Kong to be flooded by ten million or more immigrants unless we negotiated some kind of secret protocol with him. I went to you, you went to the foreign secretary, the FS went to the PM and the PM had the most godawful tantrum—"

Henderson nodded, tapped his cigar on the heavy bronze ashtray. "She was about to bring us to a state of war with the PRC. They wheeled me in to speak to her myself. It took me damn near all day, and I had to lunch with her on those deeply pathetic sandwiches they eat at Number Ten these days to prove they are busy, politically correct neurotics just like everyone else. The indigestion, Milton, nearly cost me a full night's sleep."

Cuthbert refused to smile. "With your usual consummate skill you eventually persuaded Mrs. Thatcher that China was indeed not comparable to the Falklands, that even if it were possible to win a war against the People's Liberation Army using superior technology—a premise doubtful in itself—the political implications of mowing down a million or more Chinese soldiers to protect a little piece of rock we should never have stolen in the first place was too daunting for even the prime minister to contemplate. I don't know quite what she said to you, but I remember vividly how you put it to me." Henderson raised his eyebrows. "You said that throughout history empires had moved through similar stages. Stage one, pioneers from the fatherland make contact with less developed peoples in far-off lands. Stage two, the pioneers are followed by commercial adventurers eager to make profits. Stage three, the aboriginal peoples lose much of their innocence and start to demand more in return for being exploited. Stage four, the fatherland sends in the army. Stage five, the exotic foreign lands are colonized and administered by second-rate expatriates from the fatherland. Stage six, the military and political will of the fatherland begins to decline—time to get out. Stage seven, the twilight period between the decision to leave and the final exit is marked, in the case of the fatherland, by a schizophrenic need to grovel in private whilst posturing in public."

"Did I say all that? It must have been after lunch."

"I took you to mean, Michael, that I was to grovel. And that is what I've been doing. Every time that barbarian wants something, which is more or less every week, I—metaphorically speaking—go down on my knees in the name of the queen and lick his arse."

Henderson coughed on his cigar. "Good Lord."

"Only yesterday—and this is no more than an example—I had to allow five hundred million dollars to cross the border. *Half a billion!* Of course the lout's just provoking us. The only time I refused him outright was when he asked for military assistance to move his morphine from the border to his warehouses in Kowloon."

"Morphine?"

"It's in one of my minutes to you—'for your eyes only,' of course. He has a number of factories in Yunnan; he buys the opium from Burma or Thailand or, more and more frequently, grows it himself on his farms. The whole operation is overseen by the People's Liberation Army using a workforce of slaves. He sells to various Mafia groups throughout the world. It's his most lucrative operation, but of course not the only money spinner. Arms sales to the Middle East also bring in a fair profit, I daresay."

Henderson rested his eyes on Cuthbert for a long moment while he pulled on the cigar. "I daresay. In any event, you managed to avoid participating in the heroin trade without precipitating an invasion—congratulations."

"He said he didn't need us anyway; he would use the local triads instead. And so he did. We've had to watch helplessly while local organized crime, especially the 14K and Sun Yee On triad societies, has been allowed to grow and prosper under the protection of the People's Liberation Army."

Cuthbert paused. He had excluded any tone of outrage from his narrative; there was nothing Henderson loathed more in his people than an assumption of high moral ground, a vulgar exercise properly reserved for politicians.

Henderson looked at the cigar that was darkening at the end with delicious tar. He rolled it appreciatively between thumb and fore-finger, smiled.

"You know, I don't think there's anything in my life that I've ever regretted, but what I congratulate myself on most of all is having read history at Oxford. It not only gives one a sense of perspective, it provides, to the connoisseur of human blunders, a fine nose for the basic predilections of place. When I retire, I shall write a short treatise to bear out my theory. It's not people, Milton, it's something that comes out of the ground in certain parts of the world that has an effect on the human psyche, causing man to react in exactly the same way generation after generation. South China, it seems, is the corner of the world the gods ordained to be the center for piracy and, most of all, drug running. The Chinese are merely doing to us what we did to them a hundred years ago. And in exactly the same spot, down to the half inch: warehouses in Kowloon. Fascinating."

"I'll look forward to reading your treatise. However, you may find that recent events were not adumbrated by anything in history."

Henderson nodded slowly, like a rocking horse. "Pray continue."

"I've had to piece things together as best I can. My tentative conclusion is that our latter-day Genghis Khan got it into his head that he'd like an atom bomb for Christmas, and one of the local triads, the 14K, I suspect, used international criminal contacts to find a supplier of enriched uranium of warhead quality."

If Cuthbert had been hoping for a glimmer of concern, he was disappointed. Henderson merely nodded again, although Cuthbert was aware of the fat man's full attention.

"Ah!" Henderson said eventually.

"Something, I know not what, went badly wrong in the deal, because the uranium was dumped along with some small arms and other criminal artifacts that need not concern us. Apparently related to the importation of uranium into this colony was the discovery some weeks ago of a vat full of human remains—minced human remains. I'm afraid that before I was able to do anything about it, the district commander at Mongkok Police Station put his best man on to it—''

''Why afraid?''

''Because Chief Inspector Chan is a fanatic who never gives up. If it were not for him, the uranium would never have been discovered. I tried to intimidate him yesterday by implying to the ICAC that he had something to do with the importation itself—it's a long story—but he had a watertight alibi. A pity. I'd hoped both to get him off the case and to save his life.''

Henderson drew on his cigar, exhaled appreciatively, stared affectionately at the stub, knocked it on the ashtray and cleared his throat.

''Correct me if I'm wrong, but I do seem to recall reading a memo from one of our chaps to the effect that this Chan was *not* to be removed from the case?''

Cuthbert coughed. ''Yes, well, I'm afraid that the writer of that memo was not gifted with a towering intellect. Anyway, that was before the discovery of the uranium. I hardly need to emphasize how cosmically inconvenient it would be if that was made public before midnight on thirtieth June.'' On the verge of making a moral point, Cuthbert retreated into the third person. ''You know, there are those who might consider the present scenario the realization of mankind's worst nightmare.''

''You mean an atom bomb in the hands of an Asian warlord? I suppose the melodramatic would see it that way. I'm not a liberal, Milton, nor do I look with particular favor upon the contributions certain ethnic minorities have brought to our country, but there are forms of racism that to me lack any objective justification. The day of Asian Man is upon us. Can we really look upon our own day as having been so terribly successful? Two world wars, irreparable environmental damage, inner cities torn apart by social unrest, AIDS, collapse of family life, Eurosclerosis et cetera? If our friend waves his bomb under everyone's nose, Uncle Sam will take him out, I daresay. And if Uncle Sam won't do it, the Japanese will probably wake up to their regional responsibilities, given their phobia about this sort of thing.''

Cuthbert frowned. For the first time in his career it occurred to him that the fat man might not be on his side in an important Whitehall struggle. He waited while Henderson rolled smoke around his mouth.

"The connection between the human remains in the vat and the uranium?" Henderson said.

"Is Xian himself. Ever since that vat was discovered, he's been plaguing me. Hardly a day passes when he does not demand a progress report on Chan's investigation, although he never explains the reason for his interest. I think he's got it into his head that at least two of his own most senior people were the victims. I happen to know that two senior cadres were kidnapped at about the time that the murders must have taken place, although why Xian should see a connection is beyond me. Everything in Chan's investigation indicates that the victims were the importers themselves—Mafia or triad members."

Henderson seemed to concentrate for a few seconds.

"Allow me to summarize, Milton, and please don't hesitate to interrupt if I've got anything wrong. Now, Chan appears to have stumbled on, or be about to stumble on, a criminal conspiracy of fairly serious dimensions. You have been doing your damndest to deflect him, even to the point of intimidation, because as political adviser to the governor of Hong Kong your perspective transcends the mere detection of crime. Your objectives are twofold: Firstly, you must give Xian everything he wants in order to avoid any fuss before handover in less than nine weeks; secondly, you must avoid any public scandal likely to incense opinion in England and indeed worldwide that might oblige the British government to do something about Xian's activities. Correct so far?"

"Correct."

"Chief Inspector Chan is sufficiently gifted to be able to penetrate the depths of the case in hand, which will inevitably sooner or later result in just the revelations one wishes most to avoid?"

"Correct."

"You have therefore conscientiously tried to deflect, sideline or eliminate the chief inspector from the inquiry?"

"Correct."

"Now, there I lose the logic. It is right, is it not, that our friend Xian very much wants Chan to continue with the investigation—doubtless because Xian wants to be sure one way or the other if some other agency has had the mind-boggling audacity to bump off his own chaps?"

"That would appear to be it."

"Therefore, by having Chan removed from the case, you risk incurring the wrath of our master?"

"But—"

Henderson held up a fat forefinger. "The flaw in your reasoning, Milton, is to assume that a scandal will inevitably follow from Chan's solving of the mystery."

"Oh, perhaps I should have mentioned, it's in one of my minutes, Chief Inspector Chan—"

Henderson held up the same finger. "I know, has a lifelong grudge against the Commies and is unlikely to keep his mouth shut. I do sometimes read your faxes, Milton. *Et alors?*"

There followed a long silence during which Cuthbert sat dumbfounded. "I don't—" he began, then lapsed back into silence. "So your instructions are that I allow him to conclude the investigation and then take steps to ensure his silence?"

"Milton, there's an old Chinese proverb, isn't there, 'When rape is inevitable, lie back and enjoy it'? Since we have opened our legs as wide as physiologically possible, it were churlish now to complain about the size of the aggressor's member. Xian believes he's entitled to exploit the situation for historical reasons. Rape is a dangerous hobby. People get hurt, quite apart from the victim. But that, as they say, is on the rapist's account, not ours. Let's just enjoy it, shall we?"

Cuthbert watched in silence while Henderson gestured to the sommelier and ordered a *bas* Armagnac. Cuthbert refused, finding himself without appetite. At the end of the meal he said: "I'm afraid I've rather stuck my neck out in my campaign to get rid of Chan. Perhaps some written countermand would be in order?"

Henderson smiled. "Milton, your wit has not deserted you. I'll have one of the team send a stiffly worded reprimand for you to show around."

In the car after the meal Cuthbert said, "Xian got to you, didn't he?"

Henderson looked straight ahead at the crowds flowing like molasses through the heat. "Let's say that delighted though he is with the way you've conducted yourself over the past decade, there are certain matters he feels require an overview from headquarters. Nothing personal, I'm sure."

Cuthbert crunched on a molar. "But it's just a squalid murder inquiry, for God's sake!"

Henderson seemed genuinely surprised by Cuthbert's tone. "Milton, you are no mean student of colonial history yourself. Can you think of a single occasion when we've handed back a colony to someone who did *not* appear to be clinically insane?"

During the ride through the harbor tunnel Cuthbert subsided into depression. When the time came for Henderson to get out at the Peninsula Hotel, he asked quietly: "So when the time comes, will *we* silence Chan or will they?"

Henderson popped his head back inside the car. "Undecided as yet."

Before he could pull away, Cuthbert reached out with a quick, catlike movement to hold his shoulder. He leaned across the seat, closer to the fat man.

"Michael, before you go, let me share just one last thought. If Xian's suspicions are correct and two of his favorite cronies were minced up by someone or other, have you thought how very spectacular, how *telegenic* indeed his revenge is going to be?"

Henderson patted Cuthbert's hand. "Of course, my dear. Why d'you think we pay you all this money and lavish upon you a lifestyle that would be the envy of the president of the United States if not to deal with unpleasant little incidents attractive to the verminous media? Thanks for lunch, by the way. Enjoyed it enormously.''

Cuthbert watched him stride through the high brass doors held open by Chinese in white uniforms. On the way back to Central he found himself wondering what Chief Inspector Chan was doing now that he had so much time to himself.

26

Chan commuted from bed to sofa to kitchen—and back. Every two hours or so he took a vertical voyage up to the filthy roof or down to the swarming street.

Staying home was a study in domestic clichés. In the flat above a Chinese couple nurtured an eight-year-old daughter. At seven forty-five exactly the husband took the lift to go to work. Half an hour later the wife took the daughter to school. In the lift he heard her talking to a friend about money and emigrating to New Zealand. Below a French couple had fights over breakfast. The man went to work at eight-thirty while his wife stayed home. From his travels in the lift Chan knew that around ten o'clock a tall Chinese man visited her. French culture was based on adultery. He had read that somewhere.

He held out stoically against the temptation to telephone Moira in New York. Instead, he conjured those welcoming breasts in a variety of fantasies, not all of them erotic. The most tantalizing was a dream in which they appeared beside him on the bed. In the dream he dreamed he slept between them. He believed it was the closest he came to full-fledged unconsciousness. Insomnia was at its worst now that there was nothing to do during the day. At night his mind raged like a tiger on amphetamines, though he used nothing stronger than beer and nicotine.

He found that television was intended for minds exhausted by a full day's work. Now that he was cursed with an attention span, its messages had the substance of cotton candy; did anyone over the age of twelve actually *watch* MTV?

Outside, Hong Kong buzzed like a high-voltage cable. When he went out to buy cigarettes or beer, he saw the people of Mongkok as through glass, saw the frenetic energy, the tunnel obsession with the task of the moment, the exhilaration of work, the invisible joy of being free from all choices, of having one's mind harnessed by the simple, all-consuming obligation to make money. He envied them their liberation from wayward thoughts, self-obsession, doubts about the meaning of life.

He thought of the two divers who had died hating him; he thought of Higgins swollen and skinned like a monstrous pig; he thought of radiation sickness and the word "exfoliation." He thought also of the enigma of Cuthbert. At home he ransacked his library, which lay hidden in a wardrobe that could not be opened without moving the bed. When he did so, old books tumbled out like corpses, each one a mood or hope or perception he'd once entertained for a long, sleepless night, before killing it in the morning.

As an officer in the Hong Kong Police Force Chan didn't need to be secretive about his reading. No one would have believed him anyway. He rarely admitted it, but it was a fact that his father had just had time to communicate a wanderer's eclectic taste: the poetry of Rudyard Kipling, W. B. Yeats and e. e. cummings; the books of Lewis Carroll; the *Rubaiyát of Omar Khayyám*—not in book form; the Irishman had known the seventy-stanza poem off by heart. What the wanderer had really communicated, though, was a Celtic tendency to seek answers in books.

Chan had read a great deal about modern China and about the British, his colonial masters. He'd decided that the latter formed the greater enigma. Pompous, blundering fools for the most part, racist exploiters who had never begun to understand the true wealth or depth of the Oriental cultures they were plundering, yet it seemed that every now and then this insensitive people gave birth to a genius so exalted that it defied classification. The best book about China he'd ever read was by an Englishman who'd never been there and who didn't know that he was writing about the PRC. By an uncanny coincidence *1984* was published the same year that Mao founded the People's Republic of China. All the cruel perversity of Mao's regime was contained in the first sentence of the book, which he had memorized in two lines as if it were a Chinese poem:

> It was a bright cold day in April,
> And the clocks were striking thirteen.

It was from Orwell's gray hell that Mai-mai had escaped and to which she'd finally returned. Indeed it was mostly Mai-mai he looked for in the books, and she was not difficult to find. In a manner of speaking she *was* the Asian twentieth century: a simple peasant caught between two heartless systems that had ground her to dust. At three in the morning, alone with the neon leaking through the curtains, Chan wondered if the same were not happening to her son.

He should, he knew, have been concentrating on means of extricating himself from his predicament. Indeed the peculiar anguish of false accusation, a kind of spiritual nausea that clawed at the hackles, choked him from time to time with a murderous rage. Strangely, though, it passed in minutes. For long stretches of time his own case merged in his mind with that of a billion others. Frequently the image of an old Chinese man with long sparse beard and incongruous John Lennon T-shirt popped into his mind and seemed to beckon like a sage of ancient times.

Ever since boyhood Chan had recognized in himself a fatal tendency to vibrate at the same frequency as certain tragic souls. On the rare occasions that he and Jenny had gone to the movies he always emerged choked from overidentification with the hero. Jenny was always thrilled by the action; horses, guns and blood cheered her up.

Like a powerful lover, the old man was difficult to resist, but Chan foresaw only pain, embarrassment and failure. Thursday evening he dragged his feet on the way to Wanchai and took time to buy a bottle of Jack Daniel's, the sage's favorite liquor. When he arrived, the old man was alone and morose.

"What happened to your meeting, your recruits?"

The old man shrugged. "They both have New Zealand passports. What do they care about *laogai*? China, a quarter of the world's population, can go fuck itself. They think."

"How far did you get?"

"Not to the pictures. Ever since I showed them to you and you freaked out, I've been quiet about the photographs."

"I'm a special case. They killed my mother."

"Not so special. They killed a million mothers."

"Want me to go?"

"I wanted you to be on time. You might have made a difference."

"Sorry."

The old man was working himself up to an unsagelike fury. "Why does nobody care? The Chinese prison system, the *laogaidui*, uses slaves, *slaves*, to produce wine, tea, paper, cars, opium, heroin that it sells to the West. Over fifty million people have been imprisoned in *laogai* since 1949; that's almost the population of England. And nobody gives a fuck. Why? When Solzhenitsyn wrote about the Soviet gulag, they practically beatified him."

"You know why. We're yellow, Asiatic. The white man can't relate to us. In the back of his mind we're basically slave material anyway. Less than a hundred years ago we were selling each other into slavery in the West Indies and Brazil. They don't care because we don't care. Have a drink."

Chan went to the kitchen to fetch glasses. He opened the whiskey and poured two generous slugs. The old man hardly looked at the glass before knocking back half the contents. He breathed out appreciatively.

"You have your uses." He expelled some of his rage with a sigh. "You're partly right, the race thing. It's also the sheer mass: one point four billion! How do you even begin to communicate? I tell myself you've got to start somewhere. Hong Kong seemed a good place. But here everyone has other concerns. How to make money or how to escape. Or both. And then I have a credibility problem. I'm too old, too weird and not even Cantonese. I guess I come across as a pompous old fart.'' The old man finished the whiskey in one long swallow, smacked his lips and held the glass out for more. ''I'm out of sync with the times. Ezra Pound said that. Look, while we're still sober, would you listen to my presentation? I recorded it. That's what salesmen do these days, so I'm told.'' He fetched a tape recorder from one of the shelves, placed it beside him on the sofa and switched it on. His voice emerged from the machine in a slow, steady and, to Chan, haunting rhythm.

''Slavery is like malaria,'' the voice said. ''Forty years ago it seemed as if it had been eradicated worldwide except for a few small, isolated pockets. But nothing mutates like evil. The twentieth century will be remembered for many awful things, but who's predicting that it will be the century when numerically more human beings were enslaved than at any time in history? No one except me.''

Bad start, Chan thought. A shocking and difficult idea delivered pitilessly. On the tape a woman said irritably: ''You haven't told us why you were imprisoned in the first place.''

''Good question. When I was nineteen, my father had saved up enough to send me to study humanities at Harvard University in Cambridge, Massachusetts, in the United States of America. It was 1947. I specialized in English and American literature. After graduation I went back to be part of the great adventure of socialism, the finest challenge and the greatest revolution in the history of mankind.''

There was a long silence while the tape wound on; then the old man finally resumed. ''I had about a month teaching English at the University of Beijing before my first purge. See, no true Communist could believe that anyone would be dumb enough to leave the United States to return to China. I had to be a capitalist spy. From then on I was branded socially.''

Chan got up to pause the tape. ''Bad mistake.''

The old man rolled his eyes. ''I know.''

"Never tell Chinese you're branded socially. They'll brand you socially."

"I know."

"For God's sake, it was you who told me that stuff about cultures of shame, cultures of guilt."

The old man groaned. "You're a ruthless coach."

"The Chinese have a culture of shame par excellence. To be branded socially is the ultimate sanction, a kind of death penalty. That's how we've been manipulated by a ruling class for five thousand years."

The old man switched off the tape recorder. "You're right, definitely lost them there. Tons too heavy." He picked up the glass that Chan had replenished. "What the hell. Am I wrong or are they? I worry about human destiny, the obscenity of slavery in the late twentieth century. They think about what kind of washing machine they'll have in New Zealand, how life will be without a Filipina servant. My soul may be black, but at least I have a soul."

"You should be more forgiving," Chan said. "You had forty years to meditate on the human condition. They're lucky if they get five minutes on the underground on the way home."

The old man finished the whiskey again and smirked. "Don't insult my virility. Forty years thinking about the human condition, are you crazy? I spent forty years thinking about women. Why d'you think I live in the red-light district?"

Chan watched the old man laugh. He was free, this old man; behind his outrage he walked with his god. Was that the way to go? In an inverted world, stand on your head and let the gods decide who was right? Did Chan want to end up like that?

At the door the old man held his elbow for a moment.

"Answer me one question. Thirty miles north over the border they're starving girl orphans to death in state-run orphanages. Why don't we care?"

When Chan searched his face, the old man held up his hand. "I'm not being self-righteous here; it's a simple question. The peasants dump little girls down wells; the state exterminates them. You know about it, I know about it, America and Europe know about it, it was on CNN—why don't we care?''

Chan was still pondering this question the next day when the commissioner of police himself telephoned to invite him to a meeting the following morning.

27

When Chan was shown into Cuthbert's suite at Queensway Plaza, Commissioner Tsui was already there with Caxton Smith, the commissioner for security, and Roland Brown, the commissioner for the Independent Commission Against Corruption. Chan sat at the extreme end of the long table that was the main feature of the anteroom annexed to Cuthbert's office; only the political adviser and his positively vetted English secretary were allowed to enter the office itself. Cuthbert sat at the head of the table with Roland Brown on his left, Tsui and Caxton Smith on his right.

Over the years Chan had learned some of the semaphore that the English use in place of speech. Within seconds he had absorbed signals to the effect that the meeting was informal, that he was no longer in trouble, that indeed the three men staring at him were according him a measure of respect usually reserved for their own ranks; in other words, they wanted his help. Now it was time for someone to say something. Cuthbert coughed.

"I've asked the commissioner for ICAC to be here simply to underline what we all already know. Roland?"

It was Roland Brown's turn to cough. Chan watched the Englishman work himself up to the infinitely painful act of communication. Brown searched in his pockets for something that never emerged, coughed again. As the head of ICAC he had powers in the colony greater than those accorded to the head of the FBI in America, but his shyness was known to be crippling. Finally he wriggled and spoke. Chan caught the words "radiation," "death of three good men," "uranium," "panic reaction," "apology in order'' before the Englishman's whisper merged with the rattle of a tea trolley outside the office.

An English mandarin apologize? Chan was almost disappointed, as if he had watched a famous Pacific island, a landmark to shipping, subside slowly into the ocean and, with a yawn, disappear forever.

"Well, there we are then." Cuthbert beamed.

Roland Brown stood up, nodded once to Chan and left without a word. It seemed from the looks on the faces of the two remaining Englishmen and Tsui that Chan had not merely been rehabilitated but elevated to a position of intimate friendship with these three powerful men. Chan saw an opportunity to take one small advantage.

"Mind if I smoke?"

In unison the three men signaled that they were very happy for Chan to smoke. He tapped a Benson out of the box, lit up and inhaled gratefully.

Cuthbert shuffled with a piece of blank paper in front of him. "In view of the fact that I don't . . . I mean . . . you're not . . . how shall I say? . . . not on my staff, perhaps the commissioner of police would explain a little of what we have in mind."

Clearly Cuthbert had not prepared Tsui for this moment, for Tsui threw him a quick glare. He drew a cough sweet out of a tin box that was on the table in front of him, began to suck. He thought carefully, it seemed, before speaking.

"What we have in mind is simply that you, ah, carry on the good work. I think that's about it, isn't it, Milton?"

Cuthbert frowned deeply at the piece of blank paper, and Chan was sure that Tsui had failed miserably to keep his end up, as the British put it. But then the expression on the political adviser's face changed with startling abruptness. He turned to Tsui.

"D'you know, Ronny, I think it is." He smiled recklessly.

"Well, there we are," Caxton Smith said. It was the first and only time he spoke.

Startled and only halfway through his cigarette, Chan realized that he'd missed some vital part of the semaphore, and now it was too

late. As so often with this kind of Englishman, the punch line was left
out of the joke.

"Well, Milton, if that's all, I think I'll give Chief Inspector Chan
a lift back to Arsenal Street," Tsui said.

Cuthbert smiled again. "Excellent idea, Ronny, excellent."

In the back of the large Toyota Tsui started to laugh. Chan saw
that some kind of racial table had been turned. He wasn't prepared, though, for the commissioner's Cantonese expletive, ut-
tered as he took a single sheet of paper from a file that he'd been
carrying and gave it to Chan to read. "You made them look like
a bunch of jerks" would be a rough translation of what he said.
Chan studied the document, which bore the letterhead of the
British Foreign Office and a TOP SECRET stamp. It was a photocopy of a fax to the political adviser and was clearly part of a series of communications.

"Thanks for yours of 0800 yesterday, but frankly it's not clear
to us why C. I. Chan was suspected in the first place. The identity
of the victims of this atrocity, together with the exact origin, own-
ership and intended use of the items discovered in the trunk is
information of crucial importance to us at the present delicate state
of play with the PRC. If C. I. Chan is the best hope, then he must
be given every facility. Repeat, every facility."

The fax ended abruptly in an illegible signature. When Chan had
read it, Tsui took it back, still laughing.

There was no reason for Chan to follow Tsui into the police
headquarters; the copy fax from London said everything. Tsui let
him out on Lockhart Road. Crossing Wanchai to Queen's Road,
Chan waited for an old green tram to clank past. As always it was
crammed with people, their faces pressed against the dirty glass
windows. One in particular caught his eye: an old man with wispy
beard, gaunt face and eyes that had passed beyond suffering into
some other dimension. Chan waved at the old man, who smiled
and waved back as the tram trundled toward Wanchai.

28

Chan noted with approval that the top secret fax from London had had a bracing effect on the local corridors of power. Cuthbert instructed that the chief inspector should have free run of what the diplomat called the Toys Department of the local chapter of MI6, and Commissioner Tsui promised to authorize, if necessary in retrospect, any electronic surveillance that Chan deemed necessary. From an ingenious collection of eavesdropping and visual surveillance devices, Chan chose a button-size microphone/transmitter with accompanying receiver and recorder and five cameras the size and shape of a lipstick tube. He locked the microphone and receiver in his safe at work and slipped the five cameras into his pocket.

The owners of the warehouse in which the vat had been found had finally lost patience and, from Albuquerque, instructed lawyers in Hong Kong to threaten the commissioner of police with legal proceedings if he did not release their property, currently losing ten thousand dollars per day in rental income, but despite writs and threatened injunctions, the warehouse remained empty, blocked by police barricades at both entrances. Chan edged past the barricade, used keys to open the door, pressed the heavy-duty light switch. Fluorescent strips blinked and blazed. The ladder remained where he had left it, under the still-defective light.

He dragged the stepladder to a pillar ten feet from the flickering tube, took from his pocket a small tube of glue that he used to stick a Velcro pad to the top of the pillar. The cameras were wide-angle automatic focus and enclosed in Velcro jackets. Chan tried to guess the angle as he pressed the camera into the pad. He repeated the process on two other pillars, then took from his pocket a small plastic bag that he had partly filled with sugar previously ground in a mortar. He tossed the bag on the floor to dirty it, then dragged the stepladder back to the flickering light, which he dismantled in order to stow the bag. Finally he returned to each of the three cameras to switch them on. Powered by nickel cadmium batteries, they were activated by body heat, which triggered an invisible infrared flash. The batteries had to be replaced every five days.

The remaining cameras he placed at the entrances to the warehouse.

It was a long shot, based on Chan's knowledge of the behavior of addicts. To a drug addict the substance he or she abuses acquires a religious value as well as an irresistible compulsion. Chan felt the same way about nicotine. If a fellow addict had seen Clare Coletti hide her dope, it would take unusual discipline, over the long term, to resist coming back to retrieve it. True, someone could have returned already and found the stash gone; that was a risk he could do nothing about; he'd only that day been given use of the cameras. He increased the odds in his favor by leaving both doors unlocked and dismissing the two uniformed policemen at the ground-floor lift lobby who for weeks had been checking the identity cards of everyone entering the building. He walked back to the police station, where he had scheduled meetings with murderers for the rest of the day.

Chan had been through the process of interrogating underworld cognoscenti once already, when the vat was first discovered, but the records he had kept were scanty. The related deaths of three policemen from radiation sickness, though, imparted a new spirit of formality to the investigation. It was likely that in time the case records would be mulled over by security forces, diplomats, politicians and even, perhaps, historians. He wanted to be able to show that he'd questioned the usual suspects, fired up the usual informants, recorded the usual dead ends.

Although part of him resented it, he was feeling good. He was working again and officially rehabilitated, despite those who maintained that anyone that lucky could not be entirely honest. At the funerals of Higgins and the divers he had stood at the back, left early. Now Saliver Kan, foot soldier in the Sun Yee On, was sitting in the chair on the other side of Chan's desk for the second time in a month. Aston had nicknamed him the Walking Spittoon.

"I told you, Firstborn," Kan said, "this wasn't triad." A snort executed on an inhalation temporarily cleared his troubled nasal passages. "Nice work, though. Maybe we'll use a mincer on the 14K next time they try to take over Nathan Road."

"You want a Kleenex?" Chan asked.

"Fuck your mother."

"It was just a hope."

"Pass the wastepaper basket. Thanks. Heard you found the machine? Will that be, you know, auctioned, like old police cars?"

"No."

With an internal rumble Kan made a substantial contribution to the contents of the wastebasket. "Too bad. Doesn't matter, you can buy them, right?"

"Suppose there's money in it. A lot of money?"

"Money doesn't make it triad, Firstborn."

"Three people were tortured to death. There had to be screams, struggle. They had to be taken to where they were killed; then the vat had to be removed and taken to that warehouse—probably by truck with lifting gear. Somebody must have seen or heard something."

Kan sniffed loudly. "How much money?"

Chan had checked with Commissioner Tsui that morning. There was no limit to what the government was prepared to pay at this stage.

"Maybe a million Hong Kong dollars."

For the first time Chan felt he had Kan's full attention. The triad rubbed the blue singlet across his chest, hoicked thoughtfully. "Fuck your mother. For three little murders? They mince the emperor of France or something?"

"If you hear anything—"

"I'll be knocking down your door, Firstborn."

"It has to be—"

"I know. 'Information leading to the arrest' et cetera. You had a wanted poster out on me once. Five thousand you were offering, for a bank heist. Next time I'm using a mincer. A million! Fuck me slowly down the Yangtze. Wait'll I tell the red pole. He might put me on it full-time." Getting up to leave, Kan paused. "Come to think of it, maybe I won't tell the red pole. If it was, you know, really good evidence—"

"I confirm the figure's negotiable," Chan said.

Kan nodded. At the door he paused again, gathered together a bolus, which he swallowed. "Million's just the starting figure, right?"

Throughout the day the same chair was occupied by other assassins with pebble eyes, hewn-rock features and cartoon names: Fat Boy Wong; Four-Finger Bosco; High-Rise Lam.

Joker Liu said: "Maybe you're barking up the wrong tree, Chief. Maybe it was an industrial accident." He stood up to mime his theory. "Sort of thing that happens all the time. The mincer stops, so victim one sticks his hand down to fix it, like this. Whoops! It starts up of its own accord—it was a mainland model, right?—it pulls victim one down, look, headfirst. Hearing his screams, victim two rushes to the rescue, grabs victim one's foot while he still has one, like so. Hangs on too long, fuck your mother, he's trapped too. Victim three to the rescue—same thing." He sat down. "Lucky the whole of Mongkok wasn't minced, seeing as how we care about each other so much."

"We're offering a million for hard evidence."

Joker Liu paused on the brink of more black humor, nodded slowly, scratched his face. "No kidding." At the door he said: "A million—that's the starting price, right?"

Chan's standard lecture to recruits who came under his care, usually delivered at the moment of the recruit's first experience of an investigative dead end, had not varied in ten years: "Most criminals inform on their colleagues at some stage in their careers, motivated by greed, envy, spite, malice or no good reason at all beyond a love of treachery. Such one-off aberrations can be valuable, but a successful detective needs at least one source for whom informing is a vocation."

To young recruits to whom he took a liking, he would add that a detective's career could rise or fall depending on the quality of his most important informants. If you were exceptionally lucky and made contact with an informant of genius who trusted you, then you were a fool not to cultivate him, pamper him, put up with him, no matter what the price. You'd be a fool too not to make this person's identity one of the most closely guarded secrets of your life.

Chan never allowed Wheelchair Lee to come to his office and always took elaborate precautions to avoid being seen when he visited him. Leaving Aston to write out the reports of the day's interviews with some of Mongkok's more prolific killers, Chan slipped out of the police station complex, crossed Nathan Road between the bumpers of gridlocked cars, from which exhaust fumes rose steadily like steam from a throbbing morass, took turns down alleys with Chinese names only, then finally down a footpath with no name at all. The footpath led to the back of a computer store open at both ends. Chan walked through the store to exit into a small road with lockup garages more or less dedicated to the storage and onward dispatch of stolen goods and the illegal copying of computer software. A complicated knock on the heavily fortified door of one of them brought a curse in Cantonese and, eventually, the unlocking of the door, which began to open vertically. Chan ducked under before it was fully open. Lee maneuvered his wheelchair to pull the door down again once Chan was inside. A battery of lights illuminated the garage with its half dozen trestle tables piled with computer hard disks, coaxial cables, highly colored boxes of software, screens and cardboard boxes full of floppy disks.

Lee: under a navy cutaway T-shirt, the magnificent musculature of a paraplegic. Neck and arm muscles bulged as he twisted to shoot a heavy iron bolt across the steel door, then twisted his head up again to look at Chan. Overbright eyes scanned Chan's.

"How's business?" Chan asked.

Lee shrugged. "Which side? Computer repair never ends; there's a hundred beginners every day panicking because they've lost a masterpiece on their word processors or can't log on to the Internet. I have people all over town now. We charge on an hourly basis. That's the legal side. You don't want to know about the other. Illegal copies still sell like hot cakes, though."

"I need your help."

"Something new? After the Mincer Murders, what next? The Hamburger Homicides?"

"I'm still with the mincer."

Lee spit on the floor. "I told you, no one's talking about that. Everyone I speak to, they act baffled. It looks like triads, it smells like triads, but if it was triads, someone would be boasting by now. Foot soldiers never keep their mouths shut. Not unless they're very frightened anyway."

"There's more money available now—a million, maybe more."

Lee nodded slowly. "So, it *is* something special. I was right."

"There's an extra dimension. We're not talking about it, though."

"Extra dimension? Who's paying the million, government or private?"

"Government."

"So, there's a China side. Only China gets them that excited."

"Maybe."

"Anything new?"

"There were drugs found in a light fitting over the vat. Heroin. Pure white, number four."

Lee raised his eyebrows. "How pure?"

"Almost hundred percent. Uncut."

"Export quality. You don't get it on the streets, not even gross. They'd rather make the markup in New York or Amsterdam. Very strange, but at least it gives me more questions to ask."

As he was leaving, Chan said: "I'd like you to have the million. But there's competition."

Lee shrugged. "Money—who gives a shit? If I can give them pain, that's what counts." The eyes burned still brighter. The hysteria under the surface burst in him like a boil. Chan hurried to open the door. He didn't want to hear what always came next. Too late. The cripple's hand shot out to grasp Chan's arm. Lee was stronger than he looked. Even if he strained every muscle in his body, Chan could not have loosened that iron grip, not without smashing Lee in the face anyway, and the paraplegic had ways of dealing with that maneuver. Shackled to the wheelchair, Chan turned his face away while Lee hissed: "To kill a man is one thing. To cripple him is one thing. But to make him watch in a mirror—*in a mirror*—while they cut his spinal cord—*to make him watch*—you understand, Chief Inspector? You understand?"

Outside, Chan stood in the road sweating. Most informants demanded money. Lee demanded something more. He demanded the right to unnerve you, to suck you into his private agony, to make you see the world if only for an instant through eyes of total hatred. *No, I don't understand.*

It was early evening; he pushed through the crowds on his way home, automatically scanning faces. In the underworld army of Mongkok one could discern every human calling except honesty. All in all, it would be a relief to spend the next morning at the university with a lethal radioactive isotope.

29

The University of Hong Kong at Pok Fu Lam boasts some of the best colonial architecture in the territory. Neo-Roman arches beckon to cloisters and courtyards where the furious sun hardly penetrates. There is a clock tower of the kind beloved by predigital Europe. Quarters for senior academics enjoy high ceilings and an allocation of floor space of a magnitude that the commercial world reserves for the CEOs of multinationals. Even though the age of air conditioning had grafted onto it the usual low-ceiling designs from the rectangle school of architecture, the new wings were hidden as far as possible behind the original buildings.

Chan always enjoyed visiting the university, breathing the air of disinterested inquiry into the nature of reality. In a different age and with different luck he might have brought his natural flair for detection to bear on a subject more uplifting than the squalid murder of three losers in Mongkok. In any event it was a pleasant early-morning fantasy with the sun on his back as he climbed the long stairway to the science wings.

He showed his police identity card to the security guard at the block of laboratories that conducted research into radioactive substances. The three-bladed orange symbol for radiation twirled from every surface. In case the message was unclear, there was a skull and crossbones and warnings in English and Chinese. In addition to the usual security at the doors, Chan saw armed tall Englishmen in exceptional physical condition standing in twos at various points along the corridor. Cuthbert wasn't taking any chances.

He was led to room 245. Vivian Ip, thirty-three years old with cropped black hair and tiny diamonds in her ears, was bending toward a lead-glass screen. Her arms were thrust into two white concertina cylinders that penetrated the glass and ended in various steel instruments intended to replicate the functions of the human hand. She nodded to Chan, who stood and watched while she fumbled with a brush and white powder.

"This has got to be the weirdest thing anyone has ever asked me to do in a radiation lab."

On the other side of the screen Chan recognized the trunk he had first seen on the bottom of the ocean. Its lid had been left open; in front of it were its contents. Three of the world's more sophisticated small arms lay together: a Czechoslovakian Skorpion; an Israeli Uzi; an Italian Beretta. Next to them were three fragmentation grenades. To one side lay a long, narrow lead box. To another side was a small block of gold.

Chan stared at the lead box, which he knew contained a bar of uranium 235, the highly enriched isotope that had killed Higgins and the two divers. The box looked harmless enough; one could imagine a musical instrument inside, a silver flute perhaps, or a clarinet. He studied the Skorpion. Compact black with a thick snout. He'd never heard of a Skorpion in Hong Kong, but it was a Chinese as well as an English adage that money attracts the best.

He left the guns to focus on another item.

"Any idea yet what that is?" He pointed to something reddish and shapeless about the size of a paperback.

"No. It's malleable and keeps whatever shape you give it. It has absorbed a lot of radiation. There's no way I can analyze it at the moment."

Chan stared at the dust in the cabinet. "I thought you were going to use the laser?"

Vivian nodded toward an instrument with a long barrel in carbon black plastic and gleaming steel on a heavy-duty tripod. A lens gleamed like a single eye.

"Laser stands for 'light amplification through stimulated emission of radiation.' Argon ions are used to control the wavelength of the light. I'd be willing to bet my last dollar that it wouldn't have any effect whatsoever on uranium two-three-five. I'd bet there wouldn't be any reaction at all. I can't even think of a reason why there would be. Nor can anyone I've spoken to. But there's no literature on it, and I don't really want to try. Do you?''

Chan remembered the two divers in the hospital. Higgins. The funerals. ''No.''

''Exactly. So I thought I'd go back to the Stone Age.''

As she spoke, the steel pincers dropped the brush.

''Shit.''

''May I?''

Vivian removed her small hands from the cylinders. ''Sure, you've had more practice.''

Chan slipped his hands into the cabinet, tried to use the brush to paint the fingerprint dust over the handle of the Skorpion. The brush fell from the grip of the steel jaws.

''Shit.'' He withdrew his hands.

Vivian Ip cocked her head to one side. ''Just out of interest, how likely is it that any prints would be left after immersion at sea, retrieval by divers and exposure to radiation?''

''I really have no idea,'' Chan admitted. ''But as the British say, you never know. Did you try the gold? People love to handle gold.''

''Not yet. I was hoping you would be a better duster than I am.''

Chan pulled out a box of cigarettes, remembered the strict rules, replaced it in his pocket. He tried again with the steel jaws. The trick was knowing exactly how much pressure to apply. There were no nerve endings in the instruments; it was all trial and error. When he was able to maneuver the small brush, he found it easier to dust the gleaming surface of the gold than the more complicated surfaces of the guns. Little by little it became clear that there were no prints on the gold.

''I'd appreciate it if you'd keep trying.''

''But there may be no prints at all?''

Chan hesitated. ''That could be important too.'' Vivian raised her eyebrows. ''If there are not only no prints but no signs of handling except by the divers who wore gloves, that's a negative indication.''

It was difficult not to feel embarrassment under the Chinese woman's steady American gaze.

"Negative indication? Am I right in thinking that's copspeak for it would prove that someone wiped all the evidence?"

"Okay, I'll do it myself if you think it's a waste of time."

Vivian waved her hands. "No, no, please. I don't mind. It's kind of interesting. It's like science. Half the time you're setting up ways of proving you're wrong. Hoping you'll be proved right, of course."

Chan wished he could conduct the conversation over a cigarette. "The case is a puzzle. If this evidence was carefully wiped, that would at least help to confirm the nature of the puzzle."

Vivian was gazing at him again, that American stare that tested ego.

"Would you like to go outside where you can smoke? I did some lab assistance work once to help pay for my graduate degree. Nicotine on rats, withdrawal et cetera. You're showing all the signs."

"You must have learned a lot about people, working with rats."

Outside they walked across an open space to the canteen. Over a Styrofoam mug of coffee, a cigarette in his right hand, Chan watched the youth of Hong Kong. There were a few foreigners, Americans and Europeans, the odd Indian and quite a few Eurasians; the vast majority, though, were local Chinese. He wondered how they felt, growing up under one of the most aggressive capitalist systems in the world, knowing that within two months they would have to learn a new system under new masters. Probably they felt the way he felt: cheated and scared.

"What do the kids say, about June?"

Vivian looked around at the young faces in the canteen. "That they'll have to adjust. Mostly they're glad to be free of the stigma of colonial rule, but they know it's not going to be easy. I guess they don't realize how tough, though."

"You do?"

"I saw corruption in the Chinese community in the States before I came back. I can guess what it's like over the border. No one seriously expects anything else here after June thirtieth."

"These kids look so innocent."

"Actually, they are. Compared to the States, they're pure beings who only aspire to develop their minds, be good sons and daughters, bring up their children in the traditional way. They hardly drink or smoke; the drug problem is mostly related to other nationalities; they're careful about sex. I came back here from a research post in Berkeley like a good Chinese because my parents wanted me with them. I was kind of ashamed how many vices I'd managed to pick up in the States. Compared with these people, I'm contaminated by the wicked West. Tell me about your puzzle."

Chan continued to gaze at the students. He had always been envious of people with university educations. He imagined unlimited opportunity to climb up a ladder of thought built by giants to an intellectual garden of curiosities where one spent three or four years in perpetual fascination. How Chinese. What Westerner would be that naive? He sipped his coffee.

"Let's assume there are no prints on the items in your collection. If that's so, we have almost a perfect crime. The assassins minced up three bodies and left the remains in a vat. At first I thought that indicated stupidity or arrogance. Then I saw it was clever. Once they'd minced up the bodies, practically all identification was impossible. So why take further risks in disposing of the remains? DNA is eaten by bacteria. With luck the remains might be consumed before they were found, but even if they were not, what's the use of DNA without evidence to match against it? All clothing had been removed from the bodies first and probably burned. The state of the warehouse where the vat was left bears out my theory. There's not a print anywhere near the vat, no signs of struggle. Then we have the weapons and the uranium. It was a billion to one chance that we found them under a hundred and fifty feet of water near the Chinese border. From the point of view of the perpetrators, dumping those items there was an acceptable risk. Likewise the mincer. So, we have a crime by sophisticated professionals with considerable resources at their disposal, perfectly executed, except for one flaw. Against basic common sense they place three heads in a plastic bag and dump it in the sea for a tourist to discover. Thanks to the heads, we know the name of one of the victims."

"The girl?"

"Yes. An American."

"And the other two victims?"

"Chinese. Identities unknown."

"Well, that only leaves about one point four billion possibilities. Good luck. Can I make a suggestion?" Chan inhaled, nodded. "Did you ever think that maybe someone just fucked up? Sorry about the American."

Chan shrugged. "Most crimes are committed by fools. But those kind of fools don't have access to Skorpions or uranium. I'm out of my depth. Would you mind telling me about the uranium?"

Vivian Ip took a long swig of coffee, thrust her head back as if she were reading a text from the sky. "Uranium two-three-five is a rare isotope. When you build a bomb, you want to have two subcritical masses that, when brought together using conventional explosives, become supercritical. Nothing does it like uranium two-three-five or plutonium two-three-nine. The problem is getting hold of them. What the Manhattan Project was really about—the group of physicists and mathematicians under Oppenheimer who developed the atom bomb in New Mexico during World War Two—was getting hold of enough uranium two-three-five or plutonium two-three-nine. The bomb that was dropped on Hiroshima was uranium two-three-five. Fat Boy, the bomb dropped on Nagasaki, was plutonium two-three-nine."

"Extracting the uranium two-three-five is what it's all about?"

Vivian shrugged. "There are plenty of ways to sophisticate and economize on your core. The U. S. has improved the yield-to-weight ratio and the yield-to-volume ratio enormously since the fifties. But for a really crude bomb, yes, all you need is enough uranium two-three-five." She looked at him. "To be threatening, without necessarily having a whole bomb, all you'd need is proof that you had, say, twenty-five kilograms of two-three-five so long as it was highly enriched. The stuff you found is ninety percent—nearly the best."

"And how much is in that lead case?"

"About three kilos."

They looked at each other.

"Where could it have come from?"

She looked into her plastic cup, then into his eyes. "In theory, quite a few reasonably developed countries. France, England, India, Pakistan, China, Israel, United States—the list gets longer every few years."

"In practice?"

"In practice, nuclear arms development is one of the few genuine security successes of most governments. Even democratic governments illegally assassinate scientists or others who leak atomic secrets, never mind sell two-three-five. You'd have to look to a country whose security has totally collapsed."

"Russia?"

"The word is that people with the right connections can buy anything there. Anything at all. Even weapons-grade uranium and plutonium."

"What sort of people have the right connections?"

"You tell me, Chief Inspector. Sounds like a policing problem. But there's one thing that occurs to me. Okay, on first sight, all that stuff they found in that trunk on the bottom of the ocean, the guns, uranium, et cetera, it all looks pretty impressive. But if you think about it, it's all junk."

"Junk?"

"Sure. There's no ammunition for the guns, and in any case, three guns don't make an arsenal. Fragmentation grenades can be bought on the black market, I'm sure. The uranium is exotic, but three kilos are useless to anyone wanting to build a bomb. Gold aside, that trunk contained a bunch of extremely illegal, highly exotic junk. The only smart thing to do with it was to dump it. Or if it wasn't junk, how about samples?"

"Samples?"

"Why not? Suppose a criminal traveling salesman, showing samples of what he can deliver to selected clients. I guess even crooks need to have some kind of sales promotion."

Chan listened with concentration. Truly, a disciplined mind was a wonderful tool. It made him proud that she was Chinese, nervous that she was a woman, disturbed that the power of her intellect seemed to have something to do with her liberated American background.

He felt the need to speak in Cantonese. "It's an honor to share the fruits of your learning. Is there anything else you've thought of in relation to this case?"

Her quick black eyes surveyed him for a moment. "The bag you found the heads in—did you say it was *clear* plastic?"

He nodded.

"So the people who so meticulously minced the bodies didn't mind you finding the heads?"

"I've thought of that. Mutilated heads, though."

"From which you were able to construct dental profiles?"

Chan nodded again. It was a mystery.

From Vivian's office he telephoned Aston, who told him that a fresh new homicide had just come to light, a "basic Mongkok killing with your name on it," Aston explained.

30

Nobody really minded when triad foot soldiers murdered each other. Chan theorized that a self-regulating mechanism operated as it did with rats. If it had been possible to maintain daily figures for triad membership in Mongkok, then probably one would be able to tell with precision when ranks had swollen to the point where bloodletting was inevitable. If nothing else, it provided entertainment for Aston, whose squeamishness did not extend to the cruel ends frequently met by male professional killers.

Chan was in time to watch his assistant draw a chalk line around the body.

"A classic," Aston said.

The victim lay faceup on the ground in a small concrete children's park bounded by Oak Street, Anchor Street and Palm Street. Shorts and T-shirt were torn; plastic thongs lay together under a swing. Blood had gushed from a wound in the area of the jugular. A Chinese man's hard face about thirty years old, a man who had fought to the death without expecting mercy; on the victim's forearms Aston had found some of the arcane markings of the 14K. At the iron fence around the park uniformed police kept a small crowd at bay. Chan's eye scanned the park, took in the swings and seesaw embedded in the concrete. Aston watched him proudly. Nobody did triads like the chief.

Chan bent closely over the body, beckoned to the young Englishman. "What kind of tear marks, would you say?"

Aston studied the shorts and T-shirt without touching them. "Not a knife. Not really a rip at all."

"Right."

"The material's kind of worn around where it's torn." He struggled against excitement, lost. "It's just like when they throw them out of cars." He looked around the park. "They couldn't have got a vehicle in here, though."

"True. Anyway, the material's not that worn. Looks like he hit the concrete more than once."

"They chucked him around a bit, like?"

"Exactly. Did you see the beer cans?"

"Beer cans?" Aston rubbed his temple. "Sherlock, what beer cans?"

Chan did not raise his eyes from the body. His profession offered so few opportunities for practicing the art of detection in its cinematically correct form.

"By the swings, Watson. And around the perimeter fence. There's one about five yards behind your left foot too."

Aston looked around the park. "Okay, beer cans. Looks like mostly Carlsberg and Tsingtao. By the way they've been crushed and bent I would deduce that they're all empty. So what?"

"And cigarette ends. I hope you didn't miss those?"

Aston repeated his scan. "Okay, there are butts all over the place. I didn't miss them exactly; I just don't see how they help. I mean, this is a public park. Nighttime all sorts come here."

"But look at the concentrations."

Aston walked carefully around the small park. "Mostly around the edge. More than you'd expect—so?"

Chan stood and gestured at the body. "Now tell me about the bruises."

Aston brightened. "Got them down straightaway." He pulled out a small notebook. "Upper arms, forearms, all had marks consistent with being held tightly by hands. Severe bruises caused by hard object, probably metal or plastic, in the area of the abdomen. Scorch or burn marks on the thighs."

Chan nodded, paused for a moment over the legs. Long blackish lines about an inch thick streaked from both knees toward the crotch. He sighed, stood up.

"And the wound at the jugular?"

"Black and purple. Wound not caused by knife. Puncture marks consistent with biting by teeth."

"Feet?"

"Very hard, especially around the instep. A Thai kick boxer or a karate expert." Aston closed the book.

"Well done."

"So now tell me about the beer cans and the fag ends?"

Chan walked to the perimeter fence, slouched against it, facing the body, lit a cigarette, which he held in one hand, and mimed the act of drinking beer from a can.

Aston frowned, scratched at his arms. "I don't—ah! Chief, you're a genius." Chan smiled. "The boys all came to watch a fight, right? A sort of gladiatorial battle between triad foot soldiers?"

"That would be my guess." Chan watched the ambulance arrive next to the park gate. Two orderlies jumped from the back with a stretcher. At the body they asked Chan if he was finished. He gestured for them to continue. When they rolled the body onto the stretcher, Chan said: "Does his back look broken?"

An orderly ran a finger down the spine, looked at Chan and nodded. Aston stared in wonderment.

"Chief—"

"Just a lucky guess." Chan avoided Aston's gaze. "Go back to the station; fill in the forms. You're in charge for the moment. I'll be a while." He watched while the young Englishman began to issue instructions. Within minutes he found himself alone in the park with the body outline clearly drawn in white on the concrete: Death was here. The uniformed police on the outside looked to him for instructions.

"You can open the park as soon as they've been back to clean up the blood."

He walked slowly down Anchor Street, allowing himself to be carried along by the crowds. Taking precautions to ensure he was not followed, he pursued a circuitous route to a narrow alley that led to the computer store open at both ends. On the other side of the shop he walked quickly to the metal door of the lockup garage and executed an elaborate tattoo.

"I'm very angry with you," Chan said when he was inside the garage.

Wheelchair Lee looked away, seeming to find something of absorbing interest halfway up a wall. Chan crossed the floor, placed both hands on the back of the chair, leaned over to whisper forcefully in Lee's ear.

"If I had the evidence, I'd charge you, understand? You said it wouldn't happen again."

Lee whipped the chair around so fast Chan almost fell. The cripple was facing him now. His eyes glittered at the detective.

"It was a fair fight. He was a volunteer. And he had legs. Go ahead, charge me. No jury's going to convict a cripple after a straight fight with a known triad. They'll probably give me a medal."

Chan glared.

"I'm sorry, okay? Of course I refused at first, so they taunted me; you know how they are. They claimed I'd lost my nerve. And he was 14K, which is always a selling point for me. I guess I let them persuade me. What the hell, they were going to waste him anyway."

Chan lit a cigarette, walked up and down in front of Lee. "Do they share the prize money with you at these events? Just curious."

Lee leered. "I do it for love, my friend. You know that."

Chan scowled.

"Don't take it personally. Let me make it up to you. I figured you'd be cross, so I did some work." Lee rubbed his hands together, grinned. "Ever heard of half a billion dollars?"

Chan grunted. "What kind of question is that?"

"I mean, specifically, all in one lump. *Cash.* Sure, in the abstract everyone's heard of the number. But find someone who's actually seen it or touched it or charged that much for a service. No, huh?"

"Okay, no."

"Well, *I* have. I've heard of someone very naughty who overcharged someone very powerful for delivery of a certain commodity because they thought that very powerful someone was a typical PRC jerk who didn't know his ass from his elbow. And the story I heard is that the powerful PRC peasant in question got very, very angry.'' Lee smiled. ''That's as far as I've got. When I know more, I'll tell you.''

Once outside the garage, Chan hurried down the street. He could not escape his imagination that insisted on reproducing the fight, however: It's party time in Mongkok, the major triads declare a truce for a few hours before dawn; shadows move under the street-lamps that line the park; senior men post lookouts; huge sums of money change hands; rough hands of killers grab free beer from crates near the entrance; a hundred men or more, flattered to have been invited, hush and jeer in a sadistic rhythm; the 14K bosses goad the man they'd decided to waste: ''He's a cripple in a wheel-chair; you'll rub him out in five minutes.''

The homicidal freak called Lee, mad as a dog with anticipation, wheels in tight circles in his corner. In the opposite corner the triad slips off his thongs; he's proud of those killer feet. Someone hits a Buddhist gong, the triad tries a jump-kick, contemptuous of the half-man they've given him to kill. Lee grabs a foot in one hand and throws him to the ground. The triad tries again, more cautious now. Lee toys with him to entertain the troops. Too late the triad realizes he's been set up. Lee's speed in that chair is amazing: his tactics are outlandish; the power in his arms is unbelievable.

The fights were all over when Lee succeeded in grabbing his opponent around the waist. After breaking his back, he liked to make a circuit in front of the audience, still hugging the victim while dead legs dragged on the chair's wheels. He would keep his opponent alive for twenty minutes or so, a paraplegic now, just like Lee. When the money had changed hands and the party was nearly finished, Lee buried his teeth in the jugular.

It had taken Chan years to understand why the 14K, Lee's sworn enemies and the very men who had mutilated him, did not simply kill him. Graduation came when he realized that they loved him.

The triads were about violence, and Lee was an extreme example of the genre, an icon. It was part of the magic to produce him every few years at a prizefight, an example of unrestrained ferocity.

After each fight Chan wrestled with his conscience. If he scrupulously gathered evidence, he would probably find enough to charge Lee with manslaughter. Lee sensed his struggle and would become unusually forthcoming with useful information.

31

Sometimes even in hot weather Chan had to walk to think, but it wasn't easy. He had taken the tram up to the Peak and walked down footpaths to Pok Fu Lam. Now, at Connaught Road he was forced by construction hoardings to walk on the inland side of the street.

It seemed they had been reclaiming the harbor near Kennedy Town forever. Dredgers dragged up gushing buckets of sand, mud and gravel from the seabed; cylinders of waterproof cement higher than houses stood guard over a site of rolled steel girders, heavy lifting gear, mobile cranes, men in construction yellow plastic hats.

On the other side of the street Chan was forced to step into the road while a rice truck unloaded. Apart from the Toyota vehicle it could have been a street scene from Manchu times. Male Chinese bodies, naked except for black baggy trousers that stopped at the shins, shuffled in and out of two wholesale rice shops. On the return from the truck they bent under an impossible load of rice sacks, their faces gnarled with hate. A life as hard as that ground down every morality. Any one of them might have been induced for a small fee to hold a victim steady while someone else turned the power on. In Asia ad hoc executioners had always come cheap. But who had paid? And why? A PLA general angry about having been overcharged? Was anything from China that simple?

"Out of his depth" was an understatement. Chan felt like a piece of debris edging near a giant vortex. Just a little closer and the current would pick him up and suck him at an accelerating speed into the black center. Already he was aware of a fatal symptom: He couldn't stop.

He took a side street to avoid the direct glare of the sun. Off Connaught Road the streets were shadowed canyons where rivers of people ambled past pawnshops, stereo stores, Royal Hong Kong Jockey Club betting shops, five-table restaurants selling only pork, duck and rice, cooked-food stalls on the street with collapsible metal tables, open-air hairdressers, one-man stalls specializing in business cards and rubber name stamps (English or Chinese), branches of Chinese banks that had no existence outside the territory.

As he drew closer to Central, the banks expanded and took over. From small shops with single electronic tellers in the wall they grew into great palaces with banking halls as lofty as railway termini. At the heart of it all rose the futuristic Hong Kong Bank with construction tubes all on the outside like a person clothed in his own intestines. And behind it, soaring above all else, the Bank of China with its sharp angles designed by the Chinese-American I. M. Pei. People who believed in *fung shui* (Chinese geomancy) said that the sharp edges were a Chinese thorn pressing into the heart of Hong Kong.

Chan turned left down an underpass leading to the waterfront. At the machines with the steel revolving bars he inserted some coins, joined a small crowd waiting for the next Star Ferry to Kowloon.

He sat at the front of the boat with the island and its manic skyline behind him. On Kowloon side the buildings were much lower because of the flight path to the airport. A familiar advertisement for Seiko watches was obscured by the top deck of a Viking Line cruise ship that had docked for a shore visit and refit. Sampans swarmed at the bottom of its steep walls; women with gold smiles and gold Rolex watches worked like mountaineers from flimsy platforms suspended by ropes from the decks. For speed, efficiency and economy there was no better place to repaint a large ship. Even the *QE2* underwent a refit whenever she visited.

On the second floor of the Ocean City complex, under a layer of congealed sweat, he finally arrived at the Standard Bookshop, one of the few well-stocked English-language bookshops in the territory. Chan went to the travel section, tried to find authors beginning with *P*.

Western tourists favored glossy picture books about China featuring the Great Wall, the Forbidden City, the underground army of Xi'an, but the serious China section was the most active; there was a new book about Chinese history, economy, politics almost every week. Everyone wanted to know what China would do next, not least the Chinese. Marco Polo was not there though. An assistant found him in the classics section.

He liked to handle books before he bought, dipping here and there, guessing what kind of person it was who had had the gall to commit his or her thoughts to print. In the present case he had to guess too at the kind of modern young American woman who would buy such a book. Not your average drug-and-sex Bronx street kid, or a typical corporate woman either. Ever since Moira had left, he'd been having trouble with Clare, her life and times. To lay siege to the Mafia as the last bastion of male privilege was certainly quixotic, if not suicidal. Could an eight-hundred-year-old Italian help?

"Several times a year parties of traders arrive with pearls and precious stones and gold and silver and other valuables, such as cloth of gold and silk, and surrender them all to the Great Khan. The Khan then summons twelve experts, who are chosen for the task and have special knowledge of it, and bids them examine the wares that the traders have brought and pay for them what they judge to be their true value."

Not a romantic Italian after all; the book was more an early edition of the ever-popular *Trading with China*. He paid for it and telephoned his office from the bookshop. He had wanted to speak to Aston, but Riley answered. The instructions he had intended for Aston he gave to Riley. The chief superintendent seemed grateful to run the errand.

When he returned to the station late the same afternoon, he found Riley waiting in the small evidence room in the basement of Mongkok Police Station marked CHIEF INSPECTOR CHAN: MURDER

ENQUIRY, NO ADMITTANCE. It seemed to Chan that he was standing as far away as possible from the large industrial mincer that squatted like a heavy gun emplacement on a trestle table in the middle of the room. Chan looked at two plastic Eski boxes, one large and one medium size, from which Riley was also distancing himself.

"The morgue didn't have anything suitable, so I had to buy these out of petty cash. Actually, the total was over my limit for petty cash, but there wasn't anyone around to ask approval, so I went ahead anyway. Got a ten percent discount on the two."

Chan grunted.

"Perhaps you'll countersign the form in due course?"

Chan grunted again. Ever since the great police scandals of the seventies and the founding of the Independent Commission Against Corruption, senior officers had talked like checkout girls.

"Sure. You did well."

Riley tried a beam, settled for a frown. "Bit gruesome. Not that it bothers me, seen some things in my time, I can tell you. I expect it's just routine for you?"

Chan picked up the larger of the boxes, placed it on the table next to the mincer. "You should see my fridge."

He opened the box. Two frosty Chinese heads lay broken face to broken face on a misty layer of dry ice. White smoke rose from the box like a dragon. With both hands Chan lifted one head out, closed the box.

The mincer's funnel was inches out of reach.

"Would you mind?" Chan said.

Riley rushed to find a chair.

"Another. I'd like you to look."

Standing on chairs on opposite sides of the table, Riley and Chan peered into the funnel. Their nostrils filled with the hearty odor of the sea. Apart from a battering at the edges and scraps of seaweed, the machine bore no signs of its sojourn at the bottom of the ocean other than a smell like oysters. Chan studied the shape of the funnel that narrowed toward the large screw that pulled in the meat and forced it against the double grinding blades beneath. Chan held the head by its black hair, now matted with frost. Jekyll—or was it

Hyde?—had lost color during his stay in the morgue. His eyes were glazed, and his cheeks gray as stone.

Riley's nerves made him garrulous. "Seems to be grinning. I suppose that's because they cut off his lips. Damned wicked thing to do, in my view. You know, I just don't think . . . I mean—"

"You mean it's not the sort of thing a white man would do?"

"Yes—I mean no. Of course that's not what I mean."

Of course. "Imagine a nose, would you? How far out would it stick? A little Chinese nose, I mean, not a great Caucasian conk."

Riley looked at Chan's nose, which managed to be small, flat, cruel and aquiline at the same time.

"Add a half inch for ears too. Now, watch."

Chan lowered the head into the funnel. It slid in neatly until the frozen section of neck rested on the screw.

"Even with a half inch each side for ears and, say, three quarters of an inch for the nose, it would still mince—don't you think? Riley?"

Chan left the head in the bottom of the mincer, ran around to the other side of the table, caught the tottering chief superintendent.

"Steady, sir." Chan sat him down in the chair, shook him. Riley groaned.

"Good Lord." Set into a bland face, a child's frightened eyes looked up at Chan.

Chan walked back to the other side of the table, climbed back on his chair, retrieved the head from the mincer, placed it on the trestle, took out the other. Like his companion, the small Chinese fitted the bottom of the mincer with millimeters to spare. Clare's head was larger, however. It would not have minced without further mutilation.

Chan replaced Clare's head in the icebox, looked at Riley, who was staring at him.

"An interesting experiment, without any firm conclusion," Chan said.

By then Riley was on his feet, a hand over his mouth. Chan opened the door for the chief superintendent on his way to the washroom. Pensive, Chan lifted the Chinese head from the trestle by the hair. Thawed now, the jaw dropped open as if the owner had finally decided to talk. Chan noticed the broken incisors and, toward the back, tiny flecks of something dark jammed between gaps in the teeth. On checking the other two mouths, he found similar particles. From a secretary's desk outside the evidence room he called Dr. Lam. It was late Friday, but the odontologist seemed happy to meet at the morgue the following morning.

Shades of gray: steel gray for the bench top; government gray for the walls; blue-gray for the blades of butcher's instruments hanging from hooks above the postmortem table. The air, tinged with formaldehyde and ether, was gray too. Chan wouldn't have minded if he could have had access to nicotine, but a No Smoking sign was strident in blood red on stark white. He watched while Lam pulled the heads out of a gray steel box packed with dry ice and tossed them onto the bench with professional flamboyance. Frozen now, the mouth that had seemed to want to speak the day before was resolutely shut and resisted Lam's strenuous efforts to open it. Chan used his eyes and chin to indicate the door.

"Coffee?"

Only thawing would overcome postmortem *omertà*, and smoking was permitted in the gray canteen on the first floor. When they returned ten minutes later, hinge joints had warmed and freed, but new condensation on the metal table formed a piste on which the heads skied away from Lam's reach. The dentist looked around. Everything except a head clamp apparently. Chan grunted. From the opposite side of the bench he leaned over and with his face turned away held open the jaws while Lam probed. Through the bones in his hands Chan felt the vibrations as the dentist began to scrape with a steel instrument. Every few seconds Lam cleaned the point on a stiff sheet of transparent plastic. In less than ten minutes the dentist was tossing the heads back into the box.

"You're right, there are particles in the mouths that might not be food." He pointed to a minuscule pile of scrapings on the plastic.

"What could it be?"

"Impossible to say. There's not enough of it for anyone in Hong Kong to analyze properly. You'd need Scotland Yard to take it down to molecular level." He gave the scrapings a glance and shrugged. "Up to you." He adjusted the thick glasses on his nose. "You could feel pretty stupid if it turns out to be bay leaf or some herb that was in a meal they shared before they died."

At the steps of the morgue Chan lit a Benson while he watched the dentist be driven away by his chauffeur in his black Mercedes. And they said cops were insensitive. With a plastic bag in his pocket containing the scrapings he took a taxi to Arsenal Street, left the bag with forensic and walked up to Riley's office to fill out the forms: RHKPF form hm91: "request for permission to seek scientific assistance overseas (if the agency you wish to consult is not Scotland Yard, give reasons). This form should be typed in quadruplicate." Chan looked around Riley's empty office: no typewriter, no carbon sheets, only a state-of-the-art printer. He completed the form in black ballpoint and left it in Riley's in tray.

Most of the rest of Riley's corridor echoed with Saturday morning vacuum. He was surprised to see Angie on the stairs in jeans and T-shirt, taking a mug of tea back to her studio. She turned away quickly when she saw him, then changed her mind and faced him with an exaggerated pout. Brought to a halt on the stairs, Chan fidgeted, tried a grin.

"Hi."

"You bastard." She said it with a sly smile, though.

"I should have phoned. Sorry."

She sighed. "That's all right, mate. I understand. Come here a minute. I've got something to show you."

He followed her into her studio. She nodded at the easel, where she had clipped a wad of sketches. Angie sipped from her mug. "You were right about one thing."

From the easel the blond boy smiled out. It was an excellent likeness.

"Check the others."

Chan lifted the sheets one by one. Blond boy in T-shirt, blond boy in bed, blond boy with erection, blond boy in centerfold pose.

"You've captured him very well."

She curled her lips into a sneer. "At least Australians know what our bodies are for."

Chan steered a course across the room and around her, back to the door. "Sooner or later the rest of the world will catch up."

"Wanker." The word bounced off the walls as he hurried down the stairs.

32

Often on Saturday afternoons Chan went to a beach or pier to watch the human species migrate from land to water. Square miles of sea disappeared under a counterpane of sampans, junks, tiny catamarans, seventy-foot sailing yachts, snakehead boats, twin-engine motor cruisers, board sailors, swimmers, divers, snorklers, water scooters, fleets of sailboats of a specific class competing in races, very large luxury yachts that almost deserved to be called ships. There was no real need to stare and yearn; he could have bought a small dinghy or rejoined his diving club. Ever since his divorce he had tended to deprive himself of pleasure, although he could not have explained the connection.

For example, the *Emily* was a 120-foot triple-decker, the largest pleasure boat in Hong Kong, fully equipped with compressor and diving equipment, and Chan had refused the invitation to spend the weekend on it. When his sister, Jenny, had insisted, he had finally given in as a kind of social duty, like grave sweeping and writing Chinese New Year cards.

He rode the underground from Mongkok, emerged at Central and took a taxi to Aberdeen. The marina was a large crescent with floating wooden docks attached to a spacious club that sold debentures to large corporations and consulates. The biggest boats berthed along a finger that pointed at the famous three floating restaurants where all tourists must eat once. Top heavy with lions and dragons in gold, red and green, they had emerged out of Western fantasies of mysterious China and were still cashing in. The *Emily* took up a double berth at the end of one finger with her stern pointed toward the largest of them.

Chan could see her from the other side of the marina. Her hull was white with blue trim, her triple-deck superstructure blue with white trim. The paintwork was polished to a mirror finish. In the heat she undulated as if she were her own reflection. At the forward end the two lower decks ended in tinted wraparound glass. *Emily* was a billionairess in designer sunglasses.

Chan wore white shorts, T-shirt, plastic thongs and carried a light backpack with his scuba gear, change of clothes, one book.

People were spilling all over the marina, scrambling to find the boats they'd been invited to sail on or rushing with last-minute repairs to engines, sails, lines, halyards, outboards. On the *Emily*, though, a permanent crew kept the boat in readiness for the owner's whims.

Only Jenny was there to meet him. He kissed her on both cheeks, hugged her, studied her belly that seemed as flat as ever.

"When?"

"End January."

"My God, you're as beautiful as ever."

She touched his nose. "Don't flirt with your sister; it's against the law."

Chan grimaced. "Pity."

"There are twelve cabins—berths to you. Jonathan and I have chosen ours, and of course Emily will have the what d'you call it?"

"Stateroom."

"Exactly. So that leaves ten for you to choose from."

"No one else is coming?"

Jenny hesitated. "There'll be one or two. You know how these high-powered people are; they always manage to drag along someone terribly important at the last minute. But since you're so early, you can select your own accommodation."

He followed Jenny below to a narrow corridor lined with polished teak. She turned to him with a grin.

"Want to see the stateroom?"

"Sure."

A solid teak door, arched, with "Stateroom" emblazoned in brass over the arch waited at the end of the corridor. Inside Chan saw a low king-size bed with red sheets, a panoramic window in curved tinted glass, polished teak wardrobes and chests all built into the curves of the hull, a red Chinese carpet with the double happiness character in gold in the center, a nautical writing desk with brass fittings and a brass lamp screwed to the top. Inside a polished bamboo and glass cabinet were a dozen opium pipes of the kind everyone collected. He gazed at a television/video/stereo/laser disk combination opposite a white three-seater leather sofa. Chan picked up the remote control, pressed a button. A Cantopop number with exaggerated bass and treble bounced from the walls. He turned it off.

"Wow."

"Wait till you see the bridge. Of course I don't know anything about it, but everyone says what a great bridge it is."

Chan saw that Jenny and Jonathan had taken the cabin two doors away from the stateroom. The cabin next to it was therefore empty. Chan chose another, on the other side of Jenny and Jonathan, three doors away from the stateroom. It was a third the size, but there was a tiny en suite toilet and shower, a white bathrobe and an oil painting of a sampan above the bed. Looking through the porthole, he judged the water to be only two feet below.

Jenny led the way. He marveled at how easily she had adapted to wealth; the multimillion-dollar vessel could have been her boat.

On the bridge chrome beading two inches up the walls trapped a thick red carpet. Two stainless steel swivel chairs with black leather upholstery rose on deep chrome pedestals to preside over an arcade of computer screens.

"My God, there's even a fish finder," Chan said.

"Sometimes Emily has guests who like game fishing."

"Really? Like who?"

Jenny glanced at him. "Who d'you think? Nobody loves ostentatious wealth like Communist cadres. But let's not get into that.

Jonathan and I have patched things up. I promised not to offend his friends so long as we saw less of them." She wagged a finger. "So don't you start asking questions and making everyone nervous."

Chan sat in the master's chair. "Not if I'm allowed to play in here. Just one question, First Sister. Why was I invited?"

Standing close to him, Jenny frowned, pushed the throttle up and down like a toy. "First, I wanted to invite you. Apart from ten minutes at the party I haven't seen you for ages, and when I have the baby, I expect there'll be no time for anything else—that's what everyone says. And Emily specifically asked Jonathan to bring a guest who has nothing to do with his work. She remembers you from the party."

"I'm the one who investigates grotesque murders. I bet she's delighted with your choice."

"Actually she wanted you to come. Maybe you'll get lucky."

"You mean laid?"

Chan dodged but not quickly enough to avoid her jabbing elbow. In fights she'd always been quicker than he was. "Don't set your sights so low, you crude cop. She's single."

Chan grinned. "One night with me and she'll probably want to stay that way." In a sudden movement he grabbed her hand. "There's something else, isn't there?"

She looked him in the eye. "Let's leave it till later, shall we? I don't really understand, but they promised me it was in your interests to come this weekend." Chan stared until she lowered her head. "I would die rather than let anyone hurt you. You know that."

Jenny checked her watch. "I have this checklist of items I have to get ready—things the crew aren't so good at, like choosing wine and champagne. We can get it all from the club if you want to help."

Back on the walkway he helped his sister step down from the boat. They walked together along the floating dock: two Eurasians. People turned as always to look at Jenny. Her long black hair was tied up in a bun; her dark eyes were large and only faintly tilted.

With Chan's high cheekbones and fine lips in a smaller, female mold, her apparent fragility was terrifying, like a Chinese vase.

"No one would guess that you can fight like a cat. I still have scars where you scratched me down to the bone," Chan whispered in her ear.

"You were all I had, and I was jealous." She looked at him and smiled. "I'm glad you've come. I know how you hate social groups, but you can talk to me. And you can dive. Emily likes to dive too; underwater you won't have to talk to her."

He waited in the club's enormous lobby while she chose the wine and champagne. As they were about to return to the boat, Jenny murmured, "There's Emily now."

A white Rolls-Royce with blue interior slid into the forecourt to stop in front of the entrance. A chauffeur in whites stepped out to open the rear door.

Chan winced.

"Sorry," Jenny said. "She uses it only when she's entertaining someone important."

A Chinese man in his seventies got out of the car. He wore a white jacket and blue slacks, both ill-fitting. The open-neck shirt under the white jacket was black. On his feet, old sneakers had molded around his bony feet. Chan noticed the hands, heavy and gnarled like ginseng roots. Emily followed in white shorts, a blue silk blouse, red shoes with flat heels. The old man walked in front of her, then seemed to remember a local custom and stood aside to let her pass while the doorman opened the door. Chan thought that people stopped because of the Rolls and because Emily's face was often in the newspapers, but some of the Chinese looked at the old man as if they knew him too. Chan had never seen him before, although he fitted a specific category.

Jenny was watching Chan. He caught her eye. His twitch was working. She put a hand on his arm.

"I told you, I'll explain later. Stay—for me."

"Why?"

"For me. For you. I promised them you'd stay."

Chan glanced quickly at her, then nodded. "Okay. For you."
Chan picked up the plastic bag with bottles of champagne and claret,
followed Jenny across the marble lobby. Emily gave a big wave.
Jenny smiled. Out of the corner of his eye Chan saw a white Toyota
draw up behind the Rolls-Royce. Two men got out: Chinese but
not Cantonese. They were each over six feet tall with the powerful
build of the far north. The two bodyguards took up positions about
ten feet away from the old man and never took their eyes off him.

"My God, I hate you," Emily said to Jenny. She turned to Chan.
"Every time I see her she's more stunning than ever. Doesn't it
make you mad that this former Miss Hong Kong is your sister?"

"I believe you two have met," Jenny said.

"All my life," Chan said.

"This is Mr. Xian, a very close business associate of mine from
the PRC," Emily said.

She spoke to the old man in Mandarin. Chan followed one or
two words that were the same in Cantonese. He caught the word
for "detective."

The old man held out a horny hand to Jenny, gave a shark's
yellow smile. He spoke in Mandarin. Jenny shook his hand. He
turned to Chan. Chan took the hand, pressed it instead of shaking it.

He spoke softly in Cantonese. "You killed my mother."

"What did he say?"

Emily blinked. "He said, 'pleased to meet you.' " Her Mandarin
was perfect.

On the way back to the boat Chan felt Emily's eyes on him while
she conversed with Mr. Xian. He recognized the word for "dollars"
in Mandarin. She used it a lot. The old man had a way of replying
with a high-pitched laugh and a forward shake of the head like a
horse neighing. Whatever she was saying it was pleasing Mr. Xian.
Chan noticed the old man's Shanghainese accent; he pronounced x
sounds with the middle of his tongue. Through the wooden boards
Chan could feel the heavy tread of the bodyguards ten feet behind.

"I guess you had to do that," Jenny said.

"Yes," Chan said.

She shook her head. "You never change. You're all balls and no brains." But she said it with affection and let him see how her eyes were shining. "Bravo anyway."

Jenny turned to speak to Emily. "Jonathan phone you?"

Emily switched from Mandarin to English. "He's going to be about twenty minutes late. A client."

"Anyone else coming?"

"I invited Milton Cuthbert, the political adviser. D'you know him?"

"No," Jenny said.

"Slightly," Chan said.

"Oh," Emily said.

With a cigarette Chan attempted to calm the jumping nerves, the increased heartbeat, the cold sweat. He knew that he ought to feign serious illness, disappear until he had time to work out what kind of trap it was, but there was Jenny.

33

As soon as he could, Chan left the other guests in the saloon to join the captain and mate on the bridge. On the captain's hat EMILY was embossed in gold.

At a signal from the captain the boat boy let go of the two mooring lines at the bows and ran along the side to release two more. He jumped back on board using the swimming platform at the stern. Behind the boat lay a crowded playground of smaller craft maneuvering to escape from the marina to more spacious seas. Leisure made people urgent; everyone seemed to be yelling as sailboats tacked past powerboats chugging in opposite directions. The captain of the *Emily* sounded the horn three times, and as the stern bore down on them with its threshing screws, the smaller boats took avoiding action.

Once extricated from her berth, the large boat turned slowly in her own length and the diesels increased to a low throb as she made way slowly ahead. Chan left the wheelhouse to stand at the bows. Looking up at the club terraces, Chan saw that people had crowded to the rails to watch.

"Stops them in their tracks, doesn't she?"

Chan had not heard Cuthbert come up behind. He offered Chan a Turkish cigarette from an old silver case. He was wearing beige shorts with razor creases, a blue designer sailing shirt with an anchor on the single pocket, white socks and blue leather Docksides.

Chan took the cigarette. "Money does that."

Cuthbert smiled. "I believe I've not yet proffered you a full apology. I'm afraid everyone was pretty worked up. Radiation sickness scares the best of us, and one or two were looking for a scapegoat. Also, a word of thanks. You've no idea how much more manageable Jack Forte has become since you broke his nose.''

"You knew I would be on board? You arranged it?"

Cuthbert considered the smoke winding upward from the end of his cigarette.

"Not exactly. Not in the way you mean. I know Emily very well, and I have a standing invitation for weekends. I just happened to have lunch with her last week. She mentioned you. Naturally I was not going to spoil your weekend. Then, when she told me who else was coming, I thought you might need a little help.''

"I'm lost," Chan said. "I'm paid to catch crooks with room temperature IQs. Ninety percent of the homicides I investigate are husbands or wives murdered by their spouses with meat cleavers when the air conditioning fails. If they have air conditioning. I don't want to prove anything by getting into the big time.''

What was it about Cuthbert that made one want to lie? Chan had never been so intrigued by a case in his life. Somehow it was bad form to tell the truth to a diplomat, like annoying a bat with a bright light.

Cuthbert gave no sign of incredulity. "I know. That's exactly why I might be of use to you. At any rate, there's no need for us to be enemies. Not on a glorious day like this on the best boat in the fleet. Life is short.''

"It was for three people in Mongkok.''

Chan took a long draw. An interesting cigarette; it was probably how tobacco was intended to taste.

Cuthbert leaned over the rail next to Chan, pointed to something near the floating restaurants, spoke in a whisper. "Take it or leave it, my friend, but I wouldn't let her seduce you. Not this trip.'' He raised his voice. "Just there, that's where the fire was, burned for three days. D'you remember when the floating restaurant caught fire, Emily?''

Cuthbert's antennae were better than Chan's. He hadn't heard her come on deck. Yet she was not the sort of woman to make a silent entrance.

"Mmm, I was a kid." She looked slowly over the marina, then up at the club terraces.

Cuthbert said: "We have an admiring audience. Charlie and I were just talking about it."

Emily's smile flashed. "Oh, yes, they all stare when we go out. They think it's the governor's boat. Of course his is much grander. Isn't it, Milton?"

"It's a lot older. Last time I was on it we were still using a sextant."

Emily laughed, turned to Charlie. "Aren't the British cute? And smart. You can hide anything behind self-mockery."

She stood beside him at the rail so that he was caught between them. Through the deck Chan felt an increase in engine revolutions. The view was changing swiftly as they approached the harbor walls.

Cuthbert offered Emily a cigarette, which she refused. He replaced the silver case in his pocket.

"Come now, no one has mastered false modesty better than the Chinese. The first time I went to Beijing there were still restaurants calling themselves the Worst Restaurant on Earth. That was before the party purged Confucius, of course."

"But that's the point," Emily said. "It was too obvious; it didn't work. But you, you ran the largest empire in history on bluff, paternalism . . . and phony self-effacement."

"And the Maxim gun. We started giving the colonies back when everyone else got one."

The harbor walls curved around in two scythes with a gap between them toward which every boat was racing. On either side green hills plunged down to a sea choppy from conflicting bow waves. Once past the harbor walls the boat picked up speed. Chan could hear the beginnings of a turbo whine behind the roar of the diesels.

"Just out of interest, how far could you travel on a boat like this?" Chan asked. He saw Cuthbert frown.

"You'd have to ask the captain for an accurate estimate," Emily said. "Most places on the South China seaboard anyway."

"D'you take it to China much?" Chan felt in his shorts for a pack.

Emily was staring at a large two-masted yacht that was in the process of raising a mainsail. As the crew winched in the sail, the boat heeled and shot forward, a gull racing over the waves.

She looked up at Chan. "Uh-huh. Now and then. By the way, you left your cigarettes on the bridge. I brought them for you."

She took the pack from her pocket, smiled. "You don't have to worry, we're not headed for China today. We're going the other way, about fifty miles due south in the direction of the Philippines. There's a reef. It's not Palawan or Phuket, but the diving's pretty good. Milton dives, so it'll be the three of us. Jenny won't be allowed in her condition."

34

C han stood at the bows when the crew dropped anchor. It was almost night in the middle of nowhere. The galvanized scoop-shaped anchor plunged into the blackening sea, drawing a trail like a falling jet until it disappeared. The captain reversed the engines to ensure that the anchor caught on the seabed, then stilled them. Silence.

Emily's voice came over a loudspeaker. "Sorry to do this, but everyone's all over the place. Rumor has it that we're all hungry, including me. So I thought we'd eat early. Like in twenty minutes on the upper rear deck?"

She repeated the sentence in Mandarin.

The crew folded the awning away from the upper rear deck, unwrapping the first stars. Chan watched Emily light candles along the center of the table. She used a gas cigarette lighter, which illuminated her features from a different angle at each candle. Chan saw the determined jaw, tired eyes, the beginnings of age, flashes of incandescent energy, the pursed lips of regret, raw lust. Before each small explosion of light she paused to make sure he was watching.

The others drifted up from the berths below to take their places under Emily's direction. Xian sat at one end next to the stern; Emily sat at the other. Chan found himself sitting opposite Jenny, who avoided his eyes. The Sri Lankan cook arrived with the hors d'oeuvres, climbing silently up the stairs, her face so black it was invisible against the night except for her wide white eyes.

Xian cleared his throat, said something in Mandarin.

"Mr. Xian is going to say a few words," Emily translated.

"Thanks to the gods China is rising. It is my opinion that with China, the world also will rise. China is the world's new destiny. I am glad that all of you from different countries are here with me tonight to celebrate this new destiny."

"Here, here," Cuthbert said, before Emily had finished translating.

"Here, here," Jonathan repeated loudly, apparently to please Xian and Emily. Jenny also repeated the phrase, without conviction.

"I'll drink to that." Emily let a beat pass to see if Chan was going to speak, then: "To China."

Chan nodded. "To China." From the corner of his eye he saw the old man look at him and smile. He leaned over toward Emily. "Did he really say, 'Thanks to the gods'?"

Emily hesitated. "Yes, that's what he said." She held up a hand. "I know, that phrase was banned during the Cultural Revolution. Let's not push the point. He didn't say, 'Thanks to the Revolution.' Can we leave it at that?"

Xian spoke again. Emily translated into Mandarin.

"He understood what you said. He says, when he said, 'Thanks to the gods,' that's what he meant."

Chan looked at Cuthbert, who sat quietly, smiling.

Jonathan cleared his throat. "Just think, how international everyone is these days. Any one of us could be in a different country this time tomorrow. Take me, five days ago I was in Beijing."

Emily translated into Mandarin, listened to Xian's reply, then laughed.

"Mr. Xian says that there may not be national boundaries in the future, but there will always be China. China was there at the beginning and will be at the end. Didn't you feel so very Chinese when you visited Beijing?"

"Definitely, it was like a spiritual homecoming." Catching the sneer on his wife's face, Jonathan looked down.

Chan cleared his throat. "The only time I went to Beijing I felt very Chinese."

"Oh, yes?" Emily sounded surprised.

"Yes. It was late autumn. The peasants had brought all the cabbages in from the countryside. Everywhere you looked, all around Tiananmen Square: cabbages. All along Wangfujing you saw barricades and even mountains of what they were calling *aiguo cai*— 'national vegetable.' It was that dark ugly green cabbage that they use for bitter soup. All over the city stalls were selling bitter soup. Even the rich were drinking it, as a kind of fashion. The party said it should remind people of the bitter years before communism. But it was nearly fifty years after the Communist Revolution, and almost everyone still had to drink this bitter soup for the vitamin C. Of course I had to have some. It was really the most bitter thing I've ever tasted. I've never felt so Chinese."

He saw that Emily had stopped translating and everyone except Cuthbert was avoiding his eyes. He leaned forward again, this time turning toward Xian and looking him directly in the eye. At each question and answer, Emily translated.

"You must have been in the Communist party for a long time?"

"Correct."

"And I'm sure you impressed senior cadres with your grasp of Marxist-Leninism and Mao Zedong's thought?"

"Certainly, one had to know a lot about such things."

"But now China is in the hands of the gods again?"

"When you were a young cadet in the Royal Hong Kong Police Force, did you take your oath to the queen of England?"

Chan twitched and ignored the question. "Does it worry you that China is becoming increasingly corrupt?"

Xian leaned back in his chair. "We're learning capitalism. Corruption is stage one—personalized profit motive. Does it worry you that England and the United States used to be extremely corrupt and probably still are? Hong Kong owes its origin to the enforced sale of opium to our people. More than one half of the income of the United Kingdom in the nineteenth century came from the sale of opium. Capitalism has won; now the West must pay the price for forcing this system upon us." Xian leaned forward, smiled. "But don't quote me."

Only Cuthbert laughed.

• • •

Chan sat on the swimming deck under a sky of black velvet. Water lapped inches below. Between gaps in the planks it reflected the stars and occasionally offered its own green luminescence.

He knew that Jenny would join him. He heard a soft padding on the deck above, a hesitancy around the steel ladder.

"Charlie?"

How well he remembered those whispers in the night.

"Here."

"Gosh, it's black down here."

"Need any help?"

"No, I'm okay."

They almost always spoke in English, not out of deference to their father but in obedience to their mother. In Mai-mai's day even simple peasants knew you had to learn English to get on. Now everyone was scrambling to learn Mandarin.

She sat next to him, took his hand, waited before she spoke.

He badly needed to smoke. He wriggled to free the pack from the pocket under his buttock.

"I need one too."

He lit two, passed her one.

She sucked deeply, then blew the smoke out in a thick stream. "This is definitely the only one I'm going to have for the next eight months. Being on a boat with you, though, under the stars—" She dropped her voice, as if she expected him to silence her. "Remember when we took up smoking?"

"Of course. The night after Aunt told us they'd killed her. I haven't missed a day since."

"Charlie, no man is ever going to replace you in my heart, even though I'm going to have Jonathan's baby—"

"Don't start that again. I'm your brother, a dumb, hard-bitten cop. He's a fine man, rich, successful, fantastic with people—all that."

She giggled. "You're so unconvincing when you lie. Lawyers are such creeps, aren't they? The way he sucks up to Xian and Emily really gets on my nerves."

In the dark he smiled. Nothing would cure her of loose talk apparently. He tried to make his voice stern. "We shouldn't be talking like this. It's disloyal of you."

"You're the one I'm loyal to. Don't shush me; it's an accident of history. When I was a skinless bundle of hurt, you held me tight and saved me with love. When I remember that summer, it's like you were holding me tight all the time. I didn't have your strength. I was borderline psychotic. I know that now; I've been reading about trauma, victims of violence—"

"Stop! Please."

She was silent for a moment, started on another tack. "Jonathan put a lot of pressure on me to persuade you to come on this trip."

"That I guessed."

"I don't know exactly why, but it has to do with Xian. Jonathan says it's in your interests to get to know him. He's going to be running Hong Kong after June, they say. If you make him happy, you could be commissioner of police." She held up a hand to stop Chan from interrupting. "I said you didn't give a damn about that sort of thing, but Jonathan said there was something else. The old man wants your help. He'll give you anything you want, but if you won't take gifts, at least have the sense not to make an enemy of him. He's going to approach you in his own way. I don't know what he wants, something to do with that mincer case, isn't it?"

"Is it?"

"That's all I know. Jonathan said that it was important for you to meet Xian in cordial surroundings. He made it sound like things could get pretty unpleasant if you didn't play ball." He felt her squeeze his hand. "You'll be careful, won't you?"

He squeezed back. "Don't worry."

She was silent for a long moment. "Charlie, after I have the baby, I'm going to be well and truly swept up in Jonathan's world, his people, his money, his servants, you know? I just want you to tell me I'm not crazy, that something very special welded us together that summer all those years ago. I need to know that because well, the rich are so insincere. You may be the only person in my whole life I ever really trust."

How could he deny it? The intensity of that summer lay embedded in the soul like a burning ember around which the rest of his life congealed.

He lit two more cigarettes, passed her one. She accepted it despite her resolve of a few minutes before.

He inhaled, then exhaled slowly. "After Aunt told us, I dreamed of Mum every night. Except they weren't dreams, they were crossings into another world. She belonged there; she was happy. Even in broad daylight I was dreaming. It was like Mum was with us."

"Ah! So it *was* the same for you!"

He felt her body relax. They sat together smoking. Orion, which had been at the rim of the horizon when he'd sat down, had climbed under the inside of the black dome and was hanging there, a sketch of brilliant dots waiting to be joined. She was sitting close enough for the whole of one side of their bodies to be connected. Kids sat like that. She touched his biceps in the area of the faded tattoos.

"If that old man tried to harm you, I'd kill him."

Chan laughed.

"What's so funny?"

"I really think you would. It would be kind of ironic, not the end he's expecting, I'm sure."

Her hand kneaded the tattoos. "Only you and I know what they used to say."

Chan inhaled. "Your name in Chinese characters." He tapped the cigarette to drop the ash between the planks. "And the tattooist. He must know too."

She punched him on the arm as she stood, whispered, "Thank you," blew him a kiss and was gone.

35

Chan finally rose from the swimming platform. He'd been there so long his buttocks were numb and there was no feeling in his feet. He had to hold on to a stanchion to wait for the circulation to return. Orion was directly overhead now. It was after midnight. The intensity of the stars had steadily increased until they cast dim shadows. Thinking of Moira, he pulled down his shorts, dived naked into the black sea.

When he climbed out, he was wide-awake. He showered using the hose on the swimming deck, returned wet to his cabin, where he dried himself with a fresh towel, dug out the only book he'd brought with him. He lay on his bunk. Idly he read the blurb.

"His travels began in 1271 when he accompanied his father and uncle on their second visit to China. There he worked as a diplomat, undertaking numerous missions in the service of Kublai Khan. Despite piracy, shipwreck, brigandage and wild beasts, Polo moved in a world of highly organized commerce. He loved describing precious gems, spices and silks. . . ."

The book had an elusive relevance, like the Bible. Still, apart from Moira's testimony it was all he had.

Clare's American nationality was a problem. Whenever he'd looked at it on a map, America seemed so distant. New York especially seemed in the middle of nowhere stuck on the North Atlantic seaboard as far away from Asia as it was possible to be yet with an ocean between it and Europe. He hadn't known many Americans, except in the movies. They could be the opposite of Chinese people. There was no respect for age or elders; they were promiscuous; they believed firmly in self-gratification; they were individualists and in that they possessed great courage. There was something called the American Dream: two young men on Harley-Davidson motorbikes with girls riding pillion and drugs hidden in the batteries. A film.

The more he thought about it, the more elusive America became. There was a wealth of conflicting images with no center: over-muscled GIs humping weapons up jungle trails in the Vietnam War; the assassination of President Kennedy. There were alligators in the sewers; homosexual movie stars did strange things with gerbils.

There was a principle Americans talked about the way the British talked about fairness. Anyone, no matter how humble his origins, could become president. Imagine: Charlie Chan, president of the United States.

A wonderful principle, magical. Consider how it must affect fools and villains. You were brought up to believe you could be anyone you liked: Clark Gable, Abraham Lincoln, George Washington. Al Capone, Bonnie and Clyde. Just wear the right hat and buy a gun. Marco Polo? He flicked casually through the text.

"When the Sheikh desired the death of some great Lord, he would first try an experiment to find out which of his assassins were the best. He would send some off on a mission in the neighbour-hood at no great distance with orders to kill such and such a man. They went without demur and did the bidding of their lord. Then, when they had killed the man, they returned to court—those of them that escaped, for some were caught and put to death. . . . Thus it happened that no one ever escaped when the Sheikh of the Mountain desired his death."

It was a famous passage, Chan had heard it quoted in a film with Mick Jagger. But what did it mean?

He was disturbed in his thinking by sounds from Jenny and Jon-athan's cabin next door. Someone moved, groaned lightly. People didn't realize: Boats were not like houses; the walls were often millimeter-thick fiberglass moldings that amplified sound.

More groans, the sounds of bodies turning.

"Can't sleep?" It was Jenny's voice.

"No, I nodded off, but now I'm wide-awake."

"Something bothering you?"

"No."

A pause.

"Yes."

"Want to tell me?"

"Well, you disappeared tonight. Everyone wondered where you went. It was kind of rude, you know."

"I was with Charlie. He disappeared too, didn't he?"

"He's just a cop, and he's got a personality problem. You're my wife; things are expected of you."

"Personality problem? Because he doesn't suck up to people?"

"I don't like the way you look at him. It's weird."

"You want to start a fight, is that it? What's wrong with you? You're jealous of my brother?"

"Why d'you look at him like that?"

"Like what?"

"Like he's a god or something."

"We were very close as kids. We went through trauma together. He saved my mind. Some of those people you suck up to, like Xian, they killed our mother."

A pause.

"Isn't this just a little too blue-collar?"

"Huh?"

"All this vendetta stuff. I mean, okay, you had a traumatic adolescence, but life goes on. It was over twenty years ago."

"You don't understand. You have no depth of feeling."

"Depth? Is that what he has?"

"Okay, you want it straight, this is it. After they told us Red Guards had killed Mai-mai, I lost my mind. He was all I had. He dedicated his whole time to me, never went to school, never left me alone, not for a single minute. Something happens when you get that close. When I look at him, I remember. What I remember is love winning over hate. Not something a lawyer would understand."

A long pause, then Wong's voice, meaner and more dogged than when he was putting on the charm. "I guess I need you to tell me if he raped you or not."

Jenny's outraged voice: "What did you say?"

"If it happened and you were under sixteen, that's rape. Even if you consented. It happens a lot in—well, the poorer Chinese families. It's the great unreported crime of Southeast Asia. I did a lot of family law when I was starting out, I know about these things."

"You're one sick lawyer. I tell you what, Charlie would rather have died than taken advantage of me. But if he'd asked me, I would have done anything. Anything at all. And I probably would have loved it. Happy now?"

"Calm down, relax. It was a natural question."

"No, it wasn't. It was a dirty lawyer's question. You have all these artistic pretensions, but you're just another money snob, like everyone else in Hong Kong."

"Don't raise your voice. Let's just forget it, okay?"

"I won't forget it. Rape? Maybe you're the one with the problem."

Chan grinned at the wall. She always did have a way of turning things around. She wouldn't stop until she'd extorted an unconditional surrender.

"Look, I don't want an atmosphere all day tomorrow. I know how good you are at doing that. I'm very sorry I cast an aspersion on your bighearted, macho, crime-busting brother, okay? Can we drop it now?"

"Don't worry, I won't embarrass you with peasant emotions in front of your friends—or are they clients? I can never tell the difference somehow."

Chan shook his head and got up. The argument next door had stirred his thoughts, and there was no way he was going to sleep now. He pulled on some shorts and wandered up to the top deck, where he sat on the electric windlass and tried to make out the anchor line as it disappeared into the sea. It was a night of perfect calm. The line slid cleanly into the water as if set in marble. Likewise the hands that came from behind slid cleanly under his arms and lifted him up high in the air. The second bodyguard appeared also from behind and held Chan's legs just as he started to struggle.

"Be calm," a voice said in English. There was no doubt about the Beijing accent, but the owner had certainly spent time in England.

The hands set him down again after carrying him two yards toward the wheelhouse. From the shadows a gruff peasant voice spoke in Mandarin.

"We apologize," the first voice said. "We saw you leave your cabin. We've been waiting for you. We wanted you to come into the shadow so that we would not be seen talking to you." Chan assumed that this was a translation of the old man's words.

Chan shook himself, waited. The old man cleared his throat.

"You like this boat?" This time there was no translation. The old man himself had spoken. The effect of the stunted, near-unintelligible English was of brutish stupidity. It could have been the opening gambit in an argument about pig feed.

"Yes," Chan said.

"You want it?"

"No."

"How about an apartment block?"

"No."

There was a grunt. "When you find out, you tell me, okay?"

"Find out what?"

Another grunt. "What you think?"

Chan stood still. His Mandarin was good enough to understand the old man telling his bodyguards to follow him belowdecks. No more than a craggy shadow, the old man turned at the last minute.

"By the way, I don't kill your mother. Red Guards, not army. Okay?"

"No," Chan said, but he spoke into a void.

He shook himself again, only half believing. It took minutes for the mind to catch up: *I have been mugged by China.* He walked around the cabin toward the stern of the boat.

• • •

On the rear deck where they had eaten dinner he saw a single red glow move in an arc toward the deck, flicker, then rise again. Cuthbert didn't get up from the chair next to the rails or turn his head, even though Chan exaggerated the noise of his bare feet on the deck. He stood by the rail, not far from the diplomat.

"Welcome," Cuthbert finally said. "Won't you sit down?"

Chan drew up a white plastic chair. It occurred to him that voices from the swimming deck would carry this far without serious diminution in volume.

"Have you been here long?" Chan said.

"Only just arrived. Couldn't sleep."

But when the Englishman lowered his cigarette again to knock it out on an ashtray, Chan saw a small mountain of stubs. He knew that some kind of small talk was in order, but there was no point in pretending to a skill so alien to his personality.

"Why did you say that earlier? About not letting her seduce me?"

Cuthbert drew slowly on his cigarette, then took out the case and offered one to Chan without looking at him. Chan took it, lit up and waited. The extreme languor of the diplomat's movements was unusual, even for an upper-class Englishman.

"She hasn't slept with you yet. She's intrigued by most men under forty with whom she hasn't slept—not that there are too many left in Hong Kong. If I were you, I'd keep her intrigued—follow?"

Diplomats were worse than lawyers in their effortless capacity to irritate. "What do you care? What are you doing here anyway?"

Cuthbert paused on an exhalation, nodded slowly, then continued to breathe out smoke. "Emily's an interesting girl."

"You know a lot about her?"

Cuthbert seemed on the point of saying something about their hostess, then changed his mind. He sighed, then stretched out a hand in a gesture that could only be described as theatrical. "Tell me, my friend, isn't it just incredibly wonderful?"

"What?"

"To be here, at this moment, in this tropical night, ensnared by this Chinese intrigue that will outlive both of us?"

"Is that why Englishmen like you come to Southeast Asia—for Chinese intrigue?"

"I can't speak for anyone else. After my year in China perfecting the language, I took up an appointment at Magdalen. I didn't last very long. China had bitten me. I wanted the feeling of being at that point on the earth's crust where the tectonic plates are crashing together. I was in love. I even wanted more of Mao's poems, would you believe? In 1964 he published something called 'Snow,' which I learned by heart, in Mandarin, of course. I still remember the last line—"

" 'For truly great men, look to this age alone,' " Chan quoted. "I never learned it in Mandarin, only in the English translation."

Cuthbert paused with his cigarette twelve inches from his lips. "Correct. And you are indeed a surprising man, as the truly intelligent must always be." He paused, then sighed. "But when Mao talked about great men, he was talking about Asians."

Chan let a beat pass. "With regard to the Chinese intrigue, I have some information you might be interested in."

"Please go on."

"Xian probably didn't kill those three in Mongkok. Isn't that what you're so afraid of, that I'll discover he's the culprit?"

In a tone that showed only mild interest Cuthbert said, "Perhaps. But what has caused you to form this view?"

"Ten minutes ago he offered me an apartment building if I would tell him who did, when I found out. At least I think that's what he meant."

"You didn't accept this substantial offer?"

"No."

"Why ever not?"

"I'm half Chinese."

"Meaning?"

"I was waiting for him to offer me two apartment buildings."

Cuthbert threw his head back. In the dim illumination from the anchor lights Chan saw that he was laughing. Silently, like a good diplomat.

Chan returned to his cabin slightly ashamed. English humor: It was a disease. No matter how you fought against it, you ended by making the same silly jokes as they did.

36

He awoke to an almost gentle knocking on his door. Light streamed through the porthole. He dragged on a pair of shorts.

Emily was already in her dive suit; purple and green neoprene with a band of Day-Glo yellow crossing from right shoulder to left hip was unzipped to an inch above the navel. Flaps covered her breasts. Hanging on to the door, Chan blinked.

Emily smiled.

There was a relationship between confidence and wealth; which came first?

"The tanks are set up on the swimming platform. I've found you a buoyancy jacket. There's coffee in the galley."

Chan scratched his head, his shoulders, then, defiantly, his testicles. "What about the others?"

She put a hand to his cheek. "They're all asleep, Chief Inspector; there's only you and me."

He yawned, looked back into the cabin where *The Travels of Marco Polo* lay on a table illuminated by a tunnel of blinding sunshine. As sleep fell away, he allowed his features to harden into dislike. First thing in the morning it was difficult not to bristle.

"Did anyone ever tell you—"

She placed a single hand on her chest and almost succeeded in looking vulnerable. "Stop! I know, I'm being pushy. It's unforgivable at this time in the morning. I'm sorry, I have a lifelong problem with impatience. Let me try again." She lowered her head, looked up at him with big eyes and spoke in a little-girl voice. "I've been awake for over an hour just dying to get in the water and unable to think of anyone to be my scuba buddy except that gorgeous chief inspector of police in the cabin down the way, and the anticipation seems to have got the better of my manners, but please don't take it amiss, and if there's anything I can do to persuade you to please come play with me——"

Chan put up a hand. "Okay, okay."

"It's worse when I'm trying to soft-soap, isn't it?"

He let a grin grow slowly while his eyes locked with hers. "It's charming to be able to laugh at oneself."

"I copied it from the English. It's a lot easier than genuine self-reform." She fluttered her eyelashes; that really was rather funny.

He closed the door, changed from cotton shorts to swimming shorts, brushed his teeth, omitted to shave, stepped out onto the foredeck.

With the engines off and the anchor line pinning the boat to a deserted spot on the surface of the Pacific Ocean the true identity of the 120-foot luxury cruiser was unmasked: a plastic toy in the hands of Ocean, the monster god. Water stretched in every direction like a lesson in infinity. Acid light poured over the decks, the paint, the fantasies of night. At dawn the sky was too hot to contemplate, the sun a whiteness too powerful to squint at. On a gleaming white life ring in its stainless steel housing Chan read the word EMILY, etched in blue.

The air was certainly cleaner than Mongkok; too clean——he needed a cigarette. He returned to his cabin, took a pack to the galley, where the cook had left a glass jug under a dripping coffee-maker. He filled a mug, added three sugars and milk, took the coffee out to the stern deck. On the swimming platform Emily screwed regulators into air tanks. From above he watched her breasts fall forward almost out of the neoprene as she bent over the steel cylinders. She was big-boned for a Chinese, but there was no extra flesh. Hers was an athlete's body, full of health and appetites. *Don't let her seduce you*, Cuthbert had said.

She gave him a sincere smile when he joined her, touched his forearm.

"I *am* sorry for waking you like that. It's just me; I'm one of those people born without any subtlety at all. Up front, no depth, a primal type with the sense of humor of a twelve-year-old, that's me. I even crack up at knock-knock jokes."

"Knock, knock."

"Who's there?"

"Mustafer."

"Mustafer who?"

"Mustafer fag before I dive."

He watched her double up. "You don't really find that funny?"

She nodded, helpless.

Fuck Cuthbert.

Underwater with a scuba tank on her back Emily was lithe, playful, artistic, funny: a human porpoise. On the coral bed eighty feet under the boat she lay on her back, blew air rings of silver that wobbled lazily to the surface. As soon as Chan floated down to her level, he felt her hand on his thigh. He had not brought a wet suit; he wore only a T-shirt and swimming trunks. She found his testicles under his shorts. He liked her firmness of touch, her hunger, the humor of a submarine seduction.

Emily beckoned to him to follow. She stopped by the boat's anchor, pulled him toward her. He could see her eyes glittering behind her mask. People died like this.

He felt his heartbeat double as he allowed her to pull open the Velcro fastenings to his buoyancy jacket. Carefully she slid it off him, his life in her hands. He chomped firmly on the mouthpiece. She used the Velcro straps to hitch the jacket and tank to the ring of the anchor chain. He hung in the sea with only the rubber windpipe tying him to his air. Through the water he felt her lust. *Don't let her* . . . , but this was a seduction Cuthbert might have appreciated. For denizens of the edge, there was no greater aphrodisiac than the proximity of death. How had she guessed that eighty feet underwater was the one place where he would find her irresistible?

She pulled off his shorts, taking care to leave him his weight belt, tied them too, gestured for him to remove his T-shirt.

At the same time she pulled off her own buoyancy jacket, tied it next to his, managed to unzip her wet suit and remove it without losing the weight belt. Chan thought it would be funny if they lost the weights now and shot to the surface.

They sucked life from mouthpieces joined to umbilical cords joined to the tanks that had nestled next to the anchor. Between the fins and the masks they both were naked except for the weight belts: two monster frogs in a breeding ritual. Her breasts and thighs, the whole surface of her skin glistened with the liquid silk of the sea.

She clung to the anchor line in front of him, offering him her buttocks. As he reached down in slow motion, he found her hand already there ready to guide him. Without weight, without friction, he had to press her pelvic bone hard with his hand to avoid losing her to the sea. The bubbles from her mouthpiece reached a crescendo, then subsided with her slowing loins.

Wood, earth, metal, air, fire, water: Chan remembered in the Taoist system water was the origin of pleasure. He remembered too that other Taoist wisdom: Sex was the lesser climax, foreshadowing the greater one of death. He held that thought while he hung in the sea, spent.

Already Emily was replacing her wet suit. Following her, Chan watched while she fed giant rays that emerged from small hillocks in the sand of the seabed.

During breakfast on the rear deck under an awning Chan avoided the pity in Cuthbert's eyes. Jenny and Jonathan were faintly embarrassed. Curious how sensitive people could smell coitus through eighty feet of salt water. Only Xian seemed unaware of a subtle change in the social order. He slurped congee while the others ate toast with coffee.

Cuthbert broke the silence. "How was your dawn dive?"

"It was unbelievable." Chan concentrated on his toast.

"Emily, was it good?"

There was no sign of mischief in the diplomat's face, but then he was English.

"Wonderful, just wonderful. Tell them, Charlie."

"Giant rays—some of the biggest I've seen. Emily's trained them to come when she taps her tank."

"With food, I expect?" Cuthbert asked.

"Of course. They're not stupid. Whenever I come, I first tap the tank, then give them some dried shrimp. Now all I have to do is tap the tank and they rise from the sand."

"I'd like to see that," Cuthbert said.

By lunchtime the atmosphere had altered again. Prolonged immersion in fresh air and sea had released everyone's tension. Cuthbert had lost ten years.

"By God, that was something," he said when he returned from a shower. "Such beauty, makes you never want to look at a desk or a telephone again." He winked at Chan.

They ate lunch slowly, exchanging comments like a family that had been together years. Afterward they allowed their bodies to sag in sun chairs or on the swimming platform.

Chan caught subtle looks passing between Jenny and Jonathan. Emily's eyes consumed his body. Remembering the morning, he smiled. Warm water and copulation went together like duck and rice. Only Xian seemed on edge, anxious to get back to land.

Everyone except Jenny drank a beer while lounging in the sun; then one by one with sketchy apologies they retired to their cabins.

Chan returned to the swimming deck and thought about diving naked into the sea again. He was quietly smoking and staring out at the electric blue ocean when the boat boy approached with a red envelope that bore the name Chief Inspector Chan in green felt tip pen. Inside, a single sheet of paper carried a two-word message: "knock, knock?"

Chan smiled. He could feel her will dragging him in invisible chains toward her stateroom. For a moment he toyed with the amusing idea of ignoring her message and observing the savagery of her revenge, or the humor of her pleading—her reactions were hard to predict. On reflection, though, he padded back down the corridor. Abovewater perhaps she would talk.

Cuthbert lay down on his bunk. It was so hot he gave in and turned on the boat's air conditioning. He had prepared his diskman and travel alarm. He set the alarm, replaced the Gregorian chants with Mozart's Concerto for Clarinet.

When the alarm bleeped, he pressed a button that activated a radio receiver: nothing except the sound of Xian snoring. Cuthbert removed the headset. As he did so, he heard Emily's voice penetrating through the wall from the stateroom next door. Cuthbert put his ear to the wall.

"Admit it, have the guts: They turn you off, don't they?"

"I didn't say that."

"Christ, if you didn't have to be such a fucking detective, you wouldn't have noticed. Men can't feel saline; it's guaranteed."

"Let's just say I'm impotent and leave it at that."

"You weren't so fucking impotent this morning—before you knew. I saw your face when you saw the scars."

"I'm sorry, yes, I saw the scars."

"And now all you can manage is a wet fish between your legs."

"I'm practically impotent. Submarine erections are all I can manage."

"Prick."

"Look, what d'you want me to say? You have a hang-up about your tits, your implants. What do I know? Why is it my problem?"

A long pause. Then Emily's voice: "Go on, fuck off, go back to your cabin."

"D'you have to be quite such a bitch?"

A short pause.

"No, sorry. I'm upset. It's not like me. At least it is when this happens."

"So—"

"Yes, Chief Inspector, it's happened before. Chinese men have got to be the most fastidious in the world."

"Choose a South African."

"What?"

"A particularly insensitive race—up your street."

A pause.

"Come here, kiss me."

Sound of a short kiss.

"That's better. We can be friends. I'm sorry I lost it. You're right, I'm paranoid about what I did to my body for no good reason at all. I wasn't even especially flat-chested."

"Just wanted to be perfect?"

"What's wrong with that?"

"Money doesn't buy it. Or maybe it does, what do I know?"

"Why d'you keep saying that?"

"What?"

" 'What do I know?' "

"You know."

"I know?"

"Yes, you know."

"I know why you keep saying, 'What do I know?' "

"Don't you?"

Sound of laughter.

"Christ, I actually like you. How did this happen? A down-and-out cop with the world's worst nicotine habit. You'll probably be dead from lung cancer by next week."

"Maybe you like short-term relationships. Look . . ."

"Look what?"

"You want me to go?"

"No. Stay. Just a few minutes. I want to tell you something."

Cuthbert waited. The pause was so long he wondered if they'd found a way to overcome the problem, when Emily began to speak. She spoke in a precise voice, as if reciting from a briefing.

"In 1982, after Margaret Thatcher went to China and it was clear that there would have to be some deal between England and China about the future of Hong Kong, my father went to Beijing. He was part of a high-powered delegation that included some of the most successful businessmen and women in the territory. They wanted to see Deng Xiaoping, but he palmed them off on to one of his senior cadres. It doesn't matter who they actually saw, but the point the delegation wanted to make was that Hong Kong was per capita by far and away the most successful city in the world, commercially speaking. They delicately suggested that some care was needed in the handover of power if international business confidence was to be maintained. The cadre they spoke to said—and this is important—'I don't know what you're all so worried about. Look what a good job we did in Shanghai in 1949.'"

A pause. Then Chan's voice: "Shanghai was a disaster after 1949. It went from the most prosperous port on the Pacific Rim to an overpopulated Third World dump that can hardly feed itself."

"Exactly."

"So why did you tell me all that?"

"It's your reward, Chief Inspector. You thought by fucking me, you might get some clue to your murder mystery. I'm giving you a clue. You can go now. When you need another clue, you know where to come."

A pause.

"This is all a game to you?"

"Isn't that what they say about the rich, all we have to do all day is play games?"

There was a long pause.

"I'm going."

Sound of a door opening and closing. Silence.

• • •

Cuthbert frowned. What the hell was she up to? He set the alarm to interrupt him again in thirty minutes, went back to the clarinet concerto.

In the middle of the allegro the alarm sounded. He pressed the button. Chan and Emily had spoken in a mixture of English and Cantonese. Now Emily was in Xian's cabin speaking in Mandarin.

"Don't be stupid, how was I supposed to prove it anyway?"

"Underwater? What kind of Western decadence is that?"

"It was fun. And you owe me a million U.S. dollars. Why be petty? What does a million matter to you? You gamble that every day on mah-jongg when you're in Shanghai with your cronies."

A pause. Cuthbert could imagine the old man scowling.

"Okay, you win, one million off the bill. It doesn't make a lot of difference. At least I know he was in your cabin just now. He didn't stay very long."

"Long enough, though?"

A short pause. Then the general's voice: "Oh, yes, long enough."

"And when I've got him under control, what then?"

"Then we watch. They say he's a very talented detective. But I can see he's more than that. He's a Chinese who doesn't give up. Like me. Men like him and me—we cannot be defeated."

Emily's surprised voice: "You like him?"

"He reminds me of my youth." A chuckle. "I was a Communist, you know."

A long pause. The general's voice again: "You seem upset."

"It's nothing."

"You had a good time with the detective this morning? I hope you're not having another depression attack."

"Do I look as if I am?"

"I don't know, you look upset."

"What does it matter to you?"

"Not at all. Just don't forget who you owe money to. And I don't want to hear that you've been walking around your house at night telling stories to the walls. Walls have ears."

"Apparently." A long pause. Emily's voice: "I'm going now. I need some sleep."

A grunt, then the sound of a door opening and closing.

Cuthbert took off his headphones.

Entering the mouth of the harbor, the boat came within the radius of the city's thunder. To the six of them relaxing on the rear sun deck the vibrations of the metropolis were unavoidable. Like a nerve gas, it corroded all sense of comfort. Chan counted three loud sighs before giving vent to one himself. As the boat converged with other craft, he could see the same long faces on other decks. Migration back to land had begun.

At Queen's Pier good-byes were hurried. He kissed Jenny on one cheek, shook Emily's hand, waved good-bye to Cuthbert, Jonathan and Xian, disappeared down an escalator to the underground.

At Mongkok he started to walk toward his block, then changed his mind and went to the station. The traffic and operations corridors were buzzing as usual, but homicide was quiet with a skeleton staff. It was midafternoon, and most of the weekend murders happened after dark. He locked the door to his office behind him, emptied his bag out on the desk. There was a pair of wet swimming trunks, the book, his regulator with mouthpiece, mask and fins. He examined the inside of the bag, then pressed firmly over every inch. The mouthpiece was clean; the regulator did not block his breath when he blew through it; the fins were clean, as were his trunks. Someone had thoughtfully taped the cover of his book so that it would not open inside the bag. He broke the tape. The inside of the book had been carved out in a rectangle, a small package in polythene placed inside. He took out the package, opened it. Inside was a black and viscous substance the consistency of warm tar. He sniffed, took a sample on his finger to taste, then rewrapped the packet. From his desk drawer he took a roll of tape, cleaned the packet with a tissue, went to the small kitchen at the end of the floor, taped the packet under the sink at the back. He returned to his desk, carefully wiped the book with another tissue, replaced it in his bag.

At a bin two hundred yards from the station he dumped the book.

37

"Southeast Asia's like the Bermuda Triangle: People just disappear without trace," Aston said. He dumped a stack of faxes on Chan's desk.

"What d'you want me to do with these?"

Chan sifted through, glancing only at the letterheads. San Francisco Police Department, Manila CID, Royal Thai Police Force. Most of them were extracts from missing persons files with reference to the disappearance of young Caucasian women. A small number referred to Chinese males who had also disappeared.

"File them," Chan said.

"Those concerning the girl—we can forget them, right? Jekyll and Hyde, though, they could be in here somewhere."

"You know the approximate ages; check it out," Chan said.

"But there are no dental records for PI. What am I supposed to do if I find some likely candidates?"

Chan lit a cigarette, shrugged. "Positive identification is what they didn't want. That's why they shredded the bodies. You'll have to get hold of relatives to see if they have dental records. Without fingerprints dental records are everything."

"DNA?"

"Only proves that the heads fit the bodies; who they were is another problem. Unless the relatives kept locks of hair . . ."

"What?"

"Oh, nothing. Just a thought. Locks of hair."

• • •

The day when Paddy left for good Chan found a small pile of books at the end of his bed with a two-word note scrawled badly in Chinese characters: "Forgive me." He stared at the note for over an hour before he was able to accept what it meant. Then he went down to the sea with the books: the *Barrack-Room Ballads* of Rudyard Kipling; the *Selected Poems* of W. B. Yeats; *Alice in Wonderland* and *Alice Through the Looking Glass*, and the *Rubaiyát of Omar Khayyám*, which Paddy must have bought recently in Hong Kong. Inside the *Rubaiyát* he'd pasted a lock of his brown Irish hair. With tears in his eyes and fierce Chinese anger in his heart the young Eurasian boy tore up the books, by the spines at first and then page by page, piece by piece. He floated them on the water, saving the ragged corner with the hair still attached to it until last. He watched it float until it sank somewhere in the vast South China Sea. He walked back slowly to the wooden hut where they had lived, but the hut wasn't there anymore. While he had been by the sea, he had entered a time warp; a building resembling the hut in every particular was on the site where the hut had been, but the small house, imbued from floor to roof with the love that only children know for inanimate objects, was gone. Before that day he had never noticed the smallness of the shack or the stigma that attached to living in it. Afterward he began to resent it.

The half of him that was Chinese started a war with the Irish half that was to last a lifetime. Against *Alice in Wonderland* he set the *Tao-te-ching*; against the *Rubaiyát* the *I Ching* and the poet Li Po; against Kipling he set Shen Fu's *Six Records of a Floating Life*.

In the war between the selves the Chinese side always won, but never with finality. The Irishman was always there; sometimes he dreamed of him, a soft, weak, lecherous man with a charming smile and a love of poetry that almost saved him. The sterner the Chinese half became, the more frequently the Irish side turned up unexpectedly. Moira, for example. It took an Irish connoisseur of the lowlife to appreciate an alcoholic shoplifter forty-nine years old.

· · ·

Sifting once more through the faxes that Aston had brought, Chan
wondered if Paddy was dead. Without that lock of hair identification
might be difficult. Certainly he had no fingerprints or dental records
and he'd never recognize him after all these years. Among the
papers Aston had included a confirmation slip from Riley's office
in Arsenal Street: Chan's application for assistance from Scotland
Yard had been approved; the scrappings had been sent. Chan knew
it could take a month, though, for the results to be available.

There was a fax from the New York Police Department he'd
overlooked first time round. "Reference your fax of April 21, Captain Frank Delaney will arrive in Hong Kong on April 26 United
Airlines flight U.A.204 with information of interest to you. Signed:
Frank Delaney, Captain NYPD."

He showed it to Aston.

"Oh, yeah. Sorry, Chief, I forgot to mention it. Tomorrow afternoon. Want me to meet him at the airport?"

Lunchtime. Chan pushed his way through the crowds back to his
flat. It had been a weekend full of people. Granted, one could have
wished for less challenging company on a boating trip than an aging
psychopath, a sex-hungry billionairess and a scheming diplomat;
nontheless, when he found himself solitary once more, loneliness
and squalor crept into his bones like the first aches of old age. At
the same time his body was still glowing from the sun and the sea.
And then Emily had left her own particular glow. He heard her
voice, not so complacent, almost sorrowful: *When you need another
clue, you know where to come.*

Well, that would require an erection. Another hurdle.

All his life he'd been what the British called a tits man. He'd
always taken it on faith that the pleasure he derived from fondling
was in some way transmitted through the breasts and nipples to
their owner. To squeeze a plastic bag filled with saline solution was
to turn the seduction process Pavlovian. Maybe it was anyway, but
Pavlov's dogs never saw the seam.

In his mind's eye he saw again the two U-shaped scars, livid against Emily's olive skin. The billionairess who bought perfection, or tried to. But that had been *his* question: *You wanted to be perfect?* Suppose he'd been bold enough to phrase it another way: *Why did you mutilate yourself?*

From there it was only a short hop to a more intriguing question: Why did one of the world's most successful women want to discuss the murder of three people in Mongkok, but was afraid to?

At times of genuine uncertainty he consulted the oracle called the *I Ching*. It was not a process recommended in any police manual, but Chan had the greatest respect for the book's wisdom. He was gratified that in the past thirty years quantum mechanics had been able to corroborate what Chinamen had known since ancient times: God was playing dice with the universe. Consequently the sages had been connoisseurs of chance, which in their view rewarded study more than science. As Chan put it, what would you rather know, that $e = mc^2$ or that you will save your life if you leave the car at home tomorrow?

Consultation of the great book, though, was a subtle art. It was important to phrase the question in a precise and dignified manner. Thus, Is the human penis a legitimate organ of detection? He threw the coins and read the judgment: "Removing corruption promises success. If one deliberates with great care, before and after the starting point, then great undertakings are favored."

Then the image:

> *As a wind, blowing low on a mountain,*
> *Thus does the wise man remove corruption.*
> *As a wind, he first stirs up the people.*
> *As a mountain, he gives them nourishment.*

Chan lit a cigarette. Sometimes he thought that the Chinese mind knew too much. Burdened with five thousand years of conflicting insights, it was like a computer with more data than its chip could handle. Meaning was the first casualty of overload. He closed the book.

In a four-table restaurant serving duck and rice he ate lunch, exchanged curses with the owner, smoked a cigarette, drank green Chinese tea a light amber brew with almost no taste and a way of settling the stomach. Who was he kidding? Why not admit that there existed another oracle of infinitely greater precision, though less wisdom: Cuthbert? From a wall telephone he called the commissioner's office. Tsui was at home, but Chan had his home number.

"What took you so long?" Tsui said when Chan had explained what he had in mind. "Come and see me tomorrow afternoon. We'll talk about it."

38

As a bilingual Eurasian Chan suffered, and on occasion inflicted, racial prejudice from both sides of the wall; in a bigoted mood he could be ambidextrous. The English were red-faced, blustering, arrogant, poor, infantile, given to incomprehensible failures of nerve that they called compassion. On the plus side they were good administrators, fair, and their women had large breasts. The Chinese were obsessed with money, callous, slant-eyed, incorrigible litterbugs, superstitious and rude. Nevertheless, they were resourceful, industrious, respected the family unit and had a genius for making money that left the rest of the world slack-jawed with envy.

Chan had tried to explain it to his politically correct English wife, when he'd had one: In Hong Kong nothing one race said about the other could dent that other race's conviction of unassailable superiority. To weep over the nasty things the two nations sometimes said about each other was like feeling sorry for Everest because K2 called it a dwarf—or vice versa.

One frequent observation made by the Chinese about the English, though, was neutral in character and endured in the mythology of the Raj because it was true. While the Chinese only collected information that could be used in the pursuit of commerce or malice, the English compiled records for the sake of it.

As he had risen through the ranks of the Royal Hong Kong Police Force Chan had become increasingly aware of this quirk. Often it seemed to him that 90 percent of what *they* knew was not made available even to senior police officers, yet someone somewhere possessed and leaked information on a need-to-know basis.

Chan had personal experience of this Whispering Wall school of administration through the more important cases he had been given to solve. He had noticed that when failure to catch the perpetrator of a crime was particularly embarrassing to the government—a spectacular kidnapping and murder of a famous billionaire by a renegade Communist group, for example—leads and background detail fell from some exalted but invisible source with obscene plenitude. Investigations into atrocities that failed to attract publicity or lacked political overtones had to limp on without such executive-level support. It was difficult, in the end, to resist the conclusion that a small group of men at the top of government had access to a database so extensive that they knew almost everything about the six million official inhabitants of Hong Kong and used this knowledge in accordance with a logical but restrictive policy. And who more likely to control such a committee than the political adviser? So why had Chan not yet confronted the great mandarin to demand a sharing of this secret knowledge? Chan knew why.

Irrational terror of authority was not merely a Confucian virtue; it was the bones of the Master's system that had molded the Han mind since 500 B.C. Only one administrative tool had held together the imperial system with its nine grades of mandarin, its eighteen ranks of civil and military officials, its rules of precedence for princes of the blood, wives, concubines and pirates: *paranoia*. It was the flaw in Sino psychology.

Chan remembered a trial of thirty counts of rape on separate women by a slim Chinese man about five four with the physical presence of a twig. His MO was simple. He obtained the names of housewives from the telephone directory: "Good morning, Mrs. Wong, I'm from the government medical department, and I have reason to believe you are having trouble with your marriage. I would like to visit you at a convenient time to perform a medical examination. . . ." When he arrived, he always closed the curtains and turned out the lights. Rape without violence. Only thirty of more than a hundred victims would give evidence. More than half didn't know that they had been raped. Put another way, what was the difference? The Chinese had been raped by Authority for five thousand years. K'ung Fu-tse—Confucius, as the West called him—was an anal retentive who had a lot to answer for.

That's why it took me so long to get to this point, Chan muttered to himself as he was shown into the commissioner's office.

Chan smiled after he had presented his request, added: "Confucius stole my nerve."

Tsui shook his head. "Slowed you down, perhaps. Well, you're here now."

"Every facility," Chan said, still cursing his own timidity. "That fax you showed me in your car after the meeting with Cuthbert and the others said *every facility*."

The commissioner leaned back in his chair, gazed at the chief inspector.

"You'd better tell me what you know—just so that we're sure we're talking about the same thing."

"Everyone knows. The British love information. In Hong Kong there's hardly a pig roasted without the British knowing about it."

"And you think that will help your inquiry, knowing the rate of pig mortality?"

Chan thanked his Chinese genes for a condition of implacable stubbornness that turned him into rock from time to time. "Every facility. That's what the fax said."

Still half astonished at his own temerity, half ashamed at his earlier timidity, Chan lit a cigarette without asking permission.

Tsui scratched his head. "I wasn't supposed to show it to you, though. The fax, I mean." He thought for a moment, then picked up a telephone. "Get me the political adviser, please." When he had arranged a meeting with Cuthbert, Tsui looked at Chan and smiled.

At the long table in the anteroom to Cuthbert's office, Chan waited patiently for the political adviser to deny everything he had just said and was even prepared to relish the elegance of the diplomat's lie. On instructions from Tsui, Chan had not mentioned the top secret fax the commissioner had shown him.

Cuthbert tapped the table, turned to Tsui, the only other person in the room.

"What d'you say, Ronny?"

"Nothing," Tsui said.

Cuthbert pursed his lips. "Yes, I thought you'd say that." He gave the appearance of thinking hard for a moment. He turned to Chan. "Well, I know when I'm beat. I may as well face it, you've just about cornered me." He tapped his nose and winked. "Of course you realize that everything you've just told us, this fantastic notion of some sort of systematic invasion of privacy by Big Brother, is just so much nonsense?"

"Of course," Chan said, surprised. He liked the British principle of magnanimity in victory.

"It's close to lunchtime," Cuthbert said. "If you'd allow me?" He raised eyebrows at Tsui. "Ronny—"

"I'm afraid I have a lunch appointment," Tsui said, taking Cuthbert's hint. "I'll leave you two to talk." At the door the commissioner grimaced, like one who has reluctantly delivered a lamb to a tiger.

Chan was not surprised that Cuthbert led him to the car park of the government building, where he expected the political adviser to summon one of the chauffeur-driven white Toyotas that were a privilege of the most senior ranks in government. The Englishman, though, led him to a vintage Jaguar XJ6 in English racing green with properly scuffed leather upholstery and a sun roof. After opening the front passenger door for Chan, Cuthbert slipped into the driving seat with a soft aspiration of pleasure.

They were screeching around a bend on the way to the Peak when Cuthbert turned on the CD player. Male voices unaccompanied by instruments chanted through the speakers in Latin. Chan guessed it would be to a speeding green XJ6 filled with Gregorian chants that upper-class English bachelors would graduate when they died. Cuthbert, as usual, was one jump ahead.

Near the top of the mountain, above the level where Chan and Moira had once sat, exclusive settlements of low-rise, low-density, high-value apartments with spectacular views accommodated the great and the rich. About half were owned by government. Cuthbert stopped in the outdoor car park to Beauchamp Villas, led Chan to a lift that waited with open doors. On a brass plate with the list of floors the word PENTHOUSE appeared next to the number 5. Cuthbert pressed 5.

The diplomat's penthouse flat was to light, air and space what Chan's was to darkness, asphyxiation and cramp. A huge sitting room with bay windows gave views over every part of Hong Kong Island. Orchids pressed against the inside glass; bougainvillaea cascaded over wrought-iron balcony railings; hibiscus tongues licked more orchids in window boxes; frangipani danced in the sunlight. On a tripod by a window a nautical brass telescope cocked a single eye at the sky.

While Cuthbert disappeared to find someone called Hill, Chan collected other evidence of an eccentric and discerning colonial mind. Turkish kilims, Afghan and Persian rugs were scattered haphazardly over the parquet; five shelves of a polished rosewood case with glass doors held the best collection of opium pipes Chan had seen outside an antiques dealer's showroom. On one wall, a set of classic Chinese rugs and tapestries, framed and behind glass as if they were pictures. On the opposite wall in what may have been the place of honor, a nineteenth-century long-barreled rifle with its worn and torn canvas case and another, slimmer brass telescope. Cuthbert returned in an open-neck shirt and slacks, pointed to one of the rugs.

"Kansu saddle rug with fret and floral medallion, cloud band border. I imagine it on the back of a bandit's horse somewhere along the silk route between Samarkand and Beijing."

He led Chan into an annex off the sitting room where a small Italian marble table was laid for lunch. Surrounding the table were huge terra-cotta pots from which small rubber, coffee, caocao, teak and mahogany trees grew. As he sat down at the table, Chan supposed the humidity in the room was deliberate. It was like picnicking with the viceroy of India, somewhere between Maharbellapuram and Kashmir.

Hill appeared. Unlike Emily, the Englishman did not require his servants to wear uniforms. The Filipino wore jeans, an open-neck short-sleeved shirt.

"Been with me years," Cuthbert said when Hill was out of earshot. "Damned fine chap. Half Chinese, from Luzon, up in the north somewhere. Lives with his wife just down the road where she's a maid with a Chinese family. Perfect arrangement. I get Hill all day; I'm alone at night." He smiled.

This was a different Cuthbert. From the moment they had entered the apartment the diplomat's manner had subtly changed. A new kindness, an attentiveness to his guest, a commitment to some lost tradition of hospitality soothed even Chan's nerves. He agreed to a gin and tonic, along with Cuthbert.

"Emily. Smart girl," Cuthbert said suddenly, as if in answer to a question. He proceeded to butter a roll. "Of course, trying to talk to her about anything other than money is like trying to get an orangutang to play the sitar. Firmly believes she's Chinese. I keep telling her, 'You're not Chinese, dear; you're Hong Kong.' And she is. She simply couldn't have been produced anywhere else in the world. D'you know she'd made four million American dollars profit by the time she was twenty-six? On a single transaction at that."

Cuthbert sipped his gin and tonic, stared at the stem of his rubber tree. "Damn, fungus. I just don't know how we manage it, Hill. It never bothered the planters in Malaysia, I know because I once asked one. We must be doing something wrong."

Chan watched Hill cross the room with the same smile on his face. With a tolerant "yes, sir," like a batman to an officer, he placed a small earthenware hot plate filled with glowing charcoals on the table and left the room.

Chan replaced his glass on the table. "What kind of transaction?"

Cuthbert stood up, bent over another of the trees for a moment, then sat down again. "We'll have to back up a little. Emily's family, the Pings, they've been helping us for decades. Her father fled Shanghai in '49 but kept his connections there. During the sixties Beijing wasn't officially talking to us at all. To do business, we had to use go-betweens. Nothing unusual about that, the Chinese invented the go-between system—like everything else. Emily's an only child. Old Man Ping coached her to take over from him. When I was posted here twelve years ago, I gave her her first job: Xian. I knew I had to get in with him on the ground floor or the whole process of handover would be in jeopardy, and Emily seemed like a good choice. She knew Shanghainese, Xian's mother tongue, was well connected in southern China and already respected in Hong Kong." Cuthbert sipped his gin and tonic reflectively. "Women. Doesn't matter if it's business or bed, there's always a complication. Where's Hill?"

The Englishman's mind, Chan realized, raced at the same dangerous speed as his Jag. The diplomat left the room while he tried to catch up. Chan acknowledged that Cuthbert *was* answering a question: Chan's. Back in Cuthbert's office Chan had asked generally about the availability of top secret information for his inquiry; Cuthbert had commenced providing that information, using his own "need to know" criterion. Emily, it seemed, was a part of the answer.

Chan stood up to look for a bathroom. In the hall he glimpsed Cuthbert's library. Not for him a few dozen paperbacks rotting in a cupboard. Not even the cultivated man's set of bookshelves. It was a real library with shelves from floor to ceiling, a small oak stepladder, an oak lectern in front of a window for a man who liked to read standing up. Next to the lectern an ashtray on a pedestal. At another window a cigar-colored leather chesterfield awaited a reader's pleasure.

Cuthbert was back when Chan returned to the table. He resumed before Chan had sat down. Hill appeared at the same time with a wok of stewed lamb with dry bean curd, which he placed on the hot plate.

"The complication was her greed. She saw an opportunity. She'd bought the lease to a two-story Chinese house in Central out of her own money, but she didn't have the funds to redevelop. Banks weren't going to lend a twenty-six-year-old girl twenty million to build a high-rise, and her old man, being Chinese, wasn't either unless he owned a majority of the shares in the company. Spirited girl, can't deny it. Xian was only too pleased to help. He loaned her the money; she built her office block, made her four million profit—and discovered with a jolt that Xian owned her. The old devil had found the ideal way of laundering his ill-gotten gains; Hong Kong real estate. And Emily was the perfect front. Xian's not the kind of chap you say no to, not if you want to live in this part of the world. The next time he needed to find a home for a few hundred million, he used Emily. Gave her all the status, all the face, all the profit she wanted. But she wasn't free. I can't count the number of times I've had to talk her out of a suicidal depression. Lamb?''

"Emily depressed?"

Cuthbert used a large wooden spoon to serve the lamb. ''Mmm. Wouldn't believe it, would you? But you see, Xian is a life sentence. Even when he dies, she'll never be free; there's a whole army standing in line behind him. It's not that easy to live with, if you're the independent type. Of course, I couldn't use her again for anything delicate. It's part of my job to keep the lines open with Xian, though. It didn't much matter. Xian and I reached a kind of modus vivendi. We talk almost every day. There's a lot to do when you're delivering six million people to someone else for safekeeping.'' The Englishman studied Chan for a moment. ''I believe you know quite a lot about *laogai*?''

"I have a friend who does."

"I know, that tiresome old man in Wanchai."

"Who spent most of his life as a slave in the *laogaidui*."

"Quite. Then you'll understand Emily's self-disgust. She launders money for an organization that derives much of its profit from the use of slaves. Slaves to grow the opium, hump the guns, cook the morphine. Chinese slaves, just like in the Middle Ages. Poor girl, there is absolutely no way out for her. She really is a divided soul.

Tough as nails on the outside, riddled with self-loathing on the inside. Difficult to live with.''

Sometimes Chan couldn't believe how stupid he was. He should have seen it on the boat, should have caught the subtle clues in tones and eye contact, should have guessed, at least, when Cuthbert had warned him not to sleep with Emily. It was his job, after all, to detect.

He'd been misled, largely, by the Englishman's personality. One pictured him so much more easily with a cricket bat or a rifle or a leather-bound tome than a woman. The phrase "talk her out of a suicidal depression" echoed in his mind. An ex-lover's phrase; the sort of duty a gentleman acknowledges toward a woman he's dropped. Chan saw Emily, ten years younger, less promiscuous, more of a prudish Chinese girl perhaps, wandering through this bachelor's flat, trying to follow Cuthbert's encyclopedic conversation. Their arguments would have been worth listening to.

Cuthbert's revelations about Emily were fascinating but, on reflection, failed to carry the investigation any further.

"Mr. Cuthbert, I don't understand."

"Oh?"

Under the diplomat's raised eyebrows, Chan flustered. He sensed that he was being manipulated with a finesse that produced a twinge of nostalgia for the rough killers of Mongkok. He felt his chin jutting, along with other symptoms of a vulgar belligerence.

"Perhaps you're trying to help me by supplying this information about Emily Ping. But I don't see how it fits."

Cuthbert leaned back in his chair, smiled. "But surely that's *your* job, old chap?"

Chan felt his tongue start to trip on a stutter. "I—I—I thought, in fact I'm sure, there's information somewhere, secret, in a computer. . . . You know? All these people, Xian, Emily Ping, Clare Coletti—they must be known to MI6. I thought you would persuade the committee to give me access. I thought that's why I was invited here to lunch, to discuss it further."

Too late, Chan realized he'd used a fatal word.

"Committee? You mean some sort of hypersecret little group of gray men who know everything? Come on, Charlie, I thought back in my office we'd agreed that such a notion was fantastic, absurd?''

"I thought you were being ironic when you denied it."

Cuthbert wrinkled his brow, rubbed the side of his cheek. "You know, it's a hard thing for a man like me to admit, but I do believe you're just a tad too subtle for me."

Chan felt hairs prickle at the back of his neck. Cuthbert's mastery of diplomatic humility or sarcasm—with the English there was hardly a distinction—was effortless. Chan couldn't decide if it would have been worse if the political adviser were Chinese. As a Eurasian one did not always know which race one preferred to be screwed by.

"I've been told that I'm to be given every facility." Stubbornness was the last resort of the outclassed.

Cuthbert opened his arms. "Which is exactly why I invited you to lunch. Treat me like the horse's mouth. Ask away, anything you like, anything. I promise I'll do my best to answer. Haven't I just divulged half a file full of top secret information?"

"With zero risk," Chan muttered, looking away. "And I daresay nothing Emily Ping won't tell me herself when I question her. Which I suppose is why you told me at all."

That evening at his desk in Mongkok Police Station Chan wrote on a piece of scrap paper: What do General Xian, Emily Ping, Moira Coletti, Mario Coletti, Clare Coletti have in common? Were they all invented in China? Does Cuthbert know?

To clear his mind, he walked to the warehouse to check the cameras. To his surprise, some of the film had been exposed. Someone had been in the warehouse and stood close enough to the fluorescent light fixture to interrupt the infrared beam. When he called forensic the next morning, a technician told him there was a queue for the lab; development of the film would take a few days.

39

On the underground to Arsenal Street Chan watched a *gweilo* go into stress. Despite efficient air conditioning, sweat pods exploded over his red face, he started to shake and enlarged pupils indicated mounting panic. Chan wondered if he would have to be a good policeman and take the foreigner off the train, but at the next station the middle-aged white man found the control to squeeze himself out of the compartment onto the platform. Through the window Chan watched him lean against a wall and breathe deeply. Not a danger to society, apparently, just another Westerner who didn't know how to be a sardine. None of the Chinese in the vicinity had noticed that a psychological event had taken place; they remained in a compacted upright state, minding their own business like good sardines.

At police headquarters a message at reception asked him to go straight to Riley's office on the fourth floor. Riley stood up when Chan entered. So did Aston and a tall American in his fifties.

"Ah! Charlie." Riley beamed and turned to the American. "This is the best goddamn detective on the Pacific Rim." From somewhere he had acquired a cigar and an American accent. "Charlie, allow me to introduce our colleague from the other side of the world, Captain Frank Delaney of the New York Police Department."

Delaney stood up, held out a hand. He was a little over six feet, balding elegantly from the brow, a handsome man. Chan noticed the soft brown eyes, a woman's eyes, except that they fixed on him for a moment longer than was polite, performing a judgmental scan.

A cop's eyes after all. He wore a cop's suit too: police blue in creaseless artificial fiber. Under it he wore a cream shirt, no tie.

"Charlie, I was just saying how grateful I am to you guys for seeing me at such short notice—"

"Not at all." Riley waved his cigar. Chan waited.

"I saw the fax that Inspector Aston here sent off and figured the simplest thing was just to get on a damned plane. Expensive maybe, but if I can tie this one up on a twenty-four-hour trip, it frees me for more important things." Delaney grinned. "Like the World Series maybe."

Riley laughed loudly. "World Series, love it. You guys play the best kind of football."

Aston exchanged glances with Chan; both looked at Delaney, who smiled.

Riley spoke around the cigar that he had clamped between his teeth. "I've booked a conference room on the second floor; we could mosey on down." He led the way downstairs. The brass plate on the door read INTERVIEW ROOM, SENIOR OFFICERS ONLY.

They sat at a long brown table with a view over the street.

"Sure is an interesting place," Delaney said. "Never been here before. Heard a lot about it, though."

He bypassed Riley, looked to Chan for a signal.

"How can we help?" Chan said.

Delaney reached down to a slim plastic briefcase, placed it on the table. He unzipped it, took out a plain file, began leafing through.

"This is the fax Inspector Aston—"

"Dick, please," Aston said.

"Right. This is the fax you sent, Dick. Now, I understand you've positively identified the girl, right?"

"Right," Aston said. "One PI, two unidentified."

"We obtained dental records," Riley said.

Delaney nodded. "Can't argue with that. And the girl is Clare Coletti, right?"

Riley nodded vigorously. "Sure is."

"Well, we have a short file on Clare Coletti. It's short because she was only ever busted for one thing, possession of marijuana. But it's the kind of file that ties up with an awful lot of other files. Mob files. She was associated with the Corleone family in Brooklyn for about half her life. And toward the end she was associated with another kind of mob too. I guess you guys know all about the 14K Triad Society?"

Riley and Aston nodded.

"Right. Well, they have a branch in New York. All the big triads do. Most of the time they only do business within the Chinese community. They import heroin, run prostitution, run rackets, all the usual mob things. We don't have an awfully good track record in nailing them for the usual reasons. First, as a social menace they just don't compete with the local mob, or the Colombians, or the Sicilians—or the Russians these days. Second, they're real hard to penetrate. We don't have many Chinese cops who speak Cantonese or Mandarin or Chiu Chow, and we can't afford to set them up as sleepers for years on end. A lot of the time we need them for interpretation and other work with the Chinese community. And then, frankly, and don't quote me on this, there's a feeling in the NYPD that comes down from the mayor himself that if all they're doing is muscling their own people, well, let's say that's a containable problem." Delaney looked at Chan. "I don't want to cause offense here, but I guess most jurisdictions take a pragmatic view of resource allocation?"

"You betcha," Riley answered for Chan.

Chan lit a cigarette, waved a hand. Delaney gave him a second look. Chan half closed his eyes as if listening to another voice.

"But just recently there have been some disturbing—very disturbing—developments. It's like all the world's major mobs have been seeing the sense of living in peace so they can exploit the rest of us. We know there's been a number of deals between the American Mafia and the Colombians and a separate one between the Mafia and some Russian gangs. Then it became pretty obvious that our local boys were helping the 14K to shift heroin. The only way they can supply outside the Chinese community is by using the Italian mob; nobody else has the network, and the Chinese community is so insular that even the most desperate smack or crack addict doesn't think about crossing from Mott Street to Mulberry Street to get a hit. Mott Street is Little Italy; Mulberry Street is Chinatown —they're side by side in Lower Manhattan.''

"Sure,'' Riley said.

Delaney paused. "You guys mind if I take off my jacket?''

Under the jacket Chan saw an American muscle pack starting to melt, a man who had once looked after himself. His facial skin too was better than many Americans of his age; at least it was less lined, but there was a grayness underneath. Chan noticed a gold signet ring, the odd glimpse of a thin gold chain through the open neck of his shirt. Every now and then those soft brown eyes clouded and half closed in a wince. Chan wondered if the big American was fighting some kind of pain.

Aston sat on the edge of his seat.

"I can take you down the long route or the short route—I don't mind,'' Delaney said. "I guess what's coming is sort of obvious.''

Riley looked at Chan. Noncommittal, Chan took a long draw on his cigarette. Aston seemed embarrassed.

"Maybe the short route. Or even the long one,'' Riley said. "What d'you say, Charlie?''

Chan smiled at Riley. "I'll let you decide, John.''

Delaney watched Riley hesitate. "Right. Well, the short route is just this. It seems that after her one and only drug bust Clare Coletti was cut off from the mob. Particularly, she was dumped by the middle-ranking mobster she'd been having an affair with since she was in her mid-teens. We have reason to think she had a heroin habit too. She was bright, though; got a B.A. from New York University under mob patronage. That's what threw us. Why educate her, then dump her? After all, a mob isn't so different from a corporation: You make an investment in a person or a machine, you want performance, right? In retrospect we wonder if the year or so Clare spent out in the cold was a ploy to shake our interest in her. We know that during that year she got interested in China— not a natural topic for a Bronx girl like her. Then about two and a half months ago she was seen getting on a plane bound for Hong

Kong. On the same plane were two members of the New York chapter of the 14K Triad Society.''

Delaney pulled out two sheets of paper from his file, passed them to Chan. At the top of each sheet was a mug shot of a Chinese male. The sheet gave details of dates of birth, Social Security numbers. Both men were in their mid-thirties. Chan read that they were suspected White Paper Fans, finance officers. The first man's name was Yu Ningkun; the second Mao Zingfu. Both were romanizations of Mandarin names. The two men were mainlanders and Mandarin speakers. He studied what seemed to be an extract from an NYPD file. Each was suspected to be an expert money launderer and part of the narcotics side of the business. Neither had a criminal record in the United States. Farther down the page he saw that they had emigrated from Shanghai in the late 1970s, probably through triad connections using the snakehead route down the Pearl River from Guangzhou.

While Chan was reading, Delaney said: ''The fingerprints you sent us—ones you found on a plastic bag containing heroin?—they belong to these two guys.'' Delaney coughed.

''The next thing I have to tell you is kind of, ah, delicate.'' He coughed again. ''As you probably know, when it comes to mob matters, we work pretty closely with the FBI. And the bureau has, ah, resources and powers we don't have. I'd be obliged to you if you'd keep this confidential. Contrary to certain guarantees of privacy that American citizens enjoy, we were able to persuade the bureau to procure dental records, the dental records of Yu and Mao. I've brought copies for you to use.''

Aston's mouth opened. ''The FBI burgled their dentists?''

Aston reddened as he saw the long look exchanged between Chan and Delaney. Riley played with a government ballpoint.

''That's not a very diplomatic question to ask, Richard.'' Chan seemed almost amused. Not so Delaney.

Riley looked from Chan to Delaney. ''Damn right.''

''Sorry,'' Aston said.

Delaney nodded.

''We won't tell anyone,'' Chan said. He patted Aston on the

back. "He's a good cop, smart. It's just that he hasn't mastered the diplomatic side of the business yet. Not like John here."

Riley beamed.

Chan gave Aston a big smile. "Are there any other questions you have for Captain Delaney, Richard?"

Aston struggled. "No, no." He waved a hand. "I suppose I'm missing something as usual, huh?"

Chan gave Delaney a wide grin. "We'll have the dental records sent down to forensic in a minute. It should only take half an hour to get a preliminary view." Chan looked at Riley. "I have a confession, John. Every time I try to get forensic to do something on the double, they look at me as if I haven't got enough stripes to crack the whip. I wonder, someone with your authority . . ."

Riley stood up as if under orders. "Sure thing. If I have to, I'll kick ass."

When Riley had left the room, Chan said to Delaney, "Look, it's getting late. How about you leave us the dental records, go back to your hotel to freshen up, meet us for a drink later? Such a long way you've come, Dick and I would like to show you a good time. Right, Dick?"

Delaney produced a big American smile. "Well, that's good of you, Charlie, real good. To tell the truth, I was wondering what I was going to do while I was wide-awake with jet lag in the wee hours of the morning."

40

Wanchai's fame grew out of the Vietnam War. Only a couple of hours' flight from Saigon, Hong Kong was a convenient place for short R & R stops, and Wanchai was where the flesh was sold. That was before Hong Kong turned into a sophisticated financial center. Nowadays the sex was mostly in the neon: Hot Cats Topless Bar; Purple Pussycat; Sailor's Comfort; Popeye's; the Mabini Bar; Wild Cats. Punters who were serious about taking one of the girls back to a room could still do so, but for that price marriage might have been cheaper. Most of the profit was made on the drinks, fifty to a hundred times more than the price in a normal bar. The premium was for the privilege of watching Asian girls in swimming costumes gyrate around chromium poles that sprouted out of the platform behind the bar.

Chan let Aston lead the way down Lockhart Road; he and Delaney followed.

"Guess you know the area real well, hey, Dick?" Delaney called to Aston's back. He'd changed into white trousers, sneakers, a yellow short-sleeve shirt. Chan liked the way the New York cop took in the street in a snapshot, filed it away. A real pro. Chan supposed that for Delaney Wanchai held no temptations. It was mostly a light show. A forest of illuminated signs grew like incandescent mushrooms out of the walls, reaching out to the money that passed underneath.

"You can buy anything in Wanchai," Aston said over his shoulder, "any time of the day or night. Sauna, noodles, steak and chips, television set, Walkman, ticket to San Francisco—anything."

"I bet. Fascinating place."

"I suppose New York's just the same?"

Delaney looked around to give the question justice. "Oh, this is kind of easier on the mind. Very civilized actually. All I see is a lot of people letting their hair down, having a good time without losing respect for each other. Haven't noticed a single homicide in the ten minutes we've been walking."

Chan laughed. He felt comfortable with Delaney now that he understood him better. As expected, the dental records had confirmed that Jekyll and Hyde were Yu and Mao. He felt the case easing toward a conclusion. It made him feel almost light-headed. Homicide could be like that. You solved the mystery, and for no good reason in the world you felt as if you'd brought the dead back to life.

"Try Popeye's?" Aston said.

"Why not?" Delaney said. "Okay with you, Charlie?"

They crossed the road to the short concrete wall in the center. Aston hurdled over without touching the top, grinned. Chan hitched one leg over, then the other. He was surprised to see Delaney having trouble. He offered his arm as the American paused halfway across the wall.

"You okay?"

Delaney nodded. "Just don't seem to be able to take it the way I used to."

"Climbing walls?"

"Life."

He grimaced as he lifted a leg over the wall. His face was gray when they reached Popeye's. Over a beer he took out a small box of pills, swallowed one.

"Don't know what it is—first started noticing it couple of months ago. Diet doesn't seem to make any difference. Tried giving up drink, but that didn't help. Just age, I guess. Sorry to be a pooper. Maybe I should have stayed in my hotel after all."

They sat at the bar roughly on a level with the pubic bones of the dancers, who were humping invisible lovers with knees bent, legs open wide, fists punching the air in time to an old number

from Fine Young Cannibals. Chan envied their energy. Most of the
girls were Filipinas or Thais; one or two were Chinese; three came
from Vietnam. Every few weeks vice busted the bars, deported the
girls who had come on tourist visas and overstayed. Generally vice
did a good job in Wanchai, striking a balance between permissible
entertainment and serious threats to the health of the community.
Ever since AIDS people took a more sober view of Wanchai and
the bars.

"You buy me one drink?"

The Chinese woman in her late forties in a miniskirt, tank top,
high heels had drifted in behind them. Chan had seen her waiting
on the street by the door. Rouge made apples of her cheeks; her
lips were buried under red cupid bows.

"Well, I don't know, Mother." Delaney looked at Chan. "Do
we buy the lady a drink or not?"

Chan spoke rapidly to her in Cantonese, brushed her off with
twenty dollars from his wallet.

"Let's sit at a booth," Chan said.

They found a spare booth between an American serviceman who
had a girl on either side and an Englishman who was speaking
earnestly to a Vietnamese girl.

"You'll like England," Chan heard him say, "except for the rain."

"Wain? What is wain?"

"Water—from the sky."

"Oh, England wain a lot?"

"Yes. And it's cold."

"I got you. I don't care."

"I'm going to save you," the Englishman said.

Aston sat on the outside of the booth with his face to the bar.

Delaney smiled at Chan. "We gonna get any sense out of the
inspector tonight, d'you think?"

Chan shrugged. It was hard to tell where the magnetism began.
The dusky girls behind the bar had trouble keeping their eyes off

the blond young cop with deep blue eyes, and he wasn't trying too hard to put them off. His head moved up and down with their cleavage as they bounced to U2.

After the second beer Aston walked to the end of the bar to use the toilet. Chan leaned forward, twitched. "May I ask a very personal question, Frank?"

Delaney's eyes flicked over him. It took only microseconds for the street alertness to return to the captain's face. He sipped his beer.

"Sure, Charlie. What's on your mind?"

"I hope you don't think this is disrespectful after all you've done for us today, but one thought keeps crossing my mind."

"Shoot."

"Is your real name Mario Coletti?"

Aston returned from the toilet.

"How is it down there? Safe to take a leak?" Delaney asked Aston.

"Crowded. And there's a transaction going on between a punter and the mama-san in one of the men's cubicles. But yes, it's safe."

Delaney nodded. Even as he rose to his feet, the strain showed. He waited a second for dignity to return, then strode down the aisle toward the toilet. Chan saw a couple of pairs of slim naked arms reach out to him from the booths as he passed.

"Is he okay?" Aston said.

"I think he has a medical problem, Dick. You know, on reflection this wasn't such a good idea on my part. We could give him an out after this beer, maybe?"

Disappointed, Aston nodded. "I'll say I have to go—on duty?"

"That would do it. I'll say the same."

"It won't be very convincing since you're the one who invited him out."

Chan frowned at his own stupidity. "No, true. You go first; then I'll think of something."

• • •

Delaney and Chan watched Aston leave with backward glances to the dancers.

"I think he'll be back here in twenty minutes," Chan said. "Maybe we should find another bar."

Delaney got up and took out his wallet.

"No." Chan pushed Delaney's hand away. "It'll be roughly a hundred percent cheaper if I do it."

"Hundred percent?"

"They know me; at least the mama-san does."

He walked to the back, talked to a Chinese woman in her fifties for a few minutes, rejoined Delaney on the street.

"I used to work vice. In fact I think I've worked everything. Homicide, though, that's different. Some tasks in life just have your name stamped on them all the way through. You ever find that, Frank?"

In a smooth movement the American passed an arm down Chan's back. "You're not wired, are you?"

"No."

"You're sure?"

"In this heat? I don't even wear underpants."

The American sighed. "You win, Charlie. You can call me Mario."

"Maybe we need somewhere really noisy."

"I think so too," Coletti said.

In the New Makati a live Filipino band was billed to take the stage. More than a girlie bar, this was a genuine pickup joint. Filipina maids with one night a week to spend finding a second financial source, maybe even a husband, crowded near the bandstand in groups of tens, chattering and laughing, their black eyes flickering over everyone who entered. Young Western men stood at the bar, grinning like sailors who have come across shoals of fish. Couples who might have just met or been married for decades stood drinking, talking, fighting. There didn't seem to be anyone in the bar with the time or interest to eavesdrop. Chan ordered two pints of lager, took them to a small platform attached to a pillar where Coletti was standing.

"That was pretty good, Charlie. I was gonna tell you sooner or later, of course."

"Of course."

Coletti gave the first convincing laugh of his visit. "You're a real crack-up, Charlie. Okay, so I wasn't going to tell you."

"No?"

"How did you guess? Moira describe me down to the last detail? That's not like her."

"No, nothing like that."

"That famous Chinese intuition—Charlie Chan strikes again? You're an ace, you could just smell the deception, right?"

"It comes from my karate days. You develop a martial art to a fine degree, purify your mind, and your skill spreads into every area of life. Would you believe my master could castrate a fly and leave its wings still intact?"

Delaney reassessed Chan, who held his gaze.

"Wings still intact? That would have been something to see."

Chan lit a cigarette without offering one to Delaney. "Actually I checked with immigration. You used your own passport. No one called Delaney entered Hong Kong in the last twenty-four hours. Someone called Coletti did, though."

Chan sipped his beer. Coletti scanned the room.

"You know, Charlie, you might just be the smartest cop on the block. In the NYPD we all stopped thinking a long time ago— something to do with Western decadence. People just stop asking the important questions. Anything more exalted than money and flesh is a conversation killer."

Four young Filipino men with long black hair, denims cut off at the thigh, T-shirts with sunsets bursting from their solar plexuses walked onto the low stage, picked up guitars and started in to "I Just Called to Say I Love You."

The crowd of Filipinas near the stage began to sway and twist with the music.

"Hey, that's a perfect imitation." Coletti looked genuinely impressed. "And they didn't spend twenty minutes tuning their guitars."

"What's more important than money and flesh?" Chan said. "God? drugs? Family?"

Coletti popped another pill into his mouth, swallowed it with a long slug of beer.

"It's cancer, Charlie. Of the colon. Moira doesn't know, and I'd be obliged to you if you didn't tell her. I'll tell her in my own way someday soon. She didn't give anything away when she came back, by the way, but there was a cute Irish look in her eye. I was pleased for her, honest. She's had a tough ride. Since she met me, actually. She had to come and see me, of course. Clare was my daughter too."

"No cure? Chemotherapy?"

The American shrugged. "Sure, they can delay it, cut out bits of you, expose you to radiation till your hair falls out and you look like you're dying of AIDS. Some people overcome it with sheer will, so they say. But I'm Italian. I have a sense that God's telling me my time is up. Know what I mean?"

Half the young men at the bar began moving crabwise in the direction of the swaying dancers. Giggles and smiles burst out as the first contacts were made. Girls who had been dancing with girls were now half dancing with boys. Coletti was watching them.

"I don't want my youth back, Charlie. I'd only abuse it all over again. My problem was overabundance: I was spoiled. And I always wanted more. Now I'm just trying to set the record straight. Italians like to die in peace; it's important in our culture."

Chan watched the dancers too. He hadn't thought about it before, but it was in this bar that he'd first met Sandra. Not so long ago, just a few years really, he'd been like any one of those young men, who, now that he studied them, were not really so young. She'd called him with her eyes from the moment he'd walked in, although he'd gone straight to the bar and drunk for an hour before walking up to where she was waiting. Chemistry, she'd called it.

"I agree, I don't want my youth back either. I don't want to be that dumb again. What record are you trying to set straight?"

Despite what he'd said, Coletti was enjoying exchanging glances with a blonde standing at the bar whom Chan hadn't noticed before. She was thirty-five going on forty. At that age it was hard for a woman to come to a bar like this and melt into the wallpaper. Coletti took his eyes away, smiled sheepishly.

"After Moira left, I ran wild. You develop a certain skill. I guess that's what vice is in a way, an ego skill you don't want to give up. I bet I won't get looks like that after the chemotherapy." He sipped his beer. "Clare, that's the record I'd like to set straight."

"You're not here officially at all?"

"No. You could have me busted for impersonating Frank Delaney. He's a pal of mine actually; he'd probably cover for me. But somehow I don't think you will."

"Why impersonate anyone?"

"To make it look official. Embarrassment. Because you know too much about me. You did sleep with Moira, right? So she talked to you. These days Moira talks a lot." When Chan didn't reply, Coletti said, "See what I mean? In our business we don't like to admit we're human. I'm here because I'm a pathetic dumb father who failed his wife and kid and has got cancer and can't think of anything positive to do except help with the investigation. After all these years what I really want is to be a good cop. Fuck." He looked Chan full in the face. He was using his soft eyes, those deep brown woman's eyes Chan had first noticed. "If we knew that one day our values would change, that we would finally grow up, we'd be more careful how we lived our lives."

Chan watched the other man's eyes look away across the floor. The blond woman was listening to a balding young man with ginger hair who made intense thrusting gestures with his hands. Her eyes returned to Coletti every so often, but the frequency was diminishing. Coletti flung a hand in her direction.

"The number of times I've gotten myself trapped by moments like that. You wake up two years and a lot of heartache later wondering why you didn't have the sense to go to bed early that night. If I'd stuck with Moira, I wouldn't have wasted my life. She told you I was with the mob, didn't she?"

It was Chan's turn to look around the room. A small group of Filipinas was holding together chattering in Tagalog, but most of the fifty or so girls who had been standing near the bandstand were with Western men now. At the bar some more Western women had appeared. They looked around hungrily, in a hurry, perhaps, to pass on to the next stage of the evening.

Chan always found it interesting how few Chinese men came to places like this. The ones who did usually drank alone, staring intensely into their beer. Like him. That night in bed Sandra had said she was attracted by his fierce independence, the obvious strength expressed by proud solitude. She hadn't noticed the racial wall he'd had to climb or the crippling shyness that took two pints of lager to dissolve. Even on his best nights he'd been capable of no more than one overture to a Western woman. If rebuffed, he'd go home to his flat to watch kung fu videos, like a good Chinese. The truth was, Western women were terrifying. Terrifying in their promiscuity, their fearlessness. Most of all in their bodies that were the foundation of a planet-wide advertising industry. All over the world it seemed that nothing was sold, nothing was bought without a nudge from a pair of Caucasian mammary glands to help the transaction along. What was a poor Eurasian boy to do? From puberty his hormones had been focused on the tits of the West.

"I'm not too clear," Chan said. It was a direct translation of the most overused phrase in Chinese. All over the People's Republic from Tibet to Shanghai his people were avoiding issues with those magic words. He added: "She said something about it."

Coletti nodded. "I can't blame her. I never saw it her way till now. Italians, poor ones anyway, we're brought up to see the U.S. as a potentially hostile environment where we need to pull together to survive. Taking money was just a part of it. I was a member of a tribe, that's the truth. And I will be till I die, actually. As Clare grew up, it wasn't so easy to keep it from her during her weekly custody visits. And she was intrigued. Moira never understood, but I did. It was very simple. Clare was growing up in the South Bronx just off Southern Boulevard in an environment more hostile than anything Moira or I had been exposed to in our youth. Indian Country, the cops called it. Alligators grow scales; snakes use poison; cats grow claws; dogs bite. Everything in nature adapts to the environment. What was a smart, attractive blond girl supposed to do? The boys were savage; the streets were a jungle. In the Bronx the government had abdicated. Big-time crime was the only activity that *was* organized. And Clare wanted to get ahead. I still don't blame her. I blame myself. I could have done better."

"She had a long affair with a mafioso. Moira mentioned that."

Chan was startled to hear Coletti laugh. "Alberto Gambucci. Short, fat, balding, never handled a gun in his life. A laundry man. When he found Clare in bed with a black girl, he came to see me and burst into tears."

Coletti shook his head. Amusement had collected around his eyes.

Chan lit a cigarette. "Most of your daughter's life is clear to me, except for the end. Two triad members? In Hong Kong?"

"We need more drinks."

Chan watched Coletti push through the dancers to the bar. He was still a striking figure, a man who'd never been afraid of any woman. Total confidence was a winning hand, even at fifty, it seemed. Coletti was talking to the blond woman and smiling while waiting for his drinks. The young man with ginger hair was scowling at the collection of upturned bottles behind the bar, turning his head as if to read them.

Coletti collected the two pints of lager, gave the blond woman one last charming smile, returned through the crowd while she glanced after him. The ginger man tried to resume the conversation with her, but she moved away.

"She was a dreamer," Coletti said as he put the mugs down on the Formica. "Very clever, in another age might have been an academic. As a kid she wanted to know about the stars. I thought she might be some kind of scientist. And she had a smack habit.

What does that add up to?'' He shrugged. ''A brilliant smack addict who knew almost nothing of the world outside the Bronx? Can you imagine the distorted view of reality in that kid's brain? It took her a year, but in the end she sold the idea to Gambucci, who sold it to the don.''

''China?''

''Right. China. Why not? It made perfect sense. The Sicilian cousins had beaten us in getting into bed with the Russians, but nobody was even thinking about China at that stage. Most New Yorkers have only a hazy idea where it is. Why not establish contacts at an early stage in the collapse of another huge Communist empire so that this time the American mafiosi can run all the currency scams, sell the tanks to Saddam Hussein, the AK-forty-sevens to the Palestinians, the rocket launchers to the IRA, fragmentation grenades to Colombians, grab all that morphine moving from the Golden Triangle? Before the collapse of the Soviet Union it would have sounded harebrained. Afterwards it seemed inevitable.''

''But nobody spoke Mandarin?''

Coletti laughed again. ''Right. Nobody spoke Mandarin. Approaching Chinese isn't like approaching Russians. It isn't like approaching anyone. How do you climb over the wall? Clare had an answer for that. Contacts between the mob and the New York triads had been pretty good for a decade. There's a lot of respect. Admiration, you might say. Their *omertà* is a lot more intact than ours. Ever hear of a triad member testifying in front of a grand jury?''

''So Yu and Mao were recruited?''

''Yeah. They were recruited. There's a deal, an understanding. The 14K thought it was a very good idea. They saw the potential and were realistic enough to see that they would need our contacts in making the sales. Middle Eastern terrorists don't speak Mandarin either. Neither do Colombians. At the same time the 14K saw an opportunity to outstrip the Sun Yee On, United Bamboo—the competition, in other words.''

Chan's brain was racing. It wasn't so much the story Coletti was telling; it was the magnitude of the enterprise. A twentieth-century female Marco Polo opening a new Silk Road from East to West. Except that silk had nothing to do with it.

The band was playing "Born in the USA." Coletti was right: Their imitation was perfect; it could have been Springsteen at the microphone. And on the floor in front of their eyes East had been meeting West for more than an hour. Joint ventures had already been agreed, the night taken care of. The ginger man was talking to the blond woman again. Now she was listening. It was that time in the evening when people began to be afraid of going home alone.

"One thing I can't understand," Chan said, "an organization like the American Mafia sends a young woman and two triad members to negotiate on their behalf? Would they do that?"

In the middle of swallowing more beer, Coletti shook his head. "Look at it from the other direction. Sending Clare, they had nothing to lose. It was a spearhead mission. Being a woman, it would have been easy to disown her if things went wrong. If she fucked up and lost her life, what did they lose? A dyke with a habit they could do without. And she was keen, keen. It was all her idea, her baby. I can almost be proud of her for that. And one other thing, who else would have gone? Have you any idea how afraid Italians are of the mysterious East? We have no structures out here, no references. But someone had to come. Once Clare had put the idea into their heads someone had to make the gesture. They almost got into a fever about it. It was only a matter of time before the competition thought of it. If the Sicilians tied up the East as well as Russia, it would be the biggest commercial organization in the world. Notice, I didn't say criminal organization, I said *commercial*. Nothing would be bigger, not McDonald's, not Shell Oil, not Coke—nobody. They would have a yearly turnover bigger than the gross national product of any country outside the USA and Japan. The Americans sent Clare to beat our cousins in Palermo."

"But something went wrong?"

"Yeah. Something did. Don't worry, I'm not here to find out what. I'm just here to tie up loose ends. The 14K, not the FBI, got ahold of the dental records. They want to know if their guys were the ones in the vat."

"That's why you're here?"

"I guess."

"The Mafia sent you on behalf of the triads?"

"I'm her father, aren't I?"

Not helping with the inquiry, then, or trying to be a good cop. On the contrary, obeying orders even while the cancer ate his intestine. It was the only way to leave the Cosa Nostra; Chan had read that somewhere. Maybe that's why Coletti wasn't putting up much of a fight against the disease.

As they were saying good night outside Coletti's hotel, Chan said, "Did Moira go and see you before she came out to Hong Kong?"

Coletti hesitated. "Sure. She had to. I paid for all of Clare's medical bills. I was the only one with enough influence with the dentist to get the records. Moira didn't even know who the dentist was."

Dental records again, Chan thought. They'd been a blessing throughout the case. If the truth were known, all the breakthroughs had come without any effort on his part at all. But then the reality of detection was often thus. The detective was merely a lamppost around which informers gathered to do their business.

41

In the beginning was the Word. But it was sung, not spoken. Prehistoric humans from Peking Man in the East to Cro-Magnon in the West used the full range of the vocal scale to sing instructions for the hunt, sing guidance to their children, sing reverence to the gods that provided the mammoths. They would have despised the flat, dead speech of modern times for the tuneless whitterings of ghosts. A few tongues retain an echo of that Neolithic music: French has it in glacé form, Italian tries harder than most, Thai can be lyrical, Mandarin has its moments of sublime tunefulness; but the oldest language in modern usage is also the most musical. With nine tones to condition meaning Cantonese can present a challenge to a tin ear from the Bronx.

Moira played the tapes, dutifully repeated: "*Nei ho ma?* How are you? *Nei hui bin do a?* Where are you going? *M sai jaau lak.* Keep the change."

The single-syllable words were difficult to memorize, but with effort she built a modest vocabulary. Where she suspected failure was in the rising and falling tones. The textbook warned that the same word could mean "mother," "box," "opium" or something even more controversial, depending on the tone you used and whether you ended on an up beat or a down beat. Even after hours of practice she found it hard to hear the tones when the instructor used them. She doubted she was reproducing them with any accuracy.

Since returning from Hong Kong, she had installed a fax machine in her small apartment. She typed out her answers to Chan's questions, reread them before transmitting to Mongkok Police Station.

STRICTLY PRIVATE AND CONFIDENTIAL

attn Chief Inspector S. K. Chan
Criminal Investigation Department (Homicide)
Mongkok Police Station

Dear Charlie,

Got your fax. Using your numbering, the answers to your questions are:

1. Yes, Mario came to see me when he got back. He's pretty sick; in fact he had to spend a couple of days in the hospital.

2. I'm sending some books by air that explain a lot of what I've been telling you about the expansion of organized crime and deals between the various mobs. You'll see that the Russian Mafia has done some important business with our local boys since the fall of the Soviet Union (it all started a bit before that, under Brezhnev as a matter of fact). I'm also including a report from some UN committee that sort of puts it in a nutshell.

3. Yes, uranium and other valuable radioactive metals are part of a black market run by American and Sicilian Mafia (mostly the Sicilians). Enriched uranium of the sort needed to build an atomic bomb has turned up in various places in Europe, including in the trunk of someone's car. It's been in all the main English-language newspapers. A couple of crooks nearly died of radiation poisoning a few years ago because they didn't know what they were handling. Unenriched uranium is more common.

4. Mario is right when he says that Clare was a fantasist. Even as a kid she lived in a world of her own, but she was also very smart. She was able to get people to do what she wanted most of the time. She had brains (from me—ha-ha!).

5. I don't know anything about the relationship between the local Mafia and the Chinese triads, but you'll see from the books I'm sending that there seems to be something going on.
Moira Coletti

P.S. I'm learning Cantonese. I don't need to tell you why. I'd like to see you again. It's all right if you don't want to, though.

In his office Chan reread the fax, then turned to the UN report *(Special Commission Report to the United Nations Assembly, March 20, 1990):* "International criminal organizations have reached agreements and understandings to divide up geographical areas, develop new market strategies, work out forms of mutual assistance and the settlement of conflicts . . . and this on a planetary level.

"We are faced with a genuine criminal counter-power, capable of imposing its will on legitimate states, of undermining institutions and forces of law and order, of upsetting delicate economic and financial equilibrium and destroying democratic life."

"What d'you think, Chief?" Aston said when he'd read the fax.

Chan gazed out of his office window. It gave an unobstructed view of some of the dirtiest air conditioners he'd ever seen on the other side of the street. It didn't stop the amahs from hanging washing out on long colored bamboo poles, though.

"I think this is getting too big for us. Much too big."

"Too big?"

"Think about it."

Chan left Aston alone in his office while he went to buy cigarettes. Fighting through the crowds to cross Prince Edward Road, he thought: *"Too big" is not quite the phrase. Too delicate?* Put another way, why hadn't he been stopped yet? The date on Moira's fax was two days ago. Everyone would have read it before it was passed on: the commissioner, the security chiefs, Cuthbert, everyone. And it was all there: the direction of his inquiry; the implications for the present and future governments of Hong Kong; the unspoken aspersions on the conduct of the People's Liberation Army over the border. The spade was under the rock. Did Cuthbert really want that? Did the commissioner? Xian? Chan promised himself a private fax machine installed at home as soon as he got the chance.

On the other side of the street an old lady a little under five feet tall sold every internationally known brand of cigarette from shelves in a steel frame set against the wall. It was a corner where addicts gathered, sure of being able to find a clean nicotine fix. Gitanes noires, Gitanes blondes, Camel, every Philip Morris, every Players, Italian cigarettes with unpronounceable names, Turkish, Russian. For those who preferred roll-ups there was Dutch Drum tobacco. For joints there were giant cigarette papers. The little old lady knew her clients and her business.

"You have Long March? Imperial Palace?" Chan said.

She glared, spit contemptuously. "Go back where you came from. I don't serve Communists." She turned her back.

"Okay, okay, just testing. Benson. Two packs."

He paid, opened a pack, took a few steps into the crowd surging toward the underground. Stop on any corner, look in any window, there was someone who had been maimed in body or soul by the Chinese Communist party. And that was when they were honest. Xian: Where did he get his Imperial Palace? By the truckload from across the border?

Mongkok may be the best place in the world to lose a tail, even if the tail in question is British-trained in the best Le Carré tradition. Granted they had the sense to use four Chinese, one woman and three men, and they were following all the rules. Two trailed behind, two in front with frequent excuses for halts and backward glances: shopwindows, shoelaces, something fallen out of a pocket, spectacles needing wiping. Chan was no spy, but he'd served time on the streets. He had a patrolman's eye. If one person in a thousand didn't fit, the fact nagged at his mind until he understood. At first he'd thought they were a gang of robbers assessing a future opportunity. It was only when he reached Nathan Road, turned to look in a window, walked on, turned back to look in the window again, drifted along with the crowd as far as the underground, then a third time turned back to the same window that he was sure that he was the object of their attention. They were discreet, professional, but when the mark goes back to the same spot three times, it's difficult to keep the cover.

Chan made a point of looking directly into the face of the woman, then of her male companion. He turned abruptly, looked at the other two. Cuthbert, he thought.

He returned to the underground, bought a ticket, passed through the barrier, then walked the length of the underpass to exit on the other side of Nathan Road. He merged into the mass of people struggling to step around the beggars stretched out on the pavement. Nobody wanted to have to touch the leper with his sores helpfully highlighted in orange lotion. Or the old man with his trouser rolled up to expose his stump.

Near the back of the police station he lit a cigarette, paused to think. What was it the Tibetans had said when the British invaded after hundreds of years of Chinese rule? When you have known the scorpion, you're not afraid of the toad? Probably he shouldn't have embarrassed the watchers by exposing them. It was bad form, another faux pas. Cuthbert would be hurt.

Chan was not going to stop, though. Not without a direct order. Or a bullet. Indeed he expected the next day to receive the developed photographs from the film he had retrieved from the warehouse.

That evening he left work early to buy a fax machine.

42

Chan installed his fax machine in the only room with a spare shelf, the kitchen. Ten yards of flex made a trail to the telephone jack in the dining room.

Japanese, Korean, German, Italian, Chinese, French; he found the English section at the back of the Panasonic manual. There was a facility for ten autodial numbers, but Chan only needed one. He recorded Moira's fax number, slid a sheet of paper into the machine until the rollers pulled it partway through. He waited, fascinated, while the machine digested his short note, murmured to itself, confirmed with three bleeps that the transmission had reached the Bronx and pushed the sheet out again. He reread it: "Thanks for the fax. It was good to hear from you. I'd like to see you again too. *Ho lak ngoh yiu:* Well, I must go now. *Joi gin:* See you. Charlie."

Proud of his achievement, Chan shaved and went back to work, anxious for those photographs.

A messenger finally arrived at 10:00 A.M. with a large brown envelope bearing the words "On Her Majesty's Service" in bold black type. Across it someone had used a red stamp: "Police, Secret." Aston watched while Chan tore the flap and spilled a small pack of photographs onto his desk. He was about to check through them when the telephone rang. At first the noise on the line sounded like static, then acquired a more human cadence.

"It's me," Saliver Kan said, still clearing his throat. "I think I can get what you want. It'll take a few days, and it's going to be expensive."

"How expensive?" Chan used his hard bargaining voice.

"Ten million."

During the Ming dynasty, or perhaps even as early as the Warring States period, a formal procedure developed applicable to the first stages of a trade: The vendor states an absurd price; the purchaser walks out of the shop and returns only when the vendor offers to negotiate, usually in a submissive tone ("Okay, okay, come back, we'll talk"). The age of the telephone replicated this everyday piece of theater with a form of words that has become equally hallowed over the years. "Fuck your mother," Chan said, and replaced the receiver.

One by one he began to sort through the pictures. From the camera that he'd placed by an entrance, several shots taken in quick succession showed a pair of blue jeans—ragged—and bare feet in plastic thongs. The image was blurred from the speed of the subject's movement, almost a run, Chan guessed. The telephone rang again. He ignored it. From one of the pillars a camera had caught a pair of emaciated hands like claws reaching up to the strip light. Aston came to stand by his side and picked up the telephone.

"Chief's busy," he said in passable Cantonese. Chan glanced up for a second, then returned to the pictures. "He says five million," Aston said in English with his hand over the mouthpiece, but by then Chan's hearing was drowned by a rush of perception that drained the blood from his cheeks. He stared at a blurred image of slightly tilted Eurasian eyes, short, thick black hair and a fine face with which he was familiar.

"Phone back later," Aston said into the telephone, and hung up. He stood by Chan's shoulder, stared at the picture that Chan found so disturbing—and understood nothing.

In his last year of school in the New Territories Chan had participated in some Outward Bound courses, products of the character-building aspect of the English education system. One afternoon the teacher and the group had left Chan all alone in the bush with a compass, a map, a flask of water and some rations. It should have been a simple map-reading orientation exercise, but the compass was jammed. Chan wandered around in the muggy heat, pretty sure of his direction but continually frustrated by the way the paths ran. Dense cloud obscured the sun. By nighttime he was feeling desperate, though he supposed that they would come looking for him eventually. Then with the change in temperature that occurs at night the clouds dispersed and the stars came out. He checked the Big Dipper, the last two stars of which, they had told him, always pointed to the North Star. There it was, the North Star, almost precisely where he'd least expected it to be. Shaking his head, he turned the map through 180 degrees and walked in the opposite direction. He was back at camp in an hour. Detection was sometimes like that.

With Aston watching he took a small knife with retractable blade out of a drawer, cut the photograph of the Eurasian face horizontally just under the eyes and placed the lower half over a copy of the picture of Clare that Moira had brought. He glanced up at Aston, who stared, disbelieving.

"But she's dead," Aston pointed out. "It's her murder we're investigating."

Chan looked into his eyes for a moment and then away. It was a hard lesson for the young, who had such rigid views on life, that victim and perpetrator were often interchangeable roles. It was a rare case where one did not, sooner or later, acquire attributes of the other. For the murder victim to turn into possible murderer, though, that did pose problems. And of course there was no proof. What sane cop would bet a blurred photograph against dental records? But Chan knew he was right.

"Check with every cosmetic surgeon with a practice in Hong Kong," Chan said. "Start with the best, the most expensive, and work down."

As he spoke, the telephone rang again. "Three million and it's a deal," Kan said, after a long snort.

"Two," Chan said.

"Two and a half."

"Two."

"Fuck your mother." By the submissive voice in which Kan spoke, Chan knew that the deal was concluded.

Fixing himself a late lunch of fried noodles at home, he stood and watched the fax machine roll out a message: "Wow! That was a quick response. Sure do appreciate it; at my age a girl doesn't like to be kept dangling. Say, do you have any old cop stories I haven't heard? That's about the only thing I miss from NYPD, those canteen yarns. I'll trade you. Jai gin."

Chan thought for a moment, wrote his reply and watched the machine go to work. If Moira's daughter was still alive, who was dead? Who knew?

Back at his desk he tapped a Benson out of the box and stared at the blurred Eurasian face in the photograph. He put the cigarette to his mouth and dialed Emily's number at the same time. He was surprised that the billionairess answered her own telephone.

Chan lit his Benson. "Hi."

"Who is this?"

"Your scuba buddy."

He listened to her breathing.

"I've been expecting you to call."

"I know."

"Come round tonight. I have a dinner engagement that'll take most of the evening, so make it about eleven-thirty."

"Shall I bring your present?"

A long pause. "Yes, why not?"

That evening he waited until the police station was reduced to its night skeleton staff. Then he strolled to the tea room and bent down under the sink to retrieve the plastic bag he had found concealed in *The Travels of Marco Polo*, after the trip on Emily's boat.

43

Opium: Chan knew all about it. The story begins with a field of poppies in the Shan states on the border between Laos, China and Burma. Hmong tribesmen collect the sap first in small wooden bowls, then bundle it in tiny bamboo parcels: raw opium. Chinese traders of the Chiu Chow clan exchange salt, iron bars, silver coins for the harvest that begins each year in February.

As a seventeen-year-old cadet he'd taken part in busts of some of the last opium divans of yesteryear. He remembered small rooms with bunk beds, bamboo pipes with bowls a third of the way up the stem, spirit lamps and the sweet, heavy smell. Emaciated prostitutes combined the vices, selling in one market, buying in the other. Whores aside, the clients were mostly men, often middle-aged. Chan remembered his first corpse. Everyone else in the divan was so stoned they had not noticed the old man die. The old man hadn't noticed either, to judge from the look of rapture on his face.

Opium was a subtle high that left the American warrior spirit unsatisfied, so when the number of GIs stationed in Vietnam increased to the hundreds of thousands, the Chiu Chow sought ways to improve their product. Encouraged by Ho Chi Minh, who saw the proliferation of the debilitating drug among the Americans as a legitimate war aim, and even by the CIA, which participated in the opium traffic from Laos to help pay for the war, the traders saw a once-in-a-lifetime business opportunity. In factories hidden in Hong Kong, Thailand, South Vietnam, Taiwan—anywhere but Communist China during its puritanical phase—raw opium was added to drums of hot water and dissolved with lime fertilizer and ammonia:

morphine. Boil the morphine with acetic anhydride for six hours at eight-five degrees Fahrenheit: brown heroin, known as brown sugar or simply Number 3. Asians smoked it or injected it like that and were satisfied, but the West needed a bone-jarring jolt to raise it from its strange despair. Add the Number 3 to alcohol, ether and hydrochloric acid. Sometimes there was an explosion that carried away the triad "cook" and most of his factory, but if performed well, the process produced Number 4 or pure white heroin; the American armed forces had found their high.

A hundred thousand GIs took their habit home, where it multiplied. The Chiu Chow adapted quickly to the huge new market on the other side of the world. With profit margins at over 1,000 percent they hardly bothered to smuggle plain opium anymore, and as a consequence nobody used it.

Well, almost nobody. Emily's secret package continued to baffle him. A setup? A test? A gift? Why opium?

It was close to midnight by the time Chan's taxi turned into Emily's drive. Expecting a servant to open the door, he was surprised that the mistress herself stood in the doorway leaning against the frame. She held the top of a green silk kimono together with one hand.

"You're late."

"I know." Chan held up a cheap black fiberglass briefcase. "I brought your gift back."

She let him in and closed the door behind him. He watched her lock all three bolts and switch on an alarm at a console by the door. A minute red light started to flash.

"Burglars are a risk, I guess?"

"Kidnappers. You know that."

She led him through the house to the veranda at the back. On a long marble table she had set out an opium pipe and a spirit lamp. He sat at the table, unlocked the black briefcase, took out the plastic bag with its sticky black contents, which he placed in front of her, locked the briefcase again.

He said: "I thought you were setting me up."

"I was. I was going to have you busted by an ICAC officer who wants promotion after June; then I changed my mind. Wasn't that nice of me?"

"Xian told you to get me under control?"

"Something like that."

"What changed your mind?"

She touched his cheek. "Oh, you're such a pretty boy I couldn't stand to see you get into trouble." She said it without a smile, almost mournfully. "I told him it wouldn't work. You're the martyr type: better death than compromise."

Chan scowled. "Just out of interest, why opium?"

Emily looked away over the Lamma Channel. "It's a family tradition. My father smoked; so did my grandfather. I never knew that Dad indulged every Friday night until Milton Cuthbert told me. When I confronted my father, he explained that working for the British, you need something to remind you from time to time that you're Chinese. For him, smoking was a way of making contact with the ancestors. For me, it brings relief from stress."

"I should arrest you."

"Why don't you?"

"You'd tell your friend Xian. He'd threaten to explode an atom bomb in Central."

Emily winced. "I know nothing about that. I heard the rumor about weapons-grade uranium from someone in government only yesterday. That's what I wanted to tell you."

"You asked me up here just to tell me that?"

She opened the package, lifted it up to her face, inhaled, set it down again.

"You must have spoken to Milton by now. I've heard that your investigation has expanded."

"It's becoming a very Chinese investigation. It grows without progressing."

She smiled thinly without looking at him. "You think I'm the world's biggest bitch?"

"*Laogai*," Chan said.

It was like hitting a fairground target and causing loud bells to

ring, except that the bells were violent tears. Chan thought of a
child in deep pain, searching for comfort while its body contorted
with sobs. A dedicated interrogator would drive home the advantage. Chan looked away, waited.

"Excuse me." She held the tears long enough to rise from the
table and walk quickly into the house. Chan heard a door bang and
more sobs muffled by the building. It took her fifteen minutes to
recover herself and return. She had switched kimonos. This one
was an austere black drawn tightly up to her neck.

She sat down again more or less composed. "Perfect timing. I
must congratulate you."

"You wanted to know what I knew. Now you know. You want
me to go?"

Her eyes hovered over the opium. "Such a reluctant detective.
And everyone said you were a fanatic."

Chan lit a cigarette. "I don't like wasting time. You can help
my investigation because you know something about Clare Coletti.
This even a dunce like me can deduce. You are Xian's main front
in Hong Kong, so you know why he's so damn interested in this
case. Either you want to talk or you don't. I can't make you do
things. You belong to Xian. He bought you ten years ago."

Until he had spoken, Chan had not realized how angry he was.
He was begging a possible accomplice to provide information because she was rich and powerful enough to despise the law. This
was all wrong. No, it wasn't wrong; it was Chinese. Refusing to
look at her, he stared into the billion-dollar night. Below, moving
lights—red, green and white—traced the movements of tankers.
He felt her hand move over the table, slip over his own.

"Sleep with me."

"No."

"How about underwater? We can use the pool."

He faced her in surprise.

She smiled. "Joke." She touched her hair. "Is disliking me more
difficult than you thought?"

"Yes," Chan admitted. "But I won't sleep with you."

She withdrew her hand. "Then if you want your answers, you'll

JOHN BURDETT

have to share a different pleasure with me. You're right, there's nothing in the world you can do to make me talk. Only the guilt can do that. Without opium I don't think I'll have the guts; we can't all be righteous heroes. Why should I smoke alone? If you want to solve your case and save the world, a little smoke is no price at all to pay."

"No."

She held his chin between finger and thumb and pulled his head around. "That no wasn't half as convincing as the first. I think you like the edge. I think you made love to me eighty feet under water because you're as curious about death as I am. Opium can take you into death. It's a privilege the poppy offers people like us. With the body anesthetized, you walk through a door, and there it is: eternity in all its glory. Who knows what a man like you might find there?"

He watched her skilled fingers roll a tiny piece of the opium into a ball. She heated it on a pinhead over the spirit lamp. Her movements were too quick to follow. In less than a second she was holding the pipe up, tilted sideways over the spirit lamp. She sucked while jabbing the bubbling black ball with the pin to allow air to pass. She consumed the first dose in a second.

"Don't try it so you'll never know how good it is, isn't that what they say? To someone like you, though, that's an inducement. Take the pipe."

"No."

"I can tell you everything you want to know. Not just about the case. I know so much. I'm weary with all this knowledge. I want to share it with a true hero who will know what to do with it."

She touched his hair delicately with the tips of her fingers. It was eerie how her personality had begun to alter. He sensed a burden not of knowledge but of loneliness. She seemed almost shy. Her voice was softer and slower with a girlish lilt of longing. "Your friend, for example, that old man in Wanchai—I know about him."

"You do?"

"I knew about him long before I knew about you. So many times

I've been on the point of going to see him. I have information he could use, a whole head full. When you protected him, I admired you. I wanted to be like you. I wanted even more to be like that old man. Can you imagine, the purity of his soul? To live at peace with oneself like that . . ."

Her arm was around his shoulders. In her other hand she held the pipe. "It's not like sex, my friend. I promise you, you'll feel no connection, no obligation afterwards. Just a wonderful peace."

He watched her prepare the pipe again. "Imagine, eight whole hours free from the demon that drives you. It will be the only holiday of your life." She caressed his head. "Be kind to yourself for once; it's only addictive if you do it a lot."

When she had finished preparing the pipe, he hesitated, then bent forward to inhale. In the bowl of the pipe the black ball burned away.

He was disappointed to find that the drug had no apparent effect, except for a mild improvement in his patience. He slipped a hand into his pocket to flick a switch on the microphone that would activate the tape recorder and waited until she had smoked another pipe of her own. The receiver was locked with the tape recorder in the black briefcase.

"Milton told you he used me. But I'm sure he didn't tell you what for?"

"No, he didn't."

"I was a go-between. Xian wasn't happy about the Joint Declaration between London and Beijing; nobody had consulted him about it. He insisted on a secret protocol. Milton had to agree to his demands. There's no border control on anything Xian wants to move out of China into Hong Kong. That was the deal. Of course it's not the sort of thing anyone wanted written down, and neither Xian nor Milton was openly talking at that stage. That's why they used me."

Chan sat still, trying to absorb a simple phrase: *no border control*. He should have guessed; the most appalling answers are often correct. So much fell into place when the message of those three words was properly absorbed. He saw the outline of a fine historical irony:

England as reluctant comprador; a drug that was steadily corroding Western societies.

"They let him bring anything in?"

"Anything at all. And he can ship from here too. Of course, once it leaves Hong Kong, it's his risk."

"And he runs the army in southern China?"

"He and sixteen other generals. Little by little they've bought up more than half the major public companies in Hong Kong, using proxies, of course. They've bought Hong Kong. It's simple, but it's brilliant. Shanghai collapsed in '49 because the West took all its money away. They won't do that this time because half the local companies are supported by Chinese shareholders with unlimited funds. As the British found last century, nothing is more reliable than narcotics."

"You're their agent. You launder the money, procure the proxies, set up the companies. That's what you do?"

She nodded. "When it started, I didn't know anything about *laogai*. I'd like you to believe that."

It was possible. *Laogai* even now was hardly more than a rumor. The press rarely mentioned the slaves in the gulag over the border. In Mongkok it was no more than a Chinese whisper. Chan thought of an old man with wispy beard, John Lennon T-shirt and tunnels for eyes.

After the second pipe Chan felt a deep relaxation penetrate to the core of his being. Nerves that had been clenched for a lifetime stretched like cats and purred.

Emily carefully replaced the pipe on the table. "Before Milton I was a normally romantic twenty-six-year-old. I'd had only one other lover. Since him I've had hundreds, but no one even comes close. It was a bizarre triangle. I found him fascinating. Xian needed me. Milton was transfixed by Xian. At first I didn't understand. Milton's the most cultivated man I've ever met. His Mandarin is better than mine; his Cantonese is perfect; his Latin and Greek are not half bad. His main hobby is translating classical Chinese poets. Xian is a rough peasant with no education, twenty words of English and the heart of a butcher. But Xian's instinct for power is infallible.

Only Mao came close, and he's dead. Milton told me once that he'd trade a lifetime's erudition for one minute with a finger on a true lever of power. He's a bystander, and Xian's a major player; that's the difference. Another pipe.''

''No.''

''It's the price you must pay, Chief Inspector. Nothing is free in Hong Kong, and you have nothing to offer except your virginity.''

He watched while she prepared the pipe and found himself dutifully inhaling the sweet smoke once again.

''Sex and opium are the best anesthetics. With sex you forget everything for a moment; with opium you remember even your worst transgressions with pleasure.''

''Clare Coletti,'' Chan said. The words emerged slowly as if from another mouth in a graveyard tone. *''She's still alive, isn't she?''*

He had saved the question until now, expecting a dramatic reaction, but Emily appraised him as if checking his level of intoxication. She looked away, ignoring the question. ''Milton taught me to smoke, of course; Dad warned me not to. But I guess Milton knew I would need it. He said if it was good enough for Thomas De Quincey and Sherlock Holmes, it was good enough for him. He's very disciplined about it, of course.''

''Sherlock Holmes used cocaine,'' Chan said, and almost giggled. He remembered the diplomat's extreme languor on the boat that night. He felt Emily's eyes studying him.

''It had to be you; there's really no one else I can talk to. And it had to be opium because by morning this will be no more than an opium dream. You won't even be sure if you're remembering correctly. You'll have no proof.'' She gave a short, humorless laugh. ''For your purposes it really would have been preferable to screw me.''

''Clare . . .'' He found he had difficulty remembering the last name. How odd, it was a surname he'd been living with for weeks.

''Coletti.'' Emily placed both hands palms down on the marble table, stared at them for a moment. She heaved a great sigh. ''Is she still alive? Perhaps she is. Does it matter that much? Let me start at the beginning. For years Xian had been thinking about link-

ing up with an overseas organization on a permanent footing. He
started negotiations with people in New York. He never mentioned
anything to me about weapons-grade uranium. Then all of a sudden
the most ridiculous woman in the world shows up, and—''

He had been exerting all his will to concentrate on what she was
saying. He tried to convince himself that it was important, but
somewhere in the middle distance other events of far greater sig-
nificance were taking place. It was rude to ignore Emily, and there
was his professional reputation at stake; he bent his mind back to
the case. In his bending it, a tension grew that he was unable to
control.

It happened suddenly, like a door springing open that had been
locked for an age. In a blink he was not with Emily anymore. It
was a summer's day, and he was with Jenny on their old sampan.
He noticed the colors—golds, blues and greens—how perfect they
were, like the finest porcelain. Jenny was pointing to something in
the water. He followed the direction of her arm. Mai-mai floated
under the surface of an emerald sea. He thought at first that she
was dead, but she turned her head to the sky. When she saw him,
she smiled and beckoned eagerly. In slow motion he stood at the
end of the sampan, gathered his energy and sprang in a perfect dive
into the sea. He followed where she led, down, down, slowly down
into the depths of a friendly ocean.

When she saw that the chief inspector had slipped away into an
hallucination, Emily stood up. She stared at him transfixed. Under
the influence of the drug the tension that normally afflicted him had
fallen away. He looked boyish, naive—and beautiful. For a moment
she toyed with a wicked thought, before discarding it as impractical.
Some sins really were for men only. With a sigh she walked slowly
toward the swimming pool. The problem with opium was the speed
with which one built up a resistance. She would need ten pipes
before she could reach Chan's rapturous state. But for that kind of
excess, one paid a price. Sometimes in place of rapture these days
she often found demons: a line of gray, emaciated Chinese slaves

with their hair in queues, stretching to infinity. Before each ghoul she knelt to ask forgiveness, and each one promised to forgive her as soon as she had been forgiven by his neighbor. It was a form of mental torture by repetition that exhausted her, when in the past the drug had always left her refreshed.

Even with the low dosage of the drug in her blood she could feel the slave-ghosts around her, a whispering army no more substantial than wind and just as persistent, calling her name with voices dry as grass. Quickly she returned to the table and her opium pipe. The only cure for opium phantoms was more opium. Sherlock Holmes and Thomas De Quincey both knew that.

Chan emerged from the opium dream in exactly the position in which he had entered it: elbows on the marble table, leaning forward eagerly, determined not to miss some compelling drama taking place in the middle distance. Even his brow was furrowed in the same way as five hours before. It was daylight now, and as the drug receded, he began to sweat in the glare of the sun. He searched the house, which was empty. Not even a servant appeared from the quarters at the back. Suddenly remembering and delving in his pocket, he found that the miniature microphone and transmitter were gone. The black briefcase that had contained the receiver and tape recorder was under the table where he had placed it. It was open—and empty. For ten minutes he stood motionless while every word and event from the previous night, both imagined and real, faded like a construction of mist even as he tried to grab at it with the open fingers of his mind. She had made a fool of him, this billionairess who was above the law, but he was still too opiated to care.

The swimming pool was empty too, and more tempting than money. He stripped, dived naked into the perfect blue: down, down. The beauty of opium was that the next day you felt as if you'd had the best sleep of a lifetime, even if someone did steal your dignity while you were dreaming. Still beautifully relaxed, he dressed and went to work.

• • •

By early evening, though, the drug had leached every ounce of
energy from his body, and concentration had evaporated. He went
home early, lay down on his bed and fell into a heavy sleep.

In the middle of the night it seemed he reeled himself back from
limitless depths toward a droning that grew louder as he approached
full consciousness. He shook his head, levered his body out of bed,
using an elbow, and groped his way to the telephone in the living
room. Naked, he leaned against the wall while an English voice
spoke in his ear. The voice belonged to an inspector called Spruce
from Scotland Yard who wanted to know what the time was in
Hong Kong. It was a question the English often asked, as if deviation
from Greenwich mean time was hard to believe.

"Seven hours later than it is there." Chan, who had left most
of his mind in the deep faraway, had no idea what time it was.

"Not too late then, it's just turned four in the afternoon here."

"Ah."

"I hope you weren't asleep. I've been asked to communicate the
findings of our forensic laboratory to you, concerning a murder
inquiry, it says here. I tried to reach you at Mongkok Police Station,
but you'd left, sir. They said you wouldn't mind if I telephoned
you at home. I'll be sending the full report, but it's a bit lengthy.
I thought you might want to have the gist over the phone, to see
if I can help any further. Shall I read the summary?" Chan grunted.
"Not very exciting, I'm afraid." Spruce's voice dropped to a mon-
otone as he read. "The samples which are water-resistant proved
on examination to consist mostly of natural resins, probably derived
from pine, and a variety of synthetic latex. The latex has probably
been introduced in order to attain a specific degree of plasticity.
Titanium dioxide was also found in a small quantity."

"I'm sorry," Chan said, "I think I lost you at 'water-resistant.' "

"We seem to be talking about a form of gum, sir."

"Huh?"

"Resins give the consistency, latex holds it all together in one
lump in your mouth and titanium dioxide provides coloring. I

don't know the case, of course, but the likely explanation is that the victims shared a packet of chewing gum before they died.''

"Chewing gum?" Cops were inured to trivia, but it could still hurt.

"Afraid so. Of course there may be more to it; it's hard to say from here. What's the weather like over there?"

"Hot."

"I was wondering if you needed any assistance at the scene of crime itself?"

So that's why you phoned. Chan had wondered why Spruce hadn't sent a fax. "No."

"Oh, well, just a thought."

"Is it cold there?"

"Fairly chilly. And raining."

"Next time."

Spruce perked up. "You'll see the number for my direct line on the covering letter to the report, sir."

"Thanks."

Chan hung up, then lifted the receiver and let it dangle. In the dark he groped his way back to the bed, lay down and instantly fell asleep again. Then he woke with a jolt. Gum? He switched on a light this time, padded back to the telephone. It took half an hour for the Scotland Yard switchboard to locate Spruce.

"You didn't mention flavoring," Chan said. "That titanium, for coloring, right?"

"Correct."

"And the resins and the latex, they would be tasteless in themselves, I guess?"

"Correct. No flavoring is recorded here as being found on the specimens. Flavoring is the first to dissolve, though. I took up gum when I gave up cigarettes. It can be very disappointing after the first three minutes. Monotonous and tasteless. I suppose you don't use chewing gum yourself, sir?"

"I'm still with nicotine." Chan reached for a pack of Bensons on the coffee table. "Suppose there never was any flavoring. What would that give?"

"Flavorless gum, sir. No tasty lead-in period. Not an attractive commercial proposition, I would have thought. An acquired taste anyway."

"Or a specialized use. You've been a great help, Spruce. Next time I'll ask for you to bring the report personally, business class."

"Oh, thank you, sir."

44

Nine thirty A.M. in the car park of the University of Hong Kong Chan and Aston waited for Dr. Lam. Only five minutes late, the dentist's black Mercedes drew up. Lam spoke a few words to his driver, then climbed the stairs with the two policemen to the radiation laboratory. Vivian Ip was waiting. She gestured to the lead-glass cabinet. "All yours," she said to Chan.

Chan pointed to the small reddish-colored block in the far corner on the other side of the glass. "What's that?"

Lam peered through his thick spectacles. "May I?" He slipped his hands into the concertina arm sockets and manipulated the metal instruments until he was able to lift the block. He used the pincers to squeeze it and observed the dent that was retained by the material. He withdrew his hands.

"I don't know. Unless I hold it in my hands, I can't give a professional view."

Vivian Ip assessed him with her quick eyes. "So what would be a professional guess? I mean, if you came across something like that during the course of your dental practice, what would you assume it was?"

She looked at Chan, who nodded approval.

"Gum. You all must have had to bite on it at one time or another. It retains the bite so a dentist can tell which teeth are proud of the others, where the pressure points are, how to design false teeth, that sort of thing. Actually there are a hundred and one uses for it in a dentist's surgery."

"Does dental gum have the same ingredients as chewing gum?" Chan asked.

"I have no idea. Actually it doesn't much matter what you use; anything that would retain the bite would do. Something with resins and latex would be normal. Coloring to make it easier to work with."

Aston was beginning to catch up. "Could it be used to construct a dental record—you know, upper left incisor missing, that sort of thing?"

Lam looked from Aston to Chan. "Impossible." He thrust his hands in his pockets, walked up and down in front of them as if addressing a seminar. "If the purpose of the exercise was to construct a dental record from a distance without the patient's mouth to look at, gum would have only a secondary function. You'd need detailed photographs of the mouth, taken with a miniature camera; that's what one would rely on to identify crowns, fillings, et cetera. The gum would be used as a cross-check, to see if there were any special features to the bite—a gap not obvious from the pictures, half a bicuspid missing, that sort of thing. It would take a professional, of course." He adjusted his spectacles, looked at Chan and smiled. "So I was right; it wasn't food between the victims' teeth."

Chan nodded at Vivian Ip, then led Lam and Aston back down the stairs to the car park where Lam's Mercedes was waiting. The interlude had taken less than fifteen minutes and could be said to have produced a major breakthrough. On the other hand, Chan complained in the taxi to Aston, it could also be said that they were back to square one: Who were the bodies in the vat? Who were the heads in the bag? He told the taxi driver to take them to the address of a small and very exclusive surgery in a small commercial building on the Peak near the tram stop, where they had made an appointment with Hong Kong's most expensive cosmetic surgeon.

"Blond hair and blue eyes are two of mankind's less successful genes. Men can expect to be balding by their mid-thirties, and women will likely be shortsighted. Both sexes will be prone to skin cancer if they spend much time in the sun. The tendency of other races to emulate North European genes through cosmetic surgery is a function of Hollywood and the advertising industry. In Asia, though, the curve is declining rapidly. In the eighties I would do on average forty or fifty eye jobs a year. Nowadays, maybe ten.''

The speaker, Dr. Alexander Yu, smiled; as he did so, slanted lids closed tight as oyster shells. A gene, surely, designed for a race that for ten thousand years looked up from intense green paddy to squint at the sun.

''Eye jobs?'' Aston, blond and blue-eyed, said.

''The so-called epicanthic fold, also known as the Mongolian eye fold—I've got it—is an inward fold of the upper eyelid across the inner corner of the canthus; it's what makes us look slit-eyed. Everyone from Mongol extraction has it, so, as a matter of fact, do some American Indians and some Poles and Scandinavians. Now and then women pay to have it removed.'' He gestured to the wall, which was adorned with before and after photographs. Chan stood to examine them.

Well, every profession must market itself according to its skills. His stomach turned at the monstrous victims of facial burns, traffic accidents, violent assaults, all of whom had reachieved a degree of aesthetic normality at Yu's expensive hands. In between the monsters were interspersed the faces of perfectly normal Chinese women—rich Chinese women, Chan suspected—who had paid Yu to modify the so-called Mongolian fold. The result was hardly Caucasian; in the ''after'' photos eyes no rounder than Chan's peered out of distinctly flat, high-cheekboned Han faces.

''Is it a degrading castration of one's own racial identity?'' the physician continued. ''Frankly, yes. I never like doing it.''

''But you do it anyway?'' Aston said.

''I charge double for my time.'' He laughed. ''Anyway, the issue is quickly becoming academic. It's like the fad among African Americans in the late fifties to try to have the kinks removed from their hair. That sort of genuflection to the master white race has gone out of style over here too, where even maids and chauffeurs know that the future belongs to Asia. I wasn't expecting the reverse effect to begin for at least another decade, though. So far there's only been one example. That's why I knew exactly who you were talking about when you telephoned.''

At a nod from Chan Aston took out Moira's photograph of her daughter, Clare, passed it over Yu's desk.

''Yes, that's her. Before, of course.''

''D'you have an after shot? If you do, we'd really appreciate an opportunity to copy it.''

Yu shook his head. ''Alas, no. I practically begged her and offered to cut my fee, but she refused. It wasn't a bad job either. To be honest, I was going to create quite a stir in the journals, but without the pix there's no impact—not at my end of the profession.''

Chan nodded. It was an answer he'd expected. ''You only took care of the eye shape. What about the eye color and the hair?''

''Eye color is the easiest to change. Tinted contact lenses. For hair she already had a wig. Short, straight, black, thick and Asian.'' Yu grinned.

Aston took out the picture of the Eurasian reaching up to the strip light. Yu studied it.

''Definitely. Can I have a copy?''

That afternoon from home, after a shower, Chan telephoned Emily at all her numbers. Nobody, not even a servant or secretary, responded at any of them. When he was about to leave for work, his own telephone rang. He picked up the receiver.

''I love you. My prince, my benefactor.''

''What's happened?''

''You did it to make me happy, didn't you?''

''You're crazy.''

''You offered me money, imagine! I'll pay *you* if you like, anything you say. Just don't take me off the case. Not yet.''

''Get to the point, I'm in a hurry.''

Wheelchair Lee's excitement sprang out of the telephone like a demon. ''I will, I will. Oh, this is big, big, big. Big enough to hurt the 14K very badly. Just don't ask me to keep quiet. It'll take me a couple of days. I'll have someone tell you where to meet me. We have to be careful so as not to spoil the party. Watch this space.''

Lee hung up.

From the police station Chan telephoned Emily again at home and at her office. Chan supposed she'd given instructions not to be disturbed, a Hong Kong princess withdrawing behind a curtain of cash now that the thrill had faded. Anger accumulated through the day and by early evening was burning a hole in his stomach. By nighttime he had decided to take a taxi up to the Peak again. He promised himself one full-blooded slap across her face. Some satisfactions were worth a career.

45

Atop vans and cars parked aslant, magic lanterns spilled indigo light, beckoning to a police Halloween. Walkie-talkies crackled; stern male voices speaking in English and Cantonese cut across the night's cicada static. Chan had the taxi drop him a hundred yards down the hill; he walked cautiously, like a fox crossing ice. Closer, halogen lamps burned caves of light out of the tropical darkness. An ambulance waited in the drive, its back doors open, disclosing stark white sheets and crimson blankets stacked neatly at the feet of stretchers. In the intensity of one of the floodlights a tall figure turned, one hand covering its eyes; under the hand's shadow Chan made out an almost featureless face the color and texture of potato, a mouth waiting for a cue. Under the mouth the body wore the full dress uniform of a chief superintendent of the Royal Hong Kong Police Force. The mouth sagged with relief when Chan emerged from the night.

"Incredibly fast response, even for you," Riley said. "Just this minute left a message at Mongkok. Tried to get you at home too. How on earth did you get here so fast?"

"Taxi," Chan said. "What happened?"

"Unclear as yet. Damned tricky one, though. The publicity's going to be as bad as if the governor died. They're draining the pool. I called you just in case there's a connection to your mincer case. I'd heard that you intended to question her."

At back around the swimming pool more halogen lamps bored into the water, bounced brittle light off the tiled surround and painted white masks over serious English and Chinese faces. From somewhere a sucking sound accompanied the descending water level that fell perhaps an inch every thirty seconds. No one had thought it worth trying to save the naked woman in the center; she remained anchored, apparently by her neck, while her body and legs swooped toward the surface in a perfect frozen dive. Everyone in the business saw there was no life in it to save. Yellow fluid dribbled slightly from the gaping mouth; intelligence had forsaken those eyes hours ago.

When the water level sunk to waist-height, Emily turned to face him. Two U-shaped scars under her breasts revealed a secret vulnerability. Chan regretted his curses.

"For now we'd better treat it as suspect homicide?" Riley said, coming up behind him, his voice rising into a question.

"Of course." Out of the corner of his eye Chan saw the Chinese technicians dusting the Italian marble table with meticulous Oriental care. Sweaty hands on smooth surfaces made the most beautiful prints: *"Sleep with me." "No."*

When the water was at knee height, Chan jumped in, knelt to examine the chain that held her. It was padlocked through a thick patent leather belt that was buckled around her neck. An extra hole had been bored in the leather. At the other end the chain was padlocked to a cast-iron grille at the bottom of the deep end. Her hands were handcuffed behind her back. Just under her thighs on the tile surface of the pool lay three keys. First impressions were finely balanced: A suicide dressed up as murder? Murder masquerading as suicide? Or merely an elaborate suicide with an element of self-mockery: The belt around her throat was Chanel; the two padlocks were solid brass and glinted gold in the water. Chan borrowed paper and pencil from a detective constable. With Riley hovering over his shoulder he sketched the swimming pool, the position of the body.

"Of course, unless it's related to the Mincer Murders, it's out of our area. We'll have to give it to Central."

Chan stepped back, sketched the position of the house in relation to the pool. "In the morning. Until then it's ours. And if it is related, I don't want to come in cold on another detective's screwup."

"Quite."

Chan looked at Riley. "Best not touch anything, sir. I wouldn't want you to become part of the chain of evidence. Have you touched anything?"

The question had the desired effect. Riley retreated to the collection of vehicles on the other side of the house. Chan followed him. In one of the police vans he found a video recorder which he took to the pool at the back. Everyone moved out of the way when he started to shoot. It was an automatic reflex: Overall shot of area; relationship of pool to house; film closely around the perimeter; zoom in on body; pause over cigarette butts, if any, broken fencing, if any, bushes. From the corner of his eye he saw that the technicians had finished dusting the marble table. He panned slowly from pool to table: *"Sherlock Holmes used cocaine." "It had to be you; there's really no one else I can talk to."*

There was no point videoing the inside of the house. Three officers had reported that there were no signs of disturbance. Pausing over her with the camera still whirring as she lay, now faceup on the bottom of the pool, Chan acknowledged a failure of professional objectivity. Through the lens he saw a fine, strong spirit, lost in a cloud.

46

I n his twenty-five-hundred-year-old masterpiece *The Art of War* Sun-tzu exalts one principle above all others: Cover your back. Chan supposed government servants worldwide lived by that motto, whether they'd read Sun-tzu or not. At his desk in Mongkok he dictated a memorandum to the Commissioner of Police the Right Honorable Ronald Tsui, JP, copied to Chief Superintendent John Riley.

File 128/mgk/HOM/STC

The deceased, Madame Emily Ping Lin-kok, was known to me both socially and as someone who may have had information relevant to the above investigation. On 11 May 1997 at around midnight (no earlier time for the interview could be arranged) I visited her at her mansion on Old Peak Road. We sat together at a marble table on her veranda near her swimming pool. Unfortunately Madame Ping was unable or unwilling to provide any information relevant to the investigation, and I left sometime later. It is likely, therefore, that my own fingerprints will have been lifted from the aforementioned marble table.

Signed: Chan Siu-kai, Chief Inspector, Homicide

On the front page of the *South China Morning Post* Jonathan Wong read of Emily's death. The report hinted strongly at suicide although the investigation was not complete. He read the follow-up feature in the middle pages—a flattering résumé of her life with testimonials to her commercial genius (a genius that, it was suggested, may have contained seeds of imbalance)—then put the newspaper on his desk.

Poor Emily . . . just like a woman, to play hard ball harder than anyone else and then expect to be forgiven, even loved for it. My friend the bitch is dead.

He stood up, walked around his desk with an eye fixed on the newspaper article. He searched his heart for sorrow but found instead a kind of hysteria that broke on his face in the form of a grin. The empress was dead, just as the old man had predicted. Wong wondered if the old man had killed her. It seemed unlikely, somehow. He was not that kind of psychopath.

Now was the moment to make his choice. He ought to reflect, go home and discuss it with that beautiful wife whom he had rescued from the gutter and who despised him.

Instead he picked up the telephone and dialed a number that he had written on a scrap of paper, something he rarely did.

"I would like to see you," he said into the receiver. After listening for less than twenty seconds, he replaced it again. Even so are decisions made that bend souls. Well, he would not expect to be loved—or even forgiven.

He stood up, took advantage of the harbor view that was a privilege of partners in his firm. He watched a Star Ferry cross to Kowloon and a 747 take off from the airstrip that jutted into the water. Still standing, he pressed one of the internal autodial numbers on his telephone. The LED display showed that he was calling Rathbone, the senior partner.

"I'm going to need to see you. It's about the matter we discussed. You'll have to bring the other three. No, not now. When I tell you. Just stand by. And call a full partners' meeting for next week. Just do as I say."

He retrieved his jacket from a wardrobe behind his chair, walked around his desk and paused again at the view. He'd gazed upon it so often for so long it was a kind of inner landscape. There was nothing, not his flat, his wife's body, the palm of his hand, that he knew better, but it had changed overnight. It was like a bar of music that one has heard for years; suddenly someone has the idea of playing it in a different key, and the meaning is altered forever. To his eyes the harbor view was as alluring as always, but darker and infinitely more powerful. Come to think of it, it was even more entrancing than before.

"I'll be about an hour," he told his secretary, and walked quickly to the lift lobby.

On Statue Square he strolled to the Hong Kong Bank building, walked under it, crossed Queen's Road, passed in front of the Hilton until he reached Cotton Tree Drive, which he crossed; a few hundred yards later he was at the Bank of China. At the reception desk he gave his name and the name of the man he had come to see. The old security guard nodded respectfully and, after making a telephone call, gestured to the private lift at the back. A Chinese secretary arrived to escort Wong to the top floor. She spoke to him in Mandarin with a Beijing accent. Her manners were not as good as a Hong Kong secretary's would have been, but he liked the look in her eye and the way she stood: military style with legs apart, hands behind her back. Conquest was a state of mind.

Xian wore almost the same clothes as he had on Emily's boat: black shirt, creased slacks, worn sneakers that rested at angles on the Italian leather two-tone pouffe. The general was lighting a cigarette as Jonathan approached. From the glass-roofed cocktail lounge the view was much better than from Jonathan's office: higher, more panoramic, more commanding.

Xian pointed to a leather armchair. "Women have everything except strong nerves," the old man said. "You've come to accept my offer. . . ."

When Xian had finished speaking, Wong stood, bowed and left the room.

On returning to his office, his secretary told him that a meeting had been arranged with the senior partners in the main boardroom.

Rathbone stood in front of the board table with his legs planted apart and his arms folded—like a bouncer in a nightclub, Wong always thought. Ng, Watson and Savile stood in various contemplative postures around the large boadroom. Ng half leaned on a polished teak credenza near the window; success meant a saturation of harbor views. Wong could see the uncertainty in the eyes of the three Englishmen. Ng was less concerned. Wong strode to the head of the board table, where he took a chair. The others sat near him.

"I've just come from the general," Wong said. Watson looked away; Ng nodded respectfully; Savile blinked; Rathbone stared at his hands. On the way back from Xian, Wong had debated with himself how to run the meeting. He had toyed with various subtle approaches, then abandoned them. He was developing mainland ways.

"He's offering us work."

"Good," Rathbone said.

"Excellent," Ng said.

"Well done indeed," Savile said.

"You all know that Xian and his friends will be running this place after June. They practically run it already. So it's not quite an offer exactly. It's an order. The work we'll be required to do is somewhat unorthodox for a firm of solicitors."

Wong paused to look into each man's face. What he was about to say could not really shock them; they were nothing if not shrewd. They must have worked it out at least in part. He ought to have been surprised that none of them had talked about resigning. After all, they were each of them stupendously rich already, the poorest of them being worth at least ten million U.S. dollars. Greed was a fascinating study. It afflicted mediocrities more than most. It caused the mind to fixate not on what one had but upon what one was about to acquire. Even as they sat at the table, each man was silently calculating.

"With the death of Emily Ping," Wong continued, "Xian needs a representative and a comprador. This firm will fulfill that function. We shall import on his behalf. In strict secrecy, of course."

"May one inquire what?" Savile asked with a foolish beam.

"Weapons of mass destruction."

Savile looked pensive. "Something will have to be said at the full partners' meeting next week. It's going to take a little finessing."

"Tush," Wong said. "They're commercial lawyers, aren't they? Subhuman apparatchiks, in other words, powered by greed. They'll follow the money." He looked into Savile's porcine eyes. "Just like you, Cecil."

47

You're kidding me! The judge really did that? Even numbers guilty, odd numbers innocent? That is kind of Oriental. I have some great stories for you too that I'm typing out. I just wanted to scribble this to let you know I'm thinking about you. Must be all of forty-eight hours since you last heard from me.

By the way, those sneaky little Chinese characters you added to your last fax—I tried to look them up in a Chinese dictionary in the public library. If they mean what I think they mean, I feel the same way.

M.

Chan scowled at the fax, screwed it into a ball and threw it in the trash can. *Well, I don't feel that way anymore. You know she's alive. Dental records: I know you knew.*

On a summons from headquarters Chan left his office, took the underground to Admiralty and walked in the heat to Arsenal Street. At reception he called up to homicide on the third floor. An officer there said that the death of Emily Ping was being handled by Chief Inspector Jack Siu. Chan walked up the three flights of broad stairs. There was nothing on the walls except paint, nothing on the stairs except a nonslip synthetic product and no one in uniform going up or down at that particular moment, yet Chan reckoned that if he'd been transported there blindfolded, he would have known it was a police station. There was a subliminal message that went with law enforcement and attached itself to the walls and floors of police stations. Criminals learned to read it, but so did the police themselves. This was the first time Chan had been asked to assist in a death investigation other than as an investigator. Siu was waiting with his assistant, a young Chinese inspector. Siu smiled as he entered.

"Sorry to drag you over here. Unusual, isn't it?"

Chan nodded, looked around the office. The wall behind Siu was a Bayeau tapestry in photographs of one man's progress through the system: Siu as head prefect; Siu as police cadet; Siu graduating; Siu promoted to sergeant; Siu arresting two notorious triad killers; Siu promoted to senior inspector; Siu receiving a medal from the governor; Siu in full-dress uniform of chief inspector. Chan vowed to dispose of his own photograph featuring his bravery award as soon as he returned to his office. There were certain aspects of Chineseness that his Irish side couldn't take.

"We received a copy of your memo—where you mention that your prints would be on the marble top. You're right. They are."

Chan allowed his eyes to rest on Siu for a beat too long. He was not surprised that Siu had checked. He was surprised that Siu had not asked Chan personally for a card with his prints. Without it there was only one way for him to have obtained Chan's prints. Like everyone else who lived in Hong Kong, when Chan had applied for his identity card, he had submitted to fingerprinting. Normally those fingerprints were considered confidential information, not available to police except with the consent of the commissioner. Siu must have applied to Commissioner Tsui for permission to access confidential information relating to Chan. And Commissioner Tsui had consented.

Chan smiled. "Told you."

Siu nodded. "She was a friend of yours?"

"Not exactly. She was a close friend of my brother-in-law. I spent a night on her boat with my sister, her husband and a few other people."

"I'd better take the names of those other people."

Chan hesitated. Siu waited. The young Chinese inspector leaned forward. Siu leaned back in his chair. "Would you like Inspector Ng to leave the room?"

Chan felt he was losing control of the situation. Why wait for a prompt from Siu? "Yes."

With a shrug the inspector left the room and closed the door behind him. Siu took up a government issue pencil.

Chan recited: "General Xian, the political adviser, Mr. Milton Cuthbert, two bodyguards belonging to Xian, my sister, Jenny, her husband, Jonathan Wong."

"That's a pretty impressive list. Well connected for a humble cop, aren't you?"

"I told you, she was close to my brother-in-law. He's a partner in a law firm. It's his business to know people like that. Also, there were crew for the boat and a Sri Lankan cook employed by Emily Ping."

"Yes, we've spoken to the cook. She was asleep when you paid your visit. Not surprising, it was after midnight."

"I didn't see any servants, that's true."

"How about opium?"

"What?"

"We found evidence of recent opium use in the house. We expect to find some in her blood. Know anything about that?"

"No."

"Were you lovers?"

"No."

"She ever make a pass at you? She had quite a reputation."

"No, not really." Chan could not believe he'd said that.

Siu pounced. *"Not really?"*

Chan felt the blood rising to his cheeks. "She asked me to sleep with her. I refused."

"She said that?"

"Yes."

"I'd call that making a pass, wouldn't you?"

"I guess."

"And when you refused, she asked you to smoke opium with her?"

"Why d'you say that?"

"We've spoken to other men. She was notorious. Sex, drugs—the only Western decadence she didn't like was rock and roll. You visit a woman like her late at night, it's not to play mah-jongg."

"I know nothing about the opium," Chan said, not knowing why he was lying. Wrong, he knew why he was lying. To admit to knowing about the opium was one step closer to admitting he had smoked with her. He'd caught people that way. If you have no odor, the dogs can't track you, but he was ashamed to be thinking like that. There was an adage: The line between cop and crook may be too fine to be distinguished.

"Would you say she was going through some kind of change, questioning old values, the worth of her life—that kind of thing?"

"I told you, we weren't close."

"But so far as we know you were the last of her friends to see her alive. Did she use expressions of despair: 'It doesn't matter anymore,' 'What's the use?' et cetera?"

"No."

"Anything in her conversation to suggest she was abusing drugs?"

"No."

"Do you know of any previous suicide attempts?"

"No."

"Was she burdened by any heavy feelings of guilt or regret?"

"She never said so to me."

"Why didn't you screw her?"

"What?"

"You were free, divorced. She was single, the most eligible spinster in Asia, the world probably. None of the other guys said no."

"Because none of the other guys said no."

"You're special?"

"Particular."

Siu sat back in his chair, then stood up with his hands in his pockets. He gazed out of the window reflectively.

"She wasn't a whore; how could you apply that word to a billionairess? She was voracious. She dominated with her vagina; she was like a man, a pelvic colonizer. Maybe that's what you didn't like. You have a strong independent streak. Everyone says so."

"It's not illegal."

Siu nodded, forced a smile.

"Have you formed a view yet, suicide or murder?" Chan asked the question in a humble voice.

Sui shook his head. "I've never seen a case so finely balanced. To swim down to the drain in the pool, chain and lock yourself to it, then handcuff yourself behind your back"—he shrugged—"you would have to have lungs like bellows, but it could be done. Police cadets handcuff themselves for fun in all sorts of positions. You and I have done it?" Chan nodded at the half question. "Murder is a much simpler explanation, but why would a murderer leave the keys in the pool under her where there was just a chance of her retrieving them before she died?"

"Because the murderer wanted it to look like suicide? Maybe he dropped the keys in the water after she was dead."

Siu nodded. "Of course, we thought of that."

"Of course."

"But if it was murder, why no signs of struggle? She was a strong woman, athletic. Wasn't she?"

Chan reddened again. "She swam like a dolphin. Good lungs."

Siu stared at him. "Well, thanks for coming to see us. If we think it wasn't suicide, we'll need to speak to you again."

Chan got up. "Anytime."

Siu also stood. "How's the mincer case going, by the way? Are all the rumors true?"

Chan forced himself to brighten. "Rumors are always true, you know that. As a matter of fact I might even have a lead. I'm meeting an informant tomorrow night."

At the door he wished Siu good luck.

48

I f Chan had not agreed to an evening meeting, he would never
have guessed that the Walking Spittoon considered himself a
ladies' man. From a teahouse on Lan Fong Road Chan watched
Saliver Kan in white linen slacks, white and blue suede shoes, Gucci
multichrome belt, open-neck silk shirt the color of old gold. His
left arm encircled a young Chinese woman who wore nothing at
all. Well, almost nothing. Straps no thicker than shoelaces held up
a kind of bouncing crimson tea towel joined over the buttocks by
a short zip. On the other arm another woman complemented her
colleague insofar as she was dressed from neck to ankles in a flesh-
colored body stocking. Kan had emerged from a taxi and was walking the ladies slowly toward the rendezvous, a hotel of sorts that
rented out rooms by the hour.

Such establishments were known as villas and were the brothel
owners' equivalent to a tax haven: No girls were employed on
site—customers brought their own—and no offense was committed
by renting out the rooms to those with an abbreviated need for
shelter. Indeed, Chan knew that it was the proprietors' constant
dilemma whether or not to reduce the rental period to thirty
minutes. An hour was too long in roughly 80 percent of cases, but
the remaining 20 percent tended to represent the regular trade.
Over in Kowloon Tong, where villas were an important factor in
the economy, market research had resulted in a compromise: forty
minutes with a penalty for staying over the checkout time.

"Give me half an hour after you see me enter the villa," Kan had said. "Then check into room five. I'll book it and the room next door. You should bring a girl, to make it look right."

"No."

"Okay, then I'll bring two."

Chan wondered how the extra pair of hands would improve his cover, since she would be seen only with Kan. He had to admit, though, that the triad had developed a keen sense of security. Telephone calls had become nearly unintelligible because of Kan's efforts to disguise his catarrh-laden voice. Chan didn't understand what he was saying; he just knew who it was. Now Kan had insisted on a meeting on Hong Kong side, far from his usual haunts. Chan supposed that the early enthusiasm to use the reward to improve Sun Yee On finances had waned and Kan was moonlighting.

At the check-in desk Chan paid a bored middle-aged woman for an hour in room 5. Waiting for the lift, he felt her eyes upon him. Hers was an economic rather than a moral disapproval; whatever he was going to do alone, he could have done at home and saved five hundred dollars. Her gaze fixed on the flat bulge in his trouser pocket where he had slipped in his Sony Dictaphone.

The room itself was an Asian tribute to Aphrodite. The huge mirror on the ceiling reflected crimson bed linen; a note handwritten in Chinese offered a machine named magic fingers for two hundred dollars an hour, available from reception. An elaborate printed notice recorded the exceptional lengths the management went to in laundering the sheets and pointed out that the cupboard in the closet contained ten varieties of condoms in both Asian and Caucasian sizes, "on the house." Which size would an honest Eurasian choose?

The walls were mostly mirrors too; ten thousand Chans watched ten thousand Chans draw up a chair, put his feet on the end of the bed and wait.

He saw that the room was one half of a double room, divided by a folding screen (with mirrors) that reached from wall to wall and floor to ceiling. On the other side of the screen, Kan's unusual security arrangements were causing trouble.

"Ouch! Stop it"—Kan's voice.

"Son of a bitch."

"Ouch, will you tell her to stop pinching me?"

"Of course she's pinching you. We told you, a thousand dollars each."

"And I told you, I'm here on business. It's a big deal; I'll have the money early next week."

"So why hire two girls if it's business?"

"Front. It's a secret international deal. You wouldn't understand."

"So why did you make us take our clothes off?"

Silence, followed by a snort. "A man gets curious. I didn't do anything, did I?"

"Maybe you're queer."

"Don't say that. I'll get angry. And if that little bitch pinches me again, I'm going to hit her."

"You hit her, I'll scream. This place has triad protection."

"Which triad?"

"14K."

"Shit, that's all I need. Look, here's fifteen hundred dollars. It's all I've got. I'll give you the rest next week."

"Fuck your mother. Better use the rest to get your nose fixed."

"What's wrong with my nose?"

"It doesn't work properly; you keep sniffing."

"Don't get personal."

"Don't get personal? You saw my pussy, didn't you? That's personal."

"Just get out of here."

Sound of a zip being fastened, door opening and slamming.

Feet up, Chan reflected that the life of an underworld playboy was not all milk and honey. He lit a cigarette while Kan grappled with the divider. Slowly the triad emerged, shoulder to the screen, forcing it back on protesting rollers to reveal a room identical to the one Chan was in. Sweat had stained the golden silk of his shirt, and a severe red pinch mark discolored one cheek; otherwise the killer appeared unruffled, even smug.

"You hear all that?"

"Just the odd word."

"Two women—it's not easy."

"I don't know how you do it."

Kan grinned and took out a comb. A thousand Kans checked jet black coiffure, rescued a stray hair, made sure their pants fell properly at the back, hitched their Gucci belts, hoicked deeply. He examined the swelling on his cheek with regret and pride.

"Which room shall we use as an office?" Chan asked.

Kan held up a finger. Chan watched while he checked light fittings and peered into mirrors.

"These places, often they have a blackmail option," Kan explained. He spoke in a near whisper. "This thing of yours—I have information."

"Somehow I thought so."

"Somebody talked, but they want a cut."

"Two million gives you something to play with."

"I need some more."

"No."

Kan examined him for signs of weakness.

Chan remained cool, immobile and secretly intrigued. Two million dollars had focused the foot soldier's mind in a way that he found miraculous. Most killers had the attention span of goldfish; their crimes were the final expression of a buildup of rage or avarice when the personality took a backseat to primal, preintellectual man. Watching Kan conspire with something akin to applied intelligence, Chan wondered what could not be achieved in criminal reformation with the right approach. At two million a shot, though, it was cheaper to let them go on killing each other.

Kan sighed. "You're hard."

"I should never be let loose on sensitive types like you."

Kan blinked. "This is no joke. The guy I spoke to is very scared. Fear is expensive to overcome."

"I said no."

Kan's face expressed deep hurt. He leaned forward. "I'm betraying my own people. The Sun Yee On were involved."

Chan took a long draw on his cigarette. Truly the power of money was boundless. "Another two hundred thousand, and that's it."

Kan smiled. "Okay. This is it. I know what happened."

Chan nodded. "That's good."

"So, how about an advance?"

"Definitely not. You know the formula: Information leading to the arrest—"

"Okay, okay. So, three people were minced up alive by triads."

"You don't say."

Kan's whisper was fraught with sincerity. "It was a subcontract. Sun Yee On got the order, and 14K carried it out. Ever heard of anything like that before?"

Chan shook his head.

"And no foot soldiers were involved. It was top secret. Red Poles did all the work. Generals from both sides showed up to make sure it all went smoothly."

Clearly Kan was overawed. It was as if Roosevelt and Churchill had attended at an Allied ambush.

"Where did it happen?"

"New Territories. West. I'm going to find out exactly where and take you. There's a complication, though. Some people are hiding out up there. I'm not too clear on the details."

Chan masked the sudden increase in his interest with a long draw on the cigarette. "You brought me here to tell me you're not too clear?"

Kan lowered his voice still further. "No. I brought you here to arrange a rendezvous. Here's a paper with five addresses, numbered one to five. When I phone you, I'll just say a time and number and hang up. That's where you'll pick me up. Get it?"

Chan took the sheet of paper and looked at Kan. He was finally absorbing Kan's main message: The killer was scared.

"And you show up alone. In a car alone. If not, it's all off."

Chan folded the paper, put it in a pocket. "Whatever you say."

"I'm going now. You stay for another twenty minutes. When you leave, try to look like you had a good time. Frankly, you always seem like you've just spent twenty years in a monastery. Kind of dried up like a prune."

"I'll try. I just don't have your way with women."

Kan accepted the homage solemnly as he stepped back across the line between the two rooms. Chan watched him push the folding screen back into place. When he was sure that Kan had left, he took out the Sony Dictaphone, laid it on the bed. He needed another cigarette before he could face the grille. He lit up, switched on the machine.

"File one-two-eight/mgk/HOM/STC Memorandum to be classified secret and forwarded by hand to Commissioner Tsui and copied to the political adviser Mr. Milton Cuthbert. At nine P.M. on fifteenth May 1997 I attended at a meeting in a well-known villa in Lan Fong Road, Hong Kong Island, with informant Kan, a foot soldier in the Sun Yee On Triad Society. It is possible that Kan will be able to lead me to the present location of suspects Clare Coletti, Yu Ningkun and Mao Zingfu. . . ."

49

Unlike the Jackson Room, the Red Room of the Hong Kong Club accepted women guests at lunchtime. Old hands still affected to grumble, but there had been surprisingly little opposition from the membership when the rules had changed. Expensive wives demanded a place to be seen at lunchtime, and some husbands found it convenient to discuss domestic issues over a civilized lunch in the club. As a result, the tables were spaced farther apart than in the Jackson Room, and there really was little danger of being overheard. The hors d'oeuvres trolley was another good reason for having a business lunch in the Red Room; it was the best in Hong Kong.

Not that Cuthbert had had much choice. The commander in chief of British forces in Hong Kong, Major General Horace Grant, rarely accepted a lunch appointment anywhere else. There was a rumor that his wife had ordered him to boycott the Jackson Room because of the ban on women.

Cuthbert was early, knowing the "Chief" would be on time. Without needing to ask for one, the diplomat had been allocated a table by the window and was shown to a seat by the maître d'. From the seat he faced the room. He knew that the chief would sit next to him, in the other seat next to the window, also facing the room.

The political adviser confessed to himself that he was a touch nervous. Grant was not a man to be persuaded into or out of any kind of decision. Nor was he someone who gave a damn for Cuthbert's position, reputation or erudition. He came himself from Northern Irish army stock. Contempt for diplomats was a family tradition. A Grant had lost his life along with most of his regiment 150 years ago in some interminable Kabul siege that was supposed to be the fault of the Foreign Office at the time. The Protestant Northern Irish were almost Chinese in their ability to hold historical grudges. One card that Cuthbert had to play, though, might tip the balance. For once it was the diplomat who was asking for action.

The chief appeared at the door in the company of the maître d' and, seeing Cuthbert, strode briskly over, nodding here and there to people who wanted to be seen saying hello to him. Cuthbert stood up, and they shook hands.

"So kind of you to come," Cuthbert said as they sat down.

"Not a bit. Good lunch, good company—an excuse to drop in on the governor, now I'm in Central." He smiled. Cuthbert smiled back, giving the corners of his mouth a slightly humble downturn to acknowledge the subtle assertion of rank. Only the chief had the right to "drop in" on the governor; lesser mortals, the political adviser, for example, needed appointments.

They both ordered Bloody Marys. Cuthbert sipped his while Grant chewed for a moment on the stick of celery that came with it. Cuthbert adapted to his guest's military time scale. With a fellow diplomat he probably would not have come to business until the cheese course; with Grant it was important not to lose the general's interest. Even the best soldiers tended to be cursed with an abbreviated attention span. On the other hand, it would be a mistake to plunge in like an amateur. They talked about people they knew, cocktail parties they had both recently attended, the state of the governor's yacht, troop movements in southern China, cricket scores. Cuthbert came to the point when the chief finished his Bloody Mary, said "ah" loudly and let the coversation lapse

"I asked you to lunch, General, because I thought we might discuss a new development in that business with the trunk."

"Yes?"

"Perhaps you heard that Chief Inspector Chan is making progress?"

"So I'm told. Damned good man, Chan, from what I hear."

"First-class. As you know, it's possible that he can lead us to the couriers. They're hiding somewhere in the western New Territories, it seems, according to his main informant. Assuming his informant is right, of course.''

"Quite."

"The commissioner of police wanted to go in with his own unit, but I overruled him. His men are first-class, of course, SAS-trained, but they don't have—how shall I say?—the international experience. Or quite the same kind of loyalties, if you see what I mean.''

Grant gave a quick nod. "I know. Tsui's hopping mad about it, but you've persuaded the governor to recommend SAS from the UK.''

"Subject to your approval of course, General.''

"I've given it. Memo went out this morning. In fact I had them take a military flight last night, pending my final decision. They'll be landing this afternoon.''

"Yes. The governor's secretary told me just before I came to lunch. It's the way the army handles the affair that I wanted to discuss with you.''

"Ah! Well, we can discuss. Nothing wrong with that. But I suspect the boys in the field will want maximum freedom of action. You know how it is, the men on the ground have to have the final word in how to manage an operation. Not that it's likely to be especially difficult, as far as I can see.''

Grant raised his eyebrows to let Cuthbert know he was genuinely puzzled by the diplomat's concern.

"Not difficult operationally. While they're thought to be well armed—automatic pistols of some kind and possibly heavier weapons—they're not professional soldiers. Diplomatically, though, it's just a little tricky." Grant shrugged: not his problem. "I mean, the nature of what was found in the trunk is still top secret.''

"And shall remain so if I have anything to do with it.''

"Quite." Grant gave Cuthbert an impatient soldierly stare. "Which is why I didn't want the police involved." Cuthbert continued. "There would be a trial of course. Defense lawyers et cetera. Probably impossible to keep out the China dimension. London will be furious. I mean, you can imagine what the press will say: atomic threat by unreconstructed renegade Communist cadres against six million people to whom we still owe protection. Military protection."

Grant nodded. "Thought of that. Can't see how the hell it can be avoided except through an Official Secrets Act sort of trial—in camera, as they do with spies."

"Not so easy, I'm afraid. Nobody involved has signed the Official Secrets Act. The three suspects are American citizens according to the New York Police Department. You know how the Americans can be about anyone else's breach of democratic principles. The CIA can literally get away with murder, but Singapore can't cane a young American yob's backside without an international uproar."

Grant toyed with his hors d'oeuvres. He seemed to be concentrating hard, riding a train of thought. Finally he raised his head to look Cuthbert full in the face.

"I won't stand in your way, but it's not the sort of order I can give."

"Of course not, General."

"I'll let you talk to the men. But I warn you, they'll want a lot of reassurance that it won't be another Gibraltar. And you'll have to convince them that it's necessary."

Cuthbert smiled. "I'm most grateful, General." On seeing the sommelier approach again, he added, "White or red?"

"I'm having fish this time."

"Chablis then?"

Grant nodded, returned to the last of his hors d'oeuvres. One thing you had to give diplomats credit for: You never had to be explicit. God only knew how they ever managed to do something simple and direct, though. While Cuthbert tasted the Chablis, the commander in chief thought up a joke to tell the governor later: How many diplomats does it take to change a lightbulb? Twenty. One to change the bulb, nineteen to record the international implications. Chris would like that.

• • •

Cuthbert found out when the military flight was due to land and sent two cars to pick the men up. Of the five, four would be dropped at their quarters in Stanley, and the last, the most senior, was to be brought direct to Cuthbert's office. The political adviser was still debating what tack to use when his secretary showed Major Fairgood in. Cuthbert shook hands with a stereotype: fit as an athlete with something lethal around the eyes; square jaws with lean cheeks in which a single furrow had been plowed from cheekbone to just behind the mouth. Cuthbert saw the suspicion that soldiers habitually feel toward diplomats. In Fairgood's case it took the form of an almost theatrical squinting combined with a disdainful twitch of the nose.

Cuthbert invited the soldier to sit at the long table in his anteroom.

"Good of you to see me. I do apologize for taking up your time when you must want to be settling in."

"No problem. Not a complex job as far as I can see. Not a lot of settling in to do. We'll be done this time tomorrow, I expect."

"Quite. That's rather what I wanted to discuss. I don't know if the commander in chief has spoken to you?"

"No, how could he?"

"Yes, of course."

"Something came over the radio, though, while we were in the air. It doesn't take much to guess what you want."

"Ah!"

"But it can't be done. You must have heard about Gibraltar?"

"Yes indeed."

"That was orders. Between you and me."

"If I remember correctly, some known Irish Republican Army assassins were, er, killed by SAS men. The IRA had a car full of explosives but were themselves unarmed."

"Someone very senior thought it would be nice if those particular IRA terrorists never had to stand trial. They never reckoned for the media frenzy. A bloody trial for manslaughter in Gib—SAS men! We're never supposed to see the light of day. Bloody fiasco.

Some of the blokes nearly resigned. Men like you are supposed to keep us out of politics—and the newspapers. And the courts, especially the courts."

"I absolutely agree."

"Now there's an appeal to the European Court at Strasbourg by families of the IRA bastards we shot. It never ends, that sort of thing."

"Quite."

Cuthbert took out his silver cigarette case, which he offered to Fairgood, whose fuse seemed to have burned itself out. To his surprise the superfit major accepted it gratefully.

"Of course, if circumstances were different," Cuthbert said, "and if there were good reason . . ."

"It would take more than a ten-minute chat with a diplomat to convince me to risk putting my men through that, I can tell you."

Cuthbert smiled through the tobacco smoke. "Well, let me confess, Major, I don't blame you. I'm deeply grateful that you came to see me, and I shan't attempt to persuade you further. You realize that it was my duty to try—in the interests of national security, of course."

Suprised at being let off the hook so easily, Fairgood coughed on an inhalation. He stared at Cuthbert for a moment, then inhaled deeply. "You're doing your job, I can see that. And I'm doing mine."

The diplomat noticed a change in posture. Fairgood stretched his legs under the table, leaned back in the chair. For the first time since entering the room he seemed relaxed.

"Right then," Fairgood said. His eyes flicked over the room before settling on the window. "Good view."

"One of the best. Let me show you."

Fairgood stood up with Cuthbert and went to the window. "There's the airport runway; that's a Cathay flight taking off. Just behind, d'you see? the hills of Kowloon. And behind them, China."

Fairgood took it all in as if studying a battlefield. "Yes, that must be right. One knows how close it is, but one doesn't quite take it in until one arrives on the ground. They say that all the really big disasters of the next hundred years will probably be caused by China."

He smiled without warmth, finished his cigarette slowly, went back to the table to find an ashtray, drummed thoughtfully on the top.

"Just out of interest, why?"

"Partly because if there's a trial, there'll be a huge bloody public row, partly because it will jeopardize relations between China and Hong Kong and partly, I confess, a measure of personal sentiment."

"Really?"

"Radiation sickness is horrifying. There's no other word for it."

"Yes, I heard something about that. No danger for my chaps, I hope?"

"None at all as far as I can gather. The damnable part, though, is that these three will probably get off. There's only circumstantial evidence to link them to the uranium."

"Get off?"

"Murder. Look, just as background, let me show you something."

Cuthbert went to his office and returned with some photographs. He began with the two divers in the hospital. Higgins he saved to last. He watched Fairgood dwell on that one: an Englishman, a white man, fair-skinned, about his age, his body bloated and distorted like some monstrous sea creature. Fairgood nodded slowly, whistled.

"I see." He raised his eyes. Cuthbert's stratagem was pretty crude after all. "Well, I'd better be going."

"Of course," Cuthbert said. "Take the pictures if you like. Your men might want to know the kind of people they're dealing with."

Fairgood nodded again. "Just the one will do." He picked up the picture of Higgins, slid it into a pocket.

On his way out Fairgood said: "Even if the men were sympathetic, which is by no means certain, there would have to be a cast-iron guarantee of no publicity and no repercussions—especially not legal ones. Cast-iron."

Cuthbert smiled again. "This isn't Gibraltar, Major. On important issues the media do as we tell them over here. And these three
are supposed to be dead already." Fairgood raised his eyebrows.
"You have my word," Cuthbert said.

They shook hands at the door.

50

They. In Chan's dream *they* can change shape, race, sex; *they* can even manifest as animals or spirits. He has seen them pass through walls; no matter how fast he runs, they are by his side, one step to the left and half a step behind. In some legends from ancient Chinese sorcery, death approaches from the left too. Are *they* fundamentally Chinese? At first he thought so. Little by little, though, they acquired some British attributes; one of them even appeared with a red face and a monocle. They stalk him. When he can stand it no longer, he turns to face them, daring them to kill him. They seem baffled by such behavior. He turns away; they resume their positions by his side, half a step behind. It's not exactly a nightmare, not even a dream, because when he wakes, they are still there. The explanation is simple. He is going insane.

He knows why. He saw it on the face of Chief Inspector Jack Siu. Brushing past other senior officers in the corridors of Mongkok Police Station and even more so at Arsenal Street, he notices a change in manner, a subtle distaste that they try to hide. Little by little it has filtered down to the lower levels. When the rumor, whatever it is, reaches inspector level, they will pounce. Just because you're paranoid doesn't mean they're not after you. Two days after Emily's body was found he felt the atmosphere like a glass wall between him and the other officers. As he entered the police station, faces averted, then stole glances after him. In his office Aston wouldn't look up when he entered.

"Any messages?"

Aston, red-faced and embarrassed, raised his eyes. "Just something from Siu at Arsenal Street. They've made an appointment for you to go over there at eleven this morning.''

Aston lowered his eyes. In the canteen Chan saw that the rumor had descended to the tea lady. For traditional Chinese, bad luck is a social disease. She would not look in his eyes and disappeared into the pantry as soon as she had given him his tea. He heard her whispers to the other staff: *bad joss*. From the canteen he walked downstairs to the front doors and out into the street. In the crowds he found a way to bury his disgrace. He sat at a café smoking until ten-thirty, then took the underground to Arsenal Street.

At reception it was obvious that he was expected. He was shown into a large conference room where Commissioner Tsui headed a small group of senior officers, including Riley. Jack Siu was the least senior. He sat in the middle of the table with a thick file on his left. On his right lay a transparent plastic evidence bag containing a woman's black patent leather Chanel belt. Chan was told to sit at the far end of the table, opposite Tsui. Tsui said something about asking Riley to begin. A shorthand reporter whom Chan had not noticed in a corner of the room began writing with pencil in a notebook; she also used a tape recorder, which she switched on while Riley was saying something about deep regret and embarrassment. After a long, rambling speech he turned to Jack Siu.

''Your prints were on the belt that was around her neck,'' Siu said, looking Chan in the eye. ''There may be an innocent explanation. If not, we're going to charge you with murder.''

''Normally I would suspend you from duty until conclusion of this matter,'' Tsui said, avoiding Chan's eyes. ''However, in view of the pressure on the mincer case, you will proceed with that and that alone—until further notice. You'll need a lawyer. Don't try to leave Hong Kong; you're on the stop list. You can go.''

51

From Western spoors strange cultures grew. As a kid Chan had visited the west of the New Territories often, mostly to go clamming. He remembered paddy and duck ponds with fish. The symbiosis of the ponds fascinated his Chinese side: All day ducks sat on the still water and shit. Their droppings fertilized the ponds, causing algae and other vegetation to burgeon, which in turn were eaten by the fish. Either you fed the fish to the ducks or you sold the fish and the ducks at the end of the season. It was an example of money growing from nothing, Oriental magic at its best.

The ducks, though, didn't pay half so well as the container companies. Coming over a low hill, he saw it now, a horizontal city floating in the heat; closer, it was a necropolis of steel tombs, stacked two high, that came in two sizes: twenty feet by eight feet by eight feet or forty feet by eight feet by eight feet. "Roll on, roll off," abbreviated to *roro,* had entered the Cantonese language. It was a mantra that conjured money from nowhere. Nothing defecated, nothing grew, but the rent came rolling in. In twenty years Hong Kong had become the second-busiest container port in the world, after Rotterdam, and those outsize trunks had to be put somewhere. Southern China, the destination of most of the goods, had no facilities for moving containers around, so the contents were emptied onto trucks in the container yards, and the containers left to wait in the parks until a ship needed them again. *Roro, ho ho*: it had happened so quickly the government hadn't any legislation in place for regulating this particular use of land.

Photographed from the air, it could look eerily regular in layout;

on the ground a certain Chinese chaos intervened. Paths between the rectangular boxes lurched, some of the steel was rusted; in the older, discarded containers families had begun to keep pigs and chickens; some of the newer containers were raised on jacks to provide shelter for domestic pets and, occasionally, ducks. Old cars, stolen cars, disemboweled cars crouched in the shadows. The narrow corridors that were created, lengthened or closed off each time a container was parked remained uncharted and changeable; only local children were reliable guides.

Good place to hide, Chan, murder suspect, had to concede. Driving an unmarked car with Saliver Kan beside him in the passenger seat, he had no plan how to proceed. He slowed down as they came alongside the first huge double-stacked boxes, which carried the EVERGREEN logo. It was like being a child again, unable to see over the furniture.

"Shit," Saliver said, lowered the window, spit.

On the top of the car an antenna sent signals from a transmitter installed in the dashboard instead of a radio. Chan wore a smaller antenna and transmitter that he was under orders to turn on as soon as they left the car.

Chan was more than ever mystified. The Hong Kong Police Force had its own unit of highly trained men to attack, disarm and, if necessary, kill dangerous fugitives or terrorists, and Chan had heard that Commissioner Tsui had wanted to use them for this operation. Cuthbert had persuaded the governor to overrule him: the uranium again. The men receiving Chan's radio signals were all British Special Air Services officers, hard, white, fine-tuned killers with the personalities of anvils. The investigator had turned bird dog. Well, ever since his last meeting with Jack Siu and the commissioner, Chan was just thankful for any excuse to get away from the office.

His early intuition after the standoff with the Communist coast-guards that day on the police launch had been that Beijing would exert pressure and the investigation would be aborted. As with so much in this case, he had been completely wrong. All of a sudden the Raj had woken up and was in a rage; at least Cuthbert was. Chan was forced to carry a machine pistol strapped to a harness around his chest. It was heavier than it looked and under pressure from the seat belt began to chafe. When they were strapping it on, Cuthbert had whispered in his ear: "Don't be afraid to use it, Charlie. There won't be any inquiries; you have my word." There was a hunter's eagerness in his tone.

Chan shifted the harness with one hand. "I thought you knew where it was?" he said to Kan.

"Here. It's here," Kan waved at the containers. "I didn't know there were this many." He hoicked thoughtfully. "Imagine what you could hide here."

Chan slowed to fifteen miles per hour, tried to guess what Kan was thinking.

"We'll have to ask someone," Kan finally said.

"Ask them what?"

"There's a pattern made by the containers where they're hiding. Distinctive. I'm not telling you what. I know what you'd do. You'd cut me out."

Chan stopped the car for Kan. He watched while the killer crossed the pavement to talk to a young girl about twelve years old. She had large oval eyes, a fringe of hair like a black velvet curtain, a smile to melt meat cleavers. Saliver returned cursing.

"Can you believe that little bitch?" He shook his head in philosophical disbelief.

"What?"

"She wants a thousand dollars."

"So what are you waiting for?"

Saliver stared at Chan as if he were stupid. "For her to come down, of course."

Kan stood by the car with his back to the girl. Chan watched as she ambled closer, hit the murderer softly on his forearm.

"Okay, nine hundred," she said.

"It comes out of your reward," Chan said to Kan, and smiled at the child. Getting out of the car, he remembered to switch on his radio.

• • •

More abandoned cars and motorbikes. Chan's practiced eye picked out used condoms, the sites of large, small and medium-size fires, dog and cat corpses, abandoned underwear both male and female, broken Walkmans, the remains of ducks roasted in the fires, aluminum saucepans used to cook rice: East meets West.

He and Kan followed the child as she picked her nonchalant way down paths strewn with criminal rubble. Once they came upon two old mattresses, a collection of rubber bands, disposable syringes, cotton balls and wine bottle caps. American cops called them shooting galleries: rubber bands to make a vein bulge; caps to cook up the heroin; cotton balls to soak up the last drop. Chan felt they were getting closer.

Without warning the child stopped and pointed. The path was blocked by double-stacked containers. She gestured that it was necessary to make a detour; what they were looking for was on the other side. She held out her hand while reluctantly Kan counted out nine hundred Hong Kong dollars. A deal's a deal. Anyway, a chief inspector of police with a machine pistol was watching.

Chan told Kan to wait while he made the detour. He had to go back three containers, turn left, then left, then left again. On each attempt, though, the path was blocked; the center of the maze was cut off by a steel fort. Finally he came upon a ladder. His eye traced five trip wires across the ladder, probably attached to some primitive warning system. He took out the automatic pistol, climbed the ladder slowly, carefully stepping over each trip wire. Near the top of the container he could see an unexpectedly large area, perhaps a hundred feet square, open to the light but completely closed to the rest of the area by containers packed closely together. Hitched across one corner a wire held blue jeans, male and female underwear, T-shirts. On the ground, leaning with her back against a steel wall, Clare Coletti sat hump-shouldered. Heroin had aged her. On a quick take, in a crowd, he would have registered her at about fifty.

Shaved head, blue eyes, Orientalized eye sockets: it was a face out of a comic strip: Kat Woman. Her complexion was gray. With emaciated hands like claws she scratched incessantly at different parts of her body. What Chan noticed most was her head; it was on a swivel, like a video camera on a random scan. In one instant she was looking up at him but seemed not to register anything. She was sweating.

"Johnny? I mean, fuck." It was a New York accent, Bronx, but not like Moira's. Clare spoke quickly, with condescension.

"I'm cookin'."

"Yeah. Hurry up, why doncha?"

"You wanna do it?"

"I don' cook. We went through that."

"Right. Right. The Great Khan don' cook."

Johnny said something in Mandarin. There was a short laugh from another man.

"You boys thinkin' of rebellin' again? Wouldn't try it. I'm your only way outa here—just remember that."

"Right, Your Excellency, we remember." There was a sound of giggles. Clare grimaced, then broke into a short grin.

"Fuck." She shook her head. "You guys. I should have your balls cut off."

Two Chinese men came out from under the container where Chan was standing. One was carrying a bottle cap, the other a syringe. One sat down by her side, the other in front of her. The one with the syringe held the needle in the bottle cap and pulled the plunger. In a sudden, practiced movement Clare picked up a rubber band, slipped it above her forearm and twisted it over on itself several times. With her other hand she took the syringe, found a vein after a lot of probing, pressed down on the plunger. Chan watched her body contort with the shudder; groans of joy dribbled from her mouth. She slipped into a fetal position on the ground.

"Oh, *man*, fuck."

Chan waited while the two Chinese men also shot up. He knew he had about twenty minutes when they would be very high. After that they would be able to function with more normality.

Clare slowly propped herself back up against the steel wall. One of the men sat next to her, similarly held up. The other lay on the ground at their feet.

Clare spoke slowly. "Know what I just saw, except I didn't really think about it till now? I just saw someone up on the roof."

"Roof?" Johnny giggled. "Roof? Excellency, we ain't got no roof."

Clare broke into a grin, then a guffaw as the joke caught the other man as well.

"Yeah, well." She scratched her shaved head, grinned. "I guess. This is good stuff."

"Thanks to you, Excellency."

"Uh, you can lose the 'excellency.' I wouldn't mind, except you don't mean it. You should be grateful. If it wasn't for me, you'd both be dead. Fuck was that?"

Chan landed in an imperfect karate fall, rolled on the ground, knelt holding the machine pistol in front of him.

"Don't move, police, you're all under arrest."

"Huh?"

Six pupils the size of pinheads tried to focus on him.

"Wow." Clare scratched her arm, grinned. "Someone just fell from the sky."

"Fuck."

"Maybe he fell outa that chopper I can hear."

"Oh, *fuck! Choppers!* I'm outa here." Clare tried to stand. She rose up against the wall of the container, slid back down again. "Shit. I'm so friggin' stoned. Damn, I think they got us."

"Don't move," Chan repeated. "I don't want to have to hurt you."

Clare stared at him from under heavy lids. "He has one of those British accents."

"I guess they all do round here."

"Martian falls outa the sky, and fuck, he talks faggy English."

Chan hoped they wouldn't try to escape. How do you instill fear and respect in someone whose consciousness is floating in space? He knew he couldn't shoot them either. He wasn't the type to shoot sick dogs. He stood staring at them while they stared at the chopper that had reared up like a prehistoric beast apparently from nowhere. As far as the three addicts were concerned, it upstaged Chan and his gun, like a film with bigger technical effects. They were transfixed by it; their heads swiveled as it banked and hung, blowing up a small typhoon of dust at the other end of the compound.

"Man, I been dreaming about one of those coming to take us away," Clare said, staring. "Ain't much they can do us for 'cept possession."

"Ain't the cops we're worried about, remember, Excellency?"

Clare scratched her head again. "Yeah. Shit." She turned to Chan. "You got, like, witness protection over here? We got stuff we could sell, you know, make your hair stand on end. International implications definitely."

Chan watched while two SAS officers slithered down a rope at amazing speed. They hit the compound, running.

"It's okay," Chan shouted, "I've got them covered. I've arrested them. They're too stoned to move. They're unarmed. *I said I've arrested them.*" Perhaps it was the noise of the chopper. *"They're unarmed, it's okay."* The two soldiers seemed not to hear him.

They took up positions at angles to the three junkies; each knelt on one knee, held his gun in both hands with arms straight. Chan dived to the ground and watched while bullets from the two machine pistols sawed first through the bodies of Clare and her friends, then through their heads.

Under the thunder of the chopper human mush the consistency of watermelon dripped from the container wall. It must have been all of twenty seconds since Clare was speaking.

"I had them covered, there was no danger, they were unarmed, we could have questioned them." He was still saying it, jabbering almost, as they led him across the compound to where a rope was dangling from the chopper. Two more men came down the rope.

"All yours to clean up," one of the gunmen said. The new arrivals nodded and walked briskly toward the corpses.

The gunmen found a harness, which they forced him into, and he was hoisted above the steel maze to the cabin of the chopper, where rough hands hauled him in with brutal efficiency. The other two came up the rope in the same way. A few minutes later the remaining two soldiers were also hoisted aboard, and the machine banked into a turn. One of the soldiers hung on to a steel upright to speak to the pilot.

"We'll need bulldozers, heavy lifting gear—the containers are packed tight—oh, and something for a fire."

The pilot flicked a switch; static crackled from a radio. "Operation Kidgloves here, are you reading?"

"Reading Kidgloves, over."

"You have the coordinates. Send bulldozers, lifting gear to shift shipping containers—and something for a quick bonfire. Something that burns hot for total incineration. Over."

"Will do. Over and out."

Chan was made to sit at the rear, the two gunmen immediately in front of him. They had taken his gun. Three others sat on the other side; it was a big chopper. Below, they seemed to be following the ribbon of road that led back toward Kowloon and Hong Kong Island.

Chan felt a gathering fury. When he'd finally caught up with Moira's enigmatic daughter, during the few minutes that he'd watched and heard her speak, the mystery had fallen away, together with the fear and awe. He knew who she was; any city cop would have recognized her and her friends: They were the eternal fantasists, the ones who from an early age know that reality will be more than they can bear. They slip into crime out of weakness and despair and deserve to be treated like common criminals, not terrorists. Whatever the connection with the uranium, those three could have been no more than couriers, that much was clear.

The gunman in front spoke to his colleague opposite. "It was a hostage situation; we had no choice. A police officer was in mortal danger."

The man opposite—he had lean cheeks in which a single furrow had been plowed from cheekbone to just behind the corner of his mouth—nodded. He turned to Chan. "Hear that? These officers saved your life. I'd like you to appreciate their efforts on your behalf.''

The gunman in front of Chan turned to look him directly in the face. ''Okay, Chinaman?''

There didn't seem to be any physical threat in the way they acted, Chan did not fear they were about to throw him from the helicopter. They seemed to rely for intimidation on the innate menace that emanated from who they were and what they'd done and, perhaps most of all, the psychopathic quirk that had driven them to volunteer for the SAS's training program in the first place. Chan was still in shock. Deeper than shock, distress. The object of policing was peace, but now Moira's daughter was dead, and so were her two companions, butchered in an unnecessary paramilitary siege. It took him minutes to wind his mind back from a condition of passive despair to deal with the man in front. Finally he leaned forward and spoke with controlled contempt.

''Put what you like in your report, soldier, but if you call me Chinaman one more time, I'll find a way to squeeze your balls in a vise. Got it, cunt face?''

Chan leaned back in his seat, feeling marginally better. On occasion infantile hostility could revive the spirit when mature self-restraint merely left one feeling depressed.

The man exchanged a glance with his colleagues but said nothing more. At Stanley, Cuthbert was waiting. He ignored Chan and locked himself in a room with the soldiers to debrief them. Chan was sent back to Central in a government car, as if he'd not been at the scene of the slaughter at all.

In his office Chan paced in front of Aston, refusing to answer questions, forcing his black hair back in a juddering motion every few seconds, trying to control the aftershock. Finally he took the Sony Dictaphone from his desk drawer, slipped it into his pocket and went home.

More in sorrow than in anger he found a piece of A4 size paper, wrote with a black ballpoint in large letters: "She's dead, Chan."

At his fax machine in the kitchen he pressed the only autodial number he had ever programmed. He watched the paper make its mournful way through the machine.

He took a beer from the fridge to steady his nerves. He was on the sofa sipping from the can when the telephone rang.

"You okay?"

"Yeah."

There was a noise of a throat being cleared. "A chopper came. I heard shots, so I ran."

"Smart."

"What about the money?"

"I think they'll pay. So long as you didn't see a chopper or hear shots."

"What chopper? What shots?"

"Good. And when you get the money, disappear. That would be my advice."

"Sure." There was a pause. "This is big, isn't it?"

"Yes."

"You remind me of a triad foot soldier. You're just obeying orders, and you don't really know where they come from. Right?"

Chan replaced the receiver without replying. *"Right."* He said it to the beer can. Two more cans later he found the strength to face the grille on the Sony Dictaphone.

"File reference one-two-eight/mgk/HOM/STC. This note is to record a development that took place in the western New Territories at about eleven A.M. seventeenth May 1997. . . ."

When he finished, he took the lift to the ground floor to walk around the block. In the lobby he remembered to empty his letter box. On a quarter sheet of paper a wheelchair had been sketched, and instructions scrawled in English. The date of the proposed meeting was May 17, around midnight.

52

At Asian borderlands immovable objects meet irresistible forces and come to arrangements. The irresistible force of communism had been reaching lucrative agreements with immovable British capitalism for almost fifty years—before Thatcher and the Joint Declaration, before and even during the Cultural Revolution.

Chan used his police ID card to cross the checkpoint into the restricted zone in the extreme northeast of the New Territories. From his taxi he recognized the first evidence. Huge quantities of cardboard boxes under corrugated iron shelters were to smuggling what aluminum foil and outsize cigarette papers were to marijuana: not conclusive proof of possession but a reliable indication. Human figures with crates moved in and out of blinding lights like stagehands.

The taxi dropped him farther down the road outside an unmanned office; the title CUSTOMS COMPOUND in English and Chinese was surely facetious. Behind the office the black Lexus on the end of a hook belonging to a small pickup truck seemed to his expert eye to have suffered damage only to its license plates; they were missing. As his vision adjusted to the mixture of halogen glare and primeval night, he saw that he stood on plain earth over which had been built a contraband town of open ironwork with sloping sheet-metal roofs. Articulated flatbeds waited with diesels running in deep shadow or under a white glare: the chiaroscuro of sophisticated crime. Instinctively he slipped into shadow from which he peered at the frontier hypermarket. The PRC section was mostly vegetables, fruit, cotton products, down-filled garments and low-quality ironware for kitchens and workshops. The nearest Hong Kong shelters stacked boxes of videos on boxes of televisions on boxes of laptops. Entrepreneurs with clients in the Communist state browsed ranks of Mercedeses, which respectful salesmen offered tax-free for cash, so long as it wasn't renminbi, the official People's currency that nobody wanted.

Despite the concentration of people, Chan was pleased to note an un-Chinese hush over the market town, a kind of lip service to nonexistent law enforcement. Apart from quietness, though, numbers of people, amounting here and there almost to a crowd, moved around with the kind of freedom that exists only in no-man's-land. With so much democratic openness, where would a man in a wheelchair hide? Chan made for the desktops warehouse fifty yards in the direction of China.

Hide a leaf in a forest, hide a spy on a border: Lee was no fool. Men dressed only in shorts and clearly in a hurry unloaded boxes bearing famous names in information technology from five large vans carrying no advertising and no illumination over their number plates, even though their lights were on and engines running. Many languages described the contents of the boxes as "monitors," "CPUs," "keyboards," "CD-ROM players" and "speakers." Lee had never told him of this other side of Wheelchair Enterprises. The sixth van was shut at the back. It waited about ten yards from the others. Chan tapped an elaborate tattoo on the rear door and climbed in when it opened. From his chair Lee beamed with a sadist's goodwill. Chan checked the interior of the van: a cripple, his wheelchair, another chair, a tower CPU on the floor, a desk and monitor glowing with the tropical colors of Windows 95.

"You work all hours," Chan said.

"For the pleasure you have brought me, I'd give up sleep for the rest of my life. It's not often a man gets the opportunity to start a war. And when the war is between the two groups he hates most in the world . . ." Lee raised his arms, kissed his fingers and dropped his hands in his lap. Chan had never seen him so close to peace.

"I know about the couriers—the American girl and her two Chinese friends," Lee said.

"They're dead."

"That's what I mean—I know."

Chan stared. *"You know?"*

"This morning some British soldiers shot them. It's the advantage of information technology: I network, people E-mail me." He opened his palms. "Kids talk to kids who talk to parents." Lee's eyes glistened. "News travels at twenty-eight thousand eight hundred bps, and that's a relatively slow modem these days."

Chan dragged the spare chair from a corner and sat.

"What else do you know?"

Lee leaned forward. "I told you, half a billion dollars: it was for a few kilos of uranium. The 14K burned him in a big, big way. He's not a total clown, though. How do you check the market price of weapons-quality uranium if you are a Communist general who has never been further west than Yunnan? Stealthily, of course. It takes weeks. By the time he was sure that he could have found another supplier to sell him the stuff for a mere few million, *he'd already paid*. Ever seen a megalomaniac lose his temper? I wish I'd been there; it must have been electric. He gave orders to kill the couriers as soon as the stuff was delivered, see?"

"Almost." Chan thought about it. "Well, not really."

"So whom does the richest and maybe most powerful man in Asia use to assassinate triad couriers in Hong Kong, all of whom are American citizens? Not the People's Liberation Army; the situation is still too sensitive for that."

"Other triads."

"Correct. And this is where it gets beautifully Chinese. He paid the Sun Yee On ten million to shred the 14K couriers as slowly as possible: revenge in the name of the people. He's a Communist with no sense of history. The Sun Yee On were the biggest supporters of the Nationalists in the Civil War and the biggest losers when they all had to flee Chongqing in '49. The Sun Yee On hate the Communists even more than the other triads do. *They took the money and leaked the deal to the 14K.* The 14K, naturally, were disappointed. They'd had a commercial arrangement; if he hadn't liked their price, he could have gone elsewhere. The 14K are passionate about market forces.''

"Market forces," Chan repeated.

"They make the world go round. The 14K pay the Sun Yee On another ten million to forget their contract with him. The 14K will take care of everything. They promise the Sun Yee On that they won't regret it. The Sun Yee On agree. The main point is that it will look just like the Sun Yee On carried out the executions.''

"Ah!"

"Probably the 14K would have gotten away with it if they hadn't been so creative. The first thing they did was fail to deliver the uranium—they made it look like something went wrong and it had to be dumped—so they could pick it up later. But that's not the best thing they did, is it? You have to admire their guts. Of course he suspected, but he had no proof, and for someone like him to act hysterically shows poor statesmanship. Even I admire their guts—can you believe I'm saying that?"

"It must have been pretty inspired, whatever they did to make you say that. And I need a cigarette before you tell me.''

Lee looked startled while Chan lit his Benson. "You mean, you still don't know? The British didn't tell you?''

"Tell me what?''

"When the three couriers first disappeared, at the same time two of his best cadres were kidnapped in Guangdong.''

Chan spoke softly. "Say that again.''

"It's true. It's known. It's probably even on the Internet. The bodies in the vat were unidentifiable, right?''

Slowly Chan exhaled. "Right.''

"So if the three couriers weren't minced . . .''

Through smoke he saw a blinding light that illuminated the past few weeks: Xian's clumsy approach on the boat, Cuthbert's obsession, the tapping of his phone, the behavior of the coastguards, five grim SAS assassins specially flown in, the whole strange fraught atmosphere of the case; simplicity wasn't always beautiful. This revelation was like looking in a shopwindow and seeing Fear, Greed, Loathing and Wrath as artifacts, carefully backlit.

"The third victim, the female? She wasn't a cadre. She was Caucasian."

"A backpacker they picked up in Thailand. Just some kid. They told her they were going to use her to smuggle heroin from Hong Kong to New York."

"And now he knows for certain that his own men were shredded?"

"After today, when you found the real couriers? Of course he knows for certain. I phoned him and told him myself, gleefully. I couldn't resist. I mean I really rubbed it in."

"You know Xian?"

Lee shrugged. "We do a little business from time to time." He spit on the floor. "So what? I do business with the 14K, but I still hate them."

Chan buried his head in his hands.

53

Forty-nine was too old to feel girlish excitement at the bleep of a fax machine—unless you happened to be a child of the sixties. One advantage of belonging to the generation that never grew up is that you never grow up. Moira guessed the fax was from Charlie. For a start, he was the only person she knew on the other side of the world working at 2:00 A.M. New York time. Secondly, he was the only person who sent her faxes, junk mail excluded. There was no reason for him not to fax at this hour; the fax machine's single ring would not have woken her. But she'd not gone to sleep. Maybe insomnia was contagious. Charlie never slept either. Maybe it was age. Just because you don't grow up doesn't mean you don't grow old, unfortunately.

She stood by the machine which she'd installed in the tiny spare bedroom—Clare's room—that she now called her office. With a sound between squeaking and rolling the thin, curly paper emerged into the tray. She started to read even before the guillotine chopped it. Surely there was more?

When the machine didn't bleep again, she reread the stark, cruel message and trembled.

She went to the kitchen to find the bourbon, downed a glass in one swallow, poured another. So she was dead after all, and Charlie had turned cold. In a way Clare had died a long time ago, and there was only so much mourning you could do for a smack addict who wasn't going to see forty. Even so, she could not stop the flashbacks. Clare had been such a cute kid, and so smart. In another city in another world she might have done something wonderful with her life. Moira went back to the living room, which was not much bigger than Charlie's. She opened a window, looked down on the street. Jump or scream? She gave the world a lungful of abuse, closed the window, finished the glass of bourbon. *There were choices, though, Clare. It wasn't all the fault of the world. I begged you to quit, begged you.*

Taking a fresh glass to Clare's room, she yelled at the walls: *I tried to save you. I gave you everything I had. Everything. I lied for you. I cheated for you. Why wasn't that enough? Love is supposed to be enough, goddamn you. Whatever the circumstances, it was the smack that killed you. Did you have to be so fucking weak?*

The glass was empty again. She returned to the kitchen, poured a fresh slug, collapsed into a chair. *I did all I could to save her.* In a way, losing Charlie was a crueler blow.

But Charlie was not cruel, merely very angry. How could she blame him? He'd caught her in another lie, a big one this time, those phony dental records they had persuaded her to take to Hong Kong. *But it's not the way you think, Charlie. I never joined the mob; I was only trying to save my baby.*

Two more bourbons later she made a decision. She had told herself she wasn't going to watch Mario die at Mount Sinai. He had had a whole life full of women who could do that for him. She didn't need more grief because grief was what *she'd* had a whole life full of. But now she would. And before he died, he would talk because she needed him to help her save her last relationship. There wasn't going to be anyone after Charlie. You knew things like that when you were pushing fifty.

Despite the hour, she telephoned the hospital. She used her old cop voice and her old cop manner to bully her way through to Mario, who wasn't asleep anyway and was glad to hear from her. He appreciated the opportunity to say good-bye to the only real love of his life he said, that schmoozer.

It was after nine in the morning by the time she had woken from a drunken sleep, washed, taken a couple of Tylenol for the hangover, telephoned for a cab, walked the four flights down from her apartment and was waiting on the pavement. She saw them in her makeup mirror as she was checking her mascara, two black kids no more than thirteen or fourteen; not small, though. You had to know the streets to read them: a downward glance exchanged, a whisper, a nod toward her handbag. She waited until they were nearly upon her in a run, then turned, kneed one in the groin and with an open palm thrust straight fingers into the other's windpipe. She had to step over them (one writhing, the other coughing, both amazed) to reach the cab that was drawing up to the curb. The driver barely stopped moving for her to get in, then accelerated away while she was still closing the door.

"You shouldn't have done that." The driver had a thick accent that Moira could not quite place. "I saw from across the street."

She scowled. "Kids around here, you know—"

"I mean, they coulda had guns. Even if they didn't have them, they could get them. Now they know where you live."

Moira smiled. She never waited outside her own apartment house. The address she'd given to the taxi company was ten doors away. Streetcraft, you never really forgot it. She was pleased with herself. Love gave you the strength to fight back; experience gave you the technique. Come to think of it, forty-nine didn't need to be such a bad age for a woman. *I've found a man worth fighting for.*

"What accent is that?" she asked the driver, to be polite.

"Georgian. Georgia, ex-USSR, not USA."

Russian to her. When she was very young, the cabdrivers had sometimes been Russian, refugees from communism. Now they were Russians again, refugees from the new capitalism. It made you feel as if you'd lived through a condensed historical cycle in which everything had happened except civilization. She'd tell Charlie; he appreciated that kind of talk. They had a faxual relationship. She forgot which of them had thought up that bad joke. Love was weird. A daughter dead again, a hangover like a hatchet through the skull, about to visit a terminally ill ex-husband—and she felt terrific because she had a fight worth winning. *Trust me, Charlie, I can explain. And don't get killed, okay?*

She talked to the driver about the Bronx—these days some of it was still like a circle of hell so famous they were selling tickets in purgatory—and looked out the window as they crossed the bridge into Manhattan. Traffic on the Harlem River crawled over slate-colored water shading up to light gray where the sun penetrated the clouds. Something about boats and rivers that didn't change the way cars and roads did. She'd been proud of this city once, still was up to a point. There were angles and perspectives, traditions even, that were timeless and gave the illusion that you were part of something of permanent value. But the truth was, its soul was shriveling. It was dirty. She'd watched while bluntness gave way to rudeness gave way to hostility gave way to homicidal rage, all in about thirty years. When brutality became the only effective means of communication with your fellow citizen, it was time to get out. Hong Kong? *You'd better do some explaining first, girl.*

The daydream stopped with the cab at Mount Sinai. When she told them what room Mario was in, the reception became tangibly more polite. She stood in the elevator, fuming just a little with an old rage: *Captain in the NYPD and he gets a five-thousand-dollar-a-night room in Mount Sinai to die in.*

The anger faded, though, when she saw him. The dextrose IV drip that stood by the bed on a pole wasn't hooked up to his body; the limpness of the plastic tube hanging down from it was a kind of analogue for the limpness of his two arms, which lay in parallel on the covers. She averted her eyes while she tried to catch up with the devastation that three short weeks had wrought on that fine body.

She bit her lip as she approached the bed. This was going to be more difficult than she'd expected. Damn it, women were different from men, no matter what they said. More than two decades before this womanizing crook had reached her, and she still didn't know how to forget that; any man would have been able to kill that soft spot she felt opening somewhere in her guts, but she couldn't. She sat down in one of the chairs by the bed. He'd lost a lot of his hair too.

"Thanks for coming." The voice was thin and faint, the smile forced. She could see from his eyes, though, that his mind was still alert.

"I'm not going to say you look terrific, Mario."

He lowered his eyes. "Just a scratch." She smiled.

"I forgot to bring you flowers. I meant to; then two kids tried to mug me, and I forgot."

"They still alive, those two kids?"

They laughed then, and tears came to her eyes. That had always been his secret, underneath the charm and good looks: It was the humor that women came back for. And maybe it showed a measure of courage, after all, to be joking at this stage.

"You were fast and mean, worse than any man. Everyone said so." He put out a hand for her to hold. It was hard to believe how much that small movement seemed to cost him.

"I've slowed down a lot."

Coletti shook his head. "I don't believe it, not you. If I'd had one ounce of sense, I would never have let you go."

"Don't do this."

"You were right, and I was wrong. The mob——" He tried to make a gesture like spitting. She nodded. "I understand. I don't approve, but I understand. I'm not twenty anymore, I know how things happen to people. You couldn't help being that kind of Italian——maybe."

Coletti shook his head. He spoke with agonizing slowness. "Don't soft-soap me. I had a choice, like anyone. You know what, my uncle was in the hospital, I was twenty-five, they'd shot him old style outside his favorite restaurant on Perry Street. It could have been a screenplay, it was that corny. When I sat on the chair near his bed, I told him I was gonna join. I said to avenge him, but I meant because I needed that machismo. He pointed to a bunch of roses they'd sent him in a vase. He said: 'What you talk of is like that rose. It is very beautiful, but it can make you bleed.' "

Moira looked around the room. Sure enough, there were small mountains of flowers against one wall. Roses too. She sighed. "Mario, honey, I don't think I ever told you what I really had against you being in the mob."

"It's evil. You were a good Catholic. You were right."

"Naw, I was just being holier than thou; it's an old Irish debating trick. What I really couldn't stand was the mob wives. So boring. The whole thing, I have to tell you, just bored the pants off me. You know, when your great-great-great-uncle went to see *his* uncle in his hospital bed way back in Palma di Montichiero when men were men, *his* uncle told that same story about the rose. It's even in books now, Mario. It's old."

The ravaged face on the pillow creased up in a chuckle. "You still know how to hurt." With effort he turned to look into her eyes. "Listen, the scam with the phony dental records? It worked. That's how come I can die in peace. Don't tell a fucking soul or they'll waste you and her both."

The effort had exhausted him. His head sank deeper into the pillow, a contented smile on his face. Moira swallowed hard.

"Why, that's great, Mario. Gonna tell me the details now? You know how an old cop like me gets to be an evidence junkie. And I really didn't appreciate being the mule, you know. If she hadn't pleaded with me over the phone to do exactly as you told me—"

He nodded. "I know. That's why I asked one of my partners to come here today to meet you. He should be here now. Open the door. He said he'd wait till I called him."

Moira crossed the floor to open the door to the corridor. The Chinese man on the bench stood up and stretched out his hand.

"Pleased to meet you, Mrs. Coletti." It was a New York accent. If she closed her eyes, he could have been an Italian American or a New York Jew.

She shook his hand without enthusiasm. He was shorter than she was, no more than five-four, in an electric blue silk suit with Italian cut. He was almost as round as he was tall with a jutting chin. At that height the air of unassailable authority was borderline absurd, except for the eyes. There was nothing phony there; they were genuine reptile. He gestured for her to return to the hospital room.

"Moira, meet Danny Chow, the real *capo di tutti capi*."

Chow half closed his eyes. "Please."

"One of the most powerful men in the Western world. Head of the 14K Triad Society worldwide. But don't tell anyone."

Chow raised a hand. "I said *please*."

"He's agreed to come here today out of respect for you as Clare's mother. Right, Danny?"

"I have the greatest admiration for your daughter, Mrs. Coletti. She is a visionary. I think you'll agree that we've gone to exceptional lengths to ensure her safety. We're a caring organization, Mrs. Coletti. We look after our people."

"That's good," Moira said.

"Tell her, Danny. Tell it all."

Chow gestured for Moira to sit down by the side of the bed while he stood.

"Communists, Mrs. Coletti." He raised a finger. "Excuse me, but *fucking* Communists. They have a criminal mentality, ma'am; their whole outlook is based on lies and deception. Other organizations have embraced the late twentieth century with intelligence and enthusiasm; we have grown. We are businessmen now; we abhor violence and use it only when strictly necessary. If the average man has difficulty in fully comprehending the nature of international commerce in our time, such that certain quaint regulations outlaw some of our activities, then that's a cross the businessman has to bear. We understand: The most advanced in any society have always to suffer the consequences of being out in front.

"But Communists, ma'am—Neanderthals, primitives, cavemen, power freaks, *criminals*, pure and simple. It was a business deal like any other. A certain figure prominent in the People's Liberation Army required a certain commodity for his purposes. Not having immediate access to that commodity myself, I contacted my good friend and business associate Mario Coletti. He in turn worked his contacts until that commodity could be located, its price verified according to the market, freight, forwarding and profit margin added, a certain sum for risk included, and a deal was struck. A deal, ma'am, is sacred. When we cease to honor deals, civilization will fail; we'll be back to bows and arrows. Now the nature of this particular commodity is such that we would not trust it to our usual couriers.

"Three of our best people were chosen, two from my firm, one from Mr. Coletti's: your daughter, Clare, courageous, beautiful, a trailblazer in her own right. All is going well. The commodity, together with certain sample items that we feel may be of interest to the purchaser, arrives safely at its destination. Handover is days away, *days away*. Then what happens? Tell Clare's mother, Mario. I'm ashamed of the primitive side of my own race and pray for the day when they shall be raised from out of their ignorance."

Moira closed her eyes while the two men shared the pleasure of explaining their scam in detail, down to the miniature camera used to photograph the victims' mouths and the sample bites in gum that the local mob dentist had insisted on. The dentist was an artist, they said. They were talking about lives, heroin, weapons-grade uranium, but the minds behind the words were adolescent; *My ex-husband has about five days left on earth, and dear God, he still hasn't grown up.*

When they had finished, Moira forced a smile. "That's brilliant. Thank you for telling me. The general, he doesn't know you diced up his own men?"

"Of course not, ma'am. He may suspect, and he may better understand that international commercial organizations such as ours are not to be trifled with, but of course he will never be sure. The possibility will be there, goading him like a thorn—and perhaps leading him eventually to the light. I'm pretty confident he will see the error of his ways, if he hasn't done so already. It may seem cruel to you, Mrs. Coletti, but in our business credibility—*face*, as we Chinese say—is everything." Chow looked at Mario with an indulgent smile. "I think it's safe to say we increased our credibility in the international community quite a bit. It was David and Goliath, and David won again."

"Unless Clare and the others are found," Moira said. "I guess the general will want to close the credibility gap if that happens."

Chow smiled benevolently. "We are a powerful, rich and well-connected organization, Mrs. Coletti. You have my word, that will never happen. We know he watches the airport, which is why we are keeping them safely for the time being in Hong Kong. They are being given plastic surgery. At an appropriate moment they will be brought back to this country and given new identities."

Moira nodded, stared at the floor for a moment, then put a hand on Mario's arm. "You did well, honey. You came up trumps."

The face on the pillow smiled gratefully.

54

D*ear Charlie,*

It's not the way you think. Read this fax. You can be wrong too, you know.

These are strange times. I wept real tears that day in your apartment because I didn't know anything except I was supposed to save Clare's life by delivering phony dental records to you. I still don't know how you guessed I was part of the scam, you really are one smart cop. But I knew next to nothing. All they told me was that she had to get a new identity real fast and those records were the only way to do it. I wept because she was the one caused suffering to three others, and because even if she lived, I knew that I'd lost her.

Take a moment to hear me out, Charlie. All that stuff you say about China raping its people—you think it doesn't apply to Americans too? Our system rapes; it just uses different concepts to do it. I spent my life patrolling the streets of this city, and it took everything I had, my husband, my daughter and even my good character. When I met you, she was all I had in the world. Nothing to be proud of, God knows, but she called me Mom. What would you have done for your flesh and blood? I think you would have held the world ransom if you'd had to.

I don't know. Bad as she was, she was more flake than sadist. Heroin, you know, makes monsters.

There I go, blowing the punch line and leaving out the details. I got it all written down. Mario and some Chinese triad boss told me everything. Soon as I got home I typed out all I could remember, which is most of it. It goes like this:

That stuff he told you about Clare convincing the mob to develop the relationship with China was mostly BS. Ever since the Sicilians multiplied their operation by opening up the Russia market, the New York boys have been looking for a way into China. It's a policy that comes from high up. They got lucky when the 14K asked them to look for best-quality uranium to supply to Xian. Apparently Xian's been trading with the 14K for a while, mostly supplying heroin. The Mob and the 14K sent a party over with the uranium and some stuff they thought might interest him—free gifts, samples, treasures to the Great Khan, whatever. . . .

Chan read on quickly to the last lines:

Why did we let these subhuman mutants get so powerful?

God help me, I love you. Whether you forgive me or not, I'm coming over on the first flight I can get tourist class. Take extraspecial care of yourself. There's more to this. I got a feeling there's something really bad—I mean, even worse—about to go down. Whatever you think of me, don't die.

                                                                    Moira

P.S. How did you know that I was conning you with those records? I could have been an innocent courier.

Chan crushed the fax into a ball, threw it in the waste bin in his kitchen. Then he took it out again, reread it. On a sheet of A4 paper he wrote: "Chinese intuition." He slipped the page into the fax machine; then, softening again, he took it out and added: "You were too good a cop not to know." It took only seconds to transmit to America.

· · ·

In his office Chan took out the Sony Dictaphone, walked up and down the length of his office while Aston watched and listened.

"File one-two-eight/mgk/HOM/STC status report continued.

I must reluctantly conclude that the overzealous action of the SAS officers stated above has made it difficult, if not impossible, to proceed with the investigation into an elaborate criminal plot of international dimensions that is almost certainly related to the discovery of weapons-grade uranium at Mirs Bay (see related sub-file A)."

He stopped under the weight of Aston's misery.

"You didn't kill her, did you, Chief?"

"No."

"So who did?"

"It's classified."

At his desk in Queen's Building Jonathan Wong opened a new black fiberglass briefcase with a centralized combination lock. He rotated the dials until he aligned three eights and the case snapped open. Three eights was not exactly good security, but there was a balance to be struck: Eight was a lucky number in Cantonese.

From inside the case he extracted an envelope with forty-four color pictures. Each photograph measured eight inches by ten inches, and each was a close-up. After examining a few of them with an expression of frozen disgust, he replaced them in the envelope. Taking a slip of paper that bore his name and the name and address of his firm, he wrote: "Mr. Chow, please be so kind as to telephone me on receipt of this package." He slipped the note into the envelope and resealed it.

Lifting his telephone, he pressed a button and asked his secretary to call a clerk who was to bring a Federal Express package and waybill. While the clerk waited, Wong filled out the waybill, giving the destination of the package with the photographs as "Stock-law Trading Company, 220 West 57th Street, New York, NY 10019, Strictly Confidential, Personal Attention only: Mr. Daniel

Chow, President.'' After slipping the original envelope inside the
FedEx cardboard package, Wong nodded to the clerk, who took it
away. It was eleven in the morning; the package would be on an
afternoon flight to New York and would arrive within three working days.

55

C han classified his unsolved cases into two groups: where the identity of the perpetrator was unknown and he had no leads and where he knew who had done it but lacked crucial evidence. With regard to the second category, in his opinion it was a mistake for the perpetrator to antagonize the investigator to the point where the latter is driven to unlawful means. Emily had been murdered by whoever had framed him. Would Xian have used a Chanel belt?

Behind a banyan tree near the drive at the entrance to Beauchamp Villas, his service revolver in an arm holster, Chan waited for two evenings for the green Jaguar to leave. On the third evening he watched from the shadows while the diplomat drove away at his usual speed at about eight in the evening. He was wearing a dinner jacket and black bow tie. With the Jag's sun roof open Chan could hear the chants of Gregorian monks fade quickly away. He emerged from behind the tree and walked up the drive. The heat was oppressive. By the end of the short walk he was sweating and out of breath, but not only from the heat. Did everyone suffer from molten bowels on his first major crime?

He used his identity card to pass the security at the gate. On the fifth floor he took thin cotton gloves from his pocket and slipped them on; his hands shook as he used a skeleton key for the deadlock and a piece of flat plastic on the Yale. *I am committing the first burglary of my career.*

Apart from dim light that filtered through from the public lamps on the sidewalk, the apartment was unlit, empty. Closing the door behind him, he breathed in the delicious cool from the silent air-conditioning unit. Sweat cooled on his face and arms. The luxury of space calmed his nerves a little. He took out a small flashlight. He had stopped shaking, but he noted a profound division in his policeman's psyche: He was an outlaw in another man's home at night.

He framed me.

What to look for and where to start? His flashlight picked out the priceless carpets and the antique rifle on the wall. The collection of opium pipes in their glass case looked as untouched as a museum piece. Where does a scholar keep his secrets? He padded softly down the hall to the library.

On the lectern facing the window an open volume of poems in Chinese waited. The Englishman had made notes and produced one full translation:

> *Blue, blue is the grass about the river*
> *And the willows have overfilled the close garden*
> *And within, the mistress, in the midmost of her youth,*
> *White, white of face, hesitates, passing the door.*
> *Slender, she puts forth a slender hand;*
>
> *And she was a courtesan in the old days,*
> *And she has married a sot,*
> *Who now goes drunkenly out*
> *And leaves her too much alone.*

Chan paused over the poem. Over the top of the page Cuthbert had scrawled the single word "Emily." Flicking through the notes, Chan found some instructions the diplomat had given himself:

"Tell Hill fix mold on trees. Service car before end month. Change for Nepal (plus get visa). Cash to safe."

Safe? His spirits fell. The ability to break into a flat or house was a skill a detective picked up during the course of business. Safe-cracking was an exotic specialization involving welding equipment, etc. Homicide didn't do safes.

He found it behind a false facade in a corner of the room. It was about four feet high, two feet thick and two and a half feet wide—and locked. He was sitting on the floor in front of it, feeling futile and foolish, when the door opened and a light flicked on.

Cuthbert's bow tie was undone and lay across the ruffs of his dress shirt. In his hand he held the largest revolver Chan had ever seen. The diplomat's face was ashen.

"I thought you'd try the library first." He strode further into the room. "You've been by the banyan tree for the past two evenings. I saw you. Telescope. You've deduced that I killed her and think perhaps I kept that tape recording." Cuthbert raised the huge revolver, pointed it vaguely in Chan's direction. "I feel as if I've been trying to get rid of you forever."

"I finally noticed," Chan said. "Big gun."

Cuthbert grunted. Keeping the gun pointed in Chan's direction, he walked over to the chesterfield, sat and emitted a long sigh. After a moment he raised the gun again, pointed it at Chan's head. "Well, this is the moment of truth. If I killed her, I would have no choice but to kill you, would I? I could say you burgled me, which is true, and I fired in self-defense. I assume that bulge under your jacket is a service revolver."

Chan closed his eyes. He heard Cuthbert pull the trigger. Chan was still shuddering seconds after the hammer clicked on the empty chamber.

Cuthbert threw the gun onto the carpet. "You really are the most unbelievable pain in the arse. And for a homicide detective, pretty damned ignorant about firearms. No ammunition has been available for the Civil War LeMat in over fifty years."

"I'm sorry," Chan said in Cantonese. "Your erudition is truly masterful. I am overwhelmed." In English he added: "Even if you didn't kill her, you framed me." He was still twitching.

"True."

"Why?"

Cuthbert spoke in a clipped, bitter voice. "Because I was allowed to. London changed its mind—after a lot of coaxing, I might add. I had to use the governor to go over Henderson's head to the minister. Henderson's hopping mad. But I was right, damn it. There was no reason at all not to delay the case until after June; I was simply keeping you out of the way until then. Of course this was before you found that American lesbian and her friends. The cat's out of the bag now. We can leave you to Xian. If we move fast, we can reinstate you prior to your assassination.''

Still in shock, Chan tried to concentrate. Bitter recrimination was not the reaction one normally expected from a murder suspect. Not in Mongkok anyway. ''Who's Henderson?''

Cuthbert sat back on the sofa, pinched the bridge of his nose. ''A fat, androgynous glutton who runs Britain.''

''And you had me framed to get me off the case?''

''I have the authorization from the minister.''

''But I was kept *on* the case?''

''Thank Commissioner Ronald Tsui for that. I underestimated him. Quite the paper warrior.''

Chan remembered the way Tsui had not looked at him when they accused him of murdering Emily.

''Tsui knew I was innocent? He knew you set me up?'' He could not suppress a note of hope. How very Chinese, to want to set the record straight with Authority as one was dragged before the firing squad.

''He knew nothing, but I think he guessed.''

''Ah, yes. Only the *white* mandarins would have shared the stratagem.'' He endured Cuthbert's stare. ''I'm going to stand up now.'' An odd thing to say; he found it difficult to believe that Cuthbert did not have some other weapon concealed, ready to attack.

''You may as well. I suppose we have things to discuss.''

Chan stood. When Cuthbert failed to produce an antique gun from his jacket, Chan flapped his arms nervously. Never burgle an Englishman; he may come home and want to talk. But Cuthbert seemed lost in thought.

''You faked the fingerprint evidence on Emily's belt? It's professional curiosity that makes me ask.''

The diplomat seemed to relax. He sat back a little on the sofa, sighed.

"MI6 are still capable of certain elementary tasks, not that one would trust them with something important. You've no idea how proud they are that they managed to break into Arsenal Street forensic laboratory without getting caught." Cuthbert scowled. "For the best description of the English psyche, look to Lewis Carroll."

Warily Chan moved around the room. He glanced back at the lectern.

"You didn't kill her? You knew I was coming? And you wrote her name at the top of that poem?"

The diplomat stared at him. "Christ." He shook his head. "I need a drink. Try not to think about anything while I'm gone. I've noticed it's when you think that things most often take a turn for the worse."

Cuthbert returned with a bottle of brandy and two balloon-shaped brandy glasses, which he placed on a coffee table near to the chesterfield. He poured until the glasses were about one-third full. Without waiting for Chan, he took two quick swallows. Chan saw that he had finished half the glass. Cuthbert took the silver cigarette case out of his jacket, threw a cigarette to Chan and lit one for himself, at the same time sitting down on the sofa. After an inhalation he swallowed the rest of the brandy and poured another glass.

"Drink," Cuthbert said. "It may stop you thinking."

Chan shrugged and picked up the glass. The Englishman had a point. Chan watched him swallow more brandy. He took a sip himself.

"Nice cognac."

Cuthbert shook his head, apparently in disbelief. "D'you know that's the only small talk I've ever heard from you? It takes a burglary, I suppose."

"Nice cigarette."

"Don't, it's painful."

Chan reached out to touch a book titled *A Photographer in Old*

Peking. With Cuthbert watching he pulled it from the shelf and flicked through it. To Chinese eyes, even a non-Communist, the pictures reflected a period of shame. Caucasian predators had flooded the Middle Kingdom. The worst sold opium and ruthlessly exploited the people; the best found it all very quaint. To understand someone like Cuthbert, one had to look with Western eyes. With the distance of time and the skillful positioning of the camera lens there was a haunting beauty in *The Opium Smoker and His Son, The Jujube Seller, The Altar of Heaven by Moonlight*. It was long before the Cultural Revolution; the old walls were there, still intact, and of course the gates that foreigners like Cuthbert lamented so deeply since Mao destroyed them: *Hsi An Men, Ti An Men, Tung An Men and Hou Men*. Chan closed the book.

"In your youth you had already decided to come East. You envisaged the life of a scholar-diplomat, with large old-fashioned Chinese-style house, servants, Chinese mistress, occasional opium smoking with gentlemen with long white beards—that sort of thing?"

"Perhaps."

"And perhaps Emily was part of this dream? True, you were over forty by then, and in Hong Kong, not China, but you had position, privilege and money. You could build your dream. It's what people do when they get money." Chan walked up to the diplomat. "She loved you like a Chinese." He hissed. "Fierce and true."

Cuthbert winced. "At first, yes."

"Until you sucked her into your game. You knew what Xian would do with her—"

"Damn and fuck Xian!" Chan stepped back when Cuthbert stood up and strode to the window. He turned to Chan. "He destroyed her. As he will destroy everything." Chan saw the upper lip tremble, before he brought it under control. Cuthbert placed both hands on the lectern and looked down at the poem. He spoke slowly, enunciating every syllable.

"There must have been a dozen times over the past ten years during her insane tantrums when I wished to God she would do herself in. Then when she did"—he paused and swallowed—"I realized that I had loved her. Last night I was drunk as usual, and I saw her soul, so different to her personality. It was like the woman in that poem . . . unspeakably lonely, very female, very Chinese.''

The Englishman breathed deeply. ''God knows why I left it lying around for you to find. Some sort of awful melodramatic reflex on my part, I suppose. I must have wanted your interrogation.'' He took out the silver cigarette case, lit another cigarette, inhaled deeply. ''She telephoned me just before, as she had on her previous suicide attempts. Unfortunately I wasn't in. She left a message on my answering machine. She was dead by the time I arrived. Women handle guilt badly. To their credit, I suppose.'' He shuffled among his papers on the lectern. ''Or am I doing her an injustice? Here, you were supposed to find this as well.''

His hand shook slightly as he handed Chan a piece of red paper. Two lines were written in green felt tip:

> *If glory could last for ever*
> *Then the waters of Han would flow northward.*

Chan looked at Cuthbert.

''It's from one of my translations of Li Po, 'The River Song.' It was on that marble table near her swimming pool. She knew I would be the one to find it. I think she meant that her brilliant day was over; she was bowing out. She'd had enough of all of us.''

Chan waited for the diplomat to recover. ''And that tape recording?''

''Of that memorable night when you smoked opium with her? She'd hidden it in her bedroom. I removed it before calling the police. It was classified information after all.''

Chan kept quiet. There was never anything to say in reply to a true confession. He moved nervously around the book-filled shelves, spoke in an unnaturally light tone. ''D'you know, I've always wanted a library like this? To have so many books, all in order on beautiful oak shelves. To be able to come in and handle them. To have the space to enjoy them. And the learning, of course. You read wenyen—classical Chinese. I don't. That's ironic.''

Cuthbert loosened a shirt button, then, seeming to make a decision, removed his jacket and threw it on the sofa. He had finished his second glass of brandy and showed no sign of drunkenness. Chan finished his.

Cuthbert poured two more. "You envy me, I envy you."

"You're mocking me."

"Not at all. I envy you all the things you don't have to think about. It must be marvelous, hunting down some half-witted murderer, preparing the evidence for court, potting him. You have a ninety percent success rate. Most people conclude you're brilliant. I would conclude you're underusing your gifts."

Chan looked at the Englishman standing by the window. "You know what's the weirdest thing of all about your culture? A morbid addiction to guilt. My ex-wife is English. She experienced no guilt herself, of course, but she could inflict it from a distance. You people can impose guilt on anything. If I listened to you, I could end up feeling guilty about solving so many crimes."

Cuthbert smiled thinly. "I was merely explaining why you should not envy me. In your profession you are given soluble problems, like a crossword. Take the Mincer Murders. To you it was simply a case of identifying the victims and the perpetrators."

"And to you?"

The diplomat seemed on the point of saying something, then stopped. He started again. "You conclude the investigation, and what was the case really all about? Answer: The general and his cronies who will be running this colony in a few weeks' time are criminals who have made stupendous fortunes out of the export of heroin and arms and are now in the process of collecting uranium for weapons of mass destruction."

"Truth can hurt. But it's still the truth."

"So you go to the media, tell the world. Six million people in Hong Kong who have been hoping for the best now know that they can expect the worst. The half who have other countries to go to flood the streets to the airport. The other three million riot. It becomes clear that Great Britain cannot contain the situation. So the People's Liberation Army comes in early to keep the peace. Don't you see? Xian cannot lose now. He's holding all the cards. There never was a case to solve. It's a power game we cannot win."

Chan felt that Cuthbert was invoking a deeper level of responsibilty and wisdom than he was accustomed to work on. He found himself preoccupied by a different problem.

"You think he'll kill me?"

Cuthbert shrugged. "It depends. Two days ago you demonstrated to his satisfaction that the 14K and Sun Yee On triad societies made a fool of him and chopped up two of his most senior cadres. I went to the length of recommending the assassination of Clare Coletti and her friends in the hope of keeping the thing secret. Of course I was aware of the futility, but one has to try. I heard today that the news has been leaked to Xian. I would guess that he won't get around to thinking about you until he's attended to what he will consider the more pressing aspects of the matter."

"You hate Xian?"

Cuthbert poured the brandy and shook his head. "I would like to, but it's difficult to hate a primal force. To hate Xian would be like hating typhoons or volcanic activity. He's simply a fact of life. A fact of life, moreover, that the Western democracies prefer not to think about. Their awakening from deep liberal sleep is going to be interesting."

"I don't understand."

Cuthbert handed him a glass. Chan lit a Benson. "Oh, I think you do. You must have noticed how the West is complacently convinced that human evolution will eventually produce worldwide democracy, a mirror of itself, in other words. They have no idea. Modern China is hardly twenty years old, if you count the Cultural Revolution as the moment when the old China was destroyed forever. That was also the moment when they destroyed old Peking—*because it was beautiful*. As a policeman you must know what animal finds beauty intolerable: the human mutant. The Beast. If the West had any sense, it would shiver in fear."

"I would like to understand you." Cuthbert looked at Chan in surprise. Spoken in Cantonese, the sentence indicated respect and genuine interest.

"You would? It's not difficult. Just assume the West is one hundred and eighty degrees wrong in its assumptions. Suppose China is not the past but the future. Suppose that over the border they murder their female babies for a reason, oh, not a thought-out reason but a collective psychological reaction to a situation humanity was never designed to endure. See?"

"Too many people?"

"One point six billion at the last count. Have you any idea of the sheer administrative will required to feed such numbers? You've been to Beijing; you know that you need a measure of ruthlessness just to get on or off a bus. And by the year 2000 eighty percent of them will be male. Young and male."

"What are you saying?"

"I'm saying that freedom, democracy, liberalism, these are quaint nineteenth-century concepts that have passed their sell-by date. In the very near future all such luxuries will be swept away by monsters who have been spawned by monsters to govern monsters. What will be required will be an extreme of callousness that will make the West faint. And there's not a force on earth that will be able to contain the problem in China. I'm saying, my friend, that Xian is not a mere thug or warlord. He's a visionary. He *is* the future."

"And this is why he needs an atom bomb? Because there are too many people?"

Cuthbert shrugged. "I doubt that he's bothered to think it through. It's a fact, though, if lebensraum is what you're after, nothing clears a space like nuclear radiation."

"I still don't understand. This monster, this beast who destroyed the woman you loved, you've spent much of your career doing as he tells you?"

Cuthbert fumbled with his cigarette case. His speech was becoming slurred. "I lick his arse." He raised the unlit cigarette in one hand and moved his weight with a slight lurch from one foot to another. The black bow tie still lay across his dress shirt; he stared at Chan. His eyes were windows to incredulity. *"I lick his arse."*

56

C han's second rehabilitation came in the form of a circular issued by Commissioner Tsui: In the Emily Ping investigation there had been serious contamination of evidence. It was now clear that Chief Inspector Chan's fingerprints had not, after all, been lifted from the belt that had been found around her neck.

To give his colleagues time to absorb the latest change in his fortunes, Chan took a day off. He was rereading *1984* when Aston called. One of the people who worked in the building where the vat had first been found had telephoned to report suspicious circumstances. When asked what exactly he found suspicious, the caller had replied, "I'm not too clear," and hung up. Determined to cover his back, Chan telephoned Riley and Cuthbert and arranged to meet them at the warehouse with Aston.

They were waiting for him on the ground floor and followed him into the lift. The police barriers were still in place, although someone had painted a red star over the "Royal" in "Royal Hong Kong Police Force." Heavy sweetness penetrated the corridor as they approached the wide industrial door, from behind which something droned. When Chan pushed the door open, the odor worsened and the drone increased to a thunder of buzzing. He was gagging as he switched on the light.

He turned on a heel and with an open hand thrust Aston's face back against the door. At the same time he pulled at Riley's shirtsleeve. Aston had started a high-pitched scream.

"Better get the boy out of here, sir. *I said better get the boy out of here, sir.''* When Riley's eyes started to roll, Chan slapped him across the face. The chief superintendent shook himself like a dog; blood trickled from a nostril. In a sudden lunge Riley put a long arm around Aston.

''Come on, Dick, I never could take the really rough stuff either. Let's get out of here.'' He maneuvered Aston out of the warehouse and toward the lift lobby while the young inspector started into another scream.

Turning back, Chan exchanged a glance with Cuthbert.

Cuthbert's eyes ran the length of the warehouse. ''Told you.''

Saliver Kan's head and torso emerged in a black halo of flies from the nearest mincer while mince from the lower part of his body oozed into a steel tray. He had bitten through most of his tongue, which hung from his mouth by a thread. Extreme pain had wrenched his jaw to one side and twisted it. Next to him Joker Liu sprouted at an angle from the second machine. To the right of Saliver Kan identical mincers held what remained of High-Rise Lam, Four-Finger Bosco and Fat Boy Wong—all members of the Sun Yee On Triad Society. Nor had the 14K been spared. Chan recognized foot soldiers and more senior officers as he walked slowly, hounded by flies, down a gallery of agony. With military precision the mincers had been placed in a perfect diagonal from one corner of the warehouse to the other.

Terminal suffering expressed itself differently on every face. Pausing before each image of death, he counted thirty-one members of the 14K and twelve members of the Sun Yee On, each with a mincer to himself. Metal trays had been placed under every outlet and were overflowing with rust-colored and black larvae that covered most of the floor. The ceiling was black and moving.

At the end of the row the only nontriad was silently laughing. With no nerves in his legs, Wheelchair Lee must have serenely bled until he expired. Lee would have known the price to be paid for taunting Genghis Khan. Perhaps he had even volunteered to be at the mincing of the 14K; death would have been a small price to pay for a ringside seat. It must have been eerie, even for hardened

killers of the PLA, to watch a man laugh while a machine ate his
legs. In a corner by a pillar Chan saw an empty wheelchair.

He rejoined Cuthbert, who ground his teeth. "Impressive," he
said eventually, covering his mouth and speaking through his hand,
"if one considers the logistics."

Outside, Riley walked Aston up and down and talked into his ear.
"Chelsea won three nil that time, but it was many years ago. I was
a kid and Jimmy Greaves was playing."

"He's a manager now," Aston said. When he turned, Chan saw
his struggle with horror.

"How many were there?"

"Forty-four," Chan said.

Aston doubled over in a cough, then straightened up. "Forty-
four. The number for death twice. Would be, wouldn't it?"

"One might have wished for greater subtlety," Cuthbert said.

Aston brushed at the front of his shirt and tried to function while
his teeth chattered. "Shall I call a van, start taking video shots,
sketch the positions, get some blokes to interview the occupants on
other floors of the building?"

Chan's face was free of his usual twitch. He turned to Cuthbert.
"You'd better ask the political adviser that question. Shall we investigate this crime, Mr. Cuthbert?" Cuthbert hesitated. "Or
would you like to tell us who did it so we can save time?"

Aston's eyes widened. Cuthbert grunted. "It's classified." They
watched him back away from them while they stared.

"Just a minute." Riley crossed the lobby. His tall body hung
over Cuthbert. "What d'you mean, 'it's classified'?" Cuthbert tried
to slide away. Riley put out a hand. "I said, *what d'you mean, 'it's
classified'*?"

Chan watched the two Englishmen struggle in a subdued stand-
up wrestling movement. Riley held the other's sleeve and would
not let go. Finally Cuthbert pulled himself away, tearing his jacket.
He strode to the lift and pressed the button. Turning to face them,

he seemed to want to explain, apologize even, to the three policemen, who were glaring at him.

"I'm sorry," he said when the lift came. "It really is classified."
He entered the lift and spoke as the doors closed. "You're not to
speak of this to any member of the press. That's official." His eyes
pleaded with Chan's. *It's China.*

57

Jonathan Wong received a telephone call in his office in Central.
When the caller was sure he was speaking to the dispatcher of the photographs, each of which consisted of a close-up of a mincer with human contents, Danny Chow's voice tightened. "What do you want?"

"I represent a client who wants to do business, Mr. Chow," Wong replied, reaching for a cigarette.

"Some client."

"I think both sides have made their points. Respect has been generated. Now's the time to deal, don't you think?"

The voice from New York sighed. "You could put it that way. What does he want?"

Wong lit his cigarette. "The commodity you procured for my client sometime ago was unfortunately never delivered. He would like to order some more. Enough for operational purposes this time. And at a more realistic price."

"Do we get to keep our couriers?"

"I think we can reach an understanding about that."

Chow sighed again. "We can probably deal. Give me two days."

"Certainly," Jonathan said, and replaced the receiver.

58

They came for Chan at lunchtime. Two tall Chinese with thick Shanghainese accents walked into Mongkok Police Station and up the stairs to his office. Neither would give his name or state his business at reception; no one had the courage to stop them, however. Chan did not resist and was not surprised to see Cuthbert in the back of the black Mercedes waiting in the car park behind the police station. He and Cuthbert found nothing to say to each other. Chan remembered a small room, an old man and black-and-white photographs hanging from a string that depicted people being taken to their executions.

At the top of the Bank of China a feast was in progress. Chan sat next to Cuthbert at a huge circular table. Xian sat directly opposite Chan. The detective had never seen any of the other sixteen men who sat around picking and sucking loudly at the crabs that ended every now and then with a soft *thuck* in a pile of shells in the middle. Chan saw that they were all about the same age as Xian. Apart from the general himself, who was wearing a black mandarin robe, the guests were in off-the-peg two-piece suits, black, gray or navy blue. None wore a necktie.

After the crab a very old man served *choi sam*, abalone, steamed rice, crispy duck. The lunch finished with soup and then sliced oranges. Chan and Cuthbert ate nothing.

The old man came around again with balloon-shaped brandy glasses, which he filled from a bottle labeled "VSO Cognac."

Xian raised his glass, said something loudly in Mandarin to which all the other old men assented.

"I give you human suffering," Cuthbert translated.

Everyone drank except Chan and Cuthbert. Xian put down his glass, stared at Chan. Whenever he spoke, Cuthbert translated.

"I see our chief inspector from Hong Kong doesn't like my toast."

There were murmurs from around the table. Xian held up one hand. The murmurs ceased. "It's all right, I understand. It's not a jolly sort of toast of the kind the British and Americans like. But that's because they are hypocrites. Open your eyes. It's never been clearer that the happiness of the few depends on the misery of the billions. This is the capitalist system that has been forced upon us. You who have one foot in the West should be pleased with our new enlightenment."

He paused for a moment in thought. His eyes rested on Chan. "In my youth, when I was only a little younger than you, I believed passionately in Marxist–Leninist–Mao Zedong Thought. So did General Wen, General Chen Yu, General Wu, General Guo, General Pu Xinyu, General Zuo, General Lao, General Tang, General Zhang, General Wang, General Li, General Yao, General Pan, General Ge, General Yu Wei." As Xian went around the table, each of the old men nodded. "We all did. In 1952 I had the honor of attending a report given by the great Zhou Enlai in the Cherishing Humanity Hall in Zhongnanhai in Beijing. I listened attentively while he spoke for seven hours. Of course I understood nothing, but how could a man who spoke for seven hours be wrong? How could Mao be wrong? How could Lenin and Marx be wrong? So for forty years we watched China grow poorer from being right, while the West grew richer from being wrong. When the Soviet Union finally disappeared, we all wondered what we had done with our lives. Worst of all, we wondered what we had done to China. How did it come about that the West was right after all? Political power came out of a gun, Mao said. Well, in China we had plenty of guns but not much power. So we started selling our guns, the other generals and I. Overnight things started to change. People we'd never met before from countries we'd never heard of came to see us, asking to buy our guns. America sells arms too. More than we do. More than anyone. The British and the French too. We had started to do things right. But it wasn't enough. Our guns are too old-fashioned, too inefficient to compare with American and British weapons.

"We sat down to lunch one day, the other generals and I, to work out what it was that was still missing. Being Chinese, we looked to history. Where had the British money come from to enable them to build the biggest empire in the world, to build their factories, their warships, their airplanes? Where had American money come from? Westerners work no harder than Chinese, but they make a thousand times more money, because of the start they have on us. What did it consist of, this start? It took us a whole lunchtime to work it out. Slaves and narcotics. After the slaves and narcotics phase of capitalism, who knows, we might even have democracy in China. But we're a long way behind, and we have to start in the way approved by history. Aren't you pleased we've taken the path to freedom?"

"No," Chan said.

He expected a blow or a bullet. Anything except the slowly accumulating rumble of laughter from the old men around the table. Xian was whinnying so hard his neighbor had to thump him on the back. He waved a hand.

"You can go, Chief Inspector. There's no harm you can do. Tell the world about us; start a revolution. We'll just march in a few weeks earlier. You're a good Chinaman—stubborn and old-fashioned. I used to be like you before the West educated me. You solved your case. While you were solving it"—Xian paused for another burst of whinnying—"we bought an atom bomb." There was an explosion of laughter around the table. "I tell you, I'm starting to like the American way. It's so easy. You don't need to study dialectical materialism; money talks. Go. The system you served so loyally is finished. All that Boy Scout stuff is over. Nobody's buying truth anymore—least of all the British and the Americans. You're in China now."

● ● ●

Chan and Cuthbert parted in the lobby on the ground floor of the Bank of China. Cuthbert turned right toward the government offices while Chan strolled slowly back to Central. A digital display in a watch shop in Queen's Road showed less than two and a half million seconds left to run: Twenty-eight days, and Xian would be emperor of Hong Kong.

It was the end of lunchtime. The sidewalks overflowed with crowds moving like debris in a river after a storm. Chan moved even more slowly because he examined every Chinese face that came into focus. Xian had called him "a good Chinaman," and so he was, despite his Caucasian features.

These were his people, he loved them; he had wanted to warn them, and this protective impulse had caused him to underestimate them. He saw now that Chinese faces had changed during the two decades that he had burned with anger. Fury had blinded him; he had acted as if he, Jenny and Mai-mai were the only victims of the Chinese holocaust. These people, fighting to return to work, with grimmer expressions than formerly—they knew what to expect. Everyone was waiting for the Beast. Some would leave, but most would stay.

Chan would stay. It was better to live an Eastern reality than a Western fantasy. The ancient master Lao-tsu had said it best: "Irrelevant that the tiger has leapt, is even now at midpoint in an arc that will certainly end in your destruction. So it is for all the ten thousand created things. Of relevance only is the curious fact that at this present instant you are alive."

At least he thought it was Lao-tsu. He checked his watch. Two-thirty. In another hour a Western woman whose breasts he much admired would land at Kai Tak Airport on a flight from New York. She was a thief and a liar, and he hoped she would enjoy living in a small flat in Mongkok, tigers and other beasts permitting.

AFTERWORD

MILTON CUTHBERT'S TRANSLATIONS were much inspired by Ezra Pound, whose rendering of the second century B.C. poet Mei Sheng has everything in common with the poem that Chan found in the diplomat's library. The quotation from "The River Song" is from Pound's translation of Li Po.

On the other hand, Chan himself possessed an original talent; that is to say, the quotation from Lao-tsu on the last page is not to be found in any of the Master's known works.

The phrase "borrowed place living on borrowed time," quoted in Chapter 2, was coined by the late Richard Hughes.